EXACTING

JUSTICE

Happy Hunting Detective!
TG Wolff

TG WOLFF

EXACTING JUSTICE

The De La Cruz Case Files

DOWN&OUT
BOOKS

Down & Out Books
3959 Van Dyke Rd, Ste. 265
Lutz, FL 33558
www.DownAndOutBooks.com

The characters and events in this book are fictitious. Any similarity to real persons, living or dead, is coincidental and not intended by the author.

Cover design by JT Lindroos

ISBN: 1-946502-50-2
ISBN-13: 978-1-946502-50-6

To my mother, Jane, who loves this story.

October 31

How do I feel?
The lady on the phone thinks I'm depressed. She's wrong. This is normal. When you lose the one you love most, you're not supposed to smile. This journal was her idea. She said to ask myself daily "how do I feel" as a way to get in touch with myself.
I tried to explain but she didn't get it. I don't feel. Haven't since the day you died.
I do think. Lying in bed this morning, I figured out five ways to kill myself. I can take pain, I just want it fast. I don't have a gun but it's easy enough to get. Point, click, done.
A knife is just as good if you know the right place to put it. Adrenaline makes the heart pump harder, draining you until it's time to sleep.
Pills. I have bottles in the bathroom. Sleeping. Pain. Heavy duty pain. Just float higher and higher until I drift away.
Poison. Got gallons of cleaner in the shop. Wonder how that one that smells like oranges tastes.
A bridge column at eighty miles an hour would do it. Just drift to the right. WHAM. Done.

CHAPTER ONE

Tuesday, November 1

Detective Jesus De La Cruz parked his police issue behind a black-and-white. He drained his go cup, bolstering the four measly hours of sleep he'd gotten with some high-test Colombian before he stepped into the ugly day. Mother Nature blanketed Cleveland with thick, ominous clouds. Welcome to winter in Northeast Ohio. The gloomy day matched his mood, and it fit the neighborhood. Urban blight had struck hard at the corner of southeast Cleveland called Slavic Village, leaving it pock-marked with ignored, abused, and run-down homes. For every spot of blight though, there was a meticulously-cared-for house loved down to the last nail, a ray of sunshine fighting through the clouds.

The dirty white house in front of him was not the latter. It needed a fresh coat of paint, and the big front window was nothing but plywood. The gate was missing from the fence, and concrete sections of the sidewalk and driveway were crooked, cracked, and crumbled. Grass grew in cracks, but the lawn was bare.

The house wasn't all grim. A bright orange pumpkin, hand-drawn, with crooked teeth, grinned from the yellow front door.

"What good are you?" The high-pitched cry escaped the house with the small boy who slipped out the door.

Cruz walked between the bumper of his car and one with

2

the driver's side window shattered. The caller reported a drive-by shooting the night before. The car needed to be swept for evidence. Across the dirt passing for a tree lawn, over the broken sidewalk, he reached the small walk to the house. From behind the thick porch post, the boy watched him approach. Cruz winked, trying to ease the worry in those young eyes—or was it suspicion?

Inside the house, a woman pitched forward at the waist, radiating hostility as she glared silently at the uniformed officer. The frenzied laughter of the Saturday morning cartoons filled the space between the two.

Cruz stepped into the small living room and took control. "Why did you wait until this morning to call?"

She jumped, her eyes wide at finding a second man in her house. Tall and scrawny, she wore pink sweatpants and a yellow T-shirt with a faded rainbow. Her dishwater-blonde hair poked out in tufts from a hastily tied tail. With a few more pounds, she could have been an attractive. "Who are you?"

"Detective Jesus De La Cruz. Could you turn the TV off?" The anorexic figures in primary colors disappeared, taking the noise with them. "Thank you. Officer, run the plates on the car in front of the house and get crime scene to sweep it."

"Yes, sir," the uniform said and set to his duties.

An impatient foot tapped. "You need to arrest the asshole who shot up my house."

He nodded as though there were all the time in the world. "I need some information to get started. You're Mrs. Parker, correct?"

The woman wrapped her arms across her stomach, her stance changing in a blink from aggressive to uncertain. "Hayley Parker." Her gaze fell to the floor and stayed there.

He had the distinct impression of a dog kicked too many times. "Why don't we sit, and you tell me what happened. I like the pumpkin on the door." He paid the compliment to put her at ease, to show he was on her side, and because he liked the pumpkin.

"Jace likes to draw and stuff."

"He's talented." With a sweep of his arm, he invited her to sit on her couch. He took the matching armchair. "Tell me what happened."

"Someone shot at my house." She sat ramrod straight and repeatedly looked to the place where the picture window should have been. "Is this going to take long?"

"No," he said, because it's the answer she wanted. "This was yesterday, Halloween. What time?"

Her head shook back-and-forth, back-and-forth. "I don't know. I wasn't looking at a clock."

"Tell me what you were doing."

"Jace and I were in the kitchen. I was making him a peanut butter and jelly sandwich to eat before trick-or-treating. He had his Halloween costume on—he was Spiderman—and climbing on the chair. I told him to get down before he fell. That's when I heard a pop and glass broke. I pulled Jace to the floor."

"Trick-or-treating began at six. Was it five? Five-thirty?"

"Five-thirty, I guess. Closer to it anyways."

"How many shots were fired?"

"I don't know. Four. Maybe five. I wasn't counting. Can't you—"

Shouting from the front porch cut her short. Low, bass notes filled with male bravado. Small words. Harsh tones.

The woman looked to the front door, covering her mouth with trembling fingers. "Christopher's home."

The front door burst open, and a lanky, white man stormed in. "Hayley. What the fuck did you do?" Christopher Parker stood a shade under six-foot, probably went all of a buck-sixty, but walked with the swagger of a stud.

Cruz stood between the wife and the cause of her anxiety. "Mr. Parker?" He asked the question, matching last names

4

were not a given.

Blocked from his wife, Parker's gaze snapped to Cruz's face. Then his eyes narrowed. "Do I know you?"

"Detective De La Cruz. Your wife reported shots fired at your home yesterday. Were you here when it happened?" Cruz dismissed the scrutinizing gaze and repeated the question. "Sir, were you here at the time of the shooting?"

Parker pressed his lips together like a four-year-old determined not to eat peas.

"Just tell him, Christopher. Let him get the bastard for what he did." Her voice quivered but had the boldness she used on the uniform.

Parker side-stepped and loomed over his wife. "I *told* you I would handle it. Don't involve the cops in my business."

"He shot at *me*, Christopher." She stood now, shouting back at her husband. "Me and Jace. I want him to pay."

Cruz raised his hand to stop Parker from silencing his wife. "Mrs. Parker, did you see who shot at the house?"

The show of strength didn't last long. Suddenly reticent, Hayley picked at the hem of her T-shirt. "I didn't, like, see him, but I know it was him. I *know*."

And that was the end. Hayley Parker shut down under her husband's reprimanding glare. She retreated into a shell where she couldn't remember the last twenty-four hours and wouldn't sign anything. Cruz left reluctantly not because he enjoyed their company, but because he was certain there was about to be an incident of domestic violence. He had done his best to warn off Parker but doubted it was good enough.

Jace Parker sat on the porch with his chin resting on his knees. He watched Cruz come out of his house with eyes too old.

"You're Jace, right? I'm Detective De La Cruz." He walked down the steps, intentionally standing on the walk so the boy wouldn't have to look up. "You can call me Cruz."

Jace had his mother's coloring and spectacularly large,

blue eyes.

He kept it casual, using the boy as an excuse to stay close to the house. Just in case. "Did you have a good Halloween?"

"It sucked." It was said without rancor by a boy who had too much experience with holidays falling short of commercial promises.

"You didn't get the candy you liked?"

Little shoulders rose and fell. "I was s'posed to go trick or treatin'. Then I didn't."

"That's rough. Hold on a minute." He jogged to his car and retrieved a bag of candy from the front seat. His nieces had made it from their own booty—primarily the candies they didn't like—topped off by his sister who preferred to rot her brother's teeth than her children's. It wasn't a lot of candy, but it might be enough to soothe the little boy. "Here you go."

Jace's blue eyes glistened as he peered in the bag. "Wow! Where did you get all this?"

The wonder at the small kindness made Cruz glad he'd thought of the candy. It was a little thing, but the boy looked at him like he was a hero. "I have nieces your age. They like to share. Are you allergic to nuts?" Unlikely as his mother had made him a PB&J the night before.

"Nah. Toby in my class, he's allergic to peanuts, but not me." His hand dove into the bag, withdrawing a prize piece of chocolate. "You don't dress like those other cops."

"No. I'm a detective." He held his badge out to the boy. "Do you know what a detective is?"

The blond head bobbed. "Inspector Gadget is a detective. Do you get all those things to track clues 'cause you're a detective?"

Cruz snorted with laughter. "I wish. I like your pumpkin. Did you make it in school?" He glanced at the door, listening for sounds saying he was needed.

"Kindergarten is fun. Ms. Williams reads us stories and teaches us numbers and she always smells good." He pulled out a purple-wrapped treat. "I'm going to give this to her."

"You like your teacher?"

Jace nodded. "She's nice and pretty. And she never yells. Even when you're doin' somethin' you're not s'pose to do. She looks sad and gives you a yellow on your card."

The wind gusted, reminding Cruz of the temperature. "Aren't you cold with just a sweatshirt on?"

"No." The boy wore jeans with a knee torn out, gym shoes, and a hooded sweatshirt. He dug into the bag again and came out up a lollipop. "I'm outside a lot. I watch for people."

"People? People like me? Police?"

"Sometimes. My mom called you to come."

"Do you know our job as policemen to help people? People like you and your mom and dad."

"Daddy says all cops do is fuck things up."

Cruz flinched. After everything he'd seen, he thought he was beyond surprise. Then, the day he expects a five-year-old to drop an f-bomb is the day he should turn in his badge. "I want to give you something, Jace. It's my card. If you need help, you call me. Any time, any day." He thought of his nieces, and how he took simple things for granted. "Do you know how to dial a phone?"

"You turn it on and push the numbers."

"Yep. These numbers here." He underlined digits. "You press these, and it'll connect to me."

"What about the two-one-six?"

"That's the area code." He added the one in front of the other digits. "You only need to dial these if you're far away. Like, in another state."

"Texas is a state." Jace handled the card reverently, as if it were a gift. He drew up his pantleg and put it in his sock. "If you catch Uncle, will you send him to Texas?"

Cruz stilled. He wouldn't question a kindergartener, but

he couldn't turn a deaf ear either. "Your uncle?"

"Not my uncle." Jace giggled. "His name is Uncle. Daddy and him go into the garage, but I'm not allowed to. Mommy says Uncle shot our house up."

Cruz was close and personal with the name. Uncle had been an up-and-comer when he first worked undercover narcotics. Cruz was skinnier then, hadn't filled out yet, with scraggly hair hanging in his face, a constant five o'clock shadow, and a thick street accent. He and Uncle came up through the ranks together, first as friends, then competitors. Both had vied for a coveted position within the organization. Cruz for the connections. Uncle for the drugs, money and women. Cruz had known there would come a time when he and Uncle would be down and dirty. Uncle got there first.

"Are you going to put him in jail?"

Cruz stroked the smooth scars at the corner of his eye. "It's not that simple." Which was a crappy answer. "Jace? Uncle is a bad man. I want you to promise me you'll stay away from him. Will you do that?" Knowing he'd already stayed too long, Cruz turned to the street. The uniformed officer was with the car owner. They would do the job, but without Hayley Parker naming Uncle, giving the case slim-to-none odds was being generous.

November 1

*I think about you every day. I wonder what you think of me.
I hope you don't hate me. I know it was my fault. If I listened to
you...If I was faster...If I knew...If*
   If
   If
   If
   If
   If
   If
   If
   If
   If
   If
   If
   If
   If
   If

CHAPTER TWO

Sunday, November 5

At age two, Rhianna DeMarco declared her uncle was her best friend. "Tito" took her to the park, kissed boo-boos, and played everything from coloring pages to soccer. Three years later, her best friends were her cat, her neighbor, but she steadfastly held onto Tito.

Cruz limped out of Sacrada Familia Catholic Church with a five-year-old barnacle looking at him like he was the best man in the world. "You're getting too big, girl. You're going to be carrying me soon."

"I can't carry you, Tito. You weigh, like, a thousand pounds."

"An elephant weighs a thousand pounds. Do I look like an elephant?" He lifted his squealing niece into the air. "What do you think, Gabby? Do I look like an elephant?"

At a sophisticated eight years old, Gabriella walked between her parents. She cocked her head, her long hair falling over her shoulder. "You used to look scary, like a monster. Now you look like...hmmm. I think you just look like Tito."

"*Elefante!*" Rhianna screamed, then faded into the laughter when his fingers tickled her.

"Jesus. Jesus!" His name raced the wind across the parking lot.

"Don't look now, Tito." Mariana, his favorite and only sister, smothered a giggle. "Mama has found another flower for you to pluck."

"*Aye Dios mio.*" The phrases in his head were so colorful, they were neon. His mother hurried across the parking lot. Running to keep up with the hand dragging her was a woman about his age with large chocolate eyes and white teeth set in an oversized grin.

"Jesus. This is Nadia. Nadia, this is my son, Jesus."

Cruz offered his hand. "Nadia. This is my sister, Mariana and her husband, Tony."

Vanessa De La Cruz shoved the jewel toward her son, cutting off the small talk. "Nadia is a secretary—"

"Administrative assistant," Nadia corrected.

"She has her own car, an apartment, and a 401(k) plan," his mother said without pause in her thick accent.

He swatted at his sister as she covered laughter with a cough. "Well, Nadia, congratulations, you are doing well."

"My son is a detective with the Cleveland police." His mother brushed the hair out of his face "The long hair isn't him. It's part of working under blankets."

He caught his mother's hand and held it, leaving his hair where it was. Six days a week, it was pulled against his head and tightly braided. Sundays, he let it hang free down his back and anywhere else it wanted to go. "Undercover, Mom. Not under blankets."

"I like your hair," Nadia said. "Is it as soft as it looks?"

"Tito," Rhianna said in a loud whine. "I have to go to the bathroom."

Mariana reached for her daughter. "Let's—"

Cruz shouldered his sister aside and lifted his niece to his hip. "Sorry, Nadia. Nature calls. You understand." He hurried toward the church without looking back.

Inside the foyer, Rhianna leapt down. "Did I do it right, Tito?"

"You were perfect." He knelt, took out his wallet, and handed Rhianna two dollar bills.

"Can we do it again?"

"With your *abuela*, we'll do it every Sunday." A throat cleared behind him. He cringed, dreading the lecture, then peeked over his shoulder. "Mari."

His sister stood with her arms crossed under her chest, her foot tapping on the carpeted floor. "I can't believe you would use my daughter this way." Her barely contained grin ruined the effect. "You better hope Mom doesn't catch you. I'm not covering your butt."

Rhianna giggled. "Butt."

"Every Sunday, Mari, every Sunday she finds a new girl to parade like, like…"

"For her, marriage and happiness are hand and glove. She wants to see you happy, that's all."

He opened the door enough to peer out. "We're clear." He took one of Rhianna's hands, his sister took the other. "A woman is not the answer to everything. Look, I know it's not *their* fault. That's why I came up with this. I make an exit, and nobody gets hurt."

At Mari and Tony's house, laughter and chatter and noise were the soundtrack to the dinner of stuffed peppers and rice Cruz prepared. This was his home for a year and a half. The room they kept for him anchored him in a world that still shifted beneath his feet. He loved those little girls, who had a sixth sense about when he hurt, when he struggled. They gave him the strength to step out on his own again.

Coming back each Sunday was a reward for making it through another week. He leaned back in his chair, content to watch the girls clear the table.

"Are you staying tonight, Tito?" Gabby asked with a broad smile.

"Please, please, please," Rhianna said, jumping with two plates in her hands.

"I stayed over Tuesday night." Cruz caught the plates before they fell, then pointed a finger between the two girls.

"Neither of you let me sleep. Four hours. That's all I got."

Gabby rolled her eyes. "It was Halloween, Tito. No-body's supposed to sleep on Halloween."

"Too many monsters." Rhianna pulled back her lips and gnashed her teeth.

"You definitely are going to keep me awake and I have to work in the morning. Plus, you know I meet Dr. Oscar on Sunday nights."

Both girls pouted, but then Gabby lifted her brows. "Will you play before you go?"

Rhianna grabbed her uncle's hand and pulled with all her might. "Yeah, yeah. Me and Gabby against Tito."

Hours later, Cruz walked into the familiar restaurant, high on life. After two years of meeting at the same table, he could find Bollier with his eyes closed.

"You have grass stains on your knees."

"I lost seventy to fifty-six. The girls cheat." As he sat, coffee appeared before him, dressed just the way he liked.

Dr. Oscar Bollier's edges were frayed: his hair too long, his shirt rumpled, his beard untrimmed. To find the man, you had to look in his eyes.

Calm. Collected. Content.

That drew Cruz to this man, the elusive Cs he wanted for himself.

"How's the office?" Cruz asked.

"Can't complain. Now, my patients, they complain. Did have something funny come in."

"Funny" was never "funny." Funny was weird or grotesque. It often oozed. It sometimes smelled. As he listened, Cruz was grateful, as he had been so many other times, that he was not eating. Even homicide detectives had their limits.

"And you," Bollier said. "Detect anything interesting lately?"

"I thought working undercover narcotics for six years I'd seen it all. Yesterday, a five-year-old dropped an f-bomb on me. Imitating his old man—a dealer."

"You knew him?"

"I'd been around him a few times. He tried to place me. The clean shave and new face throws them." He touched the scars at the corner of his eye that were his bane and had become his talisman. "He's going to try something stupid on a guy that takes pride on taking stupid shits apart. It gets so predictable, you know? There are times I'd like to see something different."

Bollier snorted derisively. "Be careful. I wished for something different once."

"What happened?"

"I got what I wished for."

November 5

No. No. No. This isn't happening. This isn't real. Don't go anywhere.

He's still dead. Maybe I'm dreaming.

I bit my tongue. I think it's bleeding.

Tastes like it. That doesn't prove I'm awake. Don't go anywhere

Not my fault. Not my fault. It was dark. Not my fault. Light flashed. Felt a thud. Not my fault. I got out to help. Not my fault. I thought it was a dog.

I should check for ID. Why didn't I think of that before?

I was right, it was a dog. The two-legged kind. The man sold drugs.

The City is better off without him.

CHAPTER THREE

Monday, November 6

Dressed for the day, Cruz leaned against the kitchen counter he'd installed himself, sipping coffee and reading the daily meditation. Weak sunlight poked through the blinds, striping the page until it was unreadable. He set the book aside. A moment later, his phone rang.

His day started with a caravan of city-issued cars parked on the northbound shoulder of I-71. The knot of concrete ribbons was the nexus of I-71, I-480, and the spurs to Cleveland Hopkins International Airport. Going through at sixty-five miles an hour, he had read the "Cleveland Corp Limit" sign hundreds of times but never noticed this triangle patch. The sign rose up behind the concrete barricade and between its legs was a post. The post wasn't interesting. It was what was on it.

"Just a head?" Cruz shouted to be heard over the white noise of traffic above, below and next to him. He swung a leg over the barricade and carefully lowered his weight to the ground. The land dropped sharply down to I-480. This wasn't a place made for walking.

"So far, Detective." One of the patrolmen on the scene, a big man named Buettner, answered him. Three others fought the wind to secure a tent screening the crime scene from the morning commute. "Had nearly a half dozen accidents with people looking at this."

"It would get my attention, even without coffee." Because he was watching his footing, he began with the ground. The post was one of the thousands sold for myriad household uses. Heavy enough gauge to be able to take some weight, small enough to be portable. The ground wasn't frozen, but it would take a mallet to drive it in deep enough to support a head. Crime scene would dust for prints. Overgrown scrub around the post was matted down but showed no footprints of the person who had stood here and planted the nightmare.

His latest customer died hard. The head was battered, scraped as though it had been bounced off pavement a few times. Something was familiar…

"Shit. Why wasn't I told his ID?"

"We don't have it yet, Detective. Can't take prints," Buettner said.

Cruz paced away. This wasn't coincidence or serendipity or even cosmic justice. This was just messed up. "His name is Alvin Hall. Street name Uncle."

Buettner's brows rose. "You know him?"

His hand lifted to his scars. "Narcotics."

"You sure it's him?"

When a guy puts you in a hospital for three months, rearranges your face, you tended to remember him. "I'm sure." Just another customer, he told himself, dropping into a squat. He looked at the dried chunk of meat that was Uncle's neck. The cut was smooth right through bone. "There's little blood on the ground. He wasn't killed or decapitated here." He stood, surveyed the surroundings, then pointed to the triangle valley between the highways. "Search that. See if you can find the rest of him."

A pair of patrol officers began the slow task of searching the uneven ground.

"What do we have on a timetable?"

"First call came in 6:45 a.m. First District responded. By the time I arrived, nine-one-one took a half dozen calls. I went south an exit and came back. It wouldn't have been visible in the dark. The bridge column shadowed it. I was on top of the thing before I saw it."

"It was cold last night. Everything is frosted. Except Uncle." Cruz made his way back to his car while they waited for crime scene. The highway was backed up as far as he could see. A man dressed for business rolled past, silently shouting and waving his hands at the police.

"Your day could be worse, buddy."

Two hours later, Cruz worked the case from the familiar confines of his desk. He cupped the hot mug of his second cup of coffee, bought en route. After this, he'd have to live on the gritty brew that passed for both coffee and tea. His fingers, stiff and cold, had yet to loosen up. He moved his entire hand when he typed, calling up the file on Alvin "Uncle" Hall.

Reports filled the screen documenting Uncle's rise on the streets. The stats were there, but not the story. To get that, he had to take a step backward. He looked up the number in the system directory. The name hung there, poking at the sore spots. He called himself a pussy and punched the numbers into his cell so hard he bobbled it. The call connected and was answered on the second ring.

"Yablonski."

The voice was the same. Ice water over sand paper. Course sand paper. Would he remember? "It's Cruz."

"Cruzie." The smile came through the phone. "How's homicide these days? Miss the action of narcotics?"

Matt Yablonski had been a friend, one of the many he walked away from to rebuild his life. There was guilt in that. "Nah, dying never goes out of style. Speaking of, came across

18

a mutual friend."

"Oh yeah? Who?"

"Uncle Hall."

"No shit. When?"

"Found his head this morning. Hoping the Medical Examiner will tell me more. I read the file but what's his story?"

"*That* was Uncle?" He said, then gave a low whistle. "He was running the Mid-Town Corridor but was getting squeezed lately."

"Squeezed? By who?"

"More like by what. Redevelopment. Gentrification. Cleveland Clinic keeps expanding west. Downtown is creeping east. Developers are buying up the old neighborhoods, replacing them with high-end townhouses. Not Uncle's type of people."

"They use, too."

"True, but those doctors can get better shit than what Uncle sells."

Cruz doodled on the margin of his legal pad. It morphed into a name. "Christopher Parker mean anything to you?"

Yablonski hesitated. "What does he mean to you?"

"His wife called in a drive-by shooting. Parker came home, unhappy to find her talking with me, said he was going to take care of the problem. Their five-year-old kid overheard his mother blame Uncle for the shooting."

"Is he at the top of your list?"

Cruz looked at the paper with only one name on it. "So far. See what you can find out for me."

"You going to pay a call?"

"Not yet. I want a reason to talk to Parker beyond what a kid says under the influence of a bag of candy. I'm going to check out Uncle's house, make the next-of-kin call. Mrs. Hall's a nice lady. I had dinner at her house once."

"That's messed up, you knowing her. You worried about being recognized?"

"Naw. It was more than three years ago, and I don't look the same."

Uncle lived in the house he grew up in—a two-story home on a narrow plot of land sandwiched between two other homes that could be touched by leaning out the double-sashed windows. Loretta Hall served Cruz meatloaf and mashed potatoes in a room with worn wallpaper and faces smiling out from pictures on the wall. It was a lot of years ago, before he and Uncle got sideways, but he tasted the tomato sauce she baked into the meatloaf.

The street had gotten rougher. Uncle stayed on, living in the neighborhood that made him his money.

A black metal fence had been installed since Cruz had last set foot on the property. Rods extending beyond the top brace were honed to a point. One gate, a super-sized black metal monster reached across the concrete drive.

Cruz stood on the sidewalk, looking for a mechanism to open the gate. He had traded his boots for leather shoes, so climbing was not on his to-do list. Still, without the electronic "open sesame," he had little choice. He took hold of two of the posts and braced his foot on a bracket.

"You don't wanna do that." The voice was male, elderly.

Foot back on the sidewalk, he turned to the voice. "Why not?"

Two hundred pounds of pissed-off dog answered. Two of them raced out from under the front porch. The male was a Rottweiler who went a buck and a quarter. His canine teeth were white daggers, ready for action. The female was a brindle mutt, small only in comparison to the Rott. Her growl rumbled deep in her chest, low and menacing.

"Easy Kobe. Down LeBron." The old man spoke with authority. "Good boy, LeBron." The Rott laid down but kept his eyes on the stranger. The mutt, Kobe by default, stood her ground, so ready to pounce that her body trembled.

He lifted the ID hanging from his neck. "Detective De La Cruz, Cleveland police."

"Walter Stanislav. Friends call me Stan." The old man had a shock of white hair on the top of his head, jowls that rivaled a St. Bernard, and glacial blue eyes with a twinkle that warned not to underestimate him. "You looking for Alvin?"

Just part of him. "Are you a friend of Mr. Hall's?"

"Neighbor. Known him all his life. Is he in trouble again?"

He ignored the question. First things first. "I'm looking for Mrs. Loretta Hall."

"She moved to a little place about two years ago. Got her address back in the house. Come on in. You want a cup of coffee? The wife makes a mean brew."

Cruz looked to Uncle's house. "I need to get in there. Any chance you can call the dogs off?"

Stan shook his head. "They know me, but not well enough."

Cruz called animal control and, accepting Stan's hospitality, waited in the comfort of a living room. Under the picture window, a low table was covered with vigorous plants and a picture of equally vigorously growing grandchildren. Looking beyond the plants, LeBron had gone back to the den under the porch, leaving Kobe on sentry duty.

"Sorry you had to wait so long." Stan came in carrying a silver tray from an era gone by. Two cups of coffee, cream, sugar, and a small purple paper were set on the coffee table. Cruz first accepted the note with Loretta Hall's address and phone number written in an elegant script, then he indulged in coffee strong enough to straighten his hair.

"You like it? It's Cuban. You Cuban?"

He stalled, sipping the coffee again, enjoying the jolt to his system and thinking, not for the first time, nobody laid it out like children and seniors. "My family is Puerto Rican."

"Puerto Ricans are all right. U.S. territory and all. No

communists. They're all right." He lifted his cup in a toast. "The wife gets it at the Hispanic grocery that opened in the plaza. They sell rice and beans and everything your folks need. You know it? Hacienda something something."

"No. You said you've known Alvin Hall for a while?"

"You should try it. Real authentic. As for Alvin, I've known him his whole life. I remember the day Loretta brought him home. The wife was pregnant with our first, and she was over there every day. She loves that boy. I let you skate by without answering me out there, but I'd like to know, is Alvin in trouble?"

Cruz measured the man behind the stern countenance. "I'm homicide. Mr. Hall was found this morning, and we are investigating. Tell me about Alvin."

Stan rubbed a calloused hand over his weathered features. His eyes glassed over, and he had to clear his voice twice before he could speak. "What's there to tell? He was a mean son-of-a-bitch. Oh, he was all right to us. Called us Mr. and Mrs. Stan. Even to this day." Stan paced his words, not rushing through what he had to say. His matter-of-fact tone didn't vary higher or lower, but he slowed some words, drawing out small ones, like "oh," out for a full two seconds. "I assume you know he sold drugs. I don't know if I'm supposed to know, but you don't live across from somebody for thirty-odd years and not know when something is rotten in Denmark."

"Did you see him sell drugs?"

"'Course not. What I saw was skeletons walking down my street. Every one of them went to Alvin's house."

"When did this start?"

"'Bout the same time he bought his mother a nice little house up in Shaker."

Uncle had taken Cruz off the streets two and a half years ago. The promotion after Cruz's accident must have made living with mommy difficult. "So you noticed odd things going on at Alvin's?"

"Detective, I don't know if you've noticed or not, but this is not what most folks consider a good neighborhood. Just because it's not a good neighborhood doesn't mean there aren't good people here. There was a time when Alvin was one of them. Drugs changed him. Made him hard. Made him mean." Stan sipped his coffee, looking absently out his picture window at the blue house across the street. "I saw him throw a woman out of his house once. She didn't touch the steps on the way down. Saw him pull a knife on a man."

"Did you call it in?"

Stan shrugged. "What was the point? It was over before it started. Nobody was going to wait around for the police to show up. Nobody saw nothing."

"Nobody ever sees anything. When was the last time you saw Alvin?"

Stan's mouth arched into a horseshoe shape. He was quiet as he thought. "Tuesday. Halloween. He left before trick or treating. I remember because I thought that was a good thing for the kids."

"How about yesterday? Did you see him then?"

"Can't say but I can ask the missus. She stays up on comings and goings more than I do." Stan stood when the animal control truck pulled in front of the house. "I guess I should have suspected something was wrong. Alvin doesn't leave those dogs outside at night. They threw up a fit around nine last night."

"Nine?" Cruz rose also but stayed for the story.

"Those dogs were going after something. I heard a slam, like a door close, and then everything quieted down. Didn't think anything of it."

"How did Alvin handle visitors? Between the gate and the dogs, how did anybody get in?"

"Well, now, that's the point of it all, isn't it? They didn't. Not without an invitation."

23

Cruz downed the last half of the damn good coffee and handed Stan the empty cup. "Thank you, Mr. Stanislav. For your help and the coffee."

"My pleasure, Detective. I'd like to call Loretta, help her any way we can."

"It would be better if you let me notify her first. Trust me, you don't want to be the first." With that, Cruz traded the warmth of the Stanislav home for the cold street and two animal control officers.

"What do we have?" one of them asked.

"Kobe." He pointed to the beast going nuts at the fence and then to the emerging Rott. "LeBron."

Skills. That's what collared the two dogs in less time than it took for the officers to get there. Cruz left them to fill out paperwork and mounted the front steps to Alvin Hall's home.

The front door was ajar.

Gun in hand, he knocked loudly, announced himself, and entered.

The carbon copy of the Stanislav home was decorated in stripper red and ass kicker black. The living room was arranged around an entertainment center featuring a television that took up half the width of the narrow wall.

The room had bachelor clutter—take-out bags, socks, shirts, a cereal bowl—and dealer clutter—bags, needles, knives, guns.

Cruz called out again. No one answered. He swept through to what used to be the dining room and was now a prep room. Interior decorating hadn't made it this far. Random strips were missing from the wall paper. The happy, smiling faces were replaced with smudges and dents, giving the room a war-torn look.

An arched doorway off the dining room was hidden behind a stained, thick, cream-colored drape. He swept in low. The room was empty. Two twin mattresses against opposite walls were unmade. Sheets and thin blankets hung in twisted ropes across the floor. More take-out bags, a box of cereal, knocked over and half spilled. Three empty Red Bull cans.

Back to the dining room and then through to the kitchen.

This was a different kind of mess. One of the kitchen chairs was on the stove, another sprawled over the sink. Anything that had been on the vintage 1960s' table was scattered over the floor.

Cruz made the call to crime scene.

He moved back through the house to the stairs and cleared the second floor. Two bedrooms. The larger room contained a wooden framed, full-sized bed, which was surprisingly feminine. His mother's? Another television, more clothes, more drugs.

The smaller room had a twin-sized mattress on a metal frame. There were no sheets but a thin navy-blue comforter. The rest of the room was empty except for posters of past NBA stars on the walls. Michael Jordan. Shaquille O'Neal. Terrell Brandon. Zydrunas Ilgauskas.

Blasts from the past.

It struck him that he and Uncle had been the same age. Cruz had just entered high school when the big "Z" stepped onto the Cleveland Cavaliers court for the first time.

He filled his time waiting for crime scene getting reacquainted with Uncle. He found proof of Uncle's drug activities but didn't find the man himself—or the rest of the man himself, as the case were. With the very public discovery of Uncles head, it wasn't long before crime scene knocked on the door.

Uncle had moved his mother to a neat and trim bungalow just inside the Shaker Heights city limits, an upscale suburb abutting Cleveland. Cruz turned off the main boulevard, through wide streets with hundred-year-old trees to a sweet little neighborhood tucked away from the rest of the world. A safe neighborhood where children's laughter competed with the birds for air time.

Pastor Michael Ashford sat in the passenger seat, watching the scenery in solemn silence. The middle-aged man was as white as a slice of bread. His thick brown hair was flecked with enough silver to garner respect and framed a full face with kind brown eyes. Cruz's gut had him calling the man who was a friend to Cleveland police. If there was such a thing as being good at this kind of stuff, Pastor Mike was.

Cruz understood the psychology of grief, but he wasn't a counselor. Words weren't his strength, and emotions he avoided. Mrs. Hall mattered. He wanted more for her than what he had to give. Too quickly, he parked in front of a picture-perfect house with a Honda Civic sitting in the driveway. The one-story, square brick house had a thick lawn, still green and weed free. On the small sandstone porch, two flower pots overflowed with brilliant orange mums. A sign hanging next to the front door said "Welcome" in seven languages.

Cruz gritted his teeth and walked up the stairs, knowing without looking that the pastor was right behind him, ready for the fall-out. He palmed his credentials and rang the bell.

The woman who answered the door was a little older than the picture in his memory, but the eyes were the same. Wide. Warm. Welcoming. She had put on a few pounds, weight that looked good on her tall frame. He remembered Loretta Hall as tired and worn. The woman in front of him looked the picture of health with her flawless, dark complexion.

Bile rose at what he was about to do to her. "Mrs. Hall?"

The welcome in her eyes dimmed. She wrapped her arms under her breasts, over the scrubs with kittens and puppies on them. "Yes?"

"I am Detective De La Cruz, Cleveland police."

"Cleveland?"

"Yes, ma'am." Say it fast and clear. It was the kindest thing to do. "I regret to inform you that—"

"Don't say it." She closed her eyes and held her hand out. "Please, don't say it."

Cruz swallowed again. "That your son, Alvin Hall, was found dead."

"When?" She whispered, her eyes still closed.

"This morning, ma'am. May we come in? This is Pastor Michael Ashford."

Mrs. Hall dropped her head and stepped backward, letting Cruz enter and Ashford behind him. Ashford quickly took the lead, guiding Ms. Hall to a sturdy chair at her dining room table. The room was small, the table with four chairs nearly filled the space. A corner cabinet snuggled next to a window held treasured glass figurines. The short spans of walls were covered with the smiling faces Cruz remembered plus a few new ones. Alvin was up there.

"We are very sorry for your loss, Mrs. Hall. Is there someone I can call to be with you?" Michael asked.

"M-my sister. My sister, Bernice." She picked up the cell phone on the table, fumbling it as dysfunctional fingers tried to touch in the right places. "A-are you sure it was Alvin?"

"Yes, ma'am," Cruz said.

"How? How did he die?"

"We are still putting together the details. His head was found this morning."

She grabbed onto the table. "Did you say...?"

"Yes, ma'am. I'm going to ask you to keep that to yourself. It's important for us to keep certain details from becoming public while we investigate the homicide. Do you understand, Mrs. Hall?"

She nodded, her head moving the slightest bit possible.

"Was Alvin having trouble with anyone? Maybe at work?

In his personal life?"

She blinked rapidly, processing what Cruz had said. "He was murdered. If it were a car accident or the like, his head would...wouldn't..." She handed the phone to Pastor Michael and left him to make the call.

Michael went into the small kitchen and spoke to the sister in quiet, calm tones.

"We are still trying to understand the circumstances. When was the last time you spoke with Alvin? May I sit?"

"Sit? Oh, good Lord. My manners. Where are my manners? Would you like something to drink? I have...what do I have?" Mrs. Hall looked to Cruz for the answer.

"A glass of water would be appreciated." He didn't want the water, but she needed a purpose for that specific moment. A respite while she digested the information.

Michael disconnected the line. "Your sister is on her way."

"Thank you. Would you like a glass of water? I'm sorry, I've forgotten your name."

"Michael." He smiled gently. "Most people call me Pastor Mike."

"Michael," she repeated. "Like the angel." The kitchen was a ten-by-ten square, broken up by three doorways and the usual appliances. The corner near the sink had a cabinet over top. Mrs. Hall opened the door and retrieved a glass. It slipped from her hand, shattering on the countertop. "Oh. Look what I've done."

Michael stilled her hands. "I'll take care of it. Sit and talk with Detective De La Cruz."

Mrs. Hall walked the six steps from the kitchen to the dining room chair, her mind disconnected from her body. She sank slowly into the chair, facing Cruz.

"Mrs. Hall, when was the last time you spoke with Alvin?"

"Yesterday. He picked up a bucket of chicken for lunch.

He always buys extra, so I can eat it during the week. I cooked for him his whole life and suddenly I can't cook for myself." She smiled as she spoke, lost in an argument that had become a running joke. A tear rolled down her cheek.

"What time did he leave?"

"Three? Maybe three?"

"Did he say where he was going?"

She shook her head. A slow movement to the left and then to the right. "I thought he was going home."

"And you aren't aware of anyone who might have wanted to hurt your son?"

Her gaze flickered with the intensity of a supernova. "I know what people say about Alvin. But they don't know him. He is a good man. He bought this house. He helped me plant my flowers. You tell me how bad a man can be that helps his mother plant flowers."

"A good man, I like to think. I help my mother with her flowers, too. She has a thing for roses."

She searched his face, then she pressed a hand to her throat, her mouth curling in distaste. "They say he sells drugs."

"My priority is finding the person who ended your son's life. The more you can tell me, the better I can do my job."

"I don't know how Alvin made his money." Mrs. Hall wouldn't look at him. "When I asked, he would say I didn't need to worry about it."

"What about friends, girlfriends? Anyone who might have been with him after he left here Sunday?"

"Maybe Gerard. They've known each other since middle school." Mrs. Hall reached for the phone again, but just couldn't seem to pick it up.

"I have it, Loretta," Pastor Mike said. "Gerard?"

She nodded. "Gerard Wallace."

"Found it. It's ringing."

Mrs. Hall accepted the phone back and held it to her ear.

29

"'Lo?" Cruz could hear the voice as clearly as if it had been on speaker phone.

"Gerard? It's Loretta Hall."

"Hey, Mrs. H. What's up?"

"Gerard. The police are here. They say that Alvin is…" She choked on the word that said she was never going to see her baby again. "They say he's dead." She shoved the phone at Cruz.

"Mr. Wallace. This is Detective De La Cruz, Cleveland police. Is there a place we can meet?"

Wallace snorted. "No place around here."

"Euclid and Mayfield. There's a coffee shop."

Silence answered.

He pressed. "For Mrs. Hall."

"Thirty minutes. You ain't there, I ain't stayin'."

When the line went dead, Cruz looked at Pastor Mike. "I have to leave."

"Go on. My wife will pick me up."

Mrs. Hall put her hand on Cruz's arm. "Please, Detective… take care of my boy."

Night had firmly taken hold as Cruz parked under the flood-light. He had made this journey one hundred twenty-four times before. The first time was hard. The next few times harder. While the journey then became easier, recovery would always be something he worked at. Inside, he silently climbed the stairs to the main floor where bad coffee and familiar faces greeted him.

"Cruz, you look cold. Coffee's hot." A man looking twenty years older than his age poured liquid sludge into a white cup and offered it.

Gratitude put the smile on Cruz's face. "You know my soft spot."

November 6

I watched the morning news. They announced "breaking news" and cut away to another reporter. They found my sign.
When the other drug dealers see it, they'll get out of my city. No one else will have to live in this hell I'm in.

CHAPTER FOUR

Wednesday, November 8

Forty-eight hours later, Cruz still collected puzzle pieces. Interviews and searches failed to connect Uncle to the drop spot. While he waited for results from the labs, he sat at a table for two, tugging on another string. He studied the placemat to distract himself from being nervous. Stupid shit. You'd think he was meeting a date instead of—

Matt Yablonski walked in, wearing his game face.

Yablonski had to stand on his toes to reach six feet. Shaped like a bullet, the polish on his shaved head gleamed in the lights. His thick neck connected ears to shoulders. Tree trunk thighs meant he swung his legs out to the side to walk. His face made up for the lack of hair on his head. The full beard, the color and texture of copper wire, would impress ZZ Top. Add eyes as grey as thunderstorm and Matt Yablonski was a thing of nightmares.

Those eyes scrutinized Cruz and then flashed with recognition. "Lookie what we have here! Didn't recognize you with that pretty face." Yablonski smiled, it was the face of a smart ass. "All that nasty, long hair gone. Your nose is straight. Who comes out of a mess like that with their nose straighter?"

"The hair's not gone, just tamed." He pulled the braid from behind his neck. "Looks like the years smacked you in the face with an ugly stick."

Yablonski drew his beefy hand down his long beard. "I'm

an acquired taste."

Laughing, Cruz stood and greeted his long-lost friend with a one-armed hug. The bear hug in return cracked his back.

"It's been too damn long, Cruzie. Too damn long."

"It has," he said as they took their seats. "I appreciate—"

"What's good here? Business before pleasure, remember?" He picked up the menu.

"I forgot how seriously you take a meal." There was no awkwardness. He had been afraid there would be. He should have known better. This was Yablonski. "Steak and eggs. Unless you're watching your girlish figure."

Yablonski ditched the menu, then patted his barrel belly. "Don't gotta do that anymore. Got myself a woman."

"The blow-up kind doesn't actually count as a woman."

He muttered unpleasantries as he pulled out a picture and held it for inspection. "Erin."

A pretty woman sat on Yablonski's lap. The look on his face said it all. "A cute nurse. I withdraw my previous remarks."

"Damn right you do." Yablonski smiled at the picture before putting it away. "How about you?"

"Appallingly single, if you ask my mother."

"Bet that pretty face of yours gets you plenty of booty."

Cruz snorted. He'd slept solo since his face got close and personal with an engine block. Turns out, ugly isn't sexy. "That's me. Every night and twice on Sundays."

The waitress came over, refilled Cruz's cup, and filled Yablonski's up. "Are you ready to order?"

"Two steak and eggs," Cruz said. "I'll take my steak medium, my eggs over easy. Make my friend's steak medium rare and scramble the eggs."

Yablonski clapped his fist over his heart. "You do remember."

"Yeah." He choked up, suddenly missing the friend three

feet away. "I remember." He sipped his coffee, watched the waitress as she turned in the order.

"Uh oh. Awkward silence." Yablonski threw a folder on the table. "Our friend Uncle was a busy man."

The mug shot sat atop the thick pages. Uncle looked like shit. Strung out. Pissed off. Yablonski talked through the years Cruz had missed.

"Uncle turned into a regular entrepreneur," Cruz said. "If he was pushing out, someone had to be pushing back."

"Lots of someones. You nail down the timeline?"

"Left his mother's house around three. Was with a woman, Candy Licious, starting around six. She swore he was alive and grinning from the happy ending she'd left him with. Neighbor heard the dog bark around nine. First call on his head came in at six-forty-five the next morning."

Breakfast arrived. New York strips with two eggs and a mountain of shredded, golden fried hash browns. Yablonski jumped in. Cruz hadn't gotten fork to steak when his cell rang. They both looked at it.

"Goddammit," Yablonski said. "Every time I have a hot meal in front of me..."

"Well, not every time." He pointed at his friend's barrel belly. "Besides, it's my phone. Keep eating." He pressed answer. It was the news he was waiting for. "All right... thanks." And he ended the call. "Christopher Parker's prints were on the chair in Uncle's house."

"Only his?"

"His were only on the chairs that were impaled on the stove and straddling the kitchen sink." Cruz cut into his steak. "Want to pay Parker a visit?"

Cruz held the storm door open and knocked on the closed front door. He knocked a second time, and the door opened slowly. Both he and Yablonski held their badges up.

"Mrs. Parker? It's Detective De La Cruz. Do you remember me?"

Hayley Parker was down five pounds she couldn't afford to lose. Her eyes were sunken with dark circles beneath; her cheek bones were more prominent. One was red, swollen, visible even through the veil of hair hiding her face. "I remember."

This was one of those times he wished he'd been wrong. "Are you hurt, Mrs. Parker?"

Her eyes grew as big as quarters. "No. No, I'm fine. I just, uh, fell. I was g-getting something. From a shelf. That's when I fell."

The lie was so pathetic it didn't qualify as a lie. If she wouldn't press charges, there wasn't much Cruz could do. At least about domestic violence.

"Fuck, Hayley, it's cold," Christopher Parker shouted from inside the house.

"Mr. Parker," Cruz said, raising his voice. "Police."

"What the fuck are you doin' here?"

Hayley Parker was jerked backward, the door ripped from her hand. Parker pushed into the space, running into Cruz.

Cruz pulled Parker out the doorway and planted his shoulder blades around a porch column.

"No! Christopher!" Hayley reached for her husband, but Yablonski's figure was a solid obstacle.

"What the fuck is goin' on!"

"You're under arrest for assaulting a police officer." Cruz spun him and cuffed him.

Parker squealed when the cuffs locked on his wrists. "I didn't."

"I witnessed it," Yablonski said. "He assaulted both you and his wife. Do you want to press charges, ma'am?"

Hayley cowered in the doorway. "What? No. Let him go. Christopher?"

Parker grunted as his chest was pressed into the cold

wood. "Fuckin' cops. Go inside, Hayley. Don't say nothin' to nobody. Fuck!"

"Extensive vocabulary you have, Mr. Parker. What is this?" Cruz pulled a gun from the waistband of the jeans, hidden under a baggy sweatshirt.

"Protection. This is a rough neighborhood."

Cruz handed the gun to Yablonski. "You have a concealed carry license?"

No answer.

"Let's take a ride downtown."

Cruz walked into the interview room with the case file in his hand and Yablonski on his heels. Damn, it felt good to have the bald-headed bastard on his side again. Cruz turned on the recording device, said the obligatory identification, reread Christopher Parker his rights.

Parker looked at Cruz with narrowed eyes filled with contempt. "This is because of Hayley? She fell, man. Not my fault she's fuckin' clumsy."

"Do you understand your rights, Mr. Parker?" Cruz asked again.

"Yeah. Whatever. I didn't hit her."

Cruz and Yablonski sat opposite Parker at a gray steel table bolted to the floor. Parker was bolted to the table, thanks to the assault charge.

"Sunday, November fifth, you went to the house of Alvin Hall—street name Uncle."

"No. I was home Sunday night," Parker said, cutting him off. "Ask Hayley."

"You were not home. I don't need to ask your wife. I have your fingerprints."

"I mighta been to his house but it wasn't Sunday. Whatever you think you found was, like, old."

Cruz took two photos from the case folder. "These chairs

had your prints on them. Not Uncle's. On the bottom side of the seat. Where you would put your hand to throw a chair at someone."

"So what? I missed. That fucker is faster than he looks."

"Sunday, November fifth, you went to the house of Alvin Hall. What time did you arrive?"

"I don't know. It was dark. He opened the door and let me in. I didn't break in. He has those dogs."

"We know you didn't break in. We know you and he fought. You ended up on top. He ended up dead." Cruz improvised, processing Parker's home spun information to fit the facts of the case.

"Wh-what? Uncle is dead?" Parker lost the cocky mask for ten seconds. "Shit, no, you just playin' cop games."

"Uncle is dead," Yablonski said, speaking for the first time. "And we got you for his murder."

Parker and Yablonski locked gazes, then Parker burst like a festered boil. "No, man. Uh uh, no way, no how. I didn't kill him. He was hit by that van. I saw. I'm like a fuckin' witness or some shit."

Cruz leaned back in his chair, crossed his arms, and gave Parker the rope to hang himself. "Let's hear it."

"I went over, like you said. To talk. That's it."

"After what happened on Halloween? You didn't go there to talk."

Parker's eyes hinted he was more dangerous than the scrawny, white guy packaging let on. "He needed to be convinced to stay away from my house."

House, Cruz noted. Not family. Not wife and son. "How did you convince Uncle?"

"He wanted something from me."

"Your territory?"

"He wanted me to work for him. He went into the kitchen. I said no with a chair or two. He ran."

"Uncle was a fighter."

"He was all talk. When he saw I wasn't havin' it, he took off. I chased that fucker through yards. I was comin' down a driveway when *puhhh*." His fingertips touched and then sprung wide in explosion. "This van nailed him."

"A van."

"It was, like, a work van. No windows. Dark. Black or somethin'."

"Did the driver stop?"

"Yeah." He wiped his mouth. "He went around the front, but Uncle wasn't there. He came out the other end."

"Was Uncle alive?"

"How the fuck do I know?" Parker's voice climbed a few decibels. "All I cared about was getting out of there."

The story was just messed up enough to be the truth, or as close to it as Parker could come. Adding to it, the damage to Uncle's head could have been done by a vehicle.

"What did you do next?" Cruz asked.

"I went back to my car. I went home."

"You're going to stay as our guest while we check out your story," Cruz said. He ended the interview and signaled for Parker to be taken to holding.

Cruz and Yablonski stood in Hall's yard, looking for the route Uncle and Parker took.

"Straight is fastest," Yablonski said and climbed the first fence. Cruz followed, crossing through to the street behind Uncle's. Slowly, methodically, the pair searched, speaking with residents as they progressed. Two streets over, a woman in a boldly flowered housedress leaned over the railing of her porch.

"Cleveland police, ma'am." Yablonski help up his badge.

"I have something for you." She came down the stairs and shoved a yellow dish towel into Cruz's hands.

From the shape and weight, he knew what it held. He

carefully unwrapped the gun. "Where did you get this?"

"In the landscaping. I found it Monday."

"Do you know how long it was there?"

"Could be a week. Mighta been a day. Someone trampled my mums."

Cruz didn't see Parker caring about ruining someone's flowers, but wouldn't he have noticed losing a gun? "Did you see a traffic accident here? Sunday night, after nine p.m.?"

She shook her head. "I was watching a show on that History Channel. You ever watch it?"

"One of my favorite channels," Yablonski said grinning. "What was the show?"

The woman's eyes lit in surprise, then she smiled. "Churchill. He was a bastard wasn't he? Smart man but a real bastard."

While Yablonski interviewed the woman, Cruz searched the street. One house away, a dark stain on the street had a splatter pattern. He dropped to his hands and knees for a worm's eye view. Against the curb was something that shouldn't have been there.

"What is it?" Yablonski asked.

"A shoe." Cruz held up a size fourteen, top of the line Nike. "I'll call crime scene."

Yablonski's phone rang. He listened, his gaze flashing up to Cruz. "I'll be there." He stowed the phone. "Gotta run. Customer of my own. Suspected overdose."

November 8

A girl died today. I heard her sister's cries. I knew them because they were mine.

It never stops. It doesn't matter what mayors say or cops do or people think. It never stops. It doesn't care if you're rich or poor or young or old. It doesn't care if you're black or white or Asian or Hispanic or whatever.

Everything would be good if drugs didn't exist.

Drugs are like….are like…A PLAGUE Yes! Ripping through the city like some…some…I need a word.

A pestilence.

A calamity.

Merriam-Webster know what they're talking about calling it black death.

I feel helpless, just like that day and every day since. The black death surrounds me. Is there really nothing that can be done to stop it?

They need to be warned. They need another sign.

CHAPTER FIVE

Saturday, December 16

Six weeks led nowhere on Uncle's case. His head had been released to his mother. Cruz ignored recommendations and attended the service filled with people who loved Loretta Hall. He hadn't given up, but the trail had gone cold. Cruz's case load, on the other hand, had heated up, pushing Uncle to "second shift."

He and Yablonski had breakfast a couple times a week. They didn't talk shop, not much. He liked having a friend again. When Yablonski asked him to throw darts for the fifth time, he finally agreed.

So here he was, palms sweating, legs trembling as he crossed the parking lot. Becky's on East 18th served food— damn good food—but it was a bar. Before that first AA meeting, he hadn't understood there wasn't a cure for addiction. For the rest of his life, he would be battling his monsters.

You can leave. He had to do this sooner or later. *Doesn't mean today.* He had to face the monster in his own territory.

Cruz pulled the door open and crossed the threshold. Hometown rock 'n' roll slapped him in the face. The sticky, sweet scent of stale alcohol hung heavy in the air, calling to him like a lover, promising to make everything better.

His demon reared, diamond-tipped claws ready to render his ass into sausage, to turn him into a pulpy memory of what he had become.

He took a deep breath, one meant to fortify but instead suffocated. He wasn't strong enough to do this. Turning tail, he had to get the hell out before he fucked up.

"Cruzie!" Yablonski's grating voice cut through the crowd and had every head turn his way. Cruz had a hand on the door when Yablonski crushed him in a one-armed hug and shoved a glass into his hand.

"Son of a bitch. You know I don't drink." He shoved the glass away as if it were a live grenade, stepping back until the door frame knocked his head.

"I thought you just gave up alcohol. How do you take a piss?"

His heart pounding in his ears, Cruz looked at the cocky grin on Yablonski's face, then at the red, fizzy drink. "Wh-what is it?"

"A Brass Ball. 7UP and cranberry juice."

Cruz took the glass, sipped it. 7UP and cranberry.

"My sister's husband drinks this. He's recovering, too. I named it, though. Any alchy who has the balls to be in a bar deserves showing what he has—big, huge, brass balls that ring when he walks. But that was too long, so I called it Brass Ball."

Cruz laughed. Deep down, core deep. The demons were chained for the night. He took the drink. "Just what I needed."

"Let's play some darts. I think you know most of the guys. You picked a good day. It's Vinnie's birthday. Free wings."

December 16

I found a paper on the sidewalk yesterday. It had the picture of an angel in a breast plate with his wings spread wide. He held the scales of justice in his left hand and readied a long sword in his right. Under his foot was a large creature with human head and shoulders, black wings, and a serpent's body. He is straining, trying to escape. The angel's face was calm. He wasn't angry. He was just doing his job, ridding the world of the demons infesting the earth.

On the back was the prayer to St. Michael, the Archangel. They are the most powerful words I've ever read.

Saint Michael the Archangel, defend me in battle. Be my protection against the malice and snares of the Devil. Through me, may God rebuke him, I humbly pray. And do Thou, o Prince of the Heavenly Host, by the power of God, thrust into Hell Satan and all evil spirits who wander through the world for the ruin of souls

I have a serpent in my sights. Today, I take up Michael's sword to end the ruin of souls.

CHAPTER SIX

Friday, December 22

Cruz leaned against the table at Becky's sipping his usual. This was the third time he'd stepped through the door. He looked forward it to now, having Yablonski waiting for him, a Brass Ball in one hand and darts in the other. Each time Cruz left—no matter the score of the matches—he won. With the help of AA and a stubborn friend, Cruz was reclaiming the life alcoholism had stolen.

Yablonski carried their team, making up for Cruz's lack of skill. That ended tonight. After his last ass kicking, he had bought tungsten tipped darts that felt like they were made for his hand. He practiced every night, no matter how late he got home.

Yablonski frowned as he scored Cruz's throw. "You put a little something in your Brass Ball? 'Cause I'm not cool with that."

"Nothing but 7UP and cranberry." The grin on his face went ear-to-ear, and he didn't care how stupid it looked.

Yablonski took his glass and sipped. Then he clapped his hands and spun to face his opponents. "Gentlemen. What do you say we make this interesting?"

Every dart went exactly where Cruz wanted. The moaning after he let each one fly eased the sting to his credit card.

Yablonski jawed as he raked in the winnings and shoved half at Cruz. "Do you need another lesson, boys?"

Cruz's phone rang. "Hold on, Yablonski. Dispatch." He walked to a quieter corner, then signaled the dart throwing portion of his night was over. He ended the call and went back to the table for his coat and to kick in for the tab.

"Whaddya got?" Yablonski asked.

"Another head."

"Like Uncle?"

Cruz shrugged. "I'll find out."

"We'll find out. I'm going with you."

At 9:30 p.m. at the end of December, I-90 westbound at the Cleveland-Euclid boarder was a brutal choice for a crime scene. Winds whipped easterly, using the highway as its personal expressway, oblivious to the straggling traffic fighting up wind. Small, icy flakes of snow were tossed in the air. They went left, right, north, south. All depending on the mood of the fickle wind—a wind that didn't just chill, it froze.

Five black and whites lined the interstate shoulder. Officers from the fifth district stood in the cold, a human barricade against rubberneckers and social media hounds. The area glowed like a radioactive snow globe under the light spillage from a nearby Honda dealership and the spinning lights of the cop cars.

"He came from over here," one of officers on the scene said as he pointed. "There's boot prints."

Excited by the possibility of evidence, Cruz hurried to the head. Markers delineated the route the killer took. Treadless prints stepped over the slop left by the snow plows, then beelined to the post planted in front of the Cleveland Corp Limit sign.

"Crime scene been called?"

"En route, sir."

Satisfied, he moved to the head mounted on another generic post, inside the fence, facing on-coming traffic. The victim was

Hispanic male with chin length, black hair much like Cruz's own when it wasn't braided tight against his head. The wind whipped wet strands around the unfeeling face. The eyes were closed, the mouth opened.

"What time was it reported," Cruz asked.

"Ten minutes before nine," the officer marking off the prints said.

Cruz looked at the road below where his car sat idling to the line of cars on the highway. A van would screen the killer from on-coming traffic. Drivers would have to look behind them to see and at full speed, with the icy flurries, most wouldn't. If they did, what would they see in the one or two second glimpse? He signaled a uniformed officer. "Go to the dealership and check out their security. It's a long shot but see if they caught the killer on security."

Yablonski stoked his beard as he studied the head. "I know him." His gaze left the familiar face and found Cruz's. "His name is Martinez. He was arrested a week ago for possession after his girlfriend OD'd."

"I want to know everyone he knew, Yablonski. Get me names."

Saturday, December 23

Cleveland Police Chief Edwin Ramsey played defensive back for the Ohio State Buckeyes for four years before going pro with the Cleveland police. The time on the force, the years behind the desk hadn't diminished the physical presence that was Win Ramsey. The chief leaned forward, his forearms on the polished dark wood of a desk as large as the man who occupied it. Behind him, the flags for the United States of America, the State of Ohio, and the City of Cleveland stood as sentries, symbols of the thin blue line between civilization and chaos.

"Is there a serial killer loose in my city, Detective?"

Cruz stood at attention, feeling the weight of his chief's authority. "We have two men killed, their heads severed and mounted on posts in public locations. Both victims had arrests for drugs—one for selling, the other for using. While it would be hard to argue the killings are not related, it is not definitive if they are serial."

Ramsey was a dark skinned black man with equally dark eyes set in flawless white marble. His wide face was proportionate to his six-foot-five frame. The high cheekbones and thick brows made the highly-educated, highly-decorated chief of police a man no one wanted to cross. "You're opinion, Doctor?"

Dr. Ming Chen, MD, PhD served as the department's resident expert in psychiatry and psychology. The Chinese-American embodied the stereotypical Asian—average height, slim build, earth brown eyes, straight as a pin black hair, but when he opened his mouth, Virginia poured out. Manassas, Virginia, where he'd been born nearly sixty years prior. "I have reviewed the case files for both Alvin Hall and Mathias Jose Martinez, Chief. We are nearly certain Martinez suffocated. The cause of death for Hall is less clear. The blunt force trauma caused by vehicular contact certainly *could* kill. But did it? We don't know. Hall's head was what I'll call 'fresh' while Martinez was kept on ice for a time, hindering the estimate of the time of death. Neither head showed sign of abuse—"

"Aside from Hall's road rash, Martinez's blue lips, and the heads being detached from the rest of the body," Chief Ramsey said.

Chen nodded his acquiescence. "I meant that the faces had not be struck, beaten. When the motivation is hate or anger, it is not uncommon to see violent damage done to the face. It's personal. The heads were taken with a sharp, smooth blade. I wouldn't go as far to say it was clinical, but it was...oh, what word am I looking for..."

"Dispassionate?" the chief offered.

"Excellent word. The crimes are vicious but dispassionate. That's my best guess, with what little we have to work with."

"Yes," the chief said, turning to Cruz. "Where are the bodies?"

Word went out and all of the Cleveland police was looking for the bodies of Hall and Martinez. "I can tell you a hundred places they aren't, sir."

"You had a man in custody after the first body."

"Yes, Christopher Parker. He was likely the last person to see Alvin Hall alive. They fought. Parker chased Hall. Parker said Hall was hit by a van. A gun was recovered. Parker's prints were on it, but it hadn't been discharged. A shoe was also recovered. Strands of hair found in the shoe were a match to Hall."

"Just one shoe?" the chief asked.

"Just one. Blood on the street was confirmed as Hall's. No other witnesses. No body. Parker's prints were found in Hall's home but not on the post used to mount the head. In fact, no prints were found at the crime scene. In the end, there just wasn't the evidence to hold Parker."

"Are you considering him for Martinez?"

"Yes. I'm waiting on the lab reports to come in. No prints were again found on the metal post, but there were boot impressions in the snow. I asked Detective Yablonski for support in looking for a connection between Hall, Parker, and Martinez."

The chief turned to Yablonski. "Have you found anything, Detective?"

"We are still working on it, sir. We have a firm connection between Parker and Hall, as Detective De La Cruz indicated. Hall's territory was getting squeezed by the expansion of the University Circle institutions and redevelopment of the old neighborhoods. Parker worked the Slavic Village and had a few boys working corners for him. He's ambitious, wants to be seen as the boss. We noticed increased tensions since last summer. While Martinez's arrest in December was for possession, he'd been on our radar for months. We suspect Martinez worked the west side—Lorain to Detroit— West Fiftieth to West Eighty-Fifth."

Cruz family's church stood in the middle of Martinez' territory. Sometimes the city was too damn small.

Yablonski continued. "A woman overdosed in his bed. Her sister found them and called us before Martinez was sober enough to stop her. I was on the scene. The sister accused Martinez of murder. We arrested him, searched the apartment. The only blow we found was the leftovers from the night before. When interviewed by the prosecutor, the sister admitted the dead woman frequently used."

"All right, I see where this is going. Ms. Hyatt, how is the media playing this?"

Alison Hyatt was the public information officer for the police department. The daughter of a career police officer, she began as a reporter and was persuaded to the other side of the microphone by her aunt, a councilwoman and staunch supporter of the Cleveland police. A slight, white woman in impeccable business attire, Alison was a skilled professional. "Hall's story died fast. It was sensational for a day with the number of people seeing the head. Hall's record with drugs and Mrs. Hall unwillingness to discuss the circumstances of her son's death killed the story. With Martinez, the papers and television are pushing."

"Social media?" the chief asked.

"Limited traffic so far. The weather and location weren't favorable for selfies. Conventional media is Facebooking it but not many are biting. Martinez's social circle hasn't broken through although we haven't confirmed his identification, pending notification of next of kin."

The chief's gaze swung back to Cruz. "When?"

"After this meeting, sir. We identified his sister, Mrs. Lydia Hernandez. I contacted Father Alejandro Ruiz of Sagrada Familia to accompany me."

"What happened to Pastor Michael Ashford?"

"Nothing, sir. In fact, Pastor Mike was indispensable with the notification of Mrs. Hall. In my opinion, though, Father Alejandro is better suited in this situation."

The chief nodded once, accepting his detective's judgment. "What is your workload like, Detective Yablonski?"

Yablonski stood a little straighter. "Nothing I can't handle, sir."

"Which means you're overloaded. Well aren't we all. I want you working this with De La Cruz. Narcotics and murder are often in bed together, but this has the potential to be explosive. De La Cruz? I want reports daily, sooner if developments warrant it. I'll brief the mayor, notify the feds. Ms. Hyatt, schedule a press conference for five p.m. Detectives, Doctor, you will be in attendance."

Lydia Martinez Hernandez waitressed at the Ritz-Carlton Hotel on Public Square. Ordinarily, Cruz avoided going to places of work. The emotional fallout was best kept behind closed doors but sometimes, there wasn't an option.

He led Yablonski and Father Alejandro to the host stand and discretely showed his identification to the man behind the podium. "I need Mrs. Lydia Hernandez and a private place to talk."

The manager's eyes grew wide. "If she's in trouble, I need to know. We have standards—"

"Lydia Hernandez and privacy." Cruz's tone brokered no debate.

The manager stumbled away from the podium, and, forgetting his manners, called across the room to a shapely woman placing plates before guests.

She turned, smiling as she looked to her manager, then her gaze drifted passed him, settling on Father Alejandro. The smile dropped from her lips. The plates fell from her hands. "My Uriel?"

Cruz glared at the manager while the padre hurried to Mrs. Hernandez. "Your office. Now."

All eyes followed as they exited the dining room. In the small office, the padre seated Mrs. Hernandez in the only guest chair, squatted before her, and broke the news. He spoke in a hushed Spanish. Cruz understood every word of the message delivered on his behalf.

Lydia Hernandez did not cry out. She simply fell back, boneless, drained. Silent tears rained down her face. "You are the police?"

"This is Detective Matt Yablonski. I am Detective Jesus De La Cruz. Homicide."

"Mathias." She whispered her brother's name, clutching the priest's hand. "How...how did he die?"

"It is not official, but we suspect he died of asphyxiation."

Her brows pressed down. "Somebody strangled him?"

"When was the last time you saw your brother?"

"Saturday. December sixteenth. I brought him dinner from work and reminded him he promised to babysit on Wednesday while I went to the doctor. I'm pregnant. He never showed." Tears poured rampantly down her face. "Was he dead? When I took my daughter to the appointment and called him every name in the book, was he dead?"

Cruz kept his chin up. "There is a lot we don't know. Did he ever mention a man named Parker?"

"Did he kill my brother?"

Cruz kept his face expressionless. "He's a person of interest. Have you heard the name?"

"No. Mathias's job put him in contact with many people, but he seldom spoke about his customers."

Cruz glanced at Yablonski, who raised an eyebrow. "What

did you brother do for a living?"

"He's an electronics salesman. You know, televisions, sound systems, speakers."

"Did you know he was arrested last month for drug possession?"

Lydia rolled her eyes. "I told him how stupid he was. Using drugs. And that poor girl. I told him if I ever found out he was using again he would never see his niece."

Her brother led a dual life. He was doing her a favor, he told himself, telling her before she heard it whispered or tweeted. "Your brother was suspected of dealing drugs."

"No. He was charged with a minor possession. He paid a fine. He made a stupid mistake, but he was not drug dealer. Is that it?"

Cruz shook his head. "He was decapitated, Mrs. Hernandez. His head put on a post and planted on I-90. People saw it, Mrs. Hernandez. The media."

"That was…" Her gaze looking to each man in the room, hoping one would dispel the idea. "Where is the rest of him?"

Using the key Mrs. Hernandez gave them, Cruz let crime scene into the apartment three floors up, behind a steel door that didn't match the wood trim. Mathias Martinez liked modern flush with technology.

"I see why she believed he was a salesman," Cruz said, pointing to one of three game systems in a built-in entertainment center. "My nieces want that system for Christmas."

Yablonski snorted. "I want that system for Christmas."

"Did you put it on your Christmas list? Maybe nurse Erin will put one in your stocking."

There was more to admire in Martinez's apartment than just the video games. There were the six wide screen televisions. The gaming computer. The top of the line appliances.

What there wasn't was the tools of the drug trade.

"We need to find his other flop," Yablonski said, pulling out his phone. "Let me see what I can do."

While Yablonski talked, Cruz walked. Across the hall, one floor down, he found Mr. Herman Wilde. Caucasian. Forty-five. IT tech at the cable company. He offered sympathy, support but no information.

The first-floor apartment opened after a second knock, filling the hallway with the happy laughter of Mickey Mouse. Cruz held his ID up to a small blonde woman with a pony tail and a chocolate milk stain on her T-shirt. Adele McDonald, twenty-six, stay-at-home mom, had known something wasn't right.

"The last time I saw him was the day after his sister visited. I carried a load of laundry to the basement after dinner. Mathias was coming up. He took the basket and carried it down for me before he went out. Don't tell my husband, but I had a little crush going on Mathias. He was always went out of his way to be nice."

Yablonski came down the steps, his heavy weight echoed like a herd of cattle. "Anything?"

Cruz gave a short nod. "Mrs. McDonald, is this the door to the basement?"

"Yes. Do you want to go down there? I can get my key."

"If you wouldn't mind, ma'am."

The basement was cold and worn, uncluttered and smelled like laundry detergent. Two sets of washers and driers sat at the end of a hallway formed by six small rooms. Each room had a wood door painted the same color as the floor with a bold number in white.

"What are these?" Cruz asked.

"Storage spaces. Each apartment comes with one. This one is ours," she said, gesturing to the door with the "1" on it.

"Thank you, Mrs. McDonald. We'll take it from here."

"Oh. Uh, okay." She stepped away self-consciously. "I

guess you know where I am if you need me."

The detectives stayed put until they heard the door close.

"Number six," Yablonski said. The plywood door had a simple padlock. Yablonski pulled a small case from his inside pocket. "You aren't seeing this."

Inside thirty seconds, the door swung opened to a cluster-fuck of holiday junk. A pair of light-up deer stared back in surprise at the strangers in the doorway. A Christmas tree was shoved in a corner. A six-foot spider clung to a wall with a skeleton hanging next to it. Storage bins were labeled *summer* in a feminine scrawl.

"Well shit," Yablonski said. "That's disappointing."

"Wait a second. Look at this." Cruz ran his fingers over the painted number. The shape of the number five could be seen behind the six. "This looks different than the others. And it's out of order."

"You think he used some trickery?"

Door five was solid wood, fitted with three locks. Beneath the five was the outline of a six. "One way to find out. Keep doing what I'm not seeing."

Yablonski knelt and got busy with tools too small for his sausage sized fingers.

Cruz crossed his arms and watched his friend work. "I can call in some guys off the street if you need help."

"This isn't as easy as it looks. Got one."

Yablonski was faster with the second one, but the third took nearly five minutes. Still, he stood with pride and opened the door. The room was the size of a jail cell, with cement block walls that went to the ceiling. A bare light bulb hung from the ceiling with a pull chain. "Bingo."

The room was as compulsively neat and organized as the apartment. One side had a built-in workbench with cabinets above and below. The workbench was clean enough to eat off. Yablonski opened a pair of overhead cabinets. White bundles were stacked tightly together.

Yablonski whistled long and low. "We have found the mother lode."

The other side of the room contained several full-size doors and three rows of cabinets. Cruz opened the doors that belonged on a kitchen pantry. "It's a gun safe. You name it, it's here." The cabinets contained shelves with hand guns, knives, packaging supplies. Money.

"Is that a grenade?" Yablonski asked.

"Clear the building."

Sunday, December 24, 2:00 a.m.

Cruz drove home, uncertain what day it was. There was always more to do than time to do it, especially at the holidays. He stayed on, working for Lydia Hernandez and Loretta Hall. If he could just figure it out the connection, he could get ahead of the game. He hadn't figured it out, but his bones ached. His eyes burned. He desperately wanted the warming dumbness of whiskey in his belly, the solid comfort of a glass in his hand.

He cut through the Steel Yards, a shopping center whose name was the only thing left of the storied history of iron on this part of the Cuyahoga River. Cruz pulled off the road and stopped. He couldn't go home. He still could name ten bars in any directions of this place. He knew he wouldn't make it passed them. Not in this condition.

He pulled out his phone and brought up Bollier's contact. All he had to do with press the button and help would be there.

Feeling calmer, he rubbed his eyes. Knowing help was there was enough. He lifted his head and one of the big box stores glowed through the winter darkness, a beacon to his weary eyes. Suddenly, he knew why he was there.

December 25

Today hurts. I didn't get a tree. I couldn't. But I see the hole where it should have been. I feel it.

I miss you. With every breath I take and every tear I cry and every part of me.

I can't take it.

There's no end to it? Am I going to be punished forever? Is this what hell is?

My hell.

My hell.

Michael.

CHAPTER SEVEN

Monday, December 25

"You cheated!" The video laughed at Cruz as loudly as the child next to him. To think he'd bought the damned thing.

"Nuh-uh!" Rhianna danced in celebration. "I'm just better. It's okay, 'cause I still love you. Let's play again."

The oven timer buzzed. "Sorry, short stuff, that's my cue. Play with your dad. You can kick his butt for a while."

The knife stilled in Mariana's hand when he walked in the kitchen. "You shouldn't let her win."

"Yeah, that's what I did. I let her win." He partially filled a stock pot with water for the potatoes Mari cut.

"She has to learn how to lose graciously as well as win graciously."

"Mari, there is nothing gracious about how your daughters win. They are exactly like you."

His sister scowled and was about to defend herself when he raised an eyebrow. "Still. You don't have to let her win."

"Mari. Look at me. I didn't let her win. That snot bucket of a five-year-old kicked my ass at Sweet Kitty Battlemania. Dinner is about thirty minutes away. What time is everyone coming?"

"Oh, any time now." Mariana snickered.

Something in her voice sent his trouble sensor to condition yellow. "What do you know that I don't?"

"Really, Tito, it's nothing. Mama just—"

Condition red. Condition red. "Oh no, Mari. Hell no."

"Mama says she's lovely. She's the nurse at her doctor's office."

"Mari," Cruz said, hearing the whine in his voice. "It's Christmas."

"Yes, it is, which means you will be nice to this woman who has no idea that she is being set up. Her, um, mother is coming, too."

The phone on his belt rang. Cruz grinned at his sister.

The knife in her hand pointed his way. "No, Jesus. It's Christmas."

He shrugged in a it's-not-in-my-control way and answered the call. "De La Cruz, at your service."

"Don't *tell* me you're hitting the nog."

Who knew salvation sounded like whiskey over gravel. "Hated that shit, even when I was drinking. Merry Christmas, Yablonski."

"Merry Christmas back at ya. Listen, I don't want to interrupt your holiday, but I got a loose connection between Parker and Martinez. Martinez is a graduate of Cleveland Central Catholic High School. Hayley Parker nee Whitley graduated the same year as Mathias Martinez."

"Nee? Where the fuck did you learn that?"

Mariana glared, the knife point swing back at him. "Tito! Watch your language."

He mouthed his apologies. Cleaning up his language when he moved in with Mari had been nearly as hard as staying sober. His mouth usually achieved a G-rating, no worse than PG-13 most days but he still slipped, especially when he was in cop mode, as Mari called it.

"My new app," Yablonski said. "It's a word of the day. I'm using it to expand my vocabulary." When Cruz laughed, Yablonski simply said, "Cretin."

"Looks like we need to pay a visit to Mrs. Parker. You in?"

"Today? You serious, Cruzie?"

The front door opened, and his mother descended upon her hapless victims. "*Hola! Feliz Navidad!*"

"Yes, Yablonski, I'm serious." The high-pitched laughter of women overflowed from the living room; the noose tightened around his neck. "Dead serious. Let's go now. I can be there in fifteen—"

"Hayley Parker isn't going anywhere. Tomorrow is soon enough. Sounds like you have a houseful. Enjoy the time with the family and we'll go out tomorrow."

"No, Yablonski, don't..." Cruz talked to dead air.

"Jesus," his mother's voice lilted across the living room. "Come meet Agnus Rivera."

Tuesday, January 2

The Lake Erie snow machine buried the eastern suburbs in depths measured in feet, while the city wasn't slowed by the inches on the streets. Under the dull light of a gray day, life had settled down. Too cold and dark to be out.

Domestic violence was the problem now. Too many people cooped up too close together at a time when emotions ran too high—or too low.

Chief Win Ramsey looked over the winterscape. A conference table sat in the corner of his office. Five somber faces waited patiently for the chief's attention.

"Detective De La Cruz, your report," he said, without turning around.

Cruz lifted the single sheet he had emailed to the chief. "We have exhausted leads on both the Hall and Martinez cases. The follow up interview I conducted with Hayley Parker confirmed that she knew Mathias Martinez from high school. She denied seeing him since their graduation six years ago. No evidence was found linking the two or connecting her husband directly with Martinez."

The interview had been mind-numbingly tedious. Parker had made his wife so afraid of talking to the police that it took a half hour to get her to admit knowing Martinez, even after confronted with the year book containing both their pictures. It saddened him to think of all the opportunities graduating senior Hayley Whitley had in front of her and the life Hayley Parker had chosen.

The bright spot in the memory was Jace. Cruz left the house after the unproductive conversation with his mother, and Jace sprang out from under the porch wearing a fall weight coat. He wanted candy.

Cruz had pilfered three candy canes from his sister's Christmas tree, knowing he was going to the house. Strawberry, orange, and fruit punch. Peppermint wasn't an option in the Moreno household. Jace had squirreled the candy into the waistband of his jeans and snuck in the side door but not before he gave Cruz a grin that took up his entire face. Making the boy smile was the only good part of the day.

He pulled his mind back to the report he was giving. "We have little material evidence. The boot prints at the Martinez scene were most likely a rubber pull over boot—like a wader—sized nine to eleven. Follow up with those who reported finding Martinez resulted in no additional information. No one saw a vehicle or person on the side of the road. Recreating the event, the suspect likely pulled off on the shoulder, putting the vehicle between his work area and westbound traffic. Although nighttime temperatures had been cold, most days have remained above freezing and the ground has not frozen yet. The post was driven in about two feet. Using a five-pound hammer, I was able to drive a similar stake in about three minutes. Like Hall, Martinez's head had been prepared and slid onto the post. The entire event would have taken less than five minutes."

"The suspect wasn't only prepared, Detective, he had to

be calm and confident. No fingerprints again? Strands of hair? DNA?"

"Only the victim's, Chief. The security camera angle from the dealership did not reach to the area where the suspect parked."

"Do you think he knew that, Detective?"

"There is no reason to expect he didn't."

"And by 'he,'" Dr. Chen said, "Detective De La Cruz is playing the odds. Clearly, the suspect has some level of physical fitness to have handled the bodies. The boot print is notably average. The average female shoe size is nine, the average male ten and a half. Historically, violent crimes of this nature are perpetrated by males but, to be clear, the evidence is silent, so far, on gender and race."

The chief turned to the table, leaning on the chair reserved for him. "Age?"

"My guess would be late teens to forties. Maybe even fifties, depending on activity level."

"Your guess, Doctor?"

"The evidence simply isn't there."

The chief's gaze roamed across the table, stopping at the narcotics detective. "Detective Yablonski. What do you have to contribute?"

"The recovery from the Martinez storage unit was significant. The lab is still processing the weapons."

"Ms. Hyatt. What say the press?"

"With the holidays, the story was short and on the back pages. The Cleveland Orchestra concert received top billing over our press conference. At this point, it had its thirty seconds in the spotlight and people have moved on."

The chief nodded curtly. "Then we'll consider this matter closed and pray to God it stays that way."

January 5

I met Rob at the grocery store. He kept dropping the ten bags of chips he was trying to carry. Drop one, pick it up, drop another, pick it up, drop a third, pick it up, drop a fourth, I picked it up.

I stacked it on top of his pile and he smiled at me. That's when I saw what he was. You can see the infestation in their eyes. He is so young. He doesn't look as bad as the others. Maybe evil hasn't fully tainted his soul yet. Maybe he can be saved.

CHAPTER EIGHT

Friday, January 5

Cruz couldn't get Jace Parker out of his mind. The only Christmas tree in the house had been the handmade one taped to the front door. The boy hadn't looked bothered by the lack of the holiday. Cruz suspected it was sadly normal. And so he was here, Fullerton Elementary, with a rounded garbage bag he carried over his shoulder, Santa Claus-style.

The principal, an older woman who radiated a don't-bull-shit-me attitude, squinted to read the fine print on his ID. "What department are you with?"

"Homicide, but this isn't an official visit," he said hastily.

"Then what is it?"

He tossed the bag on the counter and pulled out the thick winter coat, two hats, two pairs of gloves, and boots. "It's for one of your students. Jace Parker."

"I see." The principal called into an adjacent room. "Ms. Williams? Would you mind stepping out here?"

"What do you need, Mrs. Kaylor?"

Cruz had danced with the devil a time or two, but angels never crossed his path. Not until the woman walked through the door. She was tall with a riot of curls nested atop her head and skin the color of his favorite coffee. Her large, moss green eyes were as unexpected as they were mesmerizing.

"This is Detective De La Cruz with the Cleveland police," the principal said. "He is here about Jace Parker."

"I hope there isn't any trouble. I'm Aurora Williams. His teacher." She held out her hand.

He stared at it.

"Detective?"

He lifted his gaze from her hand to her face. The smile there jolted his enthralled ass back into gear. "No, Ms. Williams. No trouble. It's more like a gift. It is a gift, but he can't know it's from me."

She held up the coat. "Oh, it looks so warm. Two hats?"

"I figure kids lose them. Not in a bad way. I mean, I lose them, so why wouldn't a kid, you know?" He should shut up.

"I'm guilty of losing a few myself. This is so generous. You know Jace then?"

"Yeah. I know Jace. Can you give it to him somehow? Maybe make it seem like he won a contest or a raffle or something."

She looked at her watch. "I need to get them from gym class. Why don't you come with me? You can meet the class. It's important they have positive experiences with police officers."

Suddenly, he wasn't in a hurry to leave. "I have a safety talk I do. It only takes fifteen minutes."

"Perfect." She took his hand and pulled him away. "Come with me, Detective, and we'll corral your audience."

Ms. Williams led her class in. Curious gazes measured the stranger sitting on the tall stool. Jace came in near the end of the line, his blond hair waving as he bopped along. His eyes opened wide as recognition dawned.

"Cruz!" The boy ran over, sliding to a stop before he ran into his legs. "Do you have any candy?"

"Sorry, kiddo. Fresh out."

Jace looked sad for a brief moment and then his smile was back. "That's okay. I still got some of the candy canes you gave me. I only eat a little bit to make it last."

"Jace," Ms. Williams called. "Take your seat."

The boy obeyed immediately. If Cruz's teachers looked like Ms. Williams, he might have minded better in school, too.

"Class, we have a special guest. This is Police Detective De La Cruz. Can you say hello?"

"Hello, Detective Della Cruuuz," thirty five-year olds said in a sing-song cadence and harmonious dissonance.

"Hello back to all of you. Thank you to Ms. Williams for inviting me in today."

Thirty minutes later, Cruz was escorted to the door by a laughing Aurora Williams. "You have a gift with children. Do you have any of your own?"

"No. I'm not married. I have two nieces, though. They keep me on my toes."

"I'll bet they do. Maybe—"

His cell interrupted her. "Excuse me," he said turning away for privacy. Dispatch gave him the address for his next customer. Ending the call, he turned back to the teacher. "I have to go. Thank you for helping me with the coat."

Her hand lightly rested on his forearm. "Thank you for speaking with the class. They really enjoyed you. Stay warm out there."

He thought of her later as he climbed through a dumpster. The pretty teacher who, as Jace as said, smelled good. She made him feel warm, in a way no one had made him feel warm in a long time. Lifting his hand, he nearly touched the scars of his sewn-together face, stopping when he remembered where he was. She had to have seen them but didn't seem to care. Maybe it was time he got over the Frankenstein he saw in the mirror. Maybe. Yablonski's nurse Erin. She had friends. Maybe.

He finally reached the homeless man who passed on in the dumpster. His face was slack, serene even. And why not? He was beyond his cares.

February 13

I'm no match for the evil rooted in Rob's soul. By his own freewill he accepted it. I accept that I cannot change that. But he is trying to infect others. That I can stop.

Tonight, I'll send the serpent within him back to hell. His death won't be wasted. He'll be a sign to save others from his fate.

CHAPTER NINE

Wednesday, February 14

Cruz worked past the end of his shift. He didn't mind. He was in a rhythm. Work. Family. Work. AA. Work. Friends. Work. House projects. The balance he found kept his mind and body busy. Work never ended. There was as much as he wanted. Family was dance recitals and basketball games, dinners, and sleepovers. There, too, was as much as he wanted. AA was the rock under his feet, which he accredited with getting back his friends. When there was a gap in all of the above, he worked on his house. The update to his main bathroom was finished. Next his sights were set on a new master bedroom.

As Cruz sipped the cup of coffee, the ninth of the day. He and life were on good terms finally. He enjoyed the cold but sweet brew as he reviewed his report on the case of the lion and the antelope.

The lion walked along Euclid Avenue through the Cleveland State University campus. An antelope walked in the opposite direction, on the other side of the wide street. Gazes locked. The antelope ran; the lion chased.

The antelope pulled away, his long legs swiftly covering the concrete savannah.

The lion sprung, sweeping a bottle from the ground and flinging it at the antelope.

Struck, the antelope staggered but didn't fall. The antelope ran to the safety of the herd.

The lion turned and ran…into the arms of the police. That is how the lion ended up on Cruz's desk on the cold, wet, messy afternoon.

"I was hungry, is all." Brian Bigelow, aka the lion, explained calmly, simply as if the interlude was as mundane as ordering a cheeseburger to satisfy a craving.

Bigelow was locked up, again. The county prosecutor and the public defender had been notified, as had Bigelow's mother. The latter was bringing down the meds the lion *unprescribed* for himself.

The antelope, otherwise known as Shawn Quigley, was shaken but unharmed thanks to the quick action of a group of strangers, a cell phone, and a campus patrol car.

Cruz re-read the written statements. His cell rang, and he answered without taking his gaze from the computer screen. "De La Cruz." He sipped the coffee.

"This is Aurora Williams. Do you remember me?"

Cruz coughed as the coffee went down the wrong pipe. Remember her? He had dreams about those killer green eyes.

"Detective? Are you all right?"

"Yes." *Cough cough.* "I'm fine. Just fine."

"I don't mean to interrupt; you're probably on your way home—"

"No," Cruz said quickly, not wanting to chase her away. "Not at all. I was just finishing up a few reports."

"Oh, so you're working." The statement had an air of disappointment.

"It's nothing I can't catch up on later." He hit save, closed the report, and spun away from the screen. Nothing to distract him. "What can I do for you?"

She took a deep breath. "I was hoping you might be willing to meet me."

Hell yes. "Where?"

She named a restaurant and a time that let him finish his

reports and review new ones in from the lab. It was hard to concentrate on the medical jargon and statistical interpretation when his head kept going back to the phone call.

She lied.

She said she wanted to talk to him about her class, but it was a lie. He heard it through the phone.

Still, he was game. The only thing waiting for him that night was a gallon of paint. So, what the hell, he could paint tomorrow.

In a trendy restaurant in the resurgent Tremont neighborhood, he followed the hostess through the dining room crowded with couples in various states of dinner and merriment. In fact, the only table that was not fully occupied was set for two at the very back of the house.

Aurora stood when she saw him. She wore blue jeans and a red sweater that hugged her curves. Her hair was down, soft curls falling past her shoulders.

"Ms. Williams," Cruz said, closing the distance between them.

"Please. Call me Aurora. I appreciate you meeting me on such short notice."

He took the seat next to her. "You did me a favor. I would have been doomed to several more hours of paperwork if you hadn't called. I don't know if I would have gone into law enforcement if I knew how much paperwork there is. I always hated writing papers in school."

She laughed, maybe a little nervously, but it looked good on her. Touching the end of her hair, she smiled shyly.

A waiter came to their table. "Good evening. Can I start you with something to drink?"

"Um." Cruz looked at her glass of wine. She was clearly expecting somebody, squeezing him in to her evening. Whatever she had to say, he wouldn't have to wait long. "No, I, uh, won't be staying."

Her brows pinched together, as if she were hurt.

"Is something wrong," he asked, giving her the space to tell him the truth behind the invitation.

Her gaze drifted to the next table. "I...well, I had hoped, if you didn't have other plans...that you might consider, maybe—" her eyes found his, "—having dinner with me?"

His brows shot up. "Dinner?" Another stall tactic.

Her cheeks blushed. "I mean, you have to eat, right?"

"Right." She was sweet in her embarrassment. She didn't realize she didn't have to sugarcoat it. He'd give her whatever she needed, if he was able. Maybe there was trouble with an ex-boyfriend or issues with a landlord. "I'll take a ginger ale, if you have it."

When the waiter left, Aurora reached into her bag. "I wanted to give you these." She handed him a thick pack of brightly colored paper. "The children made them for you."

Another stall. He didn't mind. He learned patience long ago and enjoyed looking at the beautiful woman. He fingered through pages with their reds, yellows, blues, and greens.

"Your speech made a strong impression on them. It has become part of our daily routine. Talking about safety."

A woman walked into the dining room with an armful of roses. She approached the first table, where a man pulled out his wallet. The woman with him laid an appreciative hand on his arm.

Cruz watched the woman and the couple. His gaze slid to the next table and that couple and then the next. He looked at Aurora, who wouldn't meet his eyes. "What day is today?"

Her cheeks were crimson red now. "Wednesday. February, uh, fourteenth."

He read the scene again, this time with his eyes open. Dinner in a nice restaurant, a cozy table in the corner. His gaze snapped to the woman sitting next to him. "Son of a..."

"It's not what you think," she said quickly.

What he thought? He didn't have a thought. "What do you think I think?"

"That I tricked you into a dinner on Valentine's Day."

"And that's not what happened?"

"No," she said firmly. "I tricked you into doing me a favor. Totally different."

"A favor?"

"I, um, told my friends that I was spending Valentine's Day at my favorite restaurant with a handsome man. You're doing me a favor, saving me from lying."

Cruz took in the wringing hands, the eyes that wouldn't meet his, and his ego swelled to ten times its size. "Don't forget intelligent. And funny. Tell them I'm funny."

Those amazing eyes shined at him. "I will. And just so we get this out of the way, I'm buying."

"No, you're not."

"Yes, I am. I tricked you into a date. I'm paying."

Didn't that sound nice. "Now we're on a date?"

Her smile quickly vanished, her hands began wringing again. "No, I didn't mean a date. I meant a…"

He laughed. It felt incredible to have this gorgeous woman was nervous around him. "Well, just so we get this out of the way, when we go out next, I'm paying, and it is a date. This is your favorite restaurant?"

She sat a little taller, radiating happiness. "The food here is wonderful and I just love the place. I made the reservations in December to make sure to get the table."

His wheels turned. "December. We didn't meet until January. Was your plan all along to trick some unsuspecting man into a date?"

"You really are a detective, aren't you? I was seeing someone at the time. I broke up with him nearly a month ago but, well, I kept the reservation."

So, she had been seeing someone when they first met, but she wasn't now. Interesting. "I'm glad to be the man sitting with you, in your favorite restaurant. There's just one thing missing." He raised his hand and caught the attention of the flower lady.

"Oh, Detective, no." She pulled on his arm.

"Six please." Damn, he liked making her blush. "A dozen."

Aurora's eyes grew wet as the woman laid rose after rose in her arms.

"Now you can tell your friends you had dinner in your favorite restaurant with a smart, handsome, and funny man who bought you flowers."

She hugged the flowers to her chest.

They chatted and laughed over tasty appetizers, through savory dinners, and into a sweet dessert. Time didn't follow the rules. Two hours flew by in the space of minutes. He was disappointed when the dessert plates were cleared. He hesitated when Aurora reached for the bill, but she bared her teeth, staked out her territory by setting her credit card in the tray.

He held up his hands in surrender. "I didn't touch it."

The waiter returned with the slip for her to sign and then they were out on the street. The weather had taken a turn for the worse. Sleet rained down, making it impossible to walk in the heels she wore. Cruz held her close, escorting her to her car.

At her driver's door, he let her go. She didn't hurry for her keys but turned to him. "What is your name?"

"What?"

"When I tell my friends I had dinner with a smart, handsome, and funny man, they are bound to ask me his name. I can't tell them 'Detective.'"

"Cruz. Everyone calls me Cruz."

She wrinkled her nose. "What is your first name?"

"Jesus, but nobody calls me that except my mother."

"What's wrong with Jesus?"

Cruz rolled his eyes. "Hey, Jesus—" he said it *Gee-sus*, "—walk on water lately? Hey, Jesus, how about turning this water into a little wine?"

Aurora shook her head. "Children can be cruel."

"Those were cops."

"Still." Only the petals of flowers separated them. With her heels on, their mouths were scant inches apart. "I can't kiss a man I call by his last name."

His temperature spiked, steam rising as the sleet melted upon contact. "You're going to kiss me?" God help him if she didn't.

Her gaze was on his lips. "I'm thinking about it. Zeus."

Her breath was sweet on his face. "Zeus. That's what you're going to call me?" All he had to do was drop his chin and…

"If you don't mind." She popped up and her lips were on his. Her lips on his. It was the only place they touched and yet every nerve ending fired in triplicate.

She stepped back, her gaze on his mouth. "Yes. I think I will. Are you going to call me? Zeus?"

He was infatuated. Happily, willingly, totally infatuated. Wrapped around her little finger. "How long will it take you to get home? I'll call you then."

She smiled shyly, brushing her fingers briefly against his. "Give me thirty minutes."

His phone rang. He looked at the display. "Oh. Uh. How about tomorrow?"

"Work calls?"

He nodded. "Hazard of the job."

She buttoned his coat to the top, rose once again and brushed her lips against his. "I would like if you called, but I understand if you don't. Happy hunting, Detective."

Dispatch chirped in Cruz's ear, but in his mind, he was talking her into meeting him for coffee or something.

His brain cued into the voice on the phone. "What was the location?"

* * *

The party was easy to find. Five cop cars in the middle of a bridge tend to stick out at eight o'clock on a Saturday night. He drove past and pulled on the shoulder at the head of the line.

The first district had secured the scene. As he got close, one looked familiar.

"Buettner, right?"

"You got it, Detective." The big officer was fully outfitted by the Cleveland police and impervious to the weather.

"What do we have?"

"Another head job."

He took a deep breath, the cold air a shock to his lungs. This made three, assuming it wasn't a copycat. "How? We're on a bridge?"

"You gotta see it for yourself."

Roughly half way across the quarter mile long bridge on I-480 east, a sign cantilevered off the outside of the bridge barriers: CLEVELAND CORP LIMIT.

Suspended beneath it was another head. Male. Caucasian. The head hung in a cargo net sack attached with bungee cords, swaying as winter pelted it with all it had.

"When was it reported?"

"Seven-forty a call came in of a man on the bridge. I don't know if it was our friend here or the suspect. In this rotten weather, anyone with any sense is focusing on what's in front of him, not on the side of the road."

"Do we have anything for crime scene? Tire treads? Boot prints?"

"We tried to cordon off the area, but you see the weather, Detective."

Cruz looked at the slush covered concrete. "He had to park there." He pointed to a position that would have blocked the sign from the view of on-coming traffic. He leaned over the barrier, looked below, and saw nothing.

Somewhere under there was the Rocky River, but as dark

as it was, it could have been in China.

The scene was worked quickly, the head removed, and scene documented. A news van set up onto the shoulder, but Cleveland police was already on its way out.

A reporter called his name, but Cruz didn't stop. Who could hear anything over the wind?

At his desk, he reviewed the few facts available. The victim was male, Caucasian. Late teens, early twenties. The medical examiner wouldn't make a guesstimate as to the cause of death but would say the cut on the neck appeared consistent with the other two she had examined.

Yablonski hadn't answered his phone. Cruz left him a message, hoping his friend would get it after he enjoyed his Valentine's Day. Morning was only a few hours away.

Cruz had no fingerprints to run through the system. He ran the facial recognition software but came up empty.

He took a mental step back. What did he have? Three heads—all male, different ages, different ethnicities. Two of the three were drug dealers—so far. Two had connections to Christopher Parker—so far. Three were found on the interstate highways going into the city.

Cruz brought up the internet and Google Maps. All three were found at the corporate limits for the city of Cleveland.

Two interstates came into the city from the south and ended: I-71 and I-77.

Two interstates crossed the city east-west: I-480 and I-90.

That meant there was a total of six points at which the interstates came into the city limits. Except that wasn't accurate as the corporate limits darted around suburbs, meaning some of the highways entered the city multiple times.

He leaned back in his chair, tapping restless fingers on the arm rest. "What is the purpose of leaving the heads, and only the heads, at the city limits?"

Cruz scribbled dates on a sheet of scrap paper.

November 6
December 23
February 14

They are all close to holidays. Halloween. Christmas.
Valentine's Day. But then why not New Years? Why not
Hanukkah, Kwanza, Epiphany, Martin Luther King Day,
President's Day? And what happened to start it all?

Thursday, February 15

The donut Cruz ate was as stale as the coffee he drank. He
hadn't been home yet. He had twenty minutes until the
meeting in the chief's office. His cell rang, his nieces' faces
filling the screen.

"Hey, Mari. What's going on?"

"You sound tired," she said over Gabby's singing.

"Long night. Longer day."

"Ah. I was wondering if you could watch the girls this
evening. Tony's out of town at a flower show, and I just got
tagged for a double shift."

"You know I would if I could. I have no idea what time
I'll get out of here."

"And get some sleep. You are human, you know." She
sighed. "I'll call Mom. I just don't want to get stuck in a
thirty minute conversation about who she should set you up
with next."

Cruz smiled, exactly as his sister planned. "Nobody. No
one. Tell her I don't want a woman, Mari. If you love me,
you'll do it." Then he thought of Aurora and the blush on
her cheeks as he filled her arms with flowers. He touched his
lips, remembering the taste of hers.

"She's never going to stop, you know. She wants to see
you fat and happy."

"I don't want to be fat and I am happy." Cruz jerked back, shocked as he realized it was the truth. When did that happen?

"You are?" his sister said and then quickly covered. "Good. Good, Jesus. You deserve to be happy. What's her name?"

His little sister should have been a cop. She had a nose like a bloodhound. If she got wind of Aurora, there would be dinners and events and interrogations.

"What's who's name?"

"Oh, you don't fool me. You met a woman. She is a woman, right? Because, you know, it's okay if she's not."

"Mari, I have no idea what you just said. Gotta go. Love you."

"You can tell me—" and he hung up on her.

"You look like a man with a big dog biting on his ass." Matt Yablonski flopped down in the empty guest chair.

"A Puerto Rican Rottweiler. Once their jaws lock, there's no getting free."

"Anyone I know?"

"My sister."

"What does she want?"

"A sister-in-law."

Yablonski raised an eyebrow.

"Exactly. You have a good night?"

"I did. I'd brag about it but seeing as I know how you spent your night, I'll spare you the details of how I re-wrote the books romancing Valentine's Day."

"Oh. My night wasn't all bad." A smile grew despite being ordered not to.

Yablonski leaned forward and slapped Cruz's desk. "You dog."

Cruz's phone rang. A direct call from the chief. Not good any day. "Morning, Chief."

"My office, now. Call Yablonski and bring him."

It was déjà vu all over again. Chief Win Ramsey paced his office. At the conference table sat Alison Hyatt, public information officer, and Dr. Ming Chen. Homicide Commander Kurt Montoya was in attendance. Then, there was the new face, one that was pale against the navy-blue suit. His hazel eyes gave nothing away and said it all. Fed.

"Before we get started," Ramsey said, "I'll introduce Special Agent Zachary Bishop, FBI, Cleveland Bureau."

Cruz, Yablonski, and Montoya looked at each other with identical expressions. Oh, fuck no.

"Special Agent Bishop is here at *my* request, gentlemen." Ramsey left no doubt who was in control. "The Cleveland police and FBI have the same goals, and we have been working toward increased collaboration and resource sharing. I have asked them to consult on these cases. Consult, not take over. This is and will remain a Cleveland police case. Clear?" When all heads nodded, Ramsey tossed the floor to Special Agent Bishop.

"As the chief said, I'm here to consult and offer the resources of a federal bureau up until the point we are asked to take over or the crimes cross into our jurisdiction. Chief Ramsey shared your reports, and I have been thoroughly briefed on the situation."

"Thank you, Bishop." Ramsey's attention turned to Cruz. "Your report."

He ran through the events of the prior evening, few as there were. "We have yet to ID the victim."

"He isn't known to narcotics?" Ramsey asked Yablonski.

"I just arrived, sir." Yablonski accepted a photo of the face from Cruz. "I don't know him, but I'll get this circulated."

"There is going to be a next." Ramsey turned to Chen. "Is there a threat to the general public?"

"Pending identification of the latest victim, the focus is on the drug trade. If the suspect maintains current patterns, the threat is to people the suspect perceives as being part of illegal drugs. His perception. Not ours."

Ramsey pinched his chin between his thumb and fore-finger. "I want this played down until we know there is a real threat to the public, I want to take advantage of working behind the scenes. Ms. Hyatt, you know the routine. John Doe, I-480 yadda yadda. Dr. Chen, work up a profile with what we have. Bring Bishop in on it. Cruz, I want every stone on that damn bridge turned. I want to know where this kid came from, who he hung with, what he had for breakfast. Can you handle that, Detective?"

The weight landed on Cruz's shoulders, but it wasn't anything he couldn't handle. "Absolutely, sir."

He worked the thin case hard, logging so much time on the phone he considered having it surgically implanted. Corned beef and onion rings got him through noon. By four, he was crashing. The coffee wasn't doing it any more. He needed sleep.

Home, he stripped off his coat, then his tie, then his shirt. In his kitchen, he fumbled emptying his pockets, stalling out with his phone in hand. The number he had programmed last night showed on the screen. He dialed.

"Hello."

"It's...Zeus." He smiled, punch drunk on fatigue.

"Well, Detective, I wasn't sure you would call. Did you have a good night?"

"The part with you."

She cooed. "When did you get home?"

"Now."

She gasped. "Aren't you tired?"

"Exhausted, but I wanted to call you."

"Ah, well, I'm glad you did. Now get some sleep."

"Meet me. Tonight."

"Tonight's only a few hours away." A pregnant pause. "Where?"

His mind tripped and came up with nothing. "Anywhere.

You name the place."

She named a coffee shop near the restaurant Oscar Bollier ritualistically had Sunday dinner. "Eight?"

"Perfect. See you then."

"Sweet dreams, Detective."

"How could I have otherwise when I'll be dreaming of you." He cringed. Did he say that out loud? God, he was tired.

She laughed softly with a little inflection that said she was likely blushing. "Maybe I'll take a nap, dream about you, too. See you soon."

Cruz ran to the coffee shop with a porcelain lotus flower cupped in his hands. It was probably porcelain. The flower was the prettiest thing the corner pharmacy carried, and he didn't have time to stop somewhere else. It wasn't impressive, but it was the best he could do on three hours sleep. He snuck in as a couple left because he didn't have hands to work the door. He scanned the busy room and triumph blossomed. He arrived first.

Victory was sweet as he claimed one of the few empty tables and carefully set the flower down. The door was thrown open and Aurora hurried in. Her chest rose and fell beneath her coat. Her long legs had denim painted on and boots made to be taken off.

"You're late," he teased, meeting her near the door and helping her out of her coat. Beneath, she wore a black sweater with a small peak-a-boo opening over junction of her breasts. "Damn, you look good." Cruz pressed a kiss the corner of her mouth to prove he could.

"Thank you, Zeus. You look..." She pulled back, stared at his face, and stopped what she was about to say.

Taking her hand, he led her to their table. "I'm buying. Don't even think about arguing." His jeans were clean. His

black shirt promised to be wrinkle free. He rubbed his shadowed jaw, wishing he had shaved. He couldn't do anything
about his face, except shave.

Her mouth fell open into a perfect O. "What's this?"

"A lotus flower handmade by Tibetan monks, and sold to
raise funds for heating oil for the monastery."

She swallowed a smile, turning the gift in her hands. "It
says 'Made in Mexico.'"

"Mexican Tibetan monks. They're rare."

"I bet," she said, cradling the flower to her chest. "It's
perfect. Thank you." She stepped in.

"The monks made it, you know, just for you." Toe to
toe, he lowered his chin, inviting the soft brush her lips over
his. "Yeah. Coffee. I'll get coffee."

"Decaf, please. It's too late for caffeine."

He snorted. "It is never too late for caffeine."

Cruz was on his second cup while Aurora nursed her first.
She repeatedly stroked the petals of the flower. She talked,
he listened and asked questions when she would have retreated. He knew she was twenty-eight and an artist working
in oils and pastels. She had two sisters, one older, one younger.
She loved children. She was passionate about education and
the arts, about her family and friends.

"Tell me about your friends," Cruz said when her phone
signaled a text.

Aurora rolled her green eyes. She thumbed over the icons
and flipped through several images until she held the screen
to him. "Karen. Veronica. Kylie. They were impressed with
the flower." Her phone chimed again. Aurora read the text
and smiled.

"What?"

"They think you're cute."

He raised a brow. "Cute? You took my picture? Let me
see it."

She blushed, bright red. "Ah, no."

It had to be a damn good picture to bring out that color. "There's a woman waving at you." He pointed to the window over her shoulder.

"Really? I wonder who?" Aurora turned to where he pointed.

He snatched the phone from her hand.

"Zeus! Gimme it back."

"I'm not reading your texts. I just want to see the pict— it's my butt." His gaze snapped to her eyes. "You took a picture of my butt."

She dropped her eyes to her hands, her fingers dancing across a spoon. "I took the one of your face first. You were in line and, well, you have a great butt."

Cruz laughed. No one turned him inside out the way Aurora did. Unconsciously, he touched the scars by his eye. "It is my best side."

"You have a nice face. Strong. Maybe a little stubborn, but nice. What happened? To your eye?"

Cruz dropped his hand because he wanted to cover the scars. "I was injured on the job. I got hit in the face with an engine block."

Aurora dropped the spoon she was playing with. Large eyes in an expressionless face blinked at him.

"It was a few years ago. I don't remember it. Not really. I worked undercover narcotics. I arranged a buy, it was a big deal for our investigation. Things went wrong early. The guy who was my competition in the organization decided to make a move. I turned, I must have turned. Anyway, the bust went down. When it was over, I was done working undercover. The doctor said I was an inch away from losing my eye. My face...it was messed up. Anyway, I recovered, and transferred to homicide."

"Wow." Her fingers rested on the back of his hand.

"Part of my recovery was realizing that I am an alcoholic."

"Oh." Aurora's eyes widened. "You should have said

something. I didn't need the wine last night."

He shook his head. "You don't have to not drink around me. That's not why I'm telling you."

"Then why are you telling me?"

"Because I like being around you and I want to be around you more. If you're going to be around me, you need to know I'm a recovering alcoholic."

Aurora bit her lower lip. "I'm bad with money. I don't know where it all goes. Sometimes, I sell my paintings to make ends meet."

"I keep odd hours. With my job, I have to work all hours."

"I'm a horrible cook. I burned water once."

"I drink three gallons of coffee a day."

"I sleep naked."

His mouth went dry. "It's getting late. Maybe you should come home with me. We can have a sleep over."

Her eyes sparkled as she giggled, the sound sweet, like a bird. "You make me laugh, Zeus."

Yeah, he liked that. "Have dinner with me."

"When?"

Cruz thought through his schedule. Tomorrow would be no better than today. "Saturday. My place. I'll cook."

"It's a date."

February 16

I have a cold. My brain feels like a cannonball inside my skull. I wish I had some chicken soup but all that's in my kitchen is the basics. I used to like to cook. I didn't notice that I stopped. An apple and oatmeal isn't the same as chicken soup.

There hasn't been much in the news about my sign. The weather was rotten. That's probably where I caught the cold. One channel replayed a clip from the bridge where I hung the sign. It was gone but there were a few police cars. They should leave the signs up longer, so more would see them.

The reporter chased after a man. I couldn't believe it when he said the name.

Jesus De La Cruz.

CHAPTER TEN

Friday, February 16

The day was all about nothing.

Nothing in the Rocky River Valley Park a hundred feet below where the latest head was found. Nothing on the cargo net. Nothing from Yablonski and narcotics. A-a-and, nothing in his go cup. He'd call it a wrap and head home to—

The phone rang. "De La Cruz."

"This is Nelson from Missing Persons. We took a call loosely matching the description of your John Doe. Sending the details your way."

An email came through with Nelson's name on it. Cruz opened it and read it back to the man who sent it. "Bobby Mayes, nineteen years old, last seen Monday, February twelfth by his mother, Melissa Mayes. What took her so long to report him missing?"

"She thought he was staying with a friend for a few days. When he wasn't home this morning, she called the friend and learned he never showed."

"Blond hair, brown eyes. Scar on his forearm. Well, that's not going to help me. Okay. I'll let you know if this goes anywhere. Thanks, Nelson." Cruz ended the call and made a second one. "Yablonski. I have a name for you. Bobby Mayes."

"Not ringing any bells, Cruzie." A keyboard clicked in the background. "Nope. Let me knock a few heads together and I'll call you back."

An hour later, Cruz knew Robert James Mayes had a speeding ticket last November, unpaid, but no car was registered in his name. The address on his driver's license was his mother's. He worked at a pet store. His social media of choice was Twitter. Narcotics hadn't heard of him.

The image snapped by the medical examiner resembled the one taken by the Ohio Department of Motor Vehicles. Hair in the same color spectrum—one was wet, the other dry. Eye color was similar; shape couldn't be evaluated. Face shape was similar. Skin color impossible to compare.

The likelihood of a match was seventy-five percent, in his estimation.

Cruz and his tenth cup of coffee parked in front of the Mayes home at fifteen minutes before six. It was a faded, yellow house with a long front porch in the area Martinez had claimed.

A petite woman answered the door. Her black hair, streaked with gray, fell past her shoulders. She tucked it behind her ears, an obvious nervous habit. "Officer Cruz?"

"Detective De La Cruz," he corrected. "Mrs. Melissa Mayes?"

She nodded, and then stepped back. "Come in. Please." The living room was a large square. A doorway off the side of the room was covered with a curtain, a bedroom Cruz suspected. Through the living room was a dining room that was nearly the same size. A man stood in the doorway.

"Th-this is my neighbor, Sam Bell."

"Good evening, Mr. Bell."

Arms crossed over a thin chest. "I'm here to make sure Melissa is treated right. I have my cell phone recording his whole conversation."

"All right." He had no problem with keeping everybody on the up-and-up. Using his own smart phone, Cruz activated the recording app. "February sixteen, five-forty-five p.m.

Detective De La Cruz at the home of Melissa Mayes regarding the disappearance of her son, Robert. Also present, Mr. Sam Bell. Can we sit, Mrs. Mayes?"

"Yes. O-of course."

Bell led the way, pointing Cruz into a chair at the dining room table. Mrs. Mayes sat across from him, pale, trembling, unfocused. He read her as literally sick with worry. Mr. Bell sat next to him, leaning forward, ready to capture the social injustice he expected Cruz to perpetrate any second now.

Cruz set his notebook on the table. "I understand you last saw your son on Monday, is that correct?"

"Yes. He was scheduled Tuesday one to nine at the pet store. I left for work while he was still asleep. He had plans with a friend for a movie marathon."

"Do you know the name of his friend?"

"Pete Bartoli. Bobby didn't come home on last night, so I called Pete. He said Bobby was good and not to worry, but he doesn't answer his phone and he hasn't called and he's not home." Her voice trailed off. Bell covered her hands with his and she clung to him.

"I'll need an address and phone number for Pete. Does Bobby usually stay with friends in the middle of the week?"

"He is nineteen. Sometimes he stays there. Sometimes Pete and others stay here."

"I would like a list of his friends, addresses and phone numbers if you have them. Where did Bobby work?"

"Pet Carnival. He was promoted to assistant manager after he graduated high school. He was supposed to open the store today. I called at his lunch, just to check, and they said he didn't show up. He wouldn't just skip. That job means a lot, and he is doing so well. He does was much as the manager."

"Probably taking advantage of Bobby," Bell said. "Having him do the manager's work without paying him the manager's wages."

Cruz continued with his notes, not reacting to the comments. "Was there anyone Bobby was having any problems with? Work, friends, girlfriend?" When the mother shook her head, he changed angles. "Do you have a picture of Bobby that I may have?"

"Yes." Mrs. Mayes rose slowly, then went into the kitchen. She returned with a five by seven senior picture. The formal picture was taken in a park. The face smiling out was on a lanky body, sitting on a picnic table, elbows on his knees.

The picture upped the percentage to ninety percent to Cruz's mind. "Mrs. Mayes, can I see Bobby's room?"

Mrs. Mayes looked to Bell, who was reading Cruz like a book. "Better not, Melissa. Cops are always looking for a way to pin it on the victim."

"Mrs. Mayes," he said in a voice both calm and authoritative. "You called us to find your son. I need information to do that. Cleveland is a big place. Everything helps."

She led the way through the kitchen and up a narrow set of steps. The second floor consisted of a bathroom and two bedrooms. The wall between the bedrooms had been knocked down, but never finished, creating one large room. It was a teenage version of a man cave. A sixty-inch television swallowed one wall. Four gaming lounge chairs were arranged in front of it with video game controllers in the mix. Pricey shoes from the top NBA players were scattered around the room. An ionic air purifier hummed unobtrusively on the floor.

The toys in the room were just a little too nice for an assistant manager at a pet store, even one that lived with his mother. And you only used an air purifier when there was something in the air you needed to get out.

The odds just hit one-hundred percent.

One look at the anxious woman said she had no idea. "Mrs. Mayes, I'd like your permission to search the room."

Bell did not like that. "Don't do it, Melissa. You got rights.

He can't search it without a warrant." He spoke with the knowledge and confidence that came from watching every episode of *Law & Order* twice.

"Mr. Bell is correct, Mrs. Mayes, unless you give me your permission."

"I don't know, I don't." Mrs. Mayes became frantic, more uncertain with every word Bell whispered in her ear.

Cruz left fifteen minutes later without searching the room, but he did have Bobby Mayes's hairbrush and toothbrush. He left the worried mother and her defiant friend with empty words, knowing on his next visit, he would be coming as a homicide detective.

On instinct, Cruz went to Pet Carnival. The items he collected from the Mayes's home could wait an hour to be logged in. He wanted to see what Mayes did for a living.

Inside the shop, Mary Jane McNamara reached into the vat of crickets, oblivious to the jumping and chirping. She bagged and tagged the horde before ringing them up. Cruz waited for the customer to pay and leave.

"You want to know about Bobby?" The high school junior was more composed than many adults talking to a police detective. "He was nice, you know? If we were slow, he'd let me study and would schedule me around my school activities. He was good to work for."

There was a tentativeness in her voice that didn't match her words. "But?"

"There are no 'buts,' Okay, so his friend creeps me out. He smells funny and stares at me and giggles." She shivered, hands rubbing her arms to warm them. "Totally creepy."

"When did you see Bobby last?"

"Tuesday. He asked me to stay late and close for him."

"What time did he leave?"

"Just before seven. I remember because I got hit with a

rush right at seven and wished he had stayed just another fifteen minutes."

"Bobby didn't drive that night. Did you see who picked him up?"

"No, but Bobby was happy to see him."

"Him? Male?"

She shook her head. "Don't know. Bobby pushed the door open and said something like 'Are you ready to do this?'"

"What do you think he meant by that?"

"I don't know. When he asked me to close, I asked what was going on. I wasn't sticking my nose in, it was just conversation. He got quiet, like he was trying to think of a lie to tell me. I didn't really care, so I just told him I would. Why not? Like I said, he is a good manager."

"Are there security videos outside the building?"

"Just inside on the front and back doors. It's in the office." She led the way, using a key from a ring to unlock it.

"Is it always locked?"

"Unless the manager or Bobby is in. I have the key, so I can lock the cash up when I close." She pointed him to the security system, and then the bell rang in the main room. "That's a customer. Is it okay if I go help them?"

"Sure, Mary Jane. I'll come out when I'm done." The small office had another ionic air purifier running, and it still smelled of latent marijuana. Cruz did a search but came up empty. He'd get a search warrant tomorrow to do a thorough job. The smell itself was enough to confirm his suspicions.

He focused on the system that saved seven days of video before overwriting itself. He reversed through the footage until ten minutes before seven on Friday night. There was Bobby Mayes doing exactly what Mary Jane had described. The camera caught nothing but the white glare of headlights.

Cruz went back into the store. This time, Mary Jane was trying to net little fish swimming their tail fins off to evade her. The twenty-something she served didn't look like the aquarium type.

He started to sweat when he noticed the ID hanging from Cruz's neck. "You know what, skip it. I'll come back another time."

"But you said you were out of feeders." Mary Jane talked to his retreating back. "Hey! Don't you need your fish food?"

Cruz tapped a knuckle on the glass. "You sell a lot of these little guys?"

"Bobby does. He's like a fish whisperer. He even made his own fish food. We sell a bunch of it." She handed Cruz the small, white container the customer had left behind.

The light-weight container had a home printed label of two very happy fish. Cruz opened it, inhaled and stopped before he was as happy as the fish. "Do you have a phone number for the owner? I need to talk to him."

Saturday, February 17

By noon, it was official. Bobby Mayes and the I-480 John Doe were one and the same. The Pet Carnival owner was cooperating. crime scene spent the better part of the night searching the store and recovered marijuana, heroin, and a stash of prescription drugs. Pet Carnival sat at the end of a strip of five stores. Each store had their own security systems, but none caught the vehicle that picked up Mayes.

Melissa Mayes worked as an administrative assistant for downtown hotel. She returned Cruz's call in person, anxious for news of her Bobby. In one of the smaller interview rooms, he told her they had found him.

Her thin chest heaved twice, and then she rose and left the room.

Bewildered, Cruz followed her. "Mrs. Mayes. Please let me call someone for you." When she didn't acknowledge he had spoken, he reached for her shoulder. "Mrs. Mayes?"

"Detective, I'd appreciate it if you'd call me when you know anything about Bobby."

Oh. Shit.

"Mrs. Mayes. Please, sit down." He grabbed the nearest chair and put it in her path. She looked at it as if she couldn't quite remember what you used it for. "Is there someone I can call? A brother or sister?"

"There's just me. Me and Bobby."

"A friend? Mr. Bell?"

"Sam. Sam is my friend." Her hand trembled as she handed her phone to Cruz.

He asked a passing female officer to sit with Mrs. Mayes and withdrew to a corner to make the call.

"Dear Lord. Are you sure he's dead?" Sam Bell asked

"Yes, sir. We have positively identified him."

"With the hair, right? He was dead when you came to talk to Melissa."

"Yes, sir. He was a John Doe."

Bell swore with heart-felt emotion. "Melissa has got to be torn up."

"Mr. Bell, she needs a friend. She shouldn't be on her own right now."

"'Course not. I'll be there as fast as I can. If I get a ticket, you'll fix it?"

"Follow the traffic laws, Mr. Bell," he said but cracked a smile.

"Some detective," Bell said under his breath before the line went dead.

In hindsight, Cruz should have realized bringing Bell in would create more problems than it solved.

"We *demand* to see Bobby Mayes with our *own* eyes!" Bell's voice echoed off the plaster walls. "A grieving mother has the God given *right* to see her child."

Bell pushed, but Cruz stood his ground. "I understand this is hard, but it is not possible at this time. The investigation into Mr. Mayes's death is active and ongoing." Bell's antics were not helping Mrs. Mayes. The man was too busy being righteous to notice.

Bell narrowed his eyes, looking for deception in every word. "*When* are you going to release his body?"

As soon as we have it.

"As soon as possible." And that was the moment he realized he omitted the fact the Bobby Mayes had been decapitated. It wasn't intentional, but he did it. He wasn't going to undo it in front of Bell.

Bell did not go quickly or quietly. When he and Mrs. Mayes were out the door, Cruz notified everyone from his commander to the chief, including the PIO. Another meeting was hastily scheduled, and a plan developed. Then came the press conference. Cruz attended, standing dutifully behind the chief and wearing a game face to rival Yablonski's. Confidence. Resolve. Strength. Determination. Every hour of every day until a killer was behind bars.

Coming out of the press conference, he received some good news. Peter Bartoli was in an interview room. Either the young man was the luckiest kid on the planet or he knew how to not be found. Eventually his luck ran out. The kid looked strung out. Cruz let him sit for a while, let some of that fish food work its way out of his system. He wasn't interested in Bartoli's illegal smile. He was chasing a killer and needed to know what the kid knew.

The interview went on for close to an hour. Bartoli thought Mayes had a girlfriend, maybe a married one because Bartoli hadn't met her. Mayes snuck off once or twice a week to meet her. No, he didn't have a name. When pressed about the drugs, he was afflicted with a sudden bout of deaf-dumb-and-blindness. Yablonski took over from there. He had nothing Cruz wanted.

It took Cruz as long to write the details in a report as it did to talk to the guy. He wouldn't have minded the time if he'd had gotten something for it. His personal cell rang. He answered as he finished typing a sentence. "Yeah?"

"Should I be insulted, Detective?"

That voice. He recognized it and smiled inside and out. "Why would you be insulted?" A thought dawned. "Shit. What time is it? Shit. You're at my house and I'm not. Aurora, don't leave." He jumped to his feet, banged his knee, swore, hit save, and closed the program. "Whatever you do, don't leave."

She laughed, she should have been annoyed but instead she laughed. "It's a bit cold for waiting—"

"On top of the light next to the front door is a key." He had put it there for a neighbor to use when he had appliances delivered. He was glad he hadn't put it away. As Cruz listened to the sounds of his door opening and his fantasy woman walking through it, he shut the computer down, pulled on his coat, and stuffed his pockets with keys and gloves.

"Nice. Sparse but nice. Dart board in the dining room. Unconventional."

"I've been working on it one room at a time. I'm on my way now—"

"Cruz," his commander called. "My office."

"Uh, but..." There was no arguing that he should have left an hour ago. "I need to speak with the commander. Will you stay?"

"For a while."

A while, a while. How long was a while? Cruz thought about throwing on the lights and sirens. But that would be wrong. Completely inappropriate.

Taillights stretched out ahead of him.

Cruz flipped on the lights, pulling into the turn lane to bypass the congestion. Lights off, he pulled into his driveway, pinning in the little Jetta. He took the steps two at a time, bound in his front door with a child-like excitement.

Well, no, not a child.

More like with horny teenage excitement.

Except, she wasn't there.

There was a pizza box on the table. He lifted the cover. It was his usual with one slice missing.

"Aurora?"

"Up here."

Her voice came from the stairs leading to the upper floor. It was part future master bedroom, part attic storage. He sprinted past the two-by-fours caging in a porcelain throne and swung into his unfinished bedroom. His hand came away from the door frame wet.

"Painting? You're painting?"

The large space was nearly the size of his living room and dining room combined, with a little headroom lost to sloping sections of the ceiling. Aurora Williams, barefoot, roller in hand, was ten strokes away from finishing the first coat.

The smile she flashed had troublemaker written all over it. "I had to do something, and you hadn't gotten very far in here. Plus, I'm good at painting."

Cruz hadn't gotten very far because he was going to return the paint. The color he picked out was a virile blue. What was on the walls was an effeminate purple-ish color that no self-respecting man would voluntarily put on a wall of his house, let alone his bedroom.

"I just love this color. It's so...happy. Homey." She looked over her shoulder at him. "Sexy."

"That's just what I thought when I picked it out." He ate up the tarp covered floor with his long strides, capturing Aurora in his arms, pinning her to the wall as his mouth devoured hers. She shouted in surprise. He consumed that too.

It was too soon. They barely knew each other. His head knew it, but every other part of him said this was exactly right.

Except she fought his marauding hands, shoving at his shoulders. "The paint is wet!"

He lifted his head. "What?"

"I'm covered in paint and so are you."

He looked at his shoulder where her hand, complete with the roller full of purplish paint, pressed against his black dress shirt. He smiled when he looked down at her. Without those sky-high heels, her head fit just under his chin. She wore skin tight pants with a shapeless, white T-shirt. "That's my shirt."

"Well I wasn't going to paint in mine." She narrowed her eyes. "I better not have paint in my hair." She turned her head.

The thick black braid that ended between her shoulder blades had an iridescent line down the center.

"It's latex, it'll wash out. You can jump in the shower. I'll help."

She pointed the roller at him. "Two steps back, Detective."

He held his hands up and did as ordered. Aurora stepped away from the wall, turning to survey the damage. She sighed heavily, reloaded the roller with paint and went for her outline.

Cruz walked the perimeter, inspecting. There were no marks on the ceiling where the roller had kissed it. There was no purple-ish paint on the white trim of the windows or door. Even the tarp was clean. "You do nice work."

"Of course, I do. There." She handed him the roller. "You get to clean up while I shower."

He never spent less time cleaning up. She painted with the precision of, well, a painter, leaving him time to chop vegetables for a salad. He opened the door beneath the sink and pulled out his garbage can. Something black and smelling of smoke filled it. The room did smell like smoke. How did he miss it? And what was it? He poked at it, and it collapsed to dust.

"Tell me about your day," Aurora said as they sat side-by-side eating salad and reheated pizza

He couldn't think of a thing he wanted to share. His world was doom and gloom. He didn't want to be the clouds to her sun. "Nothing worth telling."

She cut him a look. "Something made you late. Do you always work on Saturdays?"

"Depends on the week. The case I'm on had a development today. I lost track of time, then the commander called me into his office."

"Are you late often?"

"I guess. I haven't had a reason to come home, so it wasn't an issue." Any other night, he'd have come home to a dark, quiet house. This was better. "Thanks for ordering pizza. I know I said I would cook…"

"There wasn't time for that. I tried to make a frozen pizza—you had one in your freezer—but it didn't turn out."

"Is that what is in my garbage can?"

Aurora's brows pressed together. "I think your oven is broken. I followed the directions and *poof*. I called the pizza delivery on your refrigerator magnet. They knew your favorite. Sausage, onion and green pepper."

"Let's try again. Come back tomorrow. You can do the second coat. I'll have a hot meal on the table by the time you're done."

She stabbed the tender greens and pointed at him. "Paying me off in food. I'll consider it."

Sunday, February 18

"You're late." Oscar Bollier chastised with his hand wrapped around a water glass, his cheeks filled with bread.

Cruz took his chair. "Bad couple of days. Took a nap this afternoon, overslept." He rubbed his hand over his day and a half old beard, reminiscing about the best day he'd had since...since the day before. Aurora had come back. They painted together, until she took his brush away after he got paint on the molding. After that, she painted while he flirted. Then she painted while he made lunch. She kept painting while he slept. He woke when she draped a blanket over him on her way out.

Bollier sat up a little straighter. "Something you need to talk about?"

"No. Not like that. It was work."

"Ah." Bollier lifted his hands to allow the waiter to set a simple white plate carrying a serving of filet mignon and several vividly green stalks of broccoli.

"Good evening, Cruz." The waiter smiled with the warmth reserved for long and well-tipping clients. "Coffee?"

He checked his watch. "Yes, and French onion soup and a salad. Could you bring more bread? Dr. Bollier seems to have eaten it all."

"It was mine to eat," Bollier said, buttering another piece of the fresh-made artisan bread. "Interesting case?" he asked, when the waiter had departed.

He reached for a piece of bread. "That's a word for it."

Bollier rapped his knuckle with the butter knife. "You have your own coming. I want to hear about your case."

Cruz rubbed his smarting hand. "You're a doctor. Don't you know slathering on the butter isn't good for you."

"My cholesterol says otherwise, mother. Carry on."

The tables were set far enough apart to ensure private conversations, especially with the jazz in the air. "I was called out Wednesday night to investigate the report of a body. It was the third time since November I'd taken a call like this."

Bollier sliced the steak and put the piece in his mouth. A surgeon for as long as Cruz had been alive, the messier side of Cruz's life not only didn't bother him, it intrigued him.

"Do tell."

"In each case, only the head was found. Mounted on the side of an interstate, right at the city's corp limit."

Bollier chewed, little lines forming between his brows. "Welcome to Cleveland. Tell me more." Over the years, Bollier had proven himself to be an excellent sounding board. Right now, Cruz needed new ideas, different takes on the information. He laid it all out.

The conversation stopped as the waiter served. Bollier dismissed him so hurriedly as to be rude. "I haven't heard anything on the radio, TV. I haven't seen anything in the paper."

"The chief had a press conference with the second discovery at Christmas. There were a few hundred words buried in the metro section."

Cruz broke through the cheese that covered the brown ceramic bowl of onion soup. Bollier cut another piece of steak, concentrating to the point his eyebrows linked together. Cruz knew that look on his sponsor's face. The brain beneath that salt-and-pepper hair spun at a hundred miles an hour.

"I'd like to see the coroner's report."

"I'd appreciate your take."

"Is there a task force on this?"

"Task force? No. I have a team." A thin one. Yablonski, when it fit his own caseload. A few extra hands when he needed it.

"Because of the drugs. If it were school teacher heads dotting the interstate, you would have a team of ten officers working with you, half of them working to keep the union at bay."

"We are taking these crimes seriously." Insult had him snapping back.

"I'm sure you are." Bollier pressed his fist to his heart. "I'm disappointed that you think I would think otherwise. I am merely pointing out the untimely and even gruesome death of drug dealers is going to have a different reaction than if it were respectable people of the community."

Bollier was brilliant but he was arrogant and could edge on elitist. He was a white doctor, top of the white food chain. Cruz often wondered if he was the only person of color Bollier could call a friend.

"Someone interrupted the lives of three men. Regardless of what they were in life, they are mine in death."

Bollier laughed. "Do you have a cape to go with that speech?"

"This isn't funny," Cruz said, teeth gnashing together.

"Who said anything about funny? You think I'm being cruel? I am only saying what most won't venture to say."

"Ever think it shouldn't be said?"

Bollier cocked his head, considering the question literally. "What isn't said, can't be talked about. What isn't talked about, can't be discussed, resolved and moved past. I firmly believe such things should be said. But, I'll concede, the way something is talked about matters." The gleam in those shiny eyes dimmed. "I...I..."

Cruz lifted his head, aware for the first time something more was wrong than an obstinate man's callousness. "What happened?"

"Hospital politics."

"You were fired?"

He waved it off. "I have too much political capital for that."

"Then what. Spill it, Doc."

"I have been moved aside. I am...a floating apex."

"Shit. When did that happen?"

"It has been happening for months. These things are neither quick nor clean."

Cruz set his silverware down. "You haven't said a thing. Week after week. You haven't said a thing." He was mad at his friend, on behalf of his friend, and at himself for not tuning into the fact that Bollier's life was as unsteady as his own.

He put it away. Drawing from his own experience, dealing with someone else's temper didn't help. "Well, now that you're talking about it, we can discuss it, resolve it, and move past it. Do you have options?"

"I'm thinking about starting a clinic of my own. The healthcare laws are opening new opportunities, especially for an eccentric old doctor with a good idea and a fat bank account. I'm going to use their money to serve the very people they say aren't worth the money." He inhaled deeply, exhaled slowly. "That is what is new in my life."

"I have something new." Interest, excitement made him smile. "I met a woman."

"She must be something. I don't think you've dated in all the time we've known each other. You asked her out?"

"She asked me, then she painted my bedroom."

Monday, February 19

Win Ramsey stood behind his desk, hands clasped behind his back, pissed. The glare weighed heaviest on Cruz, but there was plenty left over for the other invited guests—Commander Kurt Montoya, PIO Alison Hyatt, and Detective Matt Yablonski. Not even Special Agent Zachary Bishop was immune. "How did this get out this way?"

Alison lifted her chin. "Mrs. Mayes went to the Medical Examiner's office, demanding to see her son. Unfortunately, one of her staff didn't realize the condition of Mr. Mayes. Needless to say, it was a shock. Mrs. Mayes's associate, a Mr…." She fumbled through her pages for the name.

"Bell. Sam Bell," Cruz said.

"Mr. Bell called the *The Real News* ranting about a cover-up and caught Edward Lutz's attention. You'd think Lutz would get a clue after being fired from the *Plain Dealer*.

Instead that tabloid fed right into his delusions."

"Fucking Lutz," the chief said. "He gives journalists a bad name. Why did it say we were unavailable for comment?"

"I found a message on my desk this morning," Alison said. "Time stamp said seven last night."

"On your desk voice mail?"

Alison shook her head. "I forwarded my desk phone to my cell, just like every night. He didn't call my desk."

"Fucking Lutz," the chief repeated. "Cruz, where do we stand on this latest vic?"

Cruz caught the chief up. "Bobby Mayes fits the M.O. The suspect set up Mayes for a series of weeks, probably since the beginning of the year. There wasn't anything random about this."

"He was a kid, Cruz. A nineteen-year-old kid. I've taken calls from the mayor, city council and every Tom, Dick, and Harry who donated to their re-election campaigns. You tell me right now if you can't handle this—"

"It's mine, Chief." Cruz surged to his feet, teeth bared to protect his territory as Ramsey pointed to Bishop. "All of them are mine. You and the FBI can take this case from me, and they'll still be mine."

Ramsey scrutinized Cruz with his dark gaze. Cruz stood under the pressure, letting his chief see he meant every word, without hesitation. "Work this hard, Cruz," Ramsey said, enunciating each word. "Yablonski, clear your case load, you're officially glued to his hip. Montoya, make sure they have what they need. Bishop, let me know what the FBI has to offer. Stay, Ms. Hyatt. The rest of you are dismissed."

Yablonski stopped outside the chief's office, looking between Cruz and Montoya. "How long do you think we have until the next one?"

March 28

I met again with the infected soul, hoping today would be different. The evil was so close to the surface, he stank of it. Still, I had to be sure. He isn't afraid of me, just like the others. Evil makes them arrogant.

Whatever they see in me, it isn't a threat. That is my gift.

The sun is up, the birds are singing. Yes, it's going to be a good day.

CHAPTER ELEVEN

Wednesday, March 28

The upstairs master suite was now worthy of a photo spread in a home magazine. The purplish color he once thought girly had become something entirely different under Aurora's brush. He frequently touched the paint, the three-dimensional effect disappearing under his fingers. This was his favorite room, with its enormous television, leather couch, and queen-sized bed complete with a naked woman.

Aurora Williams was tangled in his sheets, the curves and valleys of her long body was his own personal wonderland. She rolled over, smooth and languid as a great cat, her dark hair spreading across his pillow. Her shapely leg raised, toes pointed to the ceiling. He wanted that leg curled around his back. Again.

And he wanted more. "Meet my family."

Her gaze snapped to his. "That sounds serious."

He crawled across the comforter, took her nipple in his mouth. "I'm very serious," he said against her skin, "when it comes to you."

She arched her back, offering her breast. He suckled, coaxing a breathy moan from those kissable lips. "I can't think when you do that."

"I don't want to you think. I want you to say you'll meet my family. This weekend. Church, dinner at my sister's home." His tongue flicked the hard, little bud and her hips rolled.

"This is coercion," she said breathlessly.

"Enticement." He settled between her hips, slowly moving down the soft expanse of her bare belly. He pushed her legs apart, trailing nipping kissed down her silky leg until he was at her very core. His tongue lapped at her, then he lifted his head.

She squirmed closer to him. "You stopped." It was a breathless whine edged with desperation.

"You haven't answered me."

"Zeus," she cried, turning the name into three syllables. "Okay, yes. Now do...something."

Twenty minutes later, Cruz opened the oven and checked the chicken. "Aurora. Dinner." He had the hot dish half way out when his cell rang. Hurriedly, put the dish on the stove and grabbed his phone. It shouldn't have surprised him, but it did nonetheless. It had been nearly six weeks since Bobby Mayes was the headline of the *Cleveland Plain Dealer* and the exhausting investigation that led nowhere. Cruz ended one call and placed another. Yablonski was breathing hard when he answered.

"It's Cruz, we have another head."

"Fuck." A milder oath echoed in the background, a female voice. "Where?"

"Northbound I-77 near Fleet. See you there." He disconnected the line and returned to the kitchen. "I have to go, baby. What are you doing?"

Aurora stood at the counter, a spatula in one hand and plastic bowl in the other. "Packing dinner. Here." The glass she pushed at him was pink as cotton candy and thick as a milkshake. "The protein shake will help you recover after all your hard work, and it'll buffer your stomach against all the coffee you're going to pour into it."

Touched, he set the strawberry concoction aside and pulled her into his arms. "Are you taking care of me, Ms. Williams?"

"I am, Detective De La Cruz."

"It's not an easy job. You sure you're up to it?"

She snorted confidently. "I can handle you."

"I like when you handle me." He kissed her throat. "You can stay here."

She shook her head. "It's easier to get ready from my own place. Call me when you can."

The weather had broken. The bitch of a lion held on to March until the last few days and then—*boom*—it was spring. In a town like Cleveland, good judgment was thrown by the wayside for the opportunity to be out of the house. It was only forty-eight degrees, but just seven days ago, it had been twenty-four. The abrupt jump in the thermometer was celebrated with shorts and T-shirts, light-weight jackets, and hanging out in the yard.

And, a head hanging in another cargo net from a neon orange sign that read: Caution Ahead.

The construction sign, another indication spring had truly come, was ten feet in front of the one Cruz had expected.

Cleveland Corp Limit.

The corporate limit sign sat in front of the Fleet Avenue bridge on I-77 northbound. One of the people who called the head in had pulled off the road. The owner stood near the still running car, bobbing and weaving like a boxer, trying to get around the officer who was tasked with baby-sitting. "It's real, isn't it? It's like, the real thing, right?"

The twenty-something with dark hair and a goatee stepped on the white stripe separating life and death. The officer grabbed a fist full of shirt and pulled the guy to the safety of the shoulder as a car drifted close to them, paying more attention to the cops than the road.

"What's your name?" Cruz snapped, furious the man has no sense of how close he just came to death.

"Brady. Brady Walkenshall." His gaze flickered between Cruz and the head like he was watching a tennis match.

Cruz snapped his fingers, commanding attention. "You called nine-one-one at eight-twenty-seven reporting a body on the interstate."

"Not a body. Just a head, I told the lady it was just a head."

"Why did you stay, Mr. Walkenshall?"

The young man blinked. "What?"

"Why did you stop your car? Why did you stay?"

"I thought I should, you know, stay until you guys showed up. It's one of those Drug Heads, isn't it?" The man vibrated with excitement. "It looks like a Drug Head."

Social media had named the killer then distorted, warped, twisted the facts until his case resembled a graphic novel. "Don't call it that. Do you know this man? The victim?"

"Me? No. I just, you know, saw him and well, he looked like a Drug Head. Like on the internet." Walkenshall's phone beeped in his hand. He looked at the screen, then grinned widely. "I just hit ten thousand likes."

"You posted a picture to the internet?"

"Oh, yeah," Walkenshall said with delight and pride.

The man was standing here, and yet it wasn't real to him. Cruz tightened his fist, then released it. "You took a picture of a crime scene and posted it to the internet?"

Walkenshall nodded, a toothy grin on his face, then the edge in Cruz's voice got through. "I, um, didn't think of it that way—"

Cruz took an advancing step forward. "Mr. Walkenshall, what is your connection to the deceased?"

"No. Like I said, I didn't know the guy. I was just driving by, like I said."

"You know what I think? I think you parked down the highway, walked back here to post your sick message. But you were seen. You were reported faster than you expected.

When you couldn't get away clean, you called it in yourself. What better way to fly under our radar then acting like a self-obsessed idiot by posting a fallen man's last stand."

Walkenshall stepped back. "No. I wouldn't do that. I'm not acting. I am an idiot."

Cruz verbally attacked. "Who but the killer wouldn't care about the man's family? Who but the killer would want the product of his work out for everyone to see? We have kept your work under wraps. That pissed you off, didn't it, Mr. Walkenshall?"

"No. No, no, no. You have this wrong. All wrong."

Cruz saw Matt Yablonski drop down the short wall and begin to cross to him. "Officer, take Mr. Walkenshall into custody. I'll finish this interview downtown."

Leaving the uniform to the suspect, Cruz turned to meet Yablonski.

"You got our guy?" Yablonski asked.

"Not likely. You want to see if you recognize the victim?"

Although the temperature had risen, the gust from each passing car was enough to chill. Yablonski ignore it, his coat hanging open, intent on the unseeing face. "Holy shit, Cruz. This is a game changer."

"Who is it?"

"You don't recognize him?" Yablonski raked a hand down his long beard. "Orion McKinley aka Bear. Nasty piece of work. He'd gotten into the big leagues, so to speak. We didn't think he was in town."

Cruz squatted, using a flashlight to dispel the shadows created by the street light far above their heads. Caucasian. Mediterranean heritage. Black hair. A lot of it. "Somebody knew he was here." Cruz stood. "What do you mean by this being a game changer?"

"Gangs. McKinley came up through the ranks of the Reapers. They ate up territory and spit out what they couldn't use, sell, or shoot. He pulled it together after your bust."

"Explains why I don't know him." When you were eating your meals through a straw, keeping track of gang turf wasn't high on the to-do list.

"We gotta keep this quiet, Cruz. There's going to be fall-out. Gang war fallout. We need to get this up the ladder."

"Don't hold your breath on the keeping it quiet. Our boy back there snapped pictures and posted to the internet."

In the darkness of night, Orion McKinley's house was a colorless mass. Colorless but not silent.

"I know he over dere, bitch. I know he over dere and I'm gonna mutha fuckin cut you up. I told you dun mess with my man." The woman stalked the length of the lit porch, shouting into the cell phone, her angry tenor the only sound in the night. She wore skin tight leggings in a small checkerboard pattern that dazzled the eyes when she walked. Most of her top half was covered in a lime green sweatshirt, cut off just below her breasts. She wasn't fat, but what she had poked out over the waistband of the leggings. She was an average-toned African-American, neither light- nor dark-skinned. Her hair was pulled severely back from her face and tied so the few inches of tail poked straight out the back of her head. Wisps and pieces that escaped radiated outward from her face. The angry words had come from an angry mouth, set in a frown so deep it reached to Cincinnati. "You tell Bear to get his cheatin' ass home before you ain't got no ass for him to get."

"Cleveland police," Cruz said as he and Yablonski approached the house.

The brows pressed down, further darkening her face. "What the fuck you want?"

"Does Orion McKinley live here?"

"Yeah. So?"

"And you are?"

"L'Tonya Simmons. His mutha fucking wife," she said, yelling into the phone again.

"Ms. Simmons, I'm sorry to tell you that Mr. McKinley was found dead this evening."

Her expression went blank. For five seconds, her face was completely empty. And then she exploded. Arms flailed as she stalked across the porch. "You think I'm stupid? Bear ain't dead. Ain't nothin' that can kill Bear. You think I'm so fuckin' stupid that I'd believe a cop 'bout anythin'?"

"Ms. Simmons, when did you see Mr. McKinley last?"

"Like you don' know." She pitched forward, hands on her hips. "This mornin'. That mutha fucker went to the store for Dew and never came back. I know he went to that bitch Sharonda. I went and looked for myself, but those cock suckers locked all the doors. Good thin' too or I'da cut dem botf."

"What is Sharonda's last name? Where does she live?"

"Dat's right. You go look there. Sharonda Smith." She didn't know the address but knew the street and described the house.

"Let's go inside, Ms. Simmons. We can talk privately," Yablonski suggested.

Her animated body stilled. "No. You ain't invited. I know my rights. You gotta have a thing if'n you wanna come in." She ran into the house, slammed the door closed, and locked it.

Yablonski dialed the phone as he walked. "She's going to clean that house before I can get a search warrant. Gotta get a sewer crew here to plug the pipe."

"Tell me I heard you right." The voice came through the night, edged with hope, glee. "Bear's dead?"

Cruz walked toward a middle-aged man standing in the shadows of a large oak tree. "And you are?"

"Antwan King. This is my house," he said, gesturing to the one behind him. "Make my year. Tell me Bear is dead."

"I'm Detective De La Cruz; this is Detective Yablonski. The investigation is still underway but, yes, Mr. McKinley was found dead this evening. When was the last time you saw him?"

"Just before eleven this morning. Squealed his tires and tore down the street. Left rubber in the road."

"Have you seen anyone out of place lately? You know, someone hanging around that didn't belong?"

"You know what Bear was, Detectives?" the man asked, lowering his chin and looking out of the tops of his eyes.

"Yeah," Yablonski said. "We know."

"Then you know he terrorized this neighborhood. Side of my house has so many bullet holes it's starting to look like Swiss cheese. You come back in the day and take a look."

"Have you seen a dark van," Yablonski said.

"Yeah. Complained to my wife it was parked too close to my driveway. I saw it the next day parked two houses down. Saw it a few times after."

"Can you describe it?"

"Like you said. Dark. Black. Plain."

"Make? Model?"

King shook his head. "I didn't care enough to look, and I don't recognize that stuff the way some guys do."

"What about the plates," Yablonski said.

"Ohio. The colorful one. Sorry, that's it."

"We appreciate it, sir." Cruz offered a card. "If you remember anything else, please give me a call."

"I will, Detective, but I gotta tell you, I'm not sad at all Bear is dead. This is a good day for this neighborhood."

"You *shut* yo mouth, ol' man." L'Tonya Simmons's roar came from her front door. "You show Bear respect and shut your mouth."

King turned toward the ugly sound and raised his voice. "I am done shutting up. I have put up with your shit for years. He's dead. Hallelujah. The Bear is dead." King danced on his front lawn.

"You sonofa bitch. You gonna pay. Bear gonna come home and then you gonna pay." She punctuated the threat with the slam of the front door.

Cruz looked from the front door to the grinning man. "Call me if you remember anything."

"I will, Detective. Y'all have a peaceful night. I know I will."

March 29

The sign I put up yesterday was seen by everyone. The news said it went viral on social media. Now they'll see the way Evil uses drugs to infect their souls.

Satan has a powerful weapon. It reminds me of Hansel and Gretel. The witch tempted the children with candy. The devil tempts with drugs.

The witch shoved the children into the oven. The devil sucks the souls into the fires of hell.

Once they go in, there's no getting out.

CHAPTER TWELVE

Thursday, March 29

The story made the front page of the *Plain Dealer* and was featured on every local television and radio news feed. The story was simple. Another head was found. I-77 near Fleet Avenue. Police are investigating. Identity of the victim is being withheld. There is no further comment at this time.

Cruz sat at his desk, reading the thick file on the life and times of Orion McKinley. He answered his phone without looking away from the screen. "De La Cruz."

"Good morning, Zeus."

"Good morning, baby." Cruz pushed the file back, welcoming the distraction. "I'm sorry. I didn't call."

"Zeus, you're fine. I didn't expect you to call. I guess I'm checking on you. Did you eat dinner?"

He liked the idea of her checking on him. "Yes, about two this morning. I was glad to have it."

"Good. I heard on the news about another Drug Head."

He winced at her use of the name. "Baby, don't call it that. Don't get tied up in the half-truth bullshit posted by people who get off on attention. These men were victims of vicious murders, not characters on the latest Netflix original."

"I'm sorry, Zeus. I didn't mean anything by it." A pause lingered. "It was found close to my school, wasn't it?"

He could have walked to her school from the scene without breaking a sweat. "Yes. Look, I want you to take precautions. If you see anyone out of place, you call."

"I will. Would you come in and talk to the children again? I would feel better if you talked to them about strangers."

"Sure, but not today. I'll have to see when I can break away."

"Will you come over tonight?"

"I don't know, but I'll try."

Fast strides carried Yablonski across the room. "Let's go. I got the warrant for McKinley's house."

Cruz was out of his chair, shrugging into his coat. "I have to go, baby. I'll call later."

McKinley's street looked different for more than just the daylight. Two fire trucks blocked the street, spraying water on the last stubborn flames licking Antwon King's home.

Cruz parked where he could.

"Anyone hurt," Yablonski asked a firefighter.

"Everyone got out. Smoke detectors did their job."

Cruz looked at McKinley's house. A sheet covering the picture window snapped back in place. He knew Yablonski was on the same page when he signaled for two uniform officers to join them.

Yablonski took the lead. "L'Tonya Simmons. Cleveland police. We have a warrant to search the property. Open the door." He tried a second time, and a third.

Cruz shrugged. "You didn't think she was going to make it easy for you."

Yablonski rolled his eyes, made sure Cruz had hold of the screen door and then planted his foot on the door. It took a few well-placed kicks, but the door swung open.

A toilet flushed from somewhere in front of them.

The four men moved through the house, quickly, efficiently, carefully. They found Simmons on her knees, surrounded by several kilograms of cocaine, working very hard to flush a block down the toilet.

Cruz swallowed a laugh. The toilet was overflowing and

the brick a uniform pulled out was three times too large for the opening.

"It ain't mine." L'Tonya shouted over the rights being read. "It belongs to a friend of Bear's. He explain everythin' when he get back. He be back real soon."

Cruz walked with the officer escorting Simmons to the car, in case he needed a hand.

Outside, her gaze flickered to the charred remains of her neighbor's home. The edge of her mouth curled into a cruel, sinister smile. "Tode you shut ya mouth."

Cruz watched and knew. Pride, satisfaction, excitement shone in her eyes. She was dying to tell someone about her hard work. "Bear would be proud of you, watching his back like that. King was disrespectful."

"Damn straight he was. He disrespected Bear. Nobody does that."

"Not with you around."

"Not with me around. I showed him. That bitch Sharonda can suck his cock, but she can't do what I did."

"Nobody but you would do that for Bear."

"'Xactly." She snorted. "You own gasoline burn you own house. Who's dancin' now ol' man? Huh? Who the fuck is dancin' now?" She yelled at her neighbor as she pulled uselessly against the officer's grip.

In the silence that followed Simmons's departure, Yablonski and crew went to work on McKinley's house. Cruz did his own search but found nothing that said where Bear went after getting his morning caffeine buzz. Eventually, he returned to the station. He had a date in the interview room.

"My client would like to make a statement," the lawyer said calmly.

Walkenshall's hands shook as he read from the handwritten paper. "I, uh, apologize for m-my behavior last n-night. Somebody died. It isn't a g-game. I know it isn't a g-game. I'm sorry I took those pictures and posted them. I'm r-really sorry I stayed around."

The night in lock-up and the lawyer got through to the guy. "Anything else?"

"Yeah. I, um, I didn't kill him. I didn't."

The lawyer leaned forward. "Come on, Detective. You know my client is guilty of nothing other than questionable judgment. It's not illegal to post photos like he did. He said he's sorry, let us get out of your way so you can get back to finding the guy who did this."

"I appreciate your interest in my caseload, but we're going to do this my way."

Detective Jesus De La Cruz knew he'd hit a wall when he poured the packet of sugar into the garbage and put the wrapper in his coffee. He left the noise and the hustle of the station for the quiet of his back seat and a few minutes of shut eye. One hour until the meeting with the chief. One hour before the hamster got back in the wheel.

"Orion McKinley was killed by a blow to the head, which was delivered after he was pepper-sprayed." Cruz stood straight and tall, looking Chief Ramsey in the eye. "He left his house about eleven to get his morning Mountain Dew. He bought the soda from a local grocery at eleven-twelve. The store had a security camera on the front door. McKinley was shown coming out of the store, looking past the camera and then walking out. His car was found in the opposite direction, on a side street. His head was first reported later that day at eight-oh-nine."

"McKinley managed to keep three gangs in check." Yablonski represented the joint gang-narcotics task force. "He made sure the drugs, money, and women flowed and drew strict lines of conduct. Anyone stepping over the line found themselves dead—or worse. With him gone, there is a power vacuum. He had six lieutenants, any of which may throw in for the promotion." He unfolded a map of the city. Thick, crude circles showed where the power centers were. "I have already contacted the district commanders. We will be working closely with them on the situation."

Aurora's school laid in the overlap of two of the areas. "The suspect is slowing ringing the city. Look." Cruz made an X on Yablonski's map where each of the heads was found. "90 West, 480 East, 71 North, 77 North."

Special Agent Bishop used a blue marker to add circles to the remaining entry points into the city. "There are only a few interstates left coming into the city." Bishop pinned Cruz with a look. "How could our suspect have not been seen?"

"He or she was seen," Cruz confirmed. "The problem is no one recognized what they saw. They saw a van on the side of the road, a driver with car trouble. We haven't found anyone who saw a killer."

"It's like we are chasing a ghost," Commander Montoya said. "Even when we have witness, they've seen nothing. Nobody's that good. Where aren't we looking?"

There was no response.

"Alison, where are we with the public?" the chief asked.

"It's quiet, sir. Even with the fuss Mr. Bell raised, we haven't fielded many calls from the public. There is more interest among the press. I have calls from several reporters on my desk. I was planning to return them this afternoon."

Ramsey leaned on the table, elbows locked, looming over the assembled team. "Lady and gentlemen, the first head was found five months ago. Someone explain to me how this vigilante is walking over us in our own house?"

* * *

118

Friday, March 30

Orion "Bear" McKinley's side piece of ass was a dead end. She didn't know the man, in the biblical sense, no matter what that insane bitch L'Tonya thought. Mavis McKinley, Bear's mother, lived in a rundown apartment building with lighting humming like a bug zapper and hallways reeking of urine. If she knew anything about the details of her son's life, she wasn't telling. She couldn't give up the people she needed for her next fix.

The run through the DMV database for black vans and truck with the "Ohio, Birthplace of Aviation" plate produced a mind-boggling number of potentials.

Bear McKinley had more than a few people who preferred him on a stick. The man had a long, violent past that left a trail of victims from the sixth-grade playground to his current day home.

Victims.

How many did Bear have? Ten? Twenty? A hundred? It wasn't out of the question when you considered each individual person had significant others, families, friends. Each paying a price for Bear's crimes.

Cruz's gut liked this. His fingers got busy on the keyboard. In the prior twelve months, there were seventy-nine homicides, three hundred fifty rapes, thirty-two hundred robberies, seventeen hundred fifty assaults and three hundred arsons in the city of Cleveland. Officially.

Cruz lived the numbers, and yet they staggered him.

There wasn't a net wide enough to snag all the fish in that lake in the hopes of getting the one they were looking for.

The chief wasn't satisfied with the progress. The water was getting warm for everyone in homicide and narcotics, but Cruz's feet were starting to blister.

Interviews, witness reports, data analyses. They all pointed to the same place.

Nowhere.

The department halls were quiet, giving Cruz space to think for the first time all day. He stroked the scars at his eye as he studied the board connecting Uncle Hall, Mathias Martinez, Bobby Mayes, and Bear McKinley. In the middle, some smart ass pinned the question mark that was the signature of the Riddler. Cruz left it because it wasn't wrong.

Riddle me this:

I see no skin color; only dealers.

I see no men; only monsters.

I see no end; only death.

What am I?

"A psychopath." He said the thought out loud. "Who's gonna be next? How can I get ahead of you?"

His phone rang. Aurora's number. His gaze snapped to the clock. Six-fifteen p.m. When did it get so late? "Hey, baby."

"You're still at work, aren't you? You aren't coming out tonight." Aurora had asked him this morning if he would go out with her and her girlfriends. They knew the guitar player of a band who was playing at a bar. The three, single women had some sort of psychic connection to each other. Aurora had been right there with them, but now that she was with him, she'd fallen a half step out of sync. He knew it bothered her. She didn't say it, but she was trading her friends for him.

Aurora had started throwing darts on Tuesday. The crowd Cruz hung with was a mishmash of singles and couples that easily absorbed her. Yablonski and his nurse Erin slid into their lives. Dinner after work. Home projects. The couples were together a few times a week. The fit easy, comfortable.

He didn't fit so easily into her crowd. He couldn't follow the conversation, let alone have something to say. They drank, he didn't. Every time they went out, Aurora had an internal battle waging in her head. Cruz saw it on her face. He encouraged her to go, not to hold back because of him.

But she did.

There wasn't anger in her voice. She was matter-of-fact. She could have been asking him if it was raining. He'd encouraged her to go out with her friends; she shouldn't have to give up her life for him. "No. I still have some things to wrap up here. Will you come to my house later?"

"Hmm. Probably."

He knew that sound. She was putting on lipstick.

"Call me if you need a designated driver."

"Uh huh, but," she paused for a moment, "I'm not planning on drinking much. Just, you know, dinner, blowing off a little steam."

"Have fun. I'll leave the door open." He refilled his go cup and sipped on the brew weak enough to pass for water in some countries as he puzzled through the cases.

Opportunity? These murders were not spontaneous. The suspect created the opportunity, getting physically close to a drug dealer in the city the size of Cleveland. How many entrepreneurs did the city have? Hundreds? Four were dead. Statistically, a drop in the bucket.

Means? What kind of tool was used to decapitate the heads? The medical examiner's best guess was some type of saw.

Motive? The obvious weren't playing out: money, position, territory. What motive had a player like Bear McKinley on the same field as Bobby Mayes?

Saturday, March 31 1:00 a.m.

"Zeus? Shhh, you'll wake him."

"Aurora. I'm awake." Cruz looked up from the physiology book he'd been reading, learning more about the neck and spine. "I'm talking to you on the phone. Where are you?"

"At this club. I may have had a teensy-wee-itty-bitty too

much to drink." Giggles in the background.

He dog-eared the page and closed the book. "What's the name of the club?" Thirty minutes later, he chauffeured four drunk women around the city. He poured the last of her friends into her apartment and headed for his home. Aurora flipped through the stations on the radio until she found a song she could sing at the top of her lungs.

Aurora was a talented painter...not so much on lead vocals.

He pulled into his driveway and put it in park.

"You." Aurora said, her hair falling in her eyes. "You are a good boyfriend. The best boyfriend. Ever. E.V.E.R. Come here."

He didn't try not to laugh but did lean over the center console. She took his face in her hands and kissed him deeply. Even drunk, she possessed a sexuality that drove him crazy. She pulled the band from his braid and ran her fingers though his hair. Every nerve ending fired in triplicate.

She tasted like alcohol. Sharp, tangy. The taste he remembered. This he had liked. Craving it as much as he craved her, he took control of the kiss, holding her still while he fed his addiction.

Aurora broke away and slid off the panties she wore under the short skirt. She climbed over the center console and onto his chest, wedging her legs on either side of him.

There wasn't going to be a lot of room. He was going to be at her mercy.

His fingers found the controls to the seat, moving it back until her ass fit between his cock and the steering wheel. She lifted her hips and slid down the hard length of him.

Her ass in his hands, the tang of liquor on her breath, her tight body clamping down on his cock nearly broke him. He ground his teeth, drawing out every movement, every moment.

She giggled. "You're holding out on me," she said in a sing-song taunt. She bit his ear. His breath caught, his body clenched as he pumped into her again and again. And then...

blessed release.

Heart still pounding, he opened his eyes, looking into her sedate face. Her eyes were closed, and her mouth held a little Mona Lisa smile that said he'd given as good as he got. Slowly she moved, her hands to his chest, her body swaying as she sat with him buried deep inside. Her eyelids flipped opened, but it wasn't sexual satisfaction he saw in her gaze. "Zeus? I, uh. I, uh. Uh oh."

He threw open the truck door, catching Aurora as she leaned to the right and emptied her stomach. Most ended up on the ground. This part he remembered too, without the fondness.

She pulled herself up, leaning too far to the left. He caught her again, pulling her against his body to keep her from falling.

"I don't feel good." She buried her face in his chest. "I think I'm sick."

He flinched as her sour breath assaulted his face, another mark on the side of sobriety. "Let's get you inside."

She snuggled into him. "I'm just gonna sleep here. Good night. I love you." His cock still buried to the hilt, she passed out.

He looked at himself, at his situation, and laughed.

Quiet permeated Cruz's home despite the lateness of the morning. Sitting at the desk in the bedroom he used as an office, he built his theory. If he moved away from the often brutal world of organized drug trafficking, then the next place to go was mental illness. The field fascinated him in college, and he interfaced with it often as a cop. He started with a hypothesis: an event triggered this behavior, in this city. No doubt there was a connection to drugs, but maybe not the business side.

He began with homicides, the fewest and most severe violent crimes.

There would be no norm for the length of time it would take from the inciting incident to the manifestation of the crimes. The latest compiled statistics indicated seventy-nine homicides occurred in the prior twelve months.

Uncle Hall's head was found in the early days of November; he began in October. Two of the months' homicides had a blatant connection to drugs. The bodies of two black males were discovered in a home the weekend before Halloween. The contents of the house had been thrown around and numerous bullets were found in the walls. A half a kilogram of heroin was found hidden in a child's toy box. The house was in Reaper territory—a connection to McKinley. The report contained interviews with gang members but, to date, no one had been charged with the murders. Cruz made note of the names and ages of the victims.

September had three drug-related homicides. A pregnant woman was killed by her boyfriend during an argument. The boyfriend was arrested and was moving through the judicial process. He pleaded not guilty despite the overwhelming physical evidence. He admitted to being high and had no memory of using the knife on his girlfriend or their unborn son.

A dispute between two drug dealers resulted in injury to two adult bystanders and the death of a child. One suspect had run onto a limited access highway and was struck and killed. The surviving dealer pled to lesser offenses when witnesses confirmed the dead man had injured the bystanders and killed the child.

The brutal August heat had worn tempers down and cost ten people their life. After buying a small quantity of marijuana, two white and one Hispanic teenaged boys pulled a knife on the dealer with the intent to rob. The dealer was faster with his gun. He was arrested and charged with manslaughter. He was claiming self-defense. The case was working its way through the system.

A Cleveland EMT died from wounds suffered on the job. He was attempting to revive a suspected overdose when the patient woke violently and severed the EMT's jugular. The resurrected assailant pleaded to lesser charges and was serving his time.

Three separate homicides occurred in early morning hours at bars. In each case, two men were involved. In each case, a small quantity of an illegal substance was found on either the suspect or the victim.

His cell rang. "De La Cruz."

"Are you working on the weekend?" Mariana's voice chirped in his ear. "I know you are because you didn't just say 'hello.'"

He leaned back in his chair, welcoming the break. "Cops motto. Crime never stops, and neither do we. How are my favorite girls?" Rhianna squealed in the background over some injustice perpetrated by Gabby. "What is the tragedy this time?"

"Dresses. We had to buy Gabby a new dress, she grows so fast I can't keep up. Rhia got a pretty flower dress that is new-to-her to wear."

A pitiful cry rang out again, then he could hear his niece. "It's ugly. I want to look pretty for Easter."

Mari sighed heavily. "A dress doesn't make you pretty. It's who you are inside."

"My insides want a new dress."

He chuckled as his sister reasoned with her lawyer-in-training of a daughter. "I can take her shopping tomorrow."

"Tito, Easter is tomorrow."

His brain stumbled. It was March the...the..."That can't be right. I was just at church—"

"Three weeks ago. Easter is tomorrow. That's why I was calling. You are coming to church, right? To the house after?"

125

"Yes. Of course, I am. I've just been a little distracted lately."

Mariana huffed. "I heard. I've been very patient with you, Tito, but a woman has her limits."

He stood, walking away from the pressure. "This case is demanding all my time, Mari."

"I'm not talking about your heads, Tito. I'm talking about your woman. When do I get to meet her?"

Dumbfounded, he said the only thing in his head. "How did you know?"

"My friend works on the same floor as Erin Davis." When he didn't say anything, she added. "Erin is dating your friend Matt."

"Erin. Right. Uh-oh."

"Yeah. Uh-oh. I want to meet her, Jesus." It was an order. "Tomorrow."

"On Easter?"

Easter. It was perfect. Lots of people to distract his mother and occupy his sister. "You'll meet Aurora tomorrow. Don't tell Mom."

"You think it's a good idea to surprise her?"

Cruz loved his mother, but she was a champion smotherer. If she knew he was bringing Aurora, he'd be on the phone the entire day answering questions he did not want to get into. "Yes. Absolutely. Definitely."

Mari laughed so hard she snorted. "Have it your way. I bought a pork shoulder to roast. I'm going to the grocery store and was calling to see what else you planned to make, but obviously, you haven't thought about it."

He dug for a clean piece of paper and rattled off ingredients to his sister. They divided up the dishes and the chores until the girls found their mother's hiding place.

"Tito," Rhianna said in a voice that rose and fell like a mountain. "Tell Mama I needa dress!"

"I could but then who would wear the princess flower

dress? It is an important part of Easter to have the princess who brings in the flowers for Jesus."

There was a moment of silence. "I could do it. In a new dress."

"No. That wouldn't work. That dress is very special. Gabby is a little tall, but I suppose—"

"I can do it, Tito. Gabby! I'm going to be the Easter Princess." Her voice trailed off as she ran to brag to her older sister.

"She grabbed the phone right out of my hand," Mariana complained. "That girl is going to have me gray before I'm forty. I have to go."

"Remember, not a word to Mom." He ended the call, and movement in the corner of his eye caught his attention. "Good morning, sleepy head."

"Shhh." Aurora fell heavily against the door jamb. "Head hurts. Bad."

"Let's see what we can do," he whispered. He sat her on the couch, fed her pain killers and a mug of cold water.

She sipped the water. "I'm sorry."

"For what?"

"For whatever I did to put that look on your face that says I did something really embarrassing that I have no memory of."

He grinned wider, tucking her hair behind her ear. "Oh. That look."

"Are you going to tell me what I did?"

"Are you sure you want to know?"

Aurora covered her face. "It's that bad?"

"No. Not bad." He took the water and set it down, then placed a kiss in her palm. "You told me you loved me." When her eyes grew wide, he knew the truth had escaped last night. Today, she looked afraid.

"We haven't exactly gotten to the I-love-you stage. It's okay if you don't—"

"I said that I was crazy in love with you." He hadn't said it, but he felt it. He had never said it to a woman. It was easier than he expected, especially when she smiled radiantly.

"That's good. Very good. Was that all?"

For all of Aurora's energy and outgoing personality, she embarrassed easily. If she knew the rest, she would be self-conscious, even ashamed. He didn't want that for her. "Yes. That was all."

"That's not so bad." She drew her fingers along his jaw. "Tricking you into a date was one of the smartest things I ever did."

He kissed her nose. "My luckiest day. Are you hungry? I need to work a little more, but I can make you a little breakfast first."

She pressed her hand to her stomach. "Don't even say that word. I'm just going to lie here, very still, and chain-watch Netflix. Go work. Don't worry about me."

He put a pillow under her head and tucked his one blanket around her. "Call me if you need anything."

Her hand appeared above the back of the couch, waving him away. "Happy hunting, Detective."

It wasn't happy hunting, but it was productive in the sense of doing something to advance the investigation beyond reacting to the strict facts of the case. The suspect he pursued was a shadow. He built a portfolio of potential suspects from those closest to the victims.

Old enough to drive but young enough for the physical exertion of managing the bodies and the discovery sites. Average build to match an average shoe size. Skills to decapitate a corpse. A doctor or nurse. A butcher. An EMT. After all, you couldn't YouTube it—he froze, wondered, then decided not to check. Somethings, even a homicide detective didn't want to know.

Sunday, April 1

"Please tell me we are not late." Aurora teetered on three-inch sunshine yellow heels as they ran across the asphalt parking lot.

"We're fashionably on-time." Cruz tugged her along as the church bells rang out over the bright Easter morning. He raced ahead of an elderly couple. "See? We aren't the last, so we aren't late." He led Aurora into the church and down an aisle.

"Tito!" Rhianna climbed onto the pew in the white summer dress with yellow and purple flowers. At her shout, his entire family turned and stared. He ignored the feeling of being mentally strip-searched by swinging his niece to his hip.

"Who's that?" she said, wrinkling her nose.

"This is Aurora. Aurora, this is my niece, Rhianna." Introductions were cut short with the rise of the music. Thank You, Jesus.

Easter was a joyful celebration for the congregation of Sagrada Familia, but this one stretched on ad infinitum. His niece strategically positioning herself between him and Aurora. His mother looked back every sixty seconds, alternating between him and the mixed-race beauty that sat almost by his side.

His sister looked over her shoulder. He read the I-told-you-so in her amused eyes.

After the service, he pulled Aurora hastily into the aisle, wanting to be outside the church where he would have room to maneuver. If there were high ground, he would have taken it.

"Jesus De La Cruz."

Busted. "*Hola*, Mama." He turned casually and bent dutifully to kiss her cheek. "Mama, this is Aurora Williams. Aurora, this is my mother, Vanessa De La Cruz. This is my brother-in-law Tony Moreno, my sister Mariana. That's

Gabby and you've met Rhianna."

"Tito, I have to go potty," Rhianna tugged on his arm.

Cruz tugged on her braid. "You're a big girl, Rhia. You know where it is."

Rhia crossed her arms and gave a huff. Vanessa De La Cruz held her hand out, speaking rapidly and with animated gestures.

Aurora's eyes took up her entire face. "I-I'm sorry. I don't speak Spanish."

The girls giggled. "That was English," Gabby said. "Why do you care about her hips, *Abuela*?"

Aurora paled and then went scarlet. "I, uh, um."

"Come," his mother said, reaching for his girlfriend.

He swept Aurora behind him. "No, Mama."

"*Si.* Woman talk." Vanessa De La Cruz circled her son.

"No, Mama." He turned again, keeping his body solidly between with mother and his woman.

A sing-song of his name came from across the yard. "Jesus. I was hoping you would be here. I've missed you the last few weeks. Your mother said—"

"No, no. He has a woman. I no need you." His mother intercepted the early-thirty something. "But, give me your number in case this one does not stick."

"Mama!" His voice cracked. Humiliated. Embarrassed. Emasculated. He looked down where Aurora cowered against his back. Except her shoulders were shaking, almost as if she were laughing. He nudged her with his elbow and gave her a warning look.

She sobered up quickly. "You even think about abandoning me and I will hurt you."

Fun as it was to tease her, he didn't feel relaxed. This was not going as planned. This was not anywhere close to the civil, respectable, *normal* introduction he imagined. No chance it would get better at Mari's house, he thought on the short drive. "We shouldn't go."

"We're going. We have to meet each other's family some-time."

"How about on our tenth wedding anniversary?" When she rolled her eyes, he let out a heavy breath. "I apologize in advance for anything my mother says or does. As her only son, she is honor-bound to torture any woman with the prospect of becoming her daughter-in-law." Pulling in front of his sister's house, he captured Aurora's hand before she reached the door. "I love you. Remember that. Use it like a shield to defend yourself."

"You're being silly." Aurora shook her head when he didn't release her. "Maybe I'm a little nervous, but they love you and you love me, so we should all be good. Let's go before I change my mind."

The door hadn't closed behind them before his sister and mother were pulling Aurora away from him. He leapt in to protect her. "Mama. Mariana. Stop."

Mari tossed her dark curls over her shoulder. "There's a pork shoulder calling your name, Tito. The faster you finish it, the faster you get her back."

Then Aurora was gone. Swept down the hall. Cruz went to the kitchen to stop himself from dragging her away from his mother's smothering and his sister's influence. With his favorite knife in hand, he got busy with the roast.

"Relax. They aren't going to eat her." Tony pulled a ginger ale from the refrigerator, opened it, then handed it to Cruz. Then he took one for himself. "They just want to get to know her."

He trimmed the fat from the roast with more gusto than grace. "Why can't they do that out here?"

He shrugged. "They're women."

"They don't have to mob her like that. They'll chase her away."

"Not likely. You know, this is the first woman you've brought home."

"That can't be right." The knife stopped, and he thought back.

"I've been part of your family for ten years and this is the first one I've ever met."

He sipped the ginger ale, his throat suddenly dry. Before his injury, his love life was a series of one-night stands, some lasting a few hours, others a few weeks. It was sex. A warm body to bury himself in, not someone you brought to Easter.

"Your mother thought you were gay."

He dropped the can of ginger ale, spilling it over a stack of clean dishes. "What!"

Tony tossed him a towel. "You were reclusive. You never talked about anyone, never brought anyone with you when you did come around."

He dried his shirt, left the dishes to Tony, and attacked the roast again. "If Mama thought I was gay, what was with the parade of women the last year?"

"She was trying to get you to, you know, change teams." Tony's stoic face crumbled. "You should have heard the conversations Mari had. Trying to convince your mother it was okay if you were gay."

"Mariana thought I was gay?" Why that hurt his feelings he didn't know.

"I don't know if she knew. I told her you weren't."

"What, I didn't set off your gaydar?"

Tony held up his hands. "You can't be mad at them for thinking you're gay and at me for thinking you're not. Is it serious? You might as well tell me your side 'cause I'm going to hear your sister's once you leave."

"Yeah, it's serious, and I don't want them scaring her away with the smothering." He looked down the hallway at the closed door. He planted the knife in the roast. "That's it. I can't take it." He invaded the sacred ground of the De La Cruz women, pulling his Aurora from the room.

His mother and sister followed, chattering for him to

mind his own business. He sat Aurora at the kitchen table, planting his hands on her shoulders to make sure she stayed put. "If you want to talk, talk out here."

His sister lifted her chin. "As we were saying...I think he's always had an oral fixation."

"*Si*," his mother said. "It is my fault. I nursed him until his was three. He always preferred milk from the breast."

Tony roared with laughter, fumbling the dishes he was cleaning.

Cruz shrunk until he stood three feet tall, his voice too thin, too high. "I should have worn my gun."

April 1

I'm disappointed. My signs aren't working. The same men are hanging out on the same street corners. Kids are walking by all that evil just to get to school.

The police can't stop them but it isn't their fault. Laws are made for men. The drug dealers are infested with evil. They are more like demons then men. They feed on the weak, taking apart their human lives until nothing is left but the shell.

I need to do something more. Something that shows people evil can be beaten.

I carry the card with Saint Michael on it. He is my protection, my inspiration. I'm trying to think like him. What would he do?

There's only one thing I know. It would be something big.

CHAPTER THIRTEEN

Monday, April 2

Yablonski stared the five profiles Cruz had laid out. "They're all so average. None of them jump off the page as serial killer."

"Exactly. Our suspect hides in plain sight. These five are so average, they could walk through a secured area and not be seen. These five are not only average, they had a close relation killed in drug-related homicides. I've only gotten through August, September, and October of last year, before we found Alvin 'Uncle' Hall in November. He freakin' planted heads on interstate highways, there were hundreds of witnesses and we got nothing. He doesn't stand out. He isn't the big one, or the little one, or the one that walks funny. He is absolutely, boringly average." He picked up the nearest paper, his gut telling him this path was the right one. "I'm going to visit Roger McCormick."

"I'll drive, you talk."

"Roger McCormick. Age twenty-seven. Mechanic by profession. His sister, Kelly, was killed last September by her boyfriend. She was five months pregnant at the time. Her boyfriend, Justin Reese, was found passed out next to her body, covered in her blood. The knife with his fingerprints in her blood was recovered. He pled not guilty. He said he'd been stoned and had no memory of hurting Kelly. The brother disrupted the courtroom when Reese started to cry over the death of Kelly and his son."

Yablonski drove west to the edge of the city. "A mechanic is a good fit. Physical work. Comfortable with power tools. Does he have a record?"

"A minor for public intoxication when he was twenty-two. Clean otherwise."

"Married? Kids?"

"No. He owns his own garage. Specializes in body work and collision repair. I checked out the property. He shares it with a junk yard."

Yablonski turned onto the quiet street and parked in front of a neat, two-story colonial. "Convenient."

Cruz took the lead, knocking on the front door.

"If you're looking for Roger, he's not home. He's at work. He's always at work." An older woman with two yappy dogs on the end of blinged-out leashes offered the information.

Cruz held out his identification. "Detectives De La Cruz and Yablonski, Cleveland PD. Who are you?"

"His neighbor, Elsie Watkins. Is Roger in trouble?"

"No, ma'am. We are just doing a follow up on people associated with violent crimes. We understand Mr. McCormick lost a sister last year."

"Oh, yes. Such a tragedy, she was such a lovely girl. She lived with him for a few weeks right before she died. He feels responsible, you can see it in his eyes. He spends too much time alone, too much time working. I tried to set him up with a girl who works in my son's office, but he wouldn't have it."

As serious as the conversation was, inside, Cruz laughed. What was it with woman of a certain age? Did they think coupling up solved everything?

"The holidays were hard. From Halloween until New Year's he hid out in that house of his, hid from the world. I pried him out for a few hours, long enough to get a decent meal in him. He's losing weight, you know."

Leaving Mrs. Watkins and her pooches, they headed to

McCormick's Body Shop, which shared a building with Tip Top Scrap. The three-acre lot was close enough to the residential neighborhood for easy customer service but kept the grittier details on the industrial side of the street.

A small bell over the front door announced their arrival. The man at the front counter looked up. "Hi, there."

Cruz held out his identification. "Detectives De La Cruz and Yablonski. Is Roger McCormick here?"

"I'm McCormick."

The man looked little like the picture of the five-foot-ten, two-hundred-pound man in the DMV picture. He'd lost at least forty pounds. His cheekbones stuck out where they used to be rounded. His hair hung down long enough to brush the tops of his shoulders. His eyes were as hollow as his cheeks.

"Is there somewhere we could talk?" Cruz said.

"My office." He led them down a narrow hall, looking over his shoulder every other step. "What's this about?"

"We understand you lost your sister last year in a drug-related incident."

McCormick stiffened. "She was stabbed to death by the junkie father of her baby."

"Did she use?"

Color tinted his cheeks. "No. Absolutely not. And if she did before she was pregnant, she definitely didn't after. She wouldn't even drink a cup of coffee."

"Did she ever talk about people her boyfriend associated with?"

"Sure. I went to a few parties over there. I knew some of them."

"Can you tell me if any of these men look familiar to you?"

Yablonski opened a folder and laid out mug shots, one by one, of the murder victims.

McCormick picked up the picture of Mathias Jose Martinez. "He looks familiar. Maybe." He shook his head. "That feels like forever ago."

Yablonski leaned forward. "If you don't mind me saying, it looks to me like you're having trouble coping with your sister's death."

McCormick laughed. A nervous, anxiety-filled little chortle that said it all.

"The two of you were close?"

"She was my baby sister. She lived with me while she was going to college. When I saw what kind of guy Reese was, I begged her to come back. She did for a while, but she said she wanted to give her baby a chance at a family. I let her go. Everything in me said it was the wrong thing to do. I didn't listen."

"Have you talked to someone?"

"Who? A counselor? No. I work. That's how I cope. I take care of business. One task at a time. No matter how hard. No matter how distasteful."

Another twenty minutes confirmed that McCormick did one thing: work. Every day in question, McCormick was working. Asked if he'd heard about the heads, no time for news, he was working.

That didn't ring for Yablonski and he let Cruz know it. Every media outlet splashed the last head for a day or two. He wanted to dive deeper on McCormick and Cruz gave him the green light.

For himself, McCormick's words followed Cruz all the way home. *I work. That's how I cope.* It was how Cruz him-self had coped with his recovery. Once his body had healed to the point where it could keep up with his mind, he had to keep it occupied. Work was what he had, what he was good at.

It didn't feel like a bad thing. So why when McCormick said the identical thing, did it sound like a rationalization? Why did it feel it was using an unhealthy tool to solve an un-healthy problem? Cruz realized he didn't know enough about grief to know what was reasonable and what was abnormal.

As the day shift was coming to an end, he placed a call.

"Is there a problem?" Bollier's voice was calm, clinical even.

"Of course, there is a problem and I need your help."

"Where are you? I'm one foot out the door."

Cruz stopped pacing. "Why?" Then it struck him. "No, Oscar, not *that* kind of problem. This one is for work." He had laid out the theory to his sponsor. "I interviewed my first profiled suspect today. I don't know what I expected, but it wasn't what McCormick gave me. I need to consult with someone who understands grief. Do you have any friends I can meet?"

"Dr. Edna Rogozinski. I'll make a call."

"I appreciate it." He knew Oscar would have the connections he needed.

"I missed our dinner last night. First one we've missed in a while. How was Easter?"

Cruz made time to talk, having the conversation they missed the night before. Work continued to be volatile for Bollier. The strain in his voice was at odds with the matter-of-fact words. Before he could press it, Bollier asked about Aurora and meeting the family. Cruz recounted the debacle while his friend howled with laughter. "I'm glad you're enjoying yourself at my expense. Now, I need to get something to eat before I head to the meeting."

"I'm glad to hear you're going. I worry about you. You take too much on yourself, you know that, right?"

"I do not." The defense was automatic. "I'm a detective. This is my job."

"That's right. It's your job. Not your life."

Tuesday, April 3

Dr. Edna Rogozinski was in Oscar Bollier's graduating class at Case Western Reserve University nearly thirty years before. She maintained an office above several store fronts, close to

Bollier's favorite restaurant on Cedar Avenue. The waiting room had a desk but not a receptionist. Just a sign that read: *The doctor will see you shortly.*

Sitting, Cruz did what the modern professional did while waiting for a meeting. He worked on his phone. The last of the lab reports came in on Bear McKinley. It had become the norm: no stray DNA, no fingerprints, nothing to give direction to his hunt.

Some days it felt like all he was good for was waiting for the next body.

"Detective De La Cruz." A short woman with big blue eyes and cherry red lips stood in the doorway. She dressed like a fashionable grandmother in clothes that were stylish but high on comfort.

He stood. "Dr. Rogozinski. Thank you for seeing me."

"Please call me Edna. Any friend of Oscar's is a friend of mine." She led him into her office where the themes of calm and comfortable continued. "Oscar said you wanted to know about the grieving process." With the wave of a hand, she directed him to a couch that wouldn't look half bad in his house.

"Specifically, I am interested in the standard ways people manage grief and when grief tips over to become...something else."

"Interesting words you used. 'Standard' and 'manage.' Study has shown there is a process, but inside process are individual people, each of whom has their custom version of standard and managing."

"Did Oscar tell you about the cases I'm working on?"

"He did, and I've read some, but I would like to hear about from you."

Cruz struggled with where to begin. He eschewed chronological order and led, instead, with the victims. They were the key to unlock this mystery. Once he began talking, he didn't end for a long time. As he relayed the information, bits and pieces arose from the reports, witness statements, his own research, and found a place in hypothesis. He was up then, moving around the limited space.

"I see where you are going," she said. "There are indicators or yellow flags, to be sure, but there isn't a strict set of rules for determining who will come through the grieving process and be able to live productively again and who will not. I've been reading, reading a lot actually. I came across a concept that just won't leave me alone. Altered reality." She rose, then crossed to her bookcase and selected a text book. "The concept is that an individual is living by a set of rules different from the rest of us." She didn't sneer exactly but distaste showed on her face as she flipped through the pages. "Living next to us, but not with us."

"You don't buy it?"

"It's a matter of degrees, I suppose. If a woman puts on a dress, looks in the mirror and thinks it is attractive, but the rest of us find it hideous, is she in an altered reality? If a man writes a book, is turned down by a hundred publishers, and he keeps submitting, is he crazy or persistent? These are simple examples, but do you see my concern? Taken on the surface, you could accuse everyone of living in an altered reality."

"But then, maybe we all are a little crazy." His fingers went to his scars as he considered how little black-and-white there was. "Can grief lead to an altered state?"

"In and of itself, it would be a rare occurrence, in my experience, but coupled with a mental health condition or susceptibility, the trauma created by the inciting incident could accelerate a decline. When I use the word 'decline,' I use it to refer to the mental state from our clinical point of view. From the patient's point of view, it is only reality— unaltered. Each day is perfectly normal."

He spun to face the doctor, his tongue sharpened by frustration. "The suspect is killing drug dealers and mounting their severed heads Vlad the Impaler-style around Cleveland.

I don't mean to be crude, Doctor, but I don't fucking understand a normal that embraces that."

Likely he wasn't the first person to spit venom in the room as she ignored all but the message. "Punishment is an obvious starting point," she said," but it doesn't work for me. From what you have shared, I would have expected more damage to the faces. That being said, we do not have the bodies, which could direct us down a different path." She tapped her finger against her cheek. "Warning is stronger. Perhaps he uses the heads as a no trespassing sign of a sort."

No Trespassing. That rang for Cruz. "Would that point to the suspect being part of the illegal drug culture."

"It is certainly a possibility. It doesn't fit with the altered reality theory, though."

He explained his inner-ring hypothesis and summarized his interview with McCormick. "I've taken hours of training on interviewing, but this didn't follow the rules. It's the old Catch-22. If you admit you're crazy, then you must not be because crazy people don't know they're crazy." He rubbed the spot between his brows. "McCormick wasn't crazy. He was heartbroken."

"Is there a difference?"

"One kills."

"Which, Detective?"

He shook his head, not willing to chase the rabbit any further. "How will I know him when I see him?"

"Based on what you have said, your suspect likely does not view himself as a criminal, so you shouldn't expect him to act as a criminal. You only hide when someone is chasing you." A delicate bell chimed. "I'm sorry, Detective, my next appointment is waiting."

He stood, offering his card and his hand. "I appreciate you squeezing me in. I hope you'll let me call on you again, if I need to."

Dr. Edna took a card from her desk and wrote on the

back. "Absolutely. Here is my cell. Call any time. Good luck, Detective."

A cup of coffee and two cheeseburgers later, Cruz sat on the edge of a weight bench, watching Deirdre "Dee Dee" Reynolds pound out deadlifts in the weight room of Fire Station 1. The thirty-one-year-old EMT was ripped and that made him feel guilty about the cheeseburgers.

Five-foot nine inches tall. He didn't try to gauge her weight. She wore skin-tight black Lycra boy-shorts and a tank top with a floral pattern that raced down either side. She was a strawberry blonde with a trimmed close cut that could also be called boy.

"No point wasting your time," she said. "Ask your questions."

"What are you training for?" It wasn't the question Cruz was supposed to ask but was the one at the front of the line.

"Regional cross-fit competition in three weeks. I took third last year. That bitch is mine this year. The tire flip got me. But I'm ready now. I can throw hundred-and-fifty pounds like it was a bag of dog food."

He didn't doubt it, watching the way her muscles bunched, then lengthened. "You lost your partner last summer."

"The fucking junkie stabbed Stephan." She stood tall then dropped the weights. They fell with a crash of metal, bouncing on the rubber mat. "We responded to an overdose call. The guy was unconscious one minute and slicing my partner to ribbons the next. It's all in the report. Why are you asking me about it now?"

"Were you and Stephan close?"

"We were partners." Her face tightened, revealing the depth of the relationship.

"Were you lovers?"

She snorted. "Stephan was gay. He kept is private life

private, except with me. He was the brother I never had."

"Your file noted you were written up for refusing to serve a patient."

Reynolds walked to the wall where a water bottle and towel waited. She retrieved both. "He was blitzed on coke and threatened to cut my tits off if I treated the cut on his head. I may not have big tits, but they're mine. He touched his head, figured out he was bleeding and changed his mind. I did not accommodate him."

"Your file said you were referred for counseling."

Reynolds took two hearty gulps of water. "I was, and I went. That was the only thing good to come out of that mess. It gave me clarity, you know? Helped me work through my feelings, to see the world in a different light. I didn't know it at the time. It took months for me to realize what I had to do."

Cruz raised a brow. "What did you have to do?"

"Set priorities. I took this job to help people. What happened couldn't stop me from doing that, or the bad guys would have won. They had me keep a journal to puzzle through it all. I did. Still do. You'll be in it tomorrow."

"Do you recognize any of these men?" Cruz laid the victim photos out over the work bench.

"I see a lot of faces, Detective, just like you." She went to the bench and took her time looking them over.

He watched her reaction. She took a good ten seconds with each photo, picking them up for a closer view. A few times her brows went up, only to fall away into a frown with a disgruntled little grunt.

"These could be a hundred guys. Some of them look familiar, but I couldn't tell you from where. What's the connection?"

"Have you followed the Drug Head murders?" He hated using the term, which had become the way the community referred to the victims.

"I hear things."

"I'm looking for connections. Connections between Stephan and any of the victims."

"Wrong tree, Detective. Stephan's drug of choice was nicotine. He'd just made the switch to e-cigs, trying to cut down on the tar. His only connection to addicts and pushers was through the job."

Cruz sat at his desk writing notes of his interview. The ambient sound that was the pulse of the department faded and he was one of few left standing.

Yablonski stepped in, pulling his jacket on. "Cruzie, shut that damn thing down. I'm hungry, thirsty, and want to see my lady."

He looked to the book on mental health he wanted to read and the file he needed review for Wednesday. "I should—"

"Seriously, put it away. That girlfriend of yours isn't going to be throwing darts alone for very long."

Aurora's long legs and inviting smile went IMAX on his mind. He shoved away from his desk so hard he hit the wall behind him. Again. "I'm the only one she throws darts with, and she damn well knows it."

Minutes later, he bull-rushed into the bar to find her on her toes, helping a SWAT officer with his aim. A dart was in her hand, with his wrapped around it.

"It's about the feel," Aurora said, moving her arm back and forth in preparation to throw. "Feel it?"

"Oh yeah, I'm feeling it," the burly officer said.

"Aurora!" Cruz snapped out her name. She jumped, planted the dart in the SWAT's free hand, then turned in the direction of her name. She stood there, a tall, cool drink in painted on jeans and heels. He was a thirsty man.

"There you are." Her mouth was upturned, inviting him

to kiss her silky lips. "I thought maybe you forgot about me."

"Impossible." He wrapped her in his arms, tipping her back until she clung to his strength, kissing her until she forgot they were in public.

Wednesday, April 4

"Cruz. In here." Commander Montoya stepped out of his office long enough to issue the order, then disappeared.

Leaving his second cup of the day on his desk, Cruz went into his supervisor's office.

"I read your report on McKinley. Is it at a dead end?"

He wanted to deny it, but it was there in print. Every lead run to a dry and dusty ground. "I have a theory I am working parallel to the organized drug angle." He laid it out, including the interviews with two profiled victims.

"You think one of them is our suspect?" Montoya sounded intrigued but not sold.

"That's what I'm trying to determine. I had to try something different. Someone did this. Someone knows or saw something. Narcotics isn't picking anything up on the street. If somebody was doing this to stake their claim, they'd be taking credit. That's not happening."

"What is happening," Montoya interrupted, "is an urban war for territory. I need you back. We're spread too thin to have one of our best out of rotation."

The off-handed compliment bounced around Cruz's head like a pinball, setting off lights and bells. It wasn't supposed to matter—the job was about the job—but damn it felt good.

"I understand, Commander. I had planned to conduct three more interviews today. I'd like to see those through."

"That's fine, but I can't guarantee the time. You're next up."

Cruz was solo as the rolling hills of the eastern suburbs raced by the window. Yablonski was back with narcotics. Neither was happy with the reassignments, but it was to be expected. For all the work they were doing, they weren't getting a lot done.

Something about this inner circle theory rang with him. He wasn't going to let it die. He would work it during the second forty, if he had to. Nights and weekends.

He hit the turn signal and exited the highway, hoping this next interview led to progress.

Anthony "Tony" Gentile, twenty-four, worked as a carpenter for a major construction company. It took a few calls to find out where Tony was that day. The construction site was forty-five minutes west of Cleveland. Gentile was rigged high above the river below, muscling wood boards into place. The superintendent spoke to him. Gentile looked to where he stood next to the unmarked police car. Methodically, efficiently, he returned to solid earth and approached them.

Though still early April, his olive skin of his thick forearms was darkened. "I heard you're looking for me."

"Detective Jesus De La Cruz." He held out his identification. "I understand you lost your brother last summer in a drug-related incident."

Surprise showed on Gentile's face. "Yeah. My little brother Joey, Joseph."

"The report said your brother was allegedly buying an illegal substance when gunfire broke out."

"That's what they told us." Anger started to rise. Gentile's words became short, clipped.

"Were you aware Joseph used?"

Tony shrugged it off. "It was just normal teenage experimenting. He said he and his buddies smoked a few joints now and then. Everybody does it. He sure as hell didn't deserve to die for it."

"The man accused of shooting him, D'Andre Lattimore,

is in custody."

"For manslaughter, for fuck's sake. Lattimore's claiming self-defense. You tell me how a thirty-year-old man can kill three unarmed teenagers and claim self-defense."

"The file said they pulled a knife."

"It was a kitchen knife. Whaddya call them? Paring knife. They were idiots, yeah, but the bastard was never in any danger. Why are you asking these questions?"

"Do you recognize any of these men?"

He flipped through and shoved the stack back. "No."

"You sure?

"I said no, the answer's no." There was steel in his voice that barely contained the rage within.

"Mr. Gentile. Have you seen anyone for help with your brother's death?"

"Hell, yeah, I called a lawyer. One of those ones that advertises on TV. He was an asshole."

"I meant more like a therapist."

"God no. No. Why would I?" Insult grew to outrage. "There is nothing wrong with me that seeing that cocksucking bastard locked away for fifty years wouldn't cure."

Cruz took it all in stride, letting Gentile's emotion wash over him like a wave in the lake. "How do you feel about drug dealers in general?"

"Fuck. Them. All. That guy who's going around, doing them all...he's my hero. I hope you never catch him."

The interview ended, and Cruz drove back downtown knowing half the city agreed with Gentile while the other half would lynch the suspect without a trial. The Drug Head Killer was becoming a folk hero, a type of Robin Hood.

It worried him. These were dangerous times.

His cell rang. "Detective De La Cruz." Heavy breathing. "Is someone there?"

"This is Jace," a young voice said.

It took a minute for the name and voice to click. "Hey,

buddy. Is something wrong? Do you need help?"

"Do you have a chocolate rabbit? Jimmy got a whole rabbit and Sasha just got the ears. I got nothin' 'n I like chocolate, too."

The kid's Easter hadn't been any better than his Halloween. "I'll see what I can do. Jace, you can call me anytime. You know that, right."

"Okay. When can I have the rabbit?"

That was focus. "Tomorrow Jace."

"Okay. Bye." And he was gone.

He'd swing by Malley's Chocolate on the way back. They had to have rabbits left over. His cell rang again. Same number. "Let me guess, jellybeans."

"Who is this?" An angry Hayley Parker shouted.

He vacillated between feeling busted and impressed with Jace. "Detective De La Cruz, Mrs. Parker."

"Why are you talking to my son? No. No. I know what you're up to, and it's not going to work. I know."

Then the line went dead. "Hell, I don't even know what I'm up to."

Back downtown, Cruz didn't go up to his desk. Instead, he went to find profile number four, Ester Moorehouse. Moorehouse's seventeen-year-old son, Thomas James "TJ," had been with Jimmy Gentile and also died of gunshot wounds, allegedly inflicted by D'Andre Lattimore. The thirty-nine-year-old community organizer was walking laps around the building where De La Cruz worked. The planned seven-day march was to raise awareness for victims of crime. With the relay-style organization, there was someone marching.

He stepped into her path. "Mrs. Moorehouse. I'm Detective De La Cruz."

She moved past him, forcing him to walk if he wanted conversation. "I know who you are." She was five-foot-ten with a solid frame. Her quick gait propelled her at a pace that would weary most quickly. The sign she carried declared

"Victims Are Not Criminals."

"Then you know what my job is."

She raised her chin. "To stop the one person in this city who is actually stopping criminals from victimizing children."

When people said things like this, Cruz treated it like a conversation on politics. He bit his tongue and moved on.

"Were you aware that TJ used?"

Ester narrowed her eyes. "Of course not. What kind of mother do you think I am? What kind of mother would let her seventeen-year-old son use drugs?"

"Did you find drugs in the house? After?"

She swallowed hard. "I flushed them down the toilet."

"We have a man in custody."

"Lattimore *was* in custody. He's out on bail while he waits for a new court date. We'll be lucky if he sees one day more behind bars. He's getting away with murder."

"The file said a knife was pulled."

"The man who killed my son said a knife was pulled. I believe that as much as I believe the Easter bunny."

He started to sweat, the pace she set wasn't meant for a shirt and tie. "You must be in good shape to move like this for hours."

"I run marathons. This is an easy day."

"What do you do for a living, Mrs. Moorehouse?"

"You know I'm a nurse practitioner. I work in an urgent care clinic."

"Stop for a moment, please." He pulled the photos from the file he carried. "Do you recognize any of these men?"

She rolled her eyes at him before standing still. She flipped disinterestedly through the pictures. "No."

"Look again. Really look."

She repeated the process, giving each image fractionally more attention. "No. I don't know any of them."

"When did you become active in community organization?"

The look in her eyes said at that moment, she hated him.

"After TJ died. That's when I learned first-hand there is nobody standing up for the victims. The job of the police is to find the guilty, not protect victims."

"How do you feel about drug dealers in general?"

"A plague upon our city, like Ebola or small pox. No one could do anything about it. Until now."

"You think the Drug Head Killer is a hero?"

For a moment, she looked tired. Not physically, but somewhere deep in her eyes. "Heroes and villains are for fairy tales, Detective. Real life just isn't that simple."

Sunday, April 8

"I'm getting better," Aurora said. "I almost understood every word your mother said. I think she likes me."

Cruz snorted as he backed out of his sister's driveway. "Likes you? She'd ask you to marry me if she could. My entire family is in love with you."

"Except Rhianna."

His younger niece had a serious case of the jealousies. Aurora could do nothing right. Mari and Tony tried, but there was no explaining it to the wall that was Rhia's denial.

"She'll get there. I stayed home with Rhia when I lived with Mari. It saved them the cost of daycare." He shrugged it off, but Rhianna was every bit his kid as his sister's. With her indomitable personality, the little girl forced Cruz to figure out how to be a man again. One confident enough for tea parties, painted nails, and swings. "My girl will get there."

The drive back to his house was filled with the frivolous chatter of a couple finding their stride. Two months felt like a day, felt like forever. Like she belonged with him. He went to his door, but she headed to her car. "You're not staying?"

"I'm going to my parents, remember? My mom wants to redecorate her office. I told her I'd help with colors."

"Right. You did say that." He didn't go in, suddenly losing interest. "Come back to my house after? We can watch a movie or...do something."

She giggled. "I know what your idea of doing something is."

"Does that mean yes?"

"Yes." She went to him, pressed her lips to his chin. "I'll be back around eight."

He dipped his head and kissed her lips. "Hurry back to me."

He stood in the driveway until she pulled away. Alone, he still didn't want to go in the house. He had something else he could do to fill the time.

The interview of Felix Sidowski, profile number five, didn't get done during the week thanks to the messy end of a gang meeting. Sunday afternoon put Cruz in a tucked away neighborhood between Detroit Avenue and the West Shoreway—a short stretch of high-speed road connecting Cleveland to the neighboring suburb of Lakewood, separating the residents from Lake Erie. He sat in his car, reviewing the file. Felix Sidowski, thirty-three, made his living as a butcher. His four-year-old son died three days after sustaining injuries when two drug dealers decided to settle a dispute Old West-style. The man who shot the boy was dead. He ran onto the Shoreway was hit by a car. The surviving drug dealer pleaded to lesser charges after witnesses and ballistics confirmed his gun had not been fired.

He walked up the steps and rang the doorbell, holding up his badge. "Felix Sidowski? I'm Detective Jesus De La Cruz, Cleveland PD. I'd like to talk to you for a moment."

The man at the door fit the label average. He was two inches under six feet with a lanky build. His short-cut sandy blond hair and cloudy blue eyes wouldn't stand out in a crowd.

"Detective? Okay. What's this about?" Sidowski pushed the screen door open to invite Cruz into his home. The living room was neat and cozy. A large armchair with an oversized ottoman looked to be Sidowski's preferred seat. Next to the television were framed photos of a smiling boy with dark brown eyes and matching hair.

He didn't know how people did it, lived with their dead so close. "I understand last August two men had an altercation resulting in the death of your son."

"Yes, Detective. It was just down the street. Jason and I were at a picnic one of the neighbors had. We had just started home when shots were fired."

Cruz watched Sidowski. His body language was quiet, resigned. He retold the story not in a disconnected manner but with acceptance. It was a palpable difference from the depression of Roger McCormick, the rage of Tony Gentile, the hostility of Dee Dee Reynolds, and the crusade of Ester Moorehouse.

He seemed to be a man who had come out the other side of grief with acceptance.

"He loved parties, my Jason loved parties. He ate so much I thought he'd explode. He pouted when I told him it was time to go home. He wanted to stay, but it was getting late."

Cruz waited for him to say he regretted not staying. Who wouldn't. But Sidowski didn't. He just sat, waiting for Cruz.

"Did you recognize the men?"

"You can't drive through the neighborhood and not see men like them. They weren't people I knew by name."

Cruz opened his file, took out the pictures of the victims and handed them to Sidowski. "Do you know any of these men?"

Sidowski flipped through the pictures, shuffling them like cards. "These are the drug dealers, right? The ones left as warning signs."

He put the pictures back, feeling the media had gotten ahead of him. "What do you do for a living?"

"I'm a butcher. I have a small shop on Detroit but most of my business comes from custom order for restaurants and private chefs."

"None of these men are customers?"

"No, Detective. I know my customers. They've been mine and my father's before me for years. Decades some of them. Why are you asking me about Jason and these men?"

"Just part of a follow-up investigation. Thank you for your time, Mr. Sidowski."

Sidowski walked him to the porch, stood on the edge to look over his neighborhood. Cruz continued down the stairs, seeing the good as he looked around. Children running, shouting with glee. Folks mowing and picking weeds. There was a peacefulness to it. Cruz glanced over his shoulder to where the man stood tall, comfortable with his place. "Mr. Sidowski, can I ask you a question? Off the record?"

Sidowski looked down from his lofty height and nodded. "Sure, Detective."

Cruz walked back to the stairs. "I've interviewed others who have lost loved ones. Some were angry, depressed, enraged, crusade-like. You're the first person I've met who seems, well, accepting. How did you get here?"

The tranquil expression waned, a glimpse of pain apparent for a moment. "I was depressed. I was suicidal to be honest with you. How did I get here? By coming to terms with the fact that I am not in control of the world. There's a reason the expression is 'fight for control.' You don't fight for acceptance; you let go." He scratched his head. "Sorry, that was a little deep, but it's the truth of it."

"Easier said than done." Cruz murmured the thought, remembering those weeks before he accepted his narcotics career was over, he wasn't going back on the streets.

"Yes, Detective, much easier said than done."

"Thank you, Mr. Sidowski. Best of luck to you." Cruz wandered through the city. With his windows down, the pulse of the people was a vibrant, living thing. Music. Noise. Hammers. Lawn mowers. Laughter.

His thoughts weighed heavily as he drove through the neighborhoods that were part of his case file. Too many loose ends. Not enough tied off. He couldn't build a picture of the suspect and it bothered him. Four men dead. Stopped at a red light, he looked at his empty hands. He had to dig deep, go back further in the files.

No man is an island. Somewhere, someone knew something.

May 9

The plan worked. I harvested five of the demons while they slept, then took them to the prep room. While I was freeing the souls, one of them woke up. He thrashed around, swearing he was a cop, then he hit his head and knocked himself out.

I haven't been around cops very much. After the murder, there were so many but I can't remember a single face. Then Jesus De La Cruz came to talk to me. He kept asking questions. I think he was worried I couldn't do my job. I saw his dedication and showed him mine.

I've never seen an undercover cop except on TV.

He needs a doctor. I keep checking on him and he isn't waking up. I have to get him back without blowing his cover. He'll need someone to watch over him. Someone kind and gentle.

I know who he needs. She's perfect.

CHAPTER FOURTEEN

Sunday, May 13

Today was huge in the world of relationships. Cruz and Aurora were hosting Mother's Day at his house—for both families. She'd met his and he met hers, but theirs hadn't met. The families were as different as fish and bicycles. His family was loud and moved at a hundred miles an hour. Her family was polished and used two forks when they set the table.

But it would be good. He was making his famous stuffed burgers and a mac-and-cheese so creamy it mooed.

"Do you think we have enough side dishes?" His cyclone of a girlfriend spun through the kitchen, leaving havoc in her path. "Maybe we should go to the grocery and get a tub of coleslaw? Should we have corn? I forgot to buy lemonade."

"Honey, it's under control." He stepped into her path and captured her racing body. "Relax. This will be fun."

"You promise?" The lines between her brows were carved deeper than the Grand Canyon.

"I promise." He kissed her forehead. "Why don't you bring up the empty cooler from the basement? We can put the pop on ice."

"Okay. I can do that." She nodded like she was selling it to herself. "Empty cooler. Ice. Pop."

He watched his nervous girlfriend walk out of the room, admiring the view. The cell phone on the counter buzzed. He looked at the screen, then snatched it and ran into his office, closing the door for privacy. "Commander."

"Detective, you're needed ASAP at Metro Health. One of our undercover narcotics officers was found in an abandoned building this morning. I leave it to you to determine if Officer Kroc is part of our case. Keep me updated."

"Yes, sir. On my way."

"No." Aurora stood in the now opened doorway, abject fear on her face. "No, no, no. You can't leave."

"I have to, baby. You know I wouldn't if I didn't have to."

"Zeus, we have twenty people coming in two hours expecting a Mother's Day dinner. I can't do it without you." Her voice trembled as it climbed. "I can't cook! I turned frozen pizza to ash. How am I going to feed twenty people?"

He reached for her, but she stepped back, looking as though she might bolt out the side door. "Most of it is ready or is cooking. I'll call Mariana. She'll help finish the dishes and grill the burgers. With a little luck, I'll be back before the families arrive."

"It's not fair. She's a mom, she shouldn't have to help. We can cancel, postpone the families meeting until you can be here."

This time when Cruz reached for Aurora, he didn't let her pull away. "We have all the food. Mariana will be happy to help, and everyone will have a great time." He rubbed his thumb over her frown. "There's nothing to worry about. My family loves you. Your family adores me. This is a party, not a test." She nodded but didn't say anything. He rested his forehead against hers. "You know this is part of my life. I have to go when I'm called, but my heart is always here with you."

She sighed heavily. "You say that mushy stuff just to get around me. It's not always going to work, you know."

Silently praying she was wrong, he pulled her close. "I better get going. I'll be home as soon as I can."

"Zeus, call Mariana? I don't want to ruin everyone's

Mother's Day."

Cruz called his sister as he pulled out of his driveway. Mari was much less understanding, coming to the defense of the woman she was courting as a sister-in-law. "Can't this wait, Tito? Today is really important to Aurora."

"Do you think I don't know that? She's been a bundle of nerves for a week. There's been a major development in a case I'm working, and I don't have the luxury of telling it to wait until my family has eaten dinner."

"Is this about those heads?"

"Mariana, I'm not talking about it. Will you help Aurora?"

His sister huffed, and Cruz knew the face with it. "Of course, I'll help Aurora. Let me put my makeup on and I'll go over."

"How about you go over now and take your makeup with you?"

"Fine."

"I'll make it up to you. I'll watch the girls next weekend, so you and Tony can have a date night."

"Friday. Seven o'clock, but it's not me you'll have to make it up to."

Cruz nearly ran a stop sign, distracted by coordinating between the women in his life. He hit his lights, figuring it was safer for everyone. Ten minutes later, he walked into the hospital room where Officer Nicholas Kroc laid on the hospital bed, still and alone. Eyes closed, his face was tipped toward the door. Strong features sat in a face too harsh to be called handsome. The nose had been broken at least once. He had a golf ball-sized knot over one eye.

Kroc eyes opened. Thick blueish circles curved under the bloodshot brown eyes.

"Officer Kroc. I'm Detective Jesus De La Cruz. Are you able to talk?"

Kroc nodded as he tried to sit up. The normally simple motion was a full-body effort, the difficulty of which showed on his face.

Cruz rushed to his side, helping his fellow officer.

"I got it," Kroc said. Using his hands on the thin mattress, he pushed his hips higher on the bed, then used the controller to raise the top of the bed until he was sitting. "Can you hand me my water, Detective?"

"Call me Cruz." He followed the gesturing hand to the meal tray and the hefty mug with a bendy straw. He handed it to Kroc then waited patiently while the man sucked it dry. "How badly are you hurt?"

"Not as bad as I feel. Dehydrated, two dislocated shoulders, and this pretty decoration on my forehead. The rest are bumps and bruises. Nothing I can't sleep off."

"Tell me what happened?"

"Friday night, we had a buy set up with a new supplier, after hours in an auto mechanic shop. There were five of us. I have no clue what happened. I remember feeling dizzy. The place spun, like I was drunk or something. I guess I passed out. I had to. The next thing I remember is a room. Cement block. Smelled like meat section of the grocery store. Everything was so fucked up. It took me forever to figure out I was hanging upside down."

"Upside down?"

"Yeah. My feet were, like, tied together." He pulled back the covers to expose thick bandages on his legs at the ankle. "The room was silent, but it wasn't, you know? I knew I wasn't alone. I turned, twisted until I could see there was a man next to me. Drew Martin. The guy I went in with. Something scraped on the floor, and I turned the other way. Another guy hung upside down. One had his wrists cut and was bleeding out into a bucket."

"Was he alive?"

"His eyes were open. Like, gravity pulled them open, you know? I heard more scraping behind me, and I felt something grip by back of my shirt. I started shouting that I was

Cleveland police. Undercover narcotics. Shit. I don't remember half of what I said. I was whipping around, trying to get free, then *pow*. Next time, I woke in the dark. Everything hurt. I was tied up and had a sack over my head. I don't know how long I was there, but the woman came not long after I woke up."

"The suspect, did you get a look at him?"

Kroc frowned as he thought. "I saw...feet in boots...jeans...white lights...gloved hands. Blue gloves. Apron. It was stained. I never saw above the person's legs."

"You started in a garage. Did you wake up in the garage?"

"I don't think so. Once I'm back on my feet, I'll check it out. I would recognize the wall, it was inches from my face. The cement block was painted grey but marked up, like the paint job was years old."

"You were found in an abandoned house a long way from the garage. Even if the room was in the garage, you still were moved. How? Were there cars in the garage? Was one a black van?"

Kroc lifted his hand to rub it through his hair, the IV tube hanging from his arm. "I don't remember a van. I was careful to scope out the scene. We didn't know the people we were meeting. There were two SUVs, one white, one black. There was a silver minivan. Then there was a Cadillac, a Honda and a Buick—all sedans."

Cruz was disappointed at the lack of a van, but it was reasonable to expect the suspect would use different vehicles.

"You said a woman found you? What woman?"

"A reporter. She came into the room. I stayed very still, not knowing who it was, where I was. I heard a sharp gasp, and then she called nine-one-one. I shouted and tried to get the bag off my head. She was talking to the operator. She pulled the bag off. I was never so happy to see the fucking sun. I was lying in a lump in the corner of a room like a bag of trash." His voice cracked.

Cruz gave Kroc the moment he needed. He'd had his own moments facing his mortality, knew how it could choke the life out of you. Kroc blinked a few times, clearing his eyes.

"What happened to the guys you were with?"

"No idea," he said. "Not a clue."

"What were they selling?"

"Anything you wanted. We were buying heroin."

"You have names?"

"Drew Martin, like I said, was with me. We were meeting with Ricky Rinada and his crew. Melvin was his muscle and a little guy called Carson. Didn't get last names."

"Who set the buy up? You?"

"No. I don't have those kind of connections, yet. A friend of Drew's set it up. A guy named Parker."

Cruz heart raced. "Christopher Parker?"

"Yeah. The shit was supposed to be there but never showed. Drew was pissed. Rinada wasn't happy either."

"You know Parker's wife? Hayley?"

Kroc shook his head, then push his mug Cruz's way. "You mind refilling this? Can't seem to get enough to drink."

"You want ice?"

"Nah. Long as it's wet, I'm good."

He filled the cup in the bathroom. "You know how I can find the woman?"

"Her card is in my pants pocket. In the closet there."

Cruz went to the tall, narrow cabinet that functioned as a closet. In it he found one set of men's clothing, neatly folded. "You know I have to take these. Evidence."

"I know. You find the card?"

"Yeah, it's here. Francesca Pelletier. *Akron Beacon-Journal.* What was she doing up here?"

"That you'll have to ask her, Detective."

* * *

Francesca Pelletier sat on the edge of her corduroy couch. Her elbows were perched on her knees, her hands clasped together.

"Ms. Pelletier—"

"Call me Frankie. Everyone calls me Frankie."

"Tell me how you happened to find a man tied up in an abandoned house in Cleveland."

She leveled misty blue eyes at him. "First, tell me how he is. I hung around the hospital, but they wouldn't tell me anything."

Cruz took measure of the woman sitting anxiously for his answer. Francesca Renee Pelletier was twenty-seven, a native of the Cleveland suburb of Highland Heights. She'd worked as a reporter in Indiana and Idaho before coming home to Ohio and the *Beacon-Journal*. The serious set to her face did not detract from her prettiness. She wore her honey-wheat blonde hair straight, parted down the middle and hanging past her shoulders. In spite of her age, her eyes were sharp, bold, unintimidated. She'd been with cops, around cops often.

"He is recovering. Do you know who he is?"

She shook her head. "No. What is his name?"

Cruz ignored the question. "How did you come to find him?"

"A call came in to my desk in the newsroom and was forwarded to my email." She pulled her smart phone from the pocket of her Butler University sweatshirt, thumbed through the screens, then held the device out for Cruz's inspection.

Cruz read the message: "3624 West 46th St. Save him."

"I didn't know what to make of it at first. I Googled the address, expecting it to be in the Akron area. But it wasn't. I stayed at my parents' house last night, Mother's Day and all, so I went over to see."

"What did you find?"

"A house with boarded up windows and doors on the first floor. It didn't look abandoned but like someone was

163

working on it. The front door was plywood and was pad-locked shut. The side door was closed but not locked. I got my flashlight and pepper spray from my car. I found him in the living room. He was so still. I called nine-one-one and he woke up kicking and shouting while I spoke to the operator."

"Why did you go inside?"

Frankie Pelletier held her hands open, palms up. "Curios-ity? I'm a reporter. I investigated. Besides, what were my other options? Call the Cleveland police and tell them I received an email to hurry to this address?"

"You didn't recognize the man? Or the address?" She shook her head. After an hour of talking with the reporter, Cruz was convinced the suspect had drawn Frankie Pelletier into his warped game.

"You think he was going to be the next Drug Head? Is he a drug dealer? Why didn't he follow through...not, uh, that I wish he had. Can't you at least tell me his name?"

"You know the drill, Miss Pelletier. His name is not being released at this time."

"Frankie, and I'm not the press. Okay, so I am the press but I'm, like, involved. Come on, Detective. If I'm going to have nightmares about him I'd at least like to have a name to scream."

She tried for sardonic humor, but more truth came through than Cruz thought she wanted him to see. "Nicholas. And he isn't a drug dealer."

"That's why he stopped, isn't it? He didn't want to hurt an innocent."

"Today's incident is under investigation and no connection has been made to prior drug-related deaths." Cruz choked back his distaste. She sounded far too sympathetic to the serial killer. "Nobody has the right to play judge, jury and executioner, Miss Pelletier."

Her expression sobered as though he'd slapped her. "It's good to know *you* know that, Detective."

* * *

Cruz cut through the crime scene tape and entered the house on West 46th Street. He flipped a light switch, happy to have the glow of bare bulbs illuminating the place. The house smelled of sawdust and paint.

The floor was thick with construction dust except from the side door to the living room, where a clear path was worn. Foot prints, gurney wheels, and the marks of something heavy being dragged. Kroc was unconscious when he was brought to this house.

Cruz thoroughly inspected the house for the wall Kroc described. The basement walls were an old white, not gray. The ceiling was just seven feet high, with not enough clearance to hang a grown man upside down.

No walls on the first or second floor matched Kroc's description. The garage was wood, the interior unfinished, and a dead end. His cell rang. "Tell me something good, Yablonski?"

"An old friend of ours accepted my invitation to dropped by."

"He lawyer up?"

"Nope."

"On my way."

Christopher Parker prowled the small interview room. He'd lost weight since Cruz had first met him. His cheekbones and collar bones now jutted out of his skin. He still walked with a bounce that had a 1970s' *chicka-bow-wow* track running through Cruz's head.

"Sampling too much of his shit," Yablonski said.

"Hard to believe that cute kid came from him." Cruz handed Yablonski the thick case file. "This could be the break we need. Make sure you—"

"Not my first rodeo. Watch and learn." Yablonski smirked

as he left the observation room. When he walked into the interview room seconds later, he had his game face on. "Please sit, Mr. Parker."

"What the fuck is this? You drag me out of my house and then leave me here for an hour? Say what you gotta say and then I'm walkin'."

"Sit down, Mr. Parker," Yablonski said again without expression.

Parker strutted across the room, his gaze fixed on Yablonski, then dropped into the metal chair.

"Friday night. You set up a meeting between Drew Martin and Ricky Rinada."

"You can't prove it."

"I can prove it. Now this is going to go a whole lot faster if you stop jerking me around about the easy stuff. You set up a meeting between Drew Martin and Ricky Rinada."

"Yeah, so what, I introduced them. Ricky was a friend of Bear McKinley. With Bear gone, Ricky was looking to make new friends. Nothing illegal about that."

"Who picked the place?"

"Ricky."

"When did you set the meet up?"

"What?"

"When? Day before. Week before, Month before."

"I don't know. I wasn't looking at a fucking calendar."

"When, Parker?"

"I set it up, like, the weekend before. The day and time. I got a text with the place an hour before."

Yablonski looked at the mirror, right where Cruz stood.

Parker draped his thin body over the steel table, a long, lean arm cradled his head. He raised a one finger salute to the mirror.

"Why didn't you show?"

"I wasn't s'posed to go. Just set it up."

"That's not the way I heard it. You didn't show. Drew

and Kroc went in a man down. Pissed Ricky off too, I heard. Probably figured a setup."

Parker lifted his head, hollow eyes bored into Yablonski's. "What the fuck are you talkin' about? I didn't set nobody up. My kid was sick. That's all."

"You tell Drew and Kroc your kid was sick?"

"Fuck no. Was none of their business. None of yours either."

Behind the mirror, Cruz dug in his coat for his phone, absently dialing the number.

"Does this mean you're on your way home, Detective?" Hope filled Aurora's voice.

He looked at his watch. Nearly 2:00 p.m. "No, baby, it doesn't. Is everyone still there?"

"Yes. We throw one hell of a Mother's Day party. Your sister is a goddess."

"I told Mari I would babysit next weekend."

"I heard."

"Aurora, was Jace Parker in school on Friday?"

"Jace?" she asked with the confusion that comes with the right name in the wrong place. "Jace Parker? No. He wasn't. Strep throat, I think. Did something happen to him?"

"No, baby. His father is spending some time with us. I'm just fact checking. I'll be home—"

"Oh no you don't. Take three minutes and wish your mother a Happy Mother's Day. Here she is."

"*Hola*, Mama." While he spared time for his mother and then Aurora's, Yablonski carried on with Parker.

"Have you talked to them since Friday? Drew? Kroc? Ricky or the others?"

"No. I texted Drew, like a hundred times. Figure he's pissed I ditched. Tried Ricky a few times, too."

"Where were you today before noon?"

"Man. I didn't get up until one. I was in my fucking bed. What the fuck is going on?"

"Something went down on Friday, Parker. Drew, Ricky, Carson, Melvin are gone. Kroc was found in a vacant house, tied and beaten, this morning."

"Why aren't you asking Kroc what when down?"

"We did. He doesn't remember anything after showing up at the garage. Except you weren't there." Yablonski's tone made the accusation.

"Like I said, my kid was sick."

"And you're such a good daddy you sat by his bed holding his hand."

Parker leapt to his feet. "I'm a good father. We ate ice cream and watched *Spider-Man*."

Yablonski narrowed his eyes. "You shoot up in front of Jace?"

Parker's jaw throbbed.

"Yeah. You're a candidate for Father of the Year."

Parker glared at Yablonski, his gaze sliding to the armed officer at the door and then back to Yablonski. "We done here?"

"I want their phone numbers. Names and numbers of anyone who knew about Friday night." Yablonski tore a sheet of paper from a legal pad, slid it across the table with a pen.

When Parker got to work, Yablonski left the room to meet Cruz. "What do you think?"

"Hell, if I can tell. I called Aurora and his kid was out of school sick."

"Our suspect was keyed into one of those men. Men like that can be paranoid. They don't like what they don't know."

"Men like that can be arrogant, too. So full of their own shit, they can't tell they are drowning in it." Cruz watched Parker shove the paper at the uniformed officer babysitting him. "What time does the sun set today?"

"Around seven-thirty. What are you thinking?"

* * *

Cruz had pushed off the reports that needed to be done, racing home instead. Following instinct, he walked into the backyard and found Aurora with her head back, laughing with his sister. She saw him then, and her smile went from beautiful to radiant.

Rushing past the welcoming embrace of his family, he went straight to her. His mouth covered hers, tasting chocolate on her lips. He nibbled, wanting more.

Aurora pulled back. "Easy, Tiger. The family."

He didn't want easy. He wanted her, all to himself. The family closed in around him, and so he played the good host, talking to everyone who had come to past the day under his roof. He played the good son, dancing with his mother to a tinny song coming from a Bluetooth speaker.

When his house was finally empty of guests, he played the good lover. It was the role he savored, coaxing breathy sighs, desperate whimpers, choked screams, explosive orgasms from the woman in his arms.

"I can't think," Aurora said, her eyes dazed. "I think you fucked me stupid."

His laughter bounced off the walls. "Best compliment ever." He dropped his head to the soft wealth of her breast.

"Zeus," she said in three syllables, arching into him. "You can't. I can't. Not again."

He hummed with her nipple between his lips. "I can't. At least not this soon. But you can. I just have to…"

Cruz patrolled I-480, making loops that passed the three locations where the highway crossed in and out of the limits of the city of Cleveland. His gaze combed the highway shoulder as the sun touched the horizon.

"Everything's quiet." Yablonski's voice came over the radio. He ran similar patrol loops on I-90. "People must be on their good behavior."

"It is Mother's Day. Not exactly a drinking holiday."

"That would depend on your mother. Mine is sweet as pie. Erin's? Now that's a different story."

"How long have you and the nurse been at it?"

"Almost a year. Her mother wants grandchildren. Seems to like I should be the sperm donor."

"What do you and Erin think?"

"I bought a ring."

"No shit. You give it to her?"

"Not yet. I was thinking on Tuesday at Becky's. All our friends will be there and, yeah, I thought she'd like that."

"Well, congratulations, my man."

"Thanks." The sigh that followed weighed a ton. "You're going to be there, right? I need someone on my side. Just in case."

"Wouldn't miss it, but there's no in case. You got this."

"Yeah. I got this," Matt said, soft and low. When he spoke again, Detective Yablonski was back. "Sun is setting. You think it's going to be tonight?"

"The other heads were found near holidays—Halloween, Christmas, Valentine's Day, Easter. He leaves them at the corporate limit posts on the interstates. Four-eighty and Ninety are the last two interstate highways into the city. If it's not tonight, it'll be soon. And it'll be here."

"Do you think he's going to do all four?"

"All together? It would take time. The more time, the better the chances of being seen. Spreading them out would be safer. We know he's patient. He had Mathias Martinez for nearly two weeks before dumping his head. Uncle and Bobby Mayes he had a few days. Bear was the same day. One tonight. That's what a smart man would do."

"What about an audacious, smart man?"

"Audacious? Is that another word-of-the-day?"

216-555-0403/ST. ARTEMIS CATHOLIC CHURCH
13MAY2018 20:30 STATUS:OK

I stand before the people as an instrument of justice.
Dispensing the evil ones from our home.
But where one head is cut off the serpent, two grow back.

The time has come for the righteous to come forward.
Protect the weak among us. Stand with those who cannot stand alone.
Send Satan on his way.
Be not afraid.

CHAPTER FIFTEEN

Evening, Sunday, May 13

Dispatch broke through their chatter, spiking Cruz's adrenalin. "Reports of a head on Inner Drive."

Cruz hit the lights and siren, racing to the next exit. "Inner Drive? Where the hell is that?"

"Cleveland Hopkins Airport. Access road to State Route 237, I-71, and I-480."

The road rose up to SR 237 where a sharp turn to the north began the on-ramp connecting the airport to I-71, and I-480. There, cars from Cleveland police and NTS funneled the airport traffic down to a single lane, securing a perimeter around the head.

Cruz parked on the shoulder and walked up the sloping road to the tent. He nodded to the uniforms and entered the secured area. The neatly mowed grass retained no impressions for him to use. Unsurprised, he stepped up to the head. Impaled on a generic post, the face welcomed visitors and residents alike.

Not welcomed. Dared. Threatened.

Yablonski stormed up the road, his game face in place. "Who is it?"

"Drew Martin. The suspect most likely parked here," he said as he pointed to the general area in front of the guard rail. "This is a one-way street. He wouldn't be seen by on-coming traffic. There are no street lights on this section of the road. The nearest one is up past the bridge at the intersection. The site was chosen carefully."

Yablonski flashed a light around. "It's not at the corporate limit. It's a deviation in his MO."

"We'll check a map. I have a feeling we aren't far from it."

"I'm going to talk to NTS. If the suspect parked here, like you said, he had to drive through the airport."

"All right. Let's get to it." The work followed procedures but was anything but routine.

"Detective." One of the uniformed officers waved Cruz over.

Cruz recognized the face but couldn't find the name. "I know you," he said.

"Buettner. I was on the scene back in November. You need to hear this. Dispatch, repeat."

"A head has been reported inbound I-480 west between I-77 and I-176."

"Shit." Cruz snatched the radio from the officer. "De La Cruz, responding. ETA fifteen."

It was Carson Tillman. His head hung from the Cleveland Corp Limit sign Cruz had driven past twenty times that evening. It wasn't an especially well-lit area. The corporate limit sign sat half way between the two nearest street lamps. The shoulder was wide enough to park on, to screen traffic from the happenings beyond.

The land rose sharply beyond the sign, thick brush and trees obscuring the top of the hill. A nest of shadows, anyone within it would disappear.

"Any idea what's up there," Cruz asked a uniform from the local district.

"It's an industrial road. Warehousing. Shipping."

"Get a car up there. Now."

With Yablonski working the airport crime scene, Cruz had this one to himself. Another crime scene unit appeared. The area was flooded with light until there was nowhere to hide.

Looking as hard as they did, there was little to find.

The grass and assorted broad leaf weeds held no prints.

The cargo bag holding the head was affixed to the sign with hardware store standard S hooks.

The whole thing didn't cost more than ten bucks.

"Detective." A uniform waved him over. "Dispatch."

Cruz frowned, his brows pressing low as he took the radio. "De La Cruz."

"Report of two heads, inbound I-90 east at the Cleveland/ Lakewood border."

"You're kidding me." Cruz needed help. More help. "Who is on-call for homicide? I need him here."

Ricky Rinada and Melvin Banks.

Everyone was accounted for.

The border of I-90 east with the City of Lakewood was the most exposed of the three locations. A street light in the center median softly lit this stretch of road. There was a lot of land between the edge of the highway and the twenty-foot barrier built for sound, but which also held back trees and shrubs. There were no easy access points to the highway. Bridges crossed the interstate a half mile forward and back with no ramps to the roadway below.

Some twenty feet off the edge of the road was a double sign reminding drivers they were on I-90 east and that hazardous cargo was prohibited. Another twenty feet past was the Cleveland Corp Limit sign. Between the two were the freshly planted stakes with the heads of Rinada and Banks.

"The suspect had to park on the shoulder," Cruz said, thinking out loud. "Access is too difficult any other way." There was no guard rail or other barrier to prevent the suspect from pulling off the roadway and onto the shoulder. He inspected the ground, moving to the location where he would have parked if he were the suspect.

The grass was flattened in two ruts, gradually coming off the highway and then more sharply returning. Maybe crime scene could get something here. Maybe.

His cell rang. He answered Yablonski's call.

"We're wrapping up here. I'm coming to you. Do you know how many times I drove by that sign tonight?"

"The same number I drove past the one on Four-eighty. No point in coming here. It'll do us more good if you get started updating the murder board. Finish pulling together the next of kin contact information. Hold on. I have another call coming in." He switched between callers. "Detective De La Cruz."

"This is Frankie Pelletier."

"I'm a little busy, Miss Pelletier. Can I call you—"

"He left another message for me."

"What?"

"Have you found another head?"

"I'm not at liberty to discuss an ongoing investigation."

"That means yes. The message said, 'I stand before the people as an instrument of justice. Dispensing the evil ones from our home. But to cut one head of the asp has two growing back. The time has come for the righteous to come forward. Protect the weak among us. Stand with those who cannot stand alone. Send Satan on his way. Be not afraid.'"

"When did you get this? How?"

"I came in about an hour ago, but it took some time to get to me. It was faxed. The stamp on the fax says St. Artemis Catholic Church. I can scan it and email it to you."

"Good, and I'll need you to come into the station in the morning."

"I can do that."

Cruz expected the reporter to argue, was happy she didn't.

"In the interest of fair play, I'm writing a story for tomorrow's paper."

"Shit." So much for happy. "I don't suppose there's any

way I can talk you out of it."

"This is news, Detective. I will report it, but I'd rather do it fairly. Give me an interview."

Shit shit shit.

"I'll call you back at this number."

"My deadline is midnight."

Cruz called his commander. No way he was stepping a foot into the realm of public engagement unless his ass was well and thoroughly covered. Commander Montoya connected with Chief Ramsey and PIO Alison Hyatt, which meant Cruz found himself in the chief's office while Yablonski finished working the third scene. He brought the senior officers up to date on the events of the day, beginning with the finding of Officer Kroc by Frankie Pelletier.

"All four?" Alison Hyatt said. "All four inside of two hours."

"The suspect was well organized. This is my preliminary on his timetable." He indicated a white board and his hand-written notes.

7:35-7:40 PM airport: first report to 9-1-1 at 7:42 PM
8:00-8:05 PM I-480: first report to 9-1-1 at 8:08 PM
8:30 PM Fax sent from St. Artemis church to Beacon Journal
8:50-8:55 PM I-90: first report to 9-1-1 at 9:00 PM

"Detective Yablonski and I were patrolling Four-eighty and Ninety," Cruz said. "It was reasonable to expect the suspect to act soon, giving the events of last Friday. I did not anticipate the deviation in the suspect's protocol and intend to meet with Dr. Chen on the topic."

"Do you think the suspect knew we would heighten patrols on the city limits?" Ramsey asked.

"We didn't find out about Friday's kidnappings until today. Not one of the victims was reported missing as of noon. Only one was a Cleveland resident. The others lived in the inner-ring suburbs. Calls to those departments found no missing person's reports."

Ramsey rolled his eyes. "I expect these are men who frequently do not return home. How much does this reporter know?"

"By now, I expect she's read everything—real and imagined—about this case. When I spoke with her this afternoon, she did not know who Officer Nick Kroc was. I confirmed only he was not a drug dealer. She speculated the suspect did not kill Kroc because he was not affiliated with drugs. She seemed sympathetic to the suspect, an opinion I tried to dissuade."

Ramsey turned to his public information officer. "Your opinion, Alison?"

"Take the lead. I'll schedule a press conference for late tomorrow. She'll get her exclusive and Monday morning headline. I suggest we draw up a statement confirming the recovery of four heads from various locations around the city. In order to avoid inciting a panic, I suggest we confirm the victims had some connection to illegal drugs and that Cleveland police does not believe there is a threat to the general public."

"Get on it, Alison. Montoya, De La Cruz is going to need more help. I want this reporter thoroughly investigated and all connections between the latest victims and past victims," Win Ramsey said, his eagle eye stare bearing down on Cruz. "This is the last time I am clearing your caseload for this suspect. I want this closed, Detective. Do I make myself clear? Finish this or you'll be finished."

Cruz's heart pounded in his throat as he left the meeting. His career as a detective was on life support. He needed to play the same game as the killer—cool, calm, and heartless. First on his list: Frankie Pelletier.

* * *

"Detective. Thanks for calling back. Does this mean I get my interview?"

"No, but I have a statement for you. The Cleveland police confirm that four heads were found—"

"Four? You said four."

"Four heads were found Sunday evening at various locations. This brings the number of heads found to eight since last November. All the victims are known to have some connection to illegal drugs. Currently, Cleveland police does not believe there is a threat to the general public. Anyone with information on these crimes should contact Cleveland police crime stoppers hotline."

"Have you recovered any of the bodies?"

"No."

"The man I found. The one that was spared, Nicholas. You said he was not connected with drugs."

"I said he isn't a drug dealer."

"So, he had a connection, but it wasn't dealing."

"I also said this wasn't an interview, Miss Pelletier. The chief will be holding a press conference at four tomorrow afternoon. He'll answer any questions then."

Frankie snorted a laugh, then quickly squelched it. "Sorry. Detective, one last question." Her tone changed, became softer, more personal. "Why did he contact me?"

"I don't know, Miss Pelletier, but it's something we need to work on. Come to my office tomorrow."

May 11

    Yesterday was a long, hard day. I feel like I fell down a flight of stairs. My arms hurt. My feet ache. My hands throb. I stayed up cleaning until four in the morning. My eyes are burning.

    It was worth it. Francesca's article was perfect. The radio and television stations broadcast the message. It went national. Every drug dealer will know the name Jesus De La Cruz. The demon seeds will retreat from the city limits and wither in the face of the justice.

    This is good.

CHAPTER SIXTEEN

Monday, May 11

Cruz reached to touch the angel in front of him. "You are so beautiful." He cupped her cheek, stroked her soft skin, ran his thumb over her down-turned lips. "Is everything okay?"

"Why are you sleeping on the couch?" Green eyes searched his face.

"I didn't want to wake you. I just got in a few hours ago." He pulled her down to him, but she resisted.

"I don't care what time you get home, you sleep in our bed. Period."

He stilled, alarmed by the tone in her voice. "I don't want to wake you."

"I do want you to wake me. I want to know you are home. Safe and sound."

"I hear you, baby." He pulled her down, and this time she came begrudgingly.

"What kept you out all night?"

He closed his eyes, simply holding her close. "Bad people doing bad things."

"You can talk to me, you know."

"Hmm. Don't want to think about it. Home with you is the one place my work can't touch me."

She snorted. "Unless it's calling you out of bed. What time to you have to get up?"

"Now." He let her go and, grunting, sat up. He ran his

hand over day old whiskers. "I'm going to hit the shower."

"Are you going to be late tonight?"

"Probably." He caressed her lower lip again.

She sucked his thumb into her mouth, nipping as he withdrew it. "Call me once a day. Whenever you can, call me. Just let me know you are alive and well and thinking of me."

"I'm thinking of you right now," Cruz said, pressing her hand to his hard-on.

Aurora squeezed him and then, laughing, pulled away. "Good."

The long shower and hot coffee had him feeling human again. Aurora had left him a toasted breakfast sandwich, which plugged the hole in his stomach. He parked in the garage, then walked to his desk, sorting through and ordering his day.

"Detective. Detective De La Cruz."

Cruz stopped the noise in his head, and he looked to the voice that called him. "Miss Pelletier. You didn't have to come in this early."

"Couldn't sleep. Brought you something, a copy of my story."

He led her into an interview room, leaving the door open. "Have a seat. Do you agree you probably have a connection to the suspect?"

She took a deep breath. "It's the only thing that makes sense. There's a chance he picked me at random, but it doesn't fit with the little I know. He's all about stopping the drug trade in the city of Cleveland. Not Greater Cleveland. Certainly not Akron. So why me? I'm telling you the truth, Detective, when I say I don't know."

"Let's run through your history. You've worked for the *Beacon Journal* for six months."

"Closer to nine. I started last summer."

For the first months, she lived with her parents to save money. She went out with friends and volunteered at Rainbows

Babies and Children's Hospital. She moved closer to Akron after the New Year and was slowly moving her life there.

She had no association with the underground drug culture. There had been some mild, recreational use in high school at parties. Same at college. Drugs were not a part of what she termed her adult life. She didn't know any of the victims and had no recognition of Christopher or Hayley Parker's names. She wasn't affiliated with St. Artemis.

He went out on a limb and asked her about the five profiled suspects he'd interviewed. The names didn't ring any bells. When he was out of ideas, he walked her out of the station, a measure of both respect and gratitude. "You'll call me if he contacts you again?"

"Absolutely. In the interest of fair play, you should know I'm going to stay with this one."

"Just remember you're also a witness. That changes the rules."

Frankie cocked her head. "Maybe that's the point," she said, pulling up the hood on her jacket. "It's pouring out there. I'll see you at the press conference."

The low, gray skies and heavy raindrops forewarned of the day coming. Cruz personally notified the next of kin. The stories of these men's lives were important to the people who loved them and to an unknowing group of people who would be the next targets. Because there would be more.

The suspect had escalated.

The rules were changing.

Grief had so many faces. Two had been expecting the visit. Maybe not that particular day, but there had been little expectation that the end would come naturally. Cruz had been able to collect a few names, a few tips.

He had been chased out of one house, accused of failing to do his job and of turning his back on people of color. It always confused Cruz, who looked at his own sun-kissed brown hands that would never be mistaken for white. He supposed the slur was leveled at the generic you—or in this case, the entire Cleveland Division of Police. Yet what did the general public actually know or understand of the Cleveland police? Snippets. Sensational ten second lead-ins designed to make you turn on the news, or buy a newspaper, or like a post. Three-week coverage on poor outcomes, losses. Three-second coverage of successes, victories.

As he was smarting from the sting of one woman's grief, he drowned in another's who begged him for justice for her brother. The acrid loss of the loved one was made unbearable by the fact that only the head had been found. He left the home of Drew Martin's sister aching for her. She'd wept silent tears for the brother who had braided her hair as a child and slept in her bed when storms gave her nightmares.

The afternoon was brutal in a completely different manner. The first hour was spent in front of the board he'd created, then taken down when the trail when cold and other priorities had risen, then put up and so on and so forth. This time it was out to stay until this business was done.

The little they had learned since the first discovery in November was posted for all to see. There were so many connections between the victims it looked like a black web had been cast over the board. In the center was a silhouette of a man, surrounded by but not connected to the web.

Not yet.

Cruz added the image of Frankie Pelletier to the board, connecting her to the suspect with a red line. Yablonski stormed into the room, his gaze intent on the board.

"I spoke with the pastor, Father Kevin O'Byrne. The church hosts what the pastor called a Souper Bowl every Sunday night. A pot-luck dinner with Bible study. Last night's began on time at six-thirty and broke up around eight-forty-five. The doors were locked, and he was back in the rectory by nine."

"That's cutting it close. The fax was stamped eight-thirty."

"The machine is one of those all-in-one fax-scan-print devices. The jobs report indicated a one page was printed the minute before the fax was sent. The original was not to be found. None of the computers had been accessed. Probably it was printed from a USB drive. Crime scene collected five sets of prints from the machine, but it's in a church office."

"He knew a lot about that church. You don't just happen across a machine that can print and fax in a church office on a Sunday night. I want the names and addresses of everyone at the Souper Bowl. Odds are he's familiar to someone at the church." Cruz went to the section of the board holding a map of Cleveland. The locations of the victim recoveries were marked with blue dots and flagged with the victim's name and date discovered. Orange dots signified other key locations: the pet store where Mayes worked, the Parker home, the garage where Kroc and company were taken from, the home where Kroc was found. Cruz added a dot for St. Artemis.

"He's all over the city. I don't see a pattern."

Montoya stepped out of his office, pulling on his jacket. "Cruz, Yablonski, let's go."

The meeting in the chief's office kicked up a notch on the intensity level. Narcotics Commander Traylor Deere leaned on the faux wood table, pointing at the map of Cleveland. "We're seeing a complete shift in the drug market. Every other corner is empty."

Montoya snorted. "You sound like that's a bad thing."

"It's unstable. So far, damage has been limited to players and property. But that's been our good luck. It's not going to last. Sooner or later somebody's kid is going to die for the crime of being in the wrong place at the wrong time."

Montoya raised his brows, acquiescing. "What do you think these latest deaths will do?"

"Rinada matters. We were investigating his connections to Mexico. He was bigger than just Cleveland. We'll see how the syndicate responds. For now, I'm expecting there'll be a shortage."

"I want to engage with the remaining leaders," Cruz said. "Follow my thinking on this. We have established a strong connection between the victims. A focused connection, given the suspect did not dispense of Kroc when he had the opportunity. We haven't found a connection between the victims to a common person, or place, or thing for that matter. But it's there. The guys on the street are our best chance of putting the pieces together on this suspect."

"The FBI concurs with your thoughts," Special Agent Bishop said. "When this is solved, people in the underground drug community are going to look at each other and wonder how it could have been Bob or José or Deonte or whatever. Not just someone they knew, but someone they trusted."

Deere chewed on his bottom lip as he considered. "My guys will talk to their informants."

Yablonski stepped up. "Cruz and I can do some drive-bys."

"We gotta try something," Montoya said. "He's drawing a fricking circle around our city."

"The note the reporter received, assuming it is from the suspect, provides significant insight into the suspect's altered reality." Chen stood as he spoke to the growing number of people gathered around the chief's conference table. "We see clearly that the suspect sees himself as an instrument of justice, not as a criminal. A man with duty and honor, protecting his home."

Cruz flashed back to the conversation with Dr. Edna Rogozinski. "A no trespassing sign."

Montoya leaned into the conversation. "Does this mean the suspect is a native Clevelander?"

Chen shrugged. "Perhaps, but he could also be someone who feels a deep connection to the city. Maybe an immigrant who was persecuted in his country of origin, or someone

185

who came here for schooling and settled. The suspect has clearly identified with the city itself."

Ramsey interrupted. "How do you explain the reporter?"

"Perhaps he sees his mission as failing in some manner. The later lines are practically a call to arms. Metaphorically, if not literally. The use of a reporter, in my opinion, is somewhat obvious, but also traditional. A reporter would get the message out. Other options, such as self-posting to social media, could accomplish a similar thing, but leave digital footprints."

Yablonski lifted a finger. "Maybe the suspect isn't comfortable using social media. He faxed the note to Ms. Pelletier. It's not exactly cutting-edge technology. It was easy to trace, the freaking number was printed on the top. He just got lucky he wasn't seen."

"Or wasn't noticed. Just like when he stood on the sides of the interstates." Cruz rubbed his face, wiping away the fog settling in. "We're chasing the Invisible Man."

Ramsey stood, signally the end of the meeting. "I have a press conference to prepare for. What I want to know is…is this going to escalate further, Doctor?"

Chen pointed to the printed text of the message. "There is no reason to expect otherwise. He clearly feels his work is unfinished."

Cruz left the chief's office, headed for the coffee. Yablonski at his side.

"If Chen said the word 'clearly' one more time, I was clearly going to show him what a size thirteen could do to a MD, PhD, M-I-C-K-E-Y M-O-U-S-E." Yablonski went for the candy machine, fed in a fiver and called for two Snickers.

"I hadn't even noticed until you said that. Man, now I'm going to hear it every time. You suck."

"Just sharing the love." Yablonski tore into the first sugar stick. "Speaking of love, you still going to Becky's tomorrow."

"I don't know if now's the time for throwing darts."

"Screw the darts. I'm proposing, remember? I'd like my best man there."

Cruz choked, and it wasn't on his coffee. "Best man."

"Well, you'll have to audition for the part, but I happen to know you have a sweet victory dance. What do you say?"

"Yeah. Hell, yeah, man. I'd be proud to stand for you."

Yablonski smiled, relaxed. "Wanna see the ring?" He dug into his pocket. The black velvet box opened to a round diamond sparkling up from a flat mounting. "It won't catch. When she wears latex gloves. See, the mounting is all smooth, so the glove will slide on and off with no problem."

Cruz whistled in appreciation. "You're carrying it with you?"

"Well, you know. I was afraid I might forget it."

"Aren't you afraid you're going to lose it?"

Yablonski glared at him and snapped the box shut. "Well, I wasn't until you said that. Shit. Where can I put this? I'll run it home."

"No time. Press conference."

"Shit. Shit. Here. You hold it."

Cruz put his hands up. "Why me?"

"You're the best man. It's your job to hold the ring."

"The wedding rings. On your wedding day."

"Tomayto tomahto. Take it."

And so, Cruz walked into the press conference with a bulge in his pocket that had nothing to do with being happy to be there.

The chief handled the press conference with his usual polish. Cruz stood straight, adorning the stage as did the Yablonski, Chen, and the others involved in the case. Even Special Agent Bishop attended, strategically squelching any speculation on the FBI's support of the Cleveland police. Chin up, shoulders straight, neutral expression. They all wore it like a uniform.

The minute he was released, Cruz hurried back to his

empty office. Information had begun flowing in. Initial findings from the medical examiner and the lab. The same blade was used on this weekend's victims as was used on the prior victims. The cuts were equally clean. Toxicology indicated sleep medication in the victims in high amounts.

"Bingo," Cruz said. The toxicology on Officer Nick Kroc wasn't back yet. There was a way around that. Twenty minutes later, he knocked on the partially opened door of Nick Kroc's hospital room.

"Come on in," Kroc called. "Cruz. I didn't expect to see you again."

"Brought you dinner." He set the brown paper bag on the tray.

Kroc wasn't polite about digging in, but he was appreciative. His eyes rolled back, his mouth full of the pork shoulder sandwich. "'Opital ood ucks."

"Understatement," Cruz said, glad he'd spend the ten minutes and ten dollars on the sandwich and onion rings. "When you getting out of here?"

"Not soon enough." He paused to finish the mouthful. "Docs aren't too happy with the circulation in my feet. I'm pushing the rehab though. Already been here too long." He took another bite.

"You up for a few questions?"

"Not going nowhere. Yet."

Cruz pulled the guest chair closer to the bed and sat. "Preliminary tox came back on the men you met with. All had high levels of prescription sleep medication."

"I thought they were just stoned. They had little twelve-ounce bottles of Mountain Dew. I sipped one. Dew ain't my soda of choice, but I wanted to make a good impression."

"You didn't eat or drink anything else with them?"

"No."

"The suspect got to Rinada or one of his men. He took a risk with drugging the soda. What if they didn't all drink it?"

"Wouldn't he have scoped that out? Provided the drink of choice? Probably there was a backup plan."

"Yeah," Cruz said, pacing the small room. "Yeah, he would have. This suspect is smart and patient. You must have surprised the hell out of him."

"For which I am eternally grateful." Kroc paused for a moment, then attacked the sandwich with a refreshed vigor.

Cruz missed his Monday night meeting, and he didn't like it. Sobriety for him was like riding a bike. He had to practice it regularly, so he didn't fall on his ass. There were other AA meetings in the city, but this one was his. He knew every face and the story behind it. But tonight, he would be looking at a different face. Three hours in a car doing a ride-along while Yablonski worked followed by too many minutes of emails had Cruz numb from the eyes down when he crossed the threshold of his home. He walked in the door, kicked his shoes off, walked up the three steps to the main floor, dropped his jacket on the floor, walked up the stairs to the second floor discarding his shirt, undershirt, belt, and pants. His socks and underwear were dropped next to the bed. Then he slid beneath the warm sheets and curled around his hot-blooded woman.

Aurora turned automatically, wrapping her arms around him. "What time is it?"

"It's late, baby. It's already tomorrow."

"Hmmph. Glad you're home."

"Me, too."

Tuesday, May 15

Cruz woke on a gasping breath. The life was being choked out of him. Instincts surfaced, and his hands went defensively to the warm...soft...arms? Hair, silky and fragrant, blinded him. "Aurora. Can't breathe."

"Sorry." She giggled, not sounding at all sorry, but released him.

"What time is it?"

"Six-thirty. I need to get going."

"You're awful perky today. Why's that?"

"Because I have you." She straddled him, kissing him until he was awake and hungry for her.

He anchored her body against his, rolling his hips against her. "Hmm. And I have something for you. Why don't you slip those panties off?"

She rolled her pelvis, grinding against him. "I can't, Detective, I'll be late."

"I'll write you a note."

She laughed, kissing him in a lazy, sultry manner that made him forget his own name. Then she ruthlessly climbed off him, slipping out of his hands. "Let's do something together tonight. Just us."

Cruz grabbed her hand. "I want to do something right now. Just us."

"I'm serious, Zeus. You've been working for two days straight. You need to take a break." She paused briefly. "I heard about your case."

Cruz groaned and rolled away from her.

"You can talk to me, you know. I may not understand all the police lingo, but I'll understand enough. I'm not stupid."

He lifted his head to gape at her and then narrowed his eyes. "Who called you that?"

"No one," she sat on the edge of the bed. "I know I'm not the smartest person in the world. I struggled for Bs and Cs in school, but I can draw and I'm good with kids and I can be a good partner to you."

Rolling back, he stroked her cheek, soothing her self-doubt. "You are a good partner. I never imagined having someone in my life like you."

"I love you." She turned her head and kissed his palm.
"Back at you."

All the radio stations, all the morning television program-
ming, all the newspapers headlined the case. Cruz listened to
the television as he dressed. Aurora had picked up after his
striptease. His shoes and belt were back in the closet. His
jacket hung from a doorknob. He silenced the noise in his
house, then in his head and read his daily meditation.

In the car, he channel-surfed from the college stations
through talk radio to morning drive-time shows. The DJs
hinted at the public's response, ranging from shocked, to curious, to outrage, to jazzed.

A collection of newspapers waited on his desk. The Torso
Murders Redux. Drug Heads Ring City. Cleveland's Bloody
Necklace.

"Some of them are pretty creative," Yablonski said.

Cruz looked over a summary report from the department
managing the tipline. "The hotline is warming up."

"The hotline isn't the only thing. One of the families is
planning a protest for today."

"Which one?"

"Mayes."

Cruz pictured Mrs. Mayes and her grief-stricken countenance. "I'll bet you a hundred bucks it's her righteous neighbor."

Yablonski pointed to the screen. "It's going viral. A couple
churches are jumping on board."

"Do they have a point?"

Yablonski snorted. "We suck, and they can do our jobs
better than we can. Isn't that always the point? Oh, yeah, and
we hate everyone and want them in jail. We get off on it."

"I better make sure the chief and commander know about
this." There went the first hours of his morning.

While satisfying a crazy jonesing for his missed second and third cups of coffee, Cruz's cell rang. "Miss Pelletier, what's new this morning?"

"Same ol', same ol'. Do you know how Nicholas is doing?"

"He's recovering. He's a good man and we need him back."

"Back? Like he's a cop? He doesn't look like a cop. Is he undercover?"

He couldn't believe he made such a stupid, idiotic, stupid, fucking mistake. "You keep this to yourself. He's still under."

Frankie was quiet, and Cruz was afraid that sharp mind was working through the machinations. "Is that why the suspect let him go? It wasn't just that he wasn't selling or using drugs, but that he was fighting them, just like our crusader is?"

"God, please do *not* call the suspect a crusader. He is a killer, short and simple. Not a fucking superhero." Crap, he just used the f-word with a witness who was also a reporter. He had to keep it together.

Undeterred by the lecture, she continued with her line of thinking. "The point is the suspect may have a sort of kinship with Nicholas. Maybe you can use that to draw him out."

"Nicholas may lose his use feet because of the son of a bitch." Exaggeration? Maybe. Maybe not.

"In his defense, he wasn't intending to maim him, he was intending to kill him. Circulation in his feet was probably the last thing the suspect was worried about."

His tightened fingers into a claw as he fantasized about reaching through the phone and strangling the woman. "I'm not having this conversation." And he ended the call.

Sure, the suspect could have identified with Kroc and, yes, there could be a way to use the connection to get the suspect to surface. But, damn it all, he hated thinking that way and hated more that Frankie Pelletier didn't sound nearly as afraid of the suspect as she sounded intrigued.

Cruz watched the rally at Public Square from a corner affording him a view. The event should have been predictable. In the beginning, it was. Speaker after speaker denouncing the police and then entreating protection for the victims. No one questioned the oxymoronic statements. The small lunchtime crowd there for the speeches cheered. Three times as many people hustled back and forth, carrying Styrofoam that kept their lunches hot.

Someone started it. No one ever saw who. Someone yelled back "Let the bastard have the drug dealers."

Then "Cleveland's better off without them."

The voice of reason bellowed over the microphone. "We are all God's children, looking for safety in our community."

To which "Maybe if you were better parents, our community would be safe," was retorted.

The mothers in the crowd took the loudest exception to the accusations. Too many of them were single, working to put food on the table and a decent roof over the family's head. They loved their children with the ferocity of a mother lion, parented with the same determination and pride. But determination and pride only went so far when the bills stacked up, when the school was out, when drugs and gangs and crime were the norm of the day, when addiction took root.

The ones who looked down their nose and scoffed didn't come home dead tired after twelve hours for minimum wage and then have to fight the uphill battles against stereotypes, the system, and limited opportunities. There were no easy days.

Six people were arrested.

The long afternoon was punctuated by Yablonski falling

heavily into the chair by Cruz's desk. "Do you think this is a mistake?"

"Yeah. I've never thought rallies were a good idea. Too explosive."

"Not that, Cruzie. Me and Erin. Getting engaged." He sat up suddenly. "You didn't lose the ring. Tell me you didn't lose the ring."

Cruz pulled the black box out of his zipped pocket. "I did not lose the ring. And no, you and Erin are not a mistake. You got nothing to be nervous about."

"Yeah. Yeah, you're right. But, still, I could put this off. You know, until the case is closed."

Cruz shut off his computer and stood. "Let's go. You got a girl to win."

He shoved Yablonski into his car and chauffeured him to Becky's. His buddy was sweating. If Yablonski hadn't been so nervous it would be funny. It would be funny in an hour when she said yes. Assuming he got the chunk of frozen meat from the sidewalk inside the bar.

"Will you move." He dropped his shoulder and shoved his friend to the door. "She adores your fat ass."

"What am I going to say? I didn't think about that." Yablonski spun so fast Cruz kissed the front door. "I should have some poetry or something."

"You don't need poetry. You need to get in there, get down on your knees, and tell that beautiful woman you're crazy about her." Cruz yanked the door open and pointed. "Go."

Yablonski swayed, looked ready to run for it. Cruz took a fistful of shirt and pulled him in.

They both stood still for a moment, letting their eyes adjust to the dark. The bartender waived and got busy making their usuals. People called their names like a scene from a movie. Cruz changed his grip to Yablonski's thick neck and walked the Tin Man down the aisle.

"There's my guy." Erin planted a kiss on Yablonski's chin.

"What's wrong?"

"Wrong?" Yablonski's voice broke. He looked at Cruz, panic in his eyes.

"Erin," Cruz said. "Matt has something to ask you, right, big guy?"

Yablonski smiled suddenly, too wide with too many teeth.

"Oh. Okay, you're scaring me," she said.

Cruz hissed in Yablonski's ear. "Get on your knees!" Yablonski dropped like a sack of potatoes. "Repeat after me. Erin."

"Erin," he said.

"You are everything to me."

"You are everything to me."

Erin gasped, pressing her fingers to her mouth.

Cruz shoved the velvet box into Yablonski's hand. "Give it to her."

Yablonski proffered the small box. Erin's fingers trembled as she took it using both hands. Tears ran down her face as she opened it. She made a sound only girls can make. The word *oh* with ten Hs said on an undulating wave of tones.

Then she launched herself at Yablonski, tackling him to the floor.

"Does that mean yes?" he asked as she choked him.

"Yes!" She alternately kissed him and shouted her answer.

Cruz looked down at the couple, so damn happy for them he could burst. "A round on me!"

For the first time in days, he had lost track of time in a good way. A party had been just what he needed.

"I'm going to remember forever that look on his face," Erin said, wiggling her fingers to watch the lights dance across the stone.

"Yeah. I wish I'd captured it on video. I could have black-mailed him for years."

Erin laughed, dancing foot to foot. "Why didn't Aurora come? I can't wait to show her."

The blood drain from Cruz's face, the ice cold of guilt replacing it. She was at home, waiting to do something special with him. Cruz leaned in and gave Erin a kiss on the cheek. "Tell Yablonski I need to go. I'll see him in the morning. Congratulations."

Cruz cursed himself the entire twelve-minute drive home. He called himself every name in the book, cursed himself again, and then started praying.

Her car was in front of his house. His house was dark except for the kitchen. Aurora was in his bed. He ran into the house, took the steps to the main floor in a single leap, and then froze. What was he going to say?

He climbed the stairs to the second floor one at a time. In the bedroom, he softly called her name. When she didn't stir, he stripped and slid in next to her.

She inhaled deeply, snuggling into the curve of his body. "What time is it?"

"I don't know. Eleven maybe."

She sighed heavily, cuddling his arm. "You can't work this late. You'll run yourself into the ground."

He closed his eyes, wanting to lie and let her believe he was working, but that would be covering his own ass, and he didn't deserve it. "I, uh, wasn't working the whole time. I went to Becky's. Yablonski and Erin got engaged. I should have called you, baby. I'm sorry."

"Matt and Erin?"

"Yeah. Hard to believe, right?" Cruz chuckled. "He was so nervous. First, he made me hold onto the ring, so he wouldn't lose it. Then he couldn't even ask her. I had to help him out a little."

"You helped him out." She dropped his hand, and her body stiffened.

"I should have called. I just didn't think. Yablonski was a fucking mess, and he messed me up. I don't have a big enough word to tell you how sorry I am."

"It's okay." Her voice was a thin string on the verge of breaking. She swiftly slid out of bed. "I'm not feeling well." She ran out of the room and locked herself in the bathroom.

Worry shoved Cruz's guilt to the backseat. "Can I get you something? I think we have some Tums."

"No. I'll be fine." Her voice, muffled by the door, did not sound fine. "Just go to bed. You need the rest."

"Are you sure? I'll wait—"

"No! Just…just go to bed. I'm going to be in here a while."

Cruz jumped back when she snapped. It wasn't like her. Maybe she was sick, but more likely she was angry. He would be. Crowding her wouldn't help. He did as she asked and went to bed, intending to wait for her, but he was asleep before he knew he was tired.

Wednesday, May 16

Morning light sliced across Cruz's face, waking him. It was six-forty-five, and he was alone. The energy that followed Aurora was missing.

It wasn't normal. She always woke him when she left. It was part of their routine. He pulled on a pair of shorts and searched the house, just to make sure she wasn't somewhere else. Maybe sick on the couch. Or in the bathroom again.

But she wasn't.

There was a note on the table.

Detective,
I didn't know if you had time to eat so I ordered a pizza. Most of it is in the refrigerator. You didn't call today. I hope it doesn't mean you had too bad of a day. Wake me when you get home. I love you. ~A.

Last night's note. "Shit." He would call today. Hell, he would call right now. He ran up the stairs, picked up his phone and called her.

It rolled to voicemail.

He brought up the messaging app. What to write? *Missing you this morning. U ok?* SEND.

No response. That's okay, he thought. She's driving. She's not supposed to be texting or reading texts for that matter. He decided he would be mad if she texted him back.

Don't read this or text me if you're driving. SEND.

He had a bad feeling, and nothing good ever came from a bad feeling. He had no choice, but to begin his day. The coffeemaker did its thing while he showered. No text back. He dressed, braided his hair. Still no text. He drank his coffee and stared at the page with the meditation. He didn't read the words, he was listening for a text. She should be at school by now.

His phone rang, and he fumbled it, adrenaline jolting his system. "Aurora?"

"Montoya," his commander said. "Chief's office. Twenty minutes."

Put it aside, he told himself. But he couldn't. This was Aurora. So, he went, taking her with him. He walked into the chief's office on time, finding the usual suspects grouped around the television. "Chief," he said to announce his arrival.

"Take a look at this." It was a local news program, and in the studio was Pastor Michael Ashford.

"What is Pastor Mike doing on there?"

Ramsey huffed like a ram about to charge. "Taking up the arms the suspect challenged him to."

"No," Cruz said. "Mike is more level-headed than that."

Ramsey raised the volume.

"I felt called by those words, Renee. 'The time has come for the righteous to come forward. Protect the weak among us. Stand with those who cannot stand alone. Send Satan on his way. Be not afraid.' It speaks to all of us to take control and responsibility for our city, for our fellow citizens. I am organizing a candle-light walk for tomorrow night at seven-thirty. We will walk through our streets, showing those who would rather us hide that there is safety and strength in being righteous. We will not be afraid."

The made-up woman with the microphone and permanent smile turned into the camera. "Thank you, Pastor Mike. We'll be right back after this break."

Ramsey killed it, setting the remote down with deliberate care and then making a large, tight fist.

"I'll talk to him," Cruz said hurriedly. He left the room before finding out the actual reason for the meeting. Getting to Pastor Mike and calling this thing off was priority number one. Using his lights and parking in a loading zone, Cruz was waiting on the street when Pastor Mike left the studio.

"Jesus. This is a surprise."

Cruz stalked to the pastor. "It shouldn't be. You go on television announcing you're going to take on the world, it tends to get police attention."

Pastor Mike's face paled. "You make it sound like I'm starting a war."

"That's what you made it sound like."

He took a step backward. "No. No, no, no. My message is non-violence. Complete non-violence."

"You just picked up a gauntlet thrown down by a killer."

"Exactly. Once it's picked up, he'll have no reason to continue with these crimes."

"Pastor Mike, you're only seeing this from one angle. Our suspect is mentally ill. He's not going to interpret your actions as an invitation to retire. He's going to see them as beefing up his team."

Pastor Mike looked at Cruz for a moment, then shook his head. "You may be right about your suspect's mental state, but the point is still valid that our streets need to be re-claimed by the people who live on them in a peaceful manner." He emphasized the last four words. "I have to go. I'm meeting with the leaders of other churches to organize this walk."

"This conversation isn't over, Mike."

"I know."

There was no end to the day. There were so many loose ends his case resembled a pom-pom. There were two good points. First, Yablonski was flying around the station on Cloud Nine, wearing a goofy grin. It was hard to feel down when the guy was flying so freaking high.

Then, Cruz brought Kroc an early dinner. Roast beef this time. Kroc had started therapy and was upbeat about the prognosis if not the additional time in the hospital. He on his own now, able to walk to the toilet. A point of pride and progress.

Cruz went for a hat trick, stopping in the hospital gift shop and buying a small bouquet of flowers that were as colorful as Aurora.

But when he pulled in his driveway, his house was dark, and her little car wasn't anywhere to be found.

He dialed her, warning heaven and hell that if she didn't answer he was going to—

"Hello?"

"Where are you?" He barked out the question, pissed she wasn't home.

"My apartment." She sounded tired, sad.

He softened his tone. "Why aren't you home?"

"I am home."

Bullshit. "My home. Our home."

"I don't know. I just..." She sighed heavily.

His worry increased. She sounded so ephemeral, as if she would just float away from him. He needed a tether. "Did you eat yet?"

"No. I don't have anything to heat up." The happiness and sunshine that was his lady was gone. She sounded like he felt. Drained. Empty. Weary.

"Aurora, is something wrong?"

She didn't answer right away. Cruz thought she wouldn't she waited so long. "I just, I have some things I need to work out."

And his heart stopped. "Come home, baby." Bribery wasn't beneath him. "I'll have dinner ready by the time you get here." She reluctantly agreed, and he got busy. His refrigerator was crammed with plastic bowls of every shape and color, holding the remnants of Mother's Day, topped with a pizza box wedged in. He reinvented left overs into a savory one pot dish. While it simmered, he set the table with the plates Aurora had bought. They were mustard yellow and pumpkin orange and the other weird colors that popped on the dark wood table he'd acquired. He took the chunky candle from their bedroom and set it in the center of the table. He stuck a plate under it. Then he put some of the pebbly things she had in a bowl around it and lit the candle.

"Music." He thumbed through what he owned. Aurora liked soulful music as she painted. His tastes ran more to Run the Jewels. He did have one album that might work: Marvin Gaye.

A car pulled in. He heard the back door open and close, followed by the soft ruffling of cloth and bags.

"Welcome home, baby."

Aurora turned her head, tucking her hair behind her ear. Her pretty eyes weren't shining. The mouth he loved to kiss wasn't smiling. "I thought you'd work later."

He shrugged it off, taking her in his arms. He buried his nose in her hair, relieved when she held him back. "Dinner's ready."

"I'm not really hungry."

Cruz took her hand, pulling her with him. "After I slaved

over a hot stove for you? At least try it." He sat her at the dining room table, then scooped a helping of the concocted dinner onto her plate.

Aurora poked at her dinner. "What is it?"

"A dish of my own creation. I call it littlebitofevery-thing." Cruz's teasing smile faded when she gave him only the faintest of grins. He scooped twice as much on his own plate, set the pan on a hot pad, and then sat. "So, what do you think?"

"About what?"

He couldn't read her expression. Not a good thing. "The littlebitofeverything."

"Oh. Not bad. Is that a chicken wing?"

He played with his food, watching her more than he ate. Her vibe was off. "How was school?"

"Fine. The kids can tell it's getting close to the end. Everybody's restless. Your little friend Jace led a revolt on the playground that earned everybody five minutes of quiet time. How was your day?"

"Same old. Come here," he said, taking her hand. "Come dance with me."

"What?"

Cruz pulled her into his arms. She was stiff at first but melted into him as he danced her around their home. "I missed you this morning."

"I missed you, too." Her breath hitched.

"Are you crying?" He leaned away, trying to see her face but, shaking her head, she tightened her arms and held on. "If this is about last night, I'm—"

"It's not." She rested her forehead on his shoulder, her breath hitching. "I just...have to work through something."

"Without me?" When she didn't answer, he held on tighter.

May 17

My life has changed so much since that first day. I read the entries from those early days and realized just how close I was to the end. It wasn't my time. I still had a purpose in this world. I don't know if I was called to this job because of the hell I lived through or if I went through hell because I was called to this job. Before that day, I didn't understand the ugly, incestuous, disgusting, merciless nature of evil.

I am not in instrument of mercy. I exact justice.

Today reminded me of the first soul. I was called to that street and so was the drug dealer. After I collected the soul, I saw a young girl hiding behind a tree. She was beautiful, innocent and would stay that way.

If I die tomorrow, I am happy knowing her life went on because I existed.

CHAPTER SEVENTEEN

Thursday, May 17

Cruz spent his second cup of coffee focusing on details. The medical examiner's findings. The lab reports. The crime scene reports and preliminaries. He read a hotline tip, thought it sounded familiar, then cursed viscously when he realized he'd read half the reports twice and the other half not at all.

He couldn't concentrate. Aurora. She stayed the night and let him make love to her, but it was different. She was sweet and clingy, not at all the demanding lover he knew. It felt like she was silently saying goodbye. She fell asleep in his arms, his leg over hers in case there was any doubt what he wanted. But this morning, he woke alone.

Yablonski crossed the room, going to the desk he'd wedged next to Cruz's. "How goes it?"

"None of this shit is worth anything." He shoved the tip-line pages, putting a quarter of them in flight. "Not when you're looking for one person in a half million."

Yablonski sat at his desk, leaving the pages where they landed. "What do you want to do?"

Wasn't that the question. "I am so sick of playing defense. I want to get back to building the profile list from drug-related murders. The first list washed out, but I stopped at August. Let's get help to finish culling through the files."

"On it. The turf war for territory is heating up. There was a shooting last night between two lieutenants. A little girl saw it, recognized one of the men. We found a blood trail. It ended in the middle of a street."

Yablonski didn't have to say it. The clock was ticking again, this time for a man named Michael "Jonesy" Jones. He hadn't shown up at any emergency room. His brother and his girlfriend were talking to the cops. Yeah, they knew the score.

By the end of the day, Cruz knew everything there was about Jonesy except where he was and if he was alive. The dead ends left him feeling like a blind rat in a maze—lost, frustrated, and forever away from the end.

He knocked on Montoya's open door. "I'm going to take a ride over to Pastor Mike's rally. I want to survey the crowd. The suspect might show just to admire his work."

"Good idea. Keep me updated. The chief is threatening to hand it all over to Special Agent Bishop and the fucking bureau of investigation." Montoya's face was calm, but his eyes glinted with hellfire. "This case stays with this department. Start making things happen, Cruz. That's an order."

"Yes, sir." He texted Yablonski his plan and then headed to the parking garage. Five o'clock flight was in full swing, so he sat as the eight-to-fivers caravanned out.

In that small, quiet space, Aurora invaded. He couldn't call or text her during the school day because she turned her phone off. It hadn't been the school day for a few hours, but he hadn't called. He couldn't remember a time in his adult life when he felt so afraid to call a woman. It was a toss-up which scared him more, her answering or not. It was a lose-lose situation. Pressing the button, he said a little prayer, promising he'd do all kinds of good deeds if only...

"Hey, Zeus."

Relief flooded through him, and he shook a fist in victory. "Hey, beautiful. Where are you?"

"At your house." Her upbeat voice put him at ease. She was past it, whatever it was. "I stopped at the grocery store and started dinner. It will be ready by six."

Shit. He closed his eyes, hating what he was about to say. "I don't think I'll make it by then. There's this march in the city I need to be at."

"Can't someone else do it?" Her tone changed to one of disappointment. "Just this once?"

"This is important." He waited for her to respond. To yell, to swear. Something. When she didn't, he pressed her. "Aurora?"

"I understand." She killed the line.

"Fuck." He wanted to call her back, but what was there to say? *You knew I was a cop when you asked me out. This is what cops do.*

If he called and said that, she'd be gone when he did get home.

If he didn't call back, would she be there?

He gripped the steering wheel hard; his knuckles turned white. He couldn't be in two places at once, and he made a commitment. In that moment, he hated the suspect like he never hated before. If he lost Aurora because of this case, the man would learn about hell and fury.

He started the car, threw it in gear, then pushed into the line. Every dumbass driver who didn't know where they were going or weren't in a hurry to get there was in front of him. Fifteen in a twenty-five. No Clevelander drove that slow. He flipped on his lights to scare the hell out of a guy paying more attention to yelling at the woman next to him than the road. And what dumbass programmed these traffic lights? He couldn't drive more than two blocks without stopping for the nobody coming out of the cross street.

Finally, he reached the burned-out patch of earth Ashford hand-picked as his launch point. It was at the corner of St. Clair and Armageddon.

"What the hell are you thinking, Mike?"

People trickled in, and there was the man personally greeting each one. He handed out candles, kissed babies, petted dogs. Sitting in his car on a side street, with a clear view of the corner, Cruz measured each person. Half were fat, another quarter too young or too old.

He'd be a loner most likely. Someone who lived on the edges. The crowd grew as daylight dimmed. He needed to get out there, mingle close up. A knock on his passenger window made him jump. He unlocked the door.

Yablonski's expression transformed from game face to smart ass. "Jumpy, Detective?"

Cruz cleared off the passenger seat so Yablonski could sit. "There's too damn many." He looked out over the steering wheel, then punched the dashboard.

"Easy, Cruzie. We'll get him. It's just a matter of time"

"Time, I don't have," he snapped.

Yablonski narrowed those sharp eyes. "What are you talking about?"

"Nothing. I'm talking about nothing."

"You might as well tell me. I'm just going to pester you until you do."

Cruz turned in his seat. "Do you know how much you sound like a woman?"

"Ah. What did you do?"

"I thought it was because I screwed up on your engagement party. I should have called her, you know? She should yell and scream, swear at me. Hell, throwing something would be better than her crying and telling me she has stuff to work through."

"Go home. I'll cover things here and call you if anything happens."

He shook his head. As much as he wanted to go, his duty was here.

Yablonski punched him in the arm. Hard. "Go. She matters."

He looked between the swelling crowd and his friend.

"The suspect is likely to be a loner. Quiet. Unassuming. Someone easy to approach. He thinks he's on a mission to protect the city. You could use that in a conversation to draw him out. Call for backup to apprehend."

Yablonski snorted. "Told you before, not my first rodeo."

Cruz took a fist full of shirt and yanked. "He's killed eight men. Eight strong, healthy, violent men. Do not underestimate him."

"I got it, Cruz. I'll call you if I get any nibbles. Okay?"

Satisfied, he let him go. "Okay. And thanks, man."

Aurora's car was in the driveway, and the lights were on in the attic space she used as a studio. His temper still ran hot. He couldn't live like this. They were going to talk this out whether she wanted to or not.

He walked in his side door. He expected blues or jazz or R&B to greet him. Instead, it was shouting.

"You're so stupid!"

Aurora was screaming, but at who? She never spoke to anyone that way. He crept up the stairs, the hair on the back of his neck on end.

Training had him reaching for his gun, but he stopped. This was his house. His girlfriend. Silently, he rounded the small landing. He saw her now. She faced a painting she had been working on. It was family picnic.

The nearly finished work now had violent splashes of a vivid blue across it.

"I *hate* when you do this!" She lashed out at the canvas and the small woman with cork screw curls.

"Aurora?"

She jumped back, startled at the sound of his voice, spun to face him, and then quickly turned away. "What are you doing here?" She'd been crying again.

"What are you doing?" he repeated back softly.

"P-painting." She cleaned her brushes, carefully ignoring his gaze. "You hungry? Dinner didn't work out—nothing new—but there's more of your leftovers."

"What is this," Cruz asked, pointing to the canvas. "Why were you yelling?"

Aurora wouldn't look at him. She tried to close the paints but ended up dropping more lids than she placed. "I, uh, had the radio on."

Cruz stepped into her way, his temper curling beneath his skin. "How dumb do you think I am?"

"I was just painting," she said, her voice hoarse from yelling. "Let it go."

"I won't let it go. What the hell has been going on with you these last few days? Is it my job? Because you knew I was a cop when you asked me out." He stalked toward her, forcing her backwards. "I'm not going to be a man at your beck and call." She flinched as if he'd hit her. "Damn it. Don't you act like you're afraid of me, like I'd ever hurt you."

She was crying now. It broke his heart and pissed him off in equal measures. She retreated, backing away until she hit the wall, then sank into a ball.

"Stop that," he said, then took a breath. "Come on. Get up."

"Leave me alone." She rocked herself.

His mind grasped at straws. Maybe she was ill, like having a mental break down. Maybe he should call nine-one-one.

His phone rang before he could dial. Yablonski. "We found Michael Jones. It's all hands-on deck."

He squeezed the cell phone, trying to smash it to a million pieces. How was he supposed to handle all this?

He picked her resisting body off the floor and carried her to their bed, where he tucked her under the warm comforter. "I'm sorry if you don't understand this, but I made a commitment. This is what got me through some very bad times.

It's the reason I didn't give up. I don't know what's wrong, but we can work our way through it. Just wait for me. I'll be back."

He wasn't surprised when she didn't respond, he only hoped she heard and that she stayed.

The little park on Doan Brook featured a water fountain, a playground, a pavilion, and ten of Cleveland's finest with their lights on. Three ambulances were on the scene, tending to people sitting about. The area had been roped off, and a tent erected to separate the scene from the curious. Uniformed officers were speaking to the crowd, taking names and eyewitness accounts. He found Ashford in the pavilion, talking quietly with a woman who was shaken by the events.

When she stepped away, Cruz stepped forward. "How are you?"

"Disturbed. On so many levels." Pastor Mike took a deep breath, looking around at those being treated by the EMTs. "In my wildest imagination, I never…I am so sorry."

"You didn't do this, Pastor Mike."

"No, but if I hadn't—"

Cruz cut him off. "It would have been somewhere else. Some other time." His phone chimed. A text from Aurora.

Sorry. Going to my parents. A

He texted back quickly. *Wait for me. Please*

"Cruz. We need you here."

Friday, May 18

"How could it be Friday morning?" Cruz rolled to the empty space next to him. The pillow smelled like her. He buried his face in it, homesick in his own house. He got up, dressed and left. He didn't shower. He didn't read his meditation. He just got the hell out.

He carried his gas station coffee into the early morning meeting with the chief. "The damage to the victim's head appears consistent with being struck by a vehicle. The suspect planned this disposal carefully. The head was mounted on a post, but a coat hung from a hanger and a hat was on the head, given the illusion, especially from a distance, of someone leaning against a tree. Two teens stumbled across the victim and started a stampede."

Ramsey leaned forward in his chair, taking every word in. "Do you have an opinion on whether this particular incident is one of opportunity?"

"The kill likely was opportunity as I strongly doubt he could have planned to have the victim walking down the middle of a road for him. The posting was planned. We are confirming the ID but suspect it to be Michael Jones."

"There is a growing sympathy for the suspect. Almost a respect."

"It's sickening," Montoya said. "I liked your proposal. Is everything set up?"

The idea had hit him at two in the morning. He'd pitched it to Montoya first thing. "Kroc is coming in this afternoon. He'll be on board."

"Good," Ramsey said. "We *finally* might make some progress."

The reproach was a sharp stab to the ego. He was working his ass off, how did nobody see that? God, his head hurt. In two short days, he'd gone blind, deaf and dumb, making him useless on a case like this. He wasn't having that. This was his case, his responsibility. If he didn't get his act together the commander or the chief would be taking it from him and that, straight up, was not happening.

He left the department, walking past the chatter and call-outs like a man on a mission. Minutes later, he stalked up the sidewalk of Fullerton Elementary School determined to have it out here and now. The secretary buzzed him in. She smiled, started with the small talk.

"I need to speak with Aurora. Now."

Her mouth fell into a perfect O. "She's teaching, Detective. Is this an emergency?"

"Yes." For him it was.

The secretary went down the hall. Moments later, Aurora hurried into the office.

"What are you doing here? Did something happen?" Her voice was low, full of concern for someone. Her concern should have been for them.

His feet wide, arms crossed over his chest, he lowered his gaze to hers. "We're getting this out in the open."

"Keep your voice down. Here," she said, poking her head in the dark office of the vice principal and led him in. "You can't just come in here—"

"What the hell is going on?"

She closed the door, keeping her back to him. "Zeus, please, lower your voice."

"You want me to lower my voice, you tell me what is going on. Why are you leaving our home? Why are you destroying your paintings?" He prowled the small office. "Is it another guy? Are you seeing someone else? Are you pregnant?"

"No, no and God no."

That was good. But not good enough. "I'm tired of this guessing game. Just fucking tell me."

"You can't use that word here. The children."

He spun around and kicked the desk; the sound carried the rage of thunder. "How am I supposed to catch a serial killer when I can't figure out what is going on in my own house?" He kicked it again.

Aurora caught his arm, trying to pull him away. "Zeus. Stop. Please."

Days' worth of exhaustion and frustration boiled over.

He yanked his arm away from her and pounded his fists on the desk. "Why can't you talk to me? What did I do?"

"You didn't do anything. I did. I did."

"I can't take it. I can't—"

"I found the ring!"

He turned, stunned. Her eyes were red and swollen, her hand covered her mouth. He replayed what he heard. It was in English, but it didn't help him understand what she meant. "What ring?"

"Erin's ring." A tear ran down her cheek. "It fell out of your pocket when I picked up your coat."

You didn't need to be a detective to know what happened from there. "Oh, baby. I'm so sor—"

"Don't say it." She cut him off, pressing her fingers to his lips. "You have nothing to be sorry for. It was me. All me. I wasn't snooping. I didn't even recognize what the box was. And then I opened it. It was so pretty, sparkling just for me." She turned away, her head hanging low. "I was...ridiculous. I daydreamed about how you would ask me. Dreaming up funny responses to watch you sweat." She laughed more than a little hysterically. "I practiced writing Aurora De La Cruz a hundred times during lunch. When you told me it was Erin's, I was so disappointed. So embarrassed. Ashamed. Jealous."

He put his hands on her shoulders. "Aurora."

She stepped away from him. "I know I should get over it. I mean, we've only known each other a few months. I was trying to get over it. I was wrong to be jealous. It was silly of me to think you would ever ask me to marry you. I was acting stupid and I hated it. Then you walked in. I was a hundred times more humiliated. A hundred times more embarrassed. I just wanted to crawl under a rock and die."

He pulled her to him, cuddling her to his chest. "I didn't know you wanted to get married."

"Neither did I." Her arms snaked around his waist. "I

don't know how to get past this. I need some time. Some distance, maybe."

"That's not the answer, this is. Talking. Trusting in each other. I am sorry you were hurt. I should have told you about the ring."

"No, Zeus." Aurora tried to pull away, but he held her tight. "You did nothing wrong. It was all me. God, I'm such a mess. It's a good thing you did forget about me. Can you imagine how badly I would have reacted watching Erin open the box?"

He flinched, pained that for even a moment, she would think his forgetting her could be good. Talking herself into believing he would be better off without her. "You can't leave me, Aurora. Tell me you're staying."

"Zeus—"

He gave her a little shake. "Just tell me you're staying. I need to hear you say it."

She whispered, defeated. "I can't do anything right."

He banded his arms across her shoulders, refusing to let her go. "You're talented and sweet and beautiful and intelligent." He pressed his lips to top of her head. "You can't leave me."

Wrapping her arms around his waist, she held onto him as strongly as he held on to her.

"You can always talk to me, baby. Always. We'll go out tonight. Somewhere nice."

"Can't. You promised your sister you would watch the girls tonight."

He'd forgotten. Damn it. He wanted to spend every minute making up. Alone. Sighing heavily, he adjusted his plan. Lifting her chin, he kissed her wet cheeks. "Come with me. After we'll have a late night coffee. Just you and me."

"Of course, you'd want coffee, but I'd like the you and me part." She stood still, letting his mouth soothe her. "I need to get back. How bad do I look?"

He let her step back but kept hold of her hand. Her eyes were red and a little swollen. "You look beautiful."

She smiled just a little. "I'm sure you're lying. Walk me to my room?"

They walked hand-in-hand. When Cruz jerked his arm, Aurora fell against him. By the third time, she was laughing. With smiles their faces, they walked into the classroom.

"Thank you, Mrs. Mueller. Class, you remember Detective De La Cruz."

The sing-song greeting broadened Cruz's smile. "Glad to see you are all paying attention and doing well." He called out a few by name he'd picked up from Aurora's stories. Most beamed at the recognition. One slid down in his seat. "How is your reading, Jace?"

Jace looked at this desk, embarrassed. He shrugged his little shoulders.

"Well, stick with it. It'll come. I have to get back to work. I'm deputizing all of you and putting you in charge of Miss Williams. Keep her happy by listening and giving your best effort on everything."

He pulled their teacher close and kissed her cheek. Thirty giggles flooded the room, then he walked to the door. "Be good for my best girl."

His swagger was on as he walked through the door to homicide. His co-workers were loosely assembled around the murder board. Grim faces met his. "What's happened? My phone didn't ring."

Yablonski pointed with his chin to the newspapers fanned out on the table.

"I saw them. We expected it sooner." He had read the *Plain Dealer* that morning as he tried not to think of Aurora. He read the *Beacon-Journal* online, noting Frankie Pelletier had another front-page byline. The coverage of the case spread from the front section to the editorial page. One editorial applauded the stand against drugs, glossing over the fact that the stand was criminal and barbaric. Another was driven by statistics, touting the number of deaths caused by heroin and the economic impact of the drug epidemic. The final one encouraged police and public organizers to work together on a solution.

Cruz had set up a Twitter account at the direction of his commander when he joined homicide. Montoya saw social media as a tool as important to modern day policing as a computer. Cruz had never tweeted. He lurked in the background, reading.

The Drug Head Murders solicited visceral responses from those who posted. It started with the simple condemning of the deaths, support for the families and the community. With the discovery of the four heads last weekend plus the one at the rally, the rhetoric exploded. The ugliest cheered the killer on, going so far as to invite the suspect to their neighborhood.

The sociologist in Cruz found the maturation of the dialog fascinating. His mind divided the posts into four major categories.

The first group used the statements in the suspect's fax to Frankie Pelletier as rallying points. Posts called neighbors to stand together against illegal drugs—a good message, Cruz thought—and to dispense the evil ones from our home—a dangerous message. Cruz lost some of the little sleep he'd been getting worrying about copycat crimes.

The misguided hype was painting the suspect as a twist on a modern-day Robin Hood or Batman. It turned Cruz's stomach that the vocal minority—and he had to believe it was a minority—cheered on a killer who decapitated his victims, using the heads for a public statement.

#DrugHeads #BeNotAfraid #InstrumentOfJustice

The second category of posts denounced the victims' activities but condemned the violence that lead to their deaths. The comments ran along the lines of "I hate what you do but defend your right to live" and "Let the justice system work."

Posts in this category included well-known local, regional, and state leaders. Pastor Michael Ashford tweeted in this category, which stunned Cruz only because he couldn't picture the Anglo pastor hash-tagging anything.

#CivilJustice #IAmNotAfraid #KeepYourHeads

The third group was the most curious to Cruz because they were the most unexpected. They were posts by people highly passionate…about other causes. Most of the posts sounded like whining along the lines of "Why do you care about this cause when you don't care about mine." Of course, this was over simplifying the statements, and most of the other causes were real civic problems. Yet the connection of the issue to the Drug Head Murders often felt square peg in a round hole.

"Cry over the Drug Heads while mothers abort their babies every day. #ProtectOurBabies."

"Domestic violence kills more women than heroin and the Drug Head killer. #DVKills."

"Cops would support Drug Head killer if all victims were people of color. #KillerCracker."

Few of those posts had more than a handful of likes and re-tweets, but there were out there to be read and thought about.

The fourth group was the band wagon. Far away people—either geographically or idealistically—who tried to come up with something witty to say in the character allowance to bring a slice of the attention onto themselves. Professional entertainers. Professional commentators. Politicos. Generally entertaining, ultimately meaningless.

Using the high of making up with Aurora, Cruz pushed hard on the idea of an interview. Kroc and Pelletier. The survivor and the messenger. The senior team sat around the chief's conference table, looking with respect on the determined face of Officer Nick Kroc.

Cruz stood, commanding the room. "We need to connect with the suspect and our best chance is sitting here. Officer Kroc is the sole survivor and, it is my opinion, may be able to initiate communication channels."

Montoya looked at Kroc. "It would mean your undercover days are over."

Kroc stood slowly but steady. "Chief, I joined the Cleveland police to serve the residents of the community. The capacity in which I do it is secondary. I am willing to engage the suspect, sir, after which, I'll transfer to another department."

"Aren't you on medical leave, Officer?"

Kroc, dressed in civilian attire, stood taller. "I am fit for duty, sir."

Ramsey inspected his officer, slowly measuring him with eyes that saw beneath the bravado and brass. Satisfied, he turned to Cruz. "How are you going to pull this off?"

"The suspect has already reached out to Francesca Pelletier of the *Beacon-Journal*. While we have not determined her connection to the suspect, it is reasonable to expect he reads her work. With Montoya's support, I arranged for Pelletier to come here tomorrow afternoon. I'm working with Alison Hyatt for local promotion on television and radio. Kroc's message will be that he understands the suspect's crusade and to invite him to talk."

Cruz was late. Aurora may have made the mistake with the ring, but the incident had shaken her confidence in them. Being late was not the reinforcement he was looking for. He pulled into an empty spot, ran up the driveway, and into his sister's house.

Happy, unadulterated laughter greeted him. He followed

it into the kitchen where smoke billowed out of the toaster. Gabby stood in the corner, waving her hand to clear the thick smoke as she giggled. "I told you putting the pizza bagel in the toaster was a bad idea."

Aurora looked bewildered as she poked the toaster with a knife. "It should have worked."

"Enough of that," he shouted, racing to the wall to unplug the appliance.

"Tito!" Rhianna attached herself to his leg. "We're making dinner."

He bent over and kissed her head. "You trying to hustle me out of a job?"

"You can have it," Gabby said. "Aurora has no idea what she's doing."

Cruz switched to Spanish and scolded his niece. "Show respect. She doesn't have to be here at all. Apologize."

Gabby wasn't used to being the one in trouble. Her face turned bright red. "Sorry, Aurora," she said in English.

"It's all right, Gabby. I can't cook, but I do other things really well. How about we do your hair and makeup while Tito makes dinner."

Gabby's eyes lit up. "Oh, yes, please."

"Go ahead, girls," he said, holding Aurora back. When they were alone, he kissed her cheeks and the tip of her nose before attending to her lips. "Sorry I'm late."

Aurora made a satisfied little sigh as she leaned into him. "I'm sorry you didn't get here before I killed their toaster." The burned cheese was still smoking.

"Don't worry about it. Go have fun with the girls. I'll find something to put together."

A half hour later, Cruz served a sophisticated dinner of scrambled eggs and pancakes to three of high societies' more important ladies. Gabrielle showed hints of the beautiful woman she would become with the dark eye make-up, fake eyelashes, blush, and pink lip gloss. Her father would choke, if he saw her.

Rhianna was dressed as queen of the cat people in a leopard-print leotard and black tights. Her face was artistically painted with spots, nose, and whiskers.

"Who wants a pancake," Cruz asked.

Gabby tossed her hair back. "I would love one, *darling*."

He slid the pancake onto her plate. "That's Tito darling to you."

"Meow. Me-ee-ow," Rhianna said, scratching playfully at his leg.

"Maybe I should open a can of tuna. Cats eat tuna, not pancakes."

She shook her head definitively and pointed at the plate. "Me-ow."

"Ah, maybe tomorrow." He served the pancake and added a generous amount of syrup. "And you, Ms. Williams?"

Aurora held her plate up. "Absolutely. I'm starving. I missed lunch today.

There were games and a TV show, more games, then it was bedtime. Once, twice, three times. Cruz stumbled into the kitchen, doubled over with laughter.

Aurora looked up from the dishes in the sink to glance at the clock on the microwave. "It's after ten. Do you think they are down for the count?"

"They are so worried about ruining their makeup they refuse to set their heads down. I rolled up towels and told them it would keep their heads up, but they had to lie very, very still."

"You think that's going to work?"

"I'm not putting money on it."

She dried her hands and leaned against the counter. "They're great girls. I think Rhianna has finally forgiven me for stealing her Tito."

"Forgiven you? I think you've unseated me. Did you see her push me aside, so she could sit next to you? She loves her

Tiarora."

"So, now that it's just the two of us...what does Tiarora mean?"

"*Tia* means aunt. Rora means they are too impatient to say Aurora."

"So, I'm been promoted to aunt, huh?"

He crossed the small kitchen, caging her against the counter and looking laughing green eyes. "I think we should do it. Make it official."

"Make what official?"

"Your status as an aunt. Let's do it. Get married."

The laughter faded. Her gaze drifted to the corner of the kitchen floor. "I'm sorry I made you feel like you had to ask me—"

"You didn't." With two fingers, he brought her gaze back to his. "Sure, maybe it put the idea in my head, but I would have got there on my own. Eventually."

"Exactly. Eventually. Not now. We'll know when the time is right."

"But you're not saying no, now. I consider this matter still open. When you're ready to get married, remember I'm your man."

He took her, then, with a kiss that started tender and grew with passion into a heat that consumed them both. Beneath his hands, her body tensed, vibrated with a sexual energy he knew would leave him drained and very satisfied. He bent her back until she had to rely on his strength to stay on her feet. Her hands pulled his shirt from his pants and burrowed under. Skin to skin. It was what he wanted, too.

"No making babies in my kitchen, Tito."

Little sisters. Even when they were grown they knew how to ruin a good plan. "Go away, Mariana."

"This is my house. You go away, Jesus."

Aurora pushed him back. "Did you have a nice dinner?"

"Very nice." Mari opened the refrigerator and set a bag

of leftovers inside. "How were the girls?"

"Tiarora spoiled them," Cruz said, braggingly. "Make-up and hair and dress-up clothes."

"They wouldn't let us wash their faces," Aurora said. "The make-up pencils on Rhia might make a mess on her pillow."

"Mama, Mama! Look at me! I'm a jaguar. Meow!" The spotted cub landed in the middle of the kitchen, grinning ear to ear.

Cruz looked at Aurora. "I told you I wouldn't put money on her staying in bed."

Mari looked at her daughter's elaborate makeup and then at Aurora. "I see why she didn't want it washed off. That's spectacular."

"Tiarora promised to do makeup for Halloween. I'm going to be a zebra." She neighed like a horse.

"Come on, jaguar girl," Tony said. "Time for bed."

"Like I've told you five times," Cruz called after them. "We should get going. See you Sunday, Mari." He kissed his sister's cheek.

"Good night, Tito." Mari pulled Aurora in for a long, tight hug, then grinned. "Good night, Tiarora."

Cruz walked her to her car. He opened the door, but she spun him around, backing him again the rear door. She took his mouth. Passionate. Demanding. Her right hand buried in his hair while her left explored further south. "Race you home."

May 18

When I was little and went to the lake, I loved to watch the waves. I'd sit on rocks the size of my bed and watch little ripples turn into crashing waves. Other kids played in the waves, jumping over them, riding them, diving under them. I liked to watch.

Today I watched as people have started picking up my message and carrying it forward. Life is about the impact we make on the lives of others. My city is learning to protect themselves. It is rewarding in a way no job could be.

I've learned my lesson, though. I have to keep working. I have to. There is only one way to go. I have to let go of the last part of my old life. I'm ready. I'm finally ready.

May 21

The angel has a story on the front page and it is filled with good news. In the battle for the city, good is winning. My heart is beating so fast, it might explode. The city is changing, people are changing. Goodness has taken root.

Nick Kroc is the police officer who stayed with me. He slept most of the time but we had good talks those days we spent together. He had a good jaw, strong and just. I would like to see him again.

I'll need to think this through. Every soldier works alone. That's the rule. I'll need to be careful. Can't break the rules. Can't break the rules.

CHAPTER EIGHTEEN

Monday, May 21

"Drug Head Murderer...or Hero?" The headline would do what they needed—capture the suspect's attention—but Cruz choked on it. His stomach turned. Not even coffee helped. He set down the go cup and pinned the article to his board.

There was nothing heroic about the atrocities the suspect perpetrated. Working through the system, with all its flaws and procedures, complexities and nuances, that was heroic. It wasn't sexy, and it wasn't fast but why should it be? People's lives were on the line. Mistakes here were devastating.

A subset of the population found what the suspect did heroic, taking out the bad guys where the cops and prosecutors, judges and juries couldn't. Frankie Pelletier's story could be a dangerous rally cry.

His cell rang, identifying the caller as Nick Kroc. "Cruz."

Heavy breathing came through the phone. "He's at the zoo. Get here. Now."

"Call dispatch," he ordered another detective. He gave him the information needed as he ran out the door, Kroc still in his ear.

A voice in the background shouted. "Sir. Stop. You can't enter without ID, a ticket or a pass."

"I'm a police officer," Kroc said. "A suspect just came in here. Black pants with a white stripe, black running shoes, black hoodie."

"Lock it down." Cruz shouted into the phone as he raced out of the station. It was a big place but their first chance to catch the suspect. "Lock the zoo down."

"Lock it down," Kroc said. "Officer Nick Kroc, Cleveland police. No one in or out. Get me some help, Cruz."

"We're on the way." With lights and sirens going, Cruz joined no less than eight cruisers straddling the brick paved entrance to the Cleveland Metroparks Zoo. The SWAT truck followed him in.

The zoo had protocols in the event of an emergency evacuation that had never before been put to a live test. Announcements over the speaker system informed people of an emergency and directed them to the nearer of the two public entrances. Armed Cleveland police searched each person before allowing them to exit.

Kroc was inside the main gates, standing on a souvenir stand to see above the impatient crowd. SWAT members raced by in full gear, guns across their chests. Children were pushed behind parents as the crowd opened a wide path.

Cruz climbed up next to Kroc. "What does he look like?"

"I didn't see his face."

"Wh-what?" He did a double take, certain he misheard.

"He wore a hood and his face was shaded. I couldn't see his features."

"But you're sure it's a him?"

"Absolutely. Under six-foot, trim build and fast."

"You're sure he's in here?"

"I saw him run in."

"Who's head of security?"

Kroc pointed to a man in his fifties walking back and forth along the front line. Cruz converged on the man at the same time as the SWAT team leader. The priority was to get the civilians out safely. Women and children were waved through more quickly. Bags were checked for clothing matching the description before leaving. Cleveland police scoured the parking lots, providing both a measure of safety and unrest to the families that raced to their vehicles.

For all the resources used, all the time spent, they came up empty-handed.

WHUMP

Win Ramsey's big hands slapped on his desk. "Whose idea was it to close down the zoo?"

"Mine, sir." Cruz stood tall, his chin lifted. There was no reason to back away, he'd do it again in a heartbeat. "Given Officer Kroc witnessing the suspect entering the zoo's main gates, it had to be done."

"Do you know what Mondays are at the zoo?"

"Free admission for county residents."

"Do you know how many people were at the zoo? Now I have the school superintendent breathing down my neck because there were school groups there. Did it occur to you locking it down could incite our suspect?"

He didn't believe the suspect would turn on the general population. It didn't fit his creed, his MO. He didn't say this to Chief Ramsey, who said beliefs were for churches and there was no place for them in policing. Facts. Information. Intelligence. That's what his police department acted on. Not beliefs.

Ramsey swung his gaze to Kroc. "The suspect approached you? Report."

"At approximately ten hundred hours, I was hitting base-balls in Brookside Park adjacent to the zoo. I observed several other people using the park for running and walking. One runner had completed two laps around the ballfields, running across the outfield grass. I was refilling the portable pitching machine I was using when I observed the runner standing at the mid-point in the fence along the first base side. He stood back from the fence, feet planted wide, hands clasped in front of him. You already have the description of his clothing."

"You saw his face?"

"I did not. The sun was behind him and his hood was up. His features were not distinct. At this point, I did not realize who the person was, still thinking it was a runner. The suspect looked at the fence. Something glinted in the sunlight. As I walked to the fence, he backed away. When I saw what hung there, I knew."

Ramsey grit his teeth. "What was it?"

"A medal on a silver chain. It was Michael, the archangel."

"Patron saint of cops." Cruz held the sealed bag to the chief. "It's clean."

Even in the evidence bag, the pendant looked a speck of dust in Ramsey's palm. "You didn't call it in?"

Kroc cleared his throat. "My phone and my keys were sitting on the third base bench. The fence was long enough that by the time I got around it, he would be gone."

"Did he talk to you?"

"No. He just looked at me. I had the impression of him smiling, like he was glad to see me. I don't know how long we stayed like that, then he backed away and ran. Not as though he were fleeing, but casually, like he was finishing his run. I went back for my keys and phone, but I could see him. He was faster than me, but I didn't give up. I came around the curve and was looking down the road when he turned into the main gate. I am absolutely, without a doubt, certain the suspect ran into the zoo."

"In the report, the only person zoo staff noted entering like he was being chased was you."

Cruz stepped forward. "The security cameras picked him up. As Kroc said, the suspect approached a gate attendant, showed ID and jogged in. The ID wasn't scanned, just verified for the county. The attendant didn't think a thing of it, runners are reportedly common early in the day. The suspect kept his head down, hood up. The attendant was only able to tell us the suspect had a Cleveland address, was quote 'lighter' skinned, and had no facial hair. He isn't picked up again on the security cameras. The working theory is he ran into a gift shop immediately inside the main gate, changing his clothes in some manner, and walked back out the gate. Six people exited the zoo between the time the suspect entered and Officer Kroc appeared."

Kroc shook his head. "I wasn't more than a minute or two behind him."

Ramsey's gaze stayed trained on Cruz. "You took a risk, Detective, the same risk I would have taken in your shoes. Be that as it may, I now have the schools, the Metroparks, and Sally Homemaker breathing down my neck. Find. Him. Dismissed."

Kroc walked out of the chief's office on fast strides. Cruz jogged to catch up, grabbed his elbow to stop him.

"There was something else, wasn't there. Something you didn't tell the chief."

Kroc looked at the scuffed floor. "It doesn't matter. If it did, I would have said something."

Cruz squeezed the arm he held. "Tell me, Kroc. I need to know."

"I asked him 'Why me.'" Kroc had the eyes of a haunted man.

"Did he answer?"

Kroc shook his head. "He made a fist and laid it over his heart. Then he left."

Cruz walked across the parking lot to his AA meeting with his head hanging low. The press conference gave him a throbbing headache. He stopped outside the door, watching people who carried the same burden step over the threshold. For the first time in two and a half years, he considered leaving. Just turning around and going home.

"One of those days, Cruz?" The woman who asked was

older by a decade, darker by a shade, and shorter by a head.

"It's been one of those weeks."

"Seems like every day is one of those weeks." She stepped back and held the door open.

Cruz walked through.

He sat in the meeting, white Styrofoam cup of weak coffee cupped in his hands. Voices spoke in turn, testimonies to ward off the demons, stories of battles won and lost. The tones droned on, melded together until they became a monotone hum seducing him into a thoughtless state.

His breathing slowed. His heart followed. Until, for a moment, there was just—his phone vibrating.

Cruz raised his lids enough to read the screen. He never took a call when in the meeting. Whatever Frankie Pelletier had to say could wait a goddamn hour.

When she called back thirty seconds later, Cruz rolled his eyes. She'd missed the press conference. Probably wanted a synopsis. It would wait.

Cruz sat up tall, tuning in to the speaker.

His phone buzzed again. A text.

SOS Drug Head found me.

Cruz snapped to his feet and sprinted out of the room. He pressed the button that rang through to Frankie's phone.

"She was here. Ohmygod she was here. In the bathroom." Panic ran the words into a single sound.

"Slow down. The suspect found you?"

"Yes. In the bathroom of a fro-yo. I flushed and then the door wouldn't open and then feet appeared on the other side and then she texted me."

"Fro-yo?"

"A frozen yogurt parlor. It's called Tasty Endings."

"Is the suspect still there?"

"I don't know. She told me to wait two minutes before I came out. That was when I called you. Do you think I can leave yet?"

He debated the idea. Frankie just might recognize the suspect and give him the break he needed. The suspect would absolutely recognize Frankie, though. It was a risk—

"I don't see her. I would recognize her shoes."

Decision made. "You went out?"

"Well, yeah. I thought maybe I could figure out who she was."

"Why do you keep saying 'she'?"

"Because she's a she!"

"She's a he."

"The person who just locked me in the bathroom was a woman. She had on women's shoes. Her voice was kinda gravelly, like listening to Janice Joplin."

"Stay where you are until the police get there. Do *not* take any more chances. I'm on my way."

It was past closing when Cruz reached the little store front business, but the lights were still on. Frankie sat at a table in the back while four of Akron's finest worked the room.

"You doing okay?" he asked, as he took the chair opposite her.

"Better now. Sorry I was freaked out on the phone. She just surprised me."

"Did he threaten you?"

"No, *she* didn't. *She* was calm."

"The suspect approached Nick this morning. He is certain it was a man."

She narrowed her gaze at him. "The suspect approached *me* thirty minutes ago. *I* am certain she was a woman."

Both of his witnesses were credible, neither had seen the suspect outright, both had full use of their faculties, neither expressed doubt. An accomplice?

"She spoke with you? What did she say?"

"We mostly texted." She pushed her phone to him. "I tried calling the number, but it just rings. No voicemail. I tried texting, but there's no response."

Even as he worked the phone, his temper lashed. "What part of 'do not take any more chances' didn't you get?"

"I'm sitting in a fro-yo surrounded by cops! How is this taking a risk?"

"The suspect knew where you were, knew your phone number. He...she...it probably knows where you live and your parents and the first boy you dated. The suspect is smart, coy, and blends in like a chameleon. You calling him, her may just make you their BFF. Did you ever think of that?"

She was quiet for a moment. "Isn't that what you wanted?"

Not this way. Shit. "Tell me the conversation."

"She liked my article. She said she is called to do what she's doing. Her job is to protect children. She believes that evil uses drugs to corrupt souls, rots them. She tried to, like, cure them, but it didn't work. The only thing she could do was free the soul. She does the post thing to warn others and to send a message to evil. It's all in the text."

He leafed through the conversation. "Five minutes. No one came into the bathroom."

"When I went out, there was a closed-for-maintenance sign in front of the door."

"You said you heard her voice. What did she say?"

"I asked her why me?" Her eyes glassed with tears. "She said I was kind. She asked me to tell Nick it was because 'he stands.'"

Wednesday, May 23

"Who is Drug Head? I'll tell you who Drug Head is. Drug Head is me!" The broad-faced black woman with her hair permed straight swung an arm out to the crowd behind her.

"Drug Head is everyone one of us who is sick and tired of the plague drugs and drug abuse are on our community."

A wiry black man nodded in agreement. "How many babies have to die before we say enough. Drug Head is doing what the cops can't do—driving drugs out of Cleveland."

A small white woman with mousy brown hair looked up at the interviewer. "It's not that we condone Drug Head's methods, but there's no dismissing his results."

A Hispanic woman looked into the camera, her hands on the shoulder of a tween. "All I know is my street is safer. The only thing on the corners are stop signs."

Win Ramsey stopped the video replay of the in-depth news program aired the previous night. "The rest are the same."

They knew that. Cruz knew everyone at the table—Dr. Chen, Alison Hyatt, Homicide Commander Montoya, Detective Matt Yablonski, Special Agent Bishop—had watched the show produced by one of the local news agencies.

The chief forwarded the video until Alison Hyatt's face filled the screen. Her styled hair, professional make up, and polished lines made a poignant statement in comparison to the raw and unrefined passion of the average man cuts. Her answers to the questions were professional, specific while being vague and as antiseptic as a bottle of Listerine.

Then came the cut away to Cruz. The news crew had caught him on the street, nagging him like a May midge, buzzing in his ear until he couldn't take it. He looked over his shoulder at the camera, his braided tail hanging to his shoulder blades. "No community is perfect. The sinners are ours every bit as much of the saints. I stand for them all."

If the average man was raw and Hyatt professional, Cruz looked dangerous. A predator on the hunt. Aurora had said it. So had the family and friends that called after it aired. At least five people stopped him on his way in to say something similar. He wished he felt as confident as the man on the screen. It would be a nice change from exhausted and frustrated.

"Nice interview, Detective," Ramsey said. "Next time, stick to the script. Where do we stand on recovering the bodies?"

"I can tell you five hundred places they aren't. It's a priority to find the bodies both for the families and for the evidence they could bring."

"Anything resulting from the Pelletier incident?"

"The shop did not have video security, but we have three things we didn't have before. White, male, clean shaven. The woman working remembered the suspect's shoes and added baggy clothes and a pulled-up hoodie. She said the suspect, male, purchased a small bowl yogurt, then sat at a table and read. When pressed on the gender, she said his hands were a man's. Rough, hair on the back and fingernails bitten low. She was working alone and hadn't noticed the bathroom being taken over. No one complained. The number that texted Pelletier was a disposable. The last cell tower ping put it at the yogurt shop."

"Doctor, has the information provided by Kroc and Ms. Pelletier been added to our profile?"

"As y'all expect, it confirmed some aspects of my theory. Clearly, the suspect is operating within an altered reality, one in which he recognizes anyone associated with the illegal drug sales, distribution and use as a physical threat to his children. We can infer, of course, by the location of the heads, he views the residents of the city as those children."

Chen consulted his notes. "The suspect has proven he is highly capable of planning and executing complex scenarios."

"Pelletier is insistent the suspect was female. How confident are we she is wrong?" Ramsey turned the conversation back to Cruz. "Have you started investigating a potential female as a suspect?"

"The only name that popped on multiple victims was Hayley Parker. We had brought her husband in for questioning twice. She had the connection to one victim through high school and then several of the others through her husband."

"Bring her in."

* * *

Yablonski had volunteered for the job of bringing Hayley Parker in. Damn but Cruz did not like Hayley for these crimes. She just wasn't together enough to pull off something this complicated without tipping someone off, somewhere.

Still, he went back through the files and mapped the connections between Hayley Parker to the victims, most through her husband. But that was an assumption. Maybe Parker met them through Hayley.

Before he knew it, Yablonski hovered over his desk. "She brought her kid with her."

"What? Why did you let her do that?" Not part of his game plan, interviewing the mother in front of the kid. Wasn't going to happen.

"There was no one to watch him. The father was out. Since we weren't arresting her, we didn't have a lot of choices."

"Where is he now?"

"In the interview room."

"Get him out here. He can eat cookies over your keyboard while I talk to the mother." He picked up the phone and told the officer on the other end to bring the kid out.

"My keyboard? You think…no, Cruzie. Ain't gonna happen."

Two minutes later, it happened. Cruz spent a few minutes with the boy sitting in Yablonski's chair playing detective.

Jace's blue eyes narrowed as he considered the man facing him. "How much is two plus two."

Cruz mirrored the boy's position. "Four."

"What song am I humming. Hmm hmm mmm mmm—"

"Twinkle twinkle."

"Which is the best ninja turtle?"

"Michelangelo."

"Wrong." Jace collapsed on the desk in laughter. "You're

going to jail, Cruz."

His interview with Hayley Parker didn't go as well. The only alibis she had needed a drug dealer or a five-year-old to corroborate.

"Have you followed the Drug Head case," he asked her.

"A bit."

"What do you think of it? Of someone killing the drug dealers, staking their heads on poles?"

She shrugged a boney shoulder, her gaze on the floor where it had been since he walked in.

"Why do you think he does it? What does he get from it?" He paused after each question, but she didn't answer. She didn't acknowledge the question.

"Somebody is out there stalking and killing drug dealers. Have you thought about what that means to you? To your son?" His words shortened, hardened in proportion to his frustration. The woman didn't have the sense of a—

"Christopher takes care of us." She rubbed her eyes with the back of her hand, but the worn-out look didn't go away. "He knows people. They don't come to the house. Where's Jace? I don't want him getting in trouble."

Knowing when to cut his losses, he wrapped it up. Getting Hayley out of the interview was simple. Getting Jace out of homicide? Much harder. It cost him a candy bar and two peppermints. The kid was a born negotiator. That was a tragedy Cruz had a hard time stomaching, the kids who never had a chance at normal.

Yablonski reclaimed his seat, adjusting the throne for his legs. "You like her for it? Being the accomplice?"

"I'm trying to picture Hayley Parker taking the family car, parking on the side of a highway, taking the stake and the head and getting busy. The ghost of a woman would have left footprints and fingerprints and likely DNA, just because she wouldn't have thought not to. We need to look somewhere else."

May 24

Today was an amazing day. I went downtown and there were so many good people there. We talked and sang and prayed. I couldn't stop moving. It was like my feet had their own mission and it was to dance. There was so much energy, the whole city vibrated.

The army of the people is rising. The message is getting out and people are listening. I have to push now, push the evil out.

CHAPTER NINETEEN

Thursday, May 24

Marches and counter-marches were the order of the morning. The accounts of the facts were overshadowed by the bling of self-promotion.

All roads through downtown weren't blocked, just one.

A pregnant woman wasn't trapped in her car. The passing Jimmy John's delivery man did not deliver the baby.

Windows weren't broken. A plant stand wasn't used as a battering ram, but one was turned over. Too many people standing on one side.

The ghost of Eliot Ness did not patrol the square. Probably. That one wasn't disproven.

But, six people were injured, and four arrests were made.

And the chief was not happy.

216-555-1255 CPL W25TH STREET
25MAY2018 15:59 SEND: COMPLETE

Saint Michael the Archangel, defend us in battle.

Be our protection against the malice and snares of the devil.

Through us, may God rebuke him I humbly pray and do thou, O Prince of the Heavenly host, by the power of God, thrust into hell Satan and all evil spirits who wander through the world for the ruin of souls.

Saint Michael the Archangel, lead us in battle.

Be our light through the dark alleys and shadows where evil thrives.

Let us be your instrument, I humbly pray.

Teach us, O mightiest of angels, to shelter the worthy while vanquishing to hell those that have been corrupted beyond redemption.

CHAPTER TWENTY

Friday, May 25

"I will not tolerate another incident with this holiday. Do you understand, Detective De La Cruz?"

Cruz bent backwards under the weight of Win Ramsey, both the man and his office. He'd worked day and night on a strategy to cover the city during the popular Memorial Day weekend. He'd been buoyed by two pots of coffee and a mug of tea because you have to have balance in your life. His stomach felt off. He needed more coffee. "To our knowledge, he does not have a victim in hand, but we have added patrols to get ahead of the suspect." He pointed to the map laid on the conference table. "We have mapped the locations considered most likely for the suspect to strike. There are two high-speed, limited-access roads remaining, the West Shoreway and I-176. I formed a team of those familiar with the case, and they will work with the Districts to stakeout the Cleveland corporate limits."

"Wasn't the last crime scene in University Circle? Last I checked, it is not a high-speed thoroughfare."

"In our opinion, University Circle was precipitated by a unique set of circumstances. We expect the suspect will return to his original pattern."

"You expect. You are aware this is Memorial Day weekend. We have the rib cook-off, the Greek festival, and a half-dozen other events." Ramsey lowered his gaze, looking at

Cruz as though he were a defensive back needing a pounding. "We can't be everywhere, Detective."

"No, sir, we can't."

"Drug Head Killer is changing our community, Cruz. Socially, economically, psychologically. The organizations key to the import of illegal drugs into the city have shifted their sales to the suburbs and other communities. Latest estimates have drug trafficked into the city last month down forty percent from a year ago. However, the street value is about the same. When supply is cut, prices go up."

"And buyers are having to go farther for their fix," Yablonski said. "Our snitches are telling us nobody wants to work the street corners these days. It's pushing sales underground and out of town."

"Which," Hyatt said, "has neighborhood groups celebrating."

The downside came from gang intervention. With turfs shrinking, the competition for control was increasing. Gang-on-gang violence had ticked up in the past months. It wasn't unlike the race for a presidential party nomination but with smaller words, fewer dollars, and politer rhetoric. Dangerously, civilians had taken stands. Injuries to date had been minor, superficial, further empowering neighborhoods to stand. Cruz worried that somewhere, sometime, the price would be deadly. But even on that point, there was not unanimity. Policing is most successful when people feel part of the system rather than subject to it. Those taking to the street were standing for the rules that made the city part of one nation, under God, indivisible, with liberty and justice for all.

Cruz raised his hand, measuring the sun's distance above the horizon. "Two inches," he said, driving through the streets with his windows down. The temperature was meant for taking a pretty woman out on the town. Aurora could put on her little black dress and the purple heels that put them eye to eye. There was a party. It was Vito's birthday and everyone would have a good time. Food. Music. Wine. They'd have wine. *She'd* have wine, but he would taste it on her lips.

"Son of a bitch. Whose car is that?"

Parked in his driveway was a Lexus. The body style was nearly a decade old, but it was in pristine condition and sitting exactly where it shouldn't be.

He stomped into his house, shutting the door loud enough to let whoever was here know he was home. And not happy.

Aurora's voice floated to him. He stalked to his living room, stopping in the doorway. If he'd been a dog, the fur on the back of his neck would be standing up. "What are you doing here?"

"Zeus!" Aurora was on her feet, bridging the distance between him and the woman sitting on his couch. Frankie Pelletier. "Where are your manners? I'm sorry, Frankie."

"Don't apologize for me," he snapped, taking Aurora's hand and pulling her behind him. "What are you doing here? How did you find me?"

Frankie Pelletier rose from his couch. Wearing blue jeans and a Cleveland Indians jersey, she wasn't dressed for the job. Her hair was pulled back in a ponytail, her face bare except for the worry it wore. "I get why you don't want to talk with me, after the whole he/she thing, but I need talk to you."

"You have my number. Go home and call me."

"Zeus!" Aurora shoved him into the room. "The Drug Head Killer contacted her again."

"It's another fax," Frankie said, "from a library I think." She held out a neatly folded paper.

Saint Michael the Archangel, defend us in battle.

Be our protection against the malice and snares of the devil.

Through us, may God rebuke him I humbly pray

and do thou, O Prince of the Heavenly host, by the power of God, thrust into hell
Satan and all evil spirits who wander through the world for the ruin of souls.

Saint Michael the Archangel, lead us in battle.
Be our light through the dark alleys and shadows where evil thrives.
Let us be your instrument, I humbly pray
Teach us, O mightiest of angels, to shelter the worthy while vanquishing to hell those that have been corrupted beyond redemption.

"Creepy," Aurora said, running her hands up and down her arms.

"I know the first part," he said. "It's the prayer of St. Michael the Archangel. The second part, I don't recognize."

"That's because it's not part of the prayer," Frankie said. "At least no version I could find."

Aurora sat on the couch, encouraging Frankie to relax again. "It's dark. Dark, heavy, and violent."

He read it twice, looking for the message between the lines. This was dangerous. He felt like he held the invitation to disaster. He let it drop to the coffee table. "Are you printing it?"

"That's what I wanted to talk to you about. I completely, one hundred fifty percent, believe in freedom of the press." Frankie popped up, pacing in a small, two-step move. "I believe that society is better when we know what is happening in the world around us. To make good decisions, right decisions, people have to be informed. Fairly, honestly, and without bias."

"I hear a but."

She slapped her palms on her denim clad thighs. "That's just it. There shouldn't be a but."

"But there is."

"But, if I reprint material sent to me by a killer, maybe not a manifesto but definitely a message, what is fair and without bias about that? There is no..." She struggled for a word. "Honor. There is no honor in being a mouthpiece for a killer."

She was in a tough place, he agreed. She would be scrutinized no matter what decision she made. Which made it a dilemma, standing on a mountaintop with long, sheer drops on all sides. "Have you talked with your editor?"

Frankie looked at his shoes. Guilt, he guessed. "I know what he's going to say. I need to decide what I'm going to do before I go to him. It could be the end of my job."

"So, you came here."

She looked up now, her blue eyes years older than when they first met. "I didn't plan to." Frankie looked down at Aurora, who jumped to her side.

"I insisted she come in."

Cruz plopped into one of his chairs, pulled his braid to the front and began to unweave it. "Talk."

"I didn't ask for this to happen," Frankie began. Cruz listened. Aurora ordered Chinese. It wasn't so different from his AA meetings, people listening to each other, in support. It was nearly Sunday when Frankie left. She still hadn't decided what she was going to do about the fax. Cruz felt otherwise.

On the front porch, he cut Frankie a break. "Don't beat yourself up on the gender thing. You saw exactly what the suspect wanted you to see. We caught our first break when he went to see you. I'll catch him, no matter what you choose to do with that."

"Thank you. I, uh, really appreciate you saying that."

Aurora opened her arms and hugged Frankie. "Call or come over anytime. Our door is always open."

They stood together, Aurora waving as their guest pulled away, then closed the house for the night.

"I'm not okay with that," he said when they were in their bedroom. "For the record, I am not okay with Frankie

Pelletier coming to our house anytime."

She stripped off her shirt, waiving off his hard line. "She needed to talk."

He peeled off his pants, throwing them into the laundry basket. "My work doesn't come here."

She shimmied out of her jeans, laughing. "You aren't serious."

He undid enough buttons to pull his shirt over his head. "Dead serious."

"Baby, your work is here every day. Twenty-four-seven. Sometimes, I think this bed isn't big enough for the three of us."

"No." He worked his ass off to keep his work life and his life with Aurora distinct and separate. "Here? It's just me and you."

In the camisole she liked best, she slid between the covers, lying on her side with her head propped on her hand. "You believe that, don't you?"

He pulled on his sleep pants, crawled into bed, and kicked the sheets into obedience until he mirrored her position. "Yes, I do."

Her fingers traced the scars by his eye. "When are you going to accept me as a part of your life? Your whole life."

"You are my life, baby. The best part." Tiring of the conversation, he pulled her against his body and got busy distracting her.

Monday, May 28

Cruz sat up in bed, reading his daily reflections with the sound of Aurora's shower in the background. This morning she sang a spiritual, a classic, "Amazing Grace." A beautiful song…except she couldn't hit the high notes.

The words resonated. He felt lost. It had been over six

months since Uncle Hall's head was found. All the advances in technology and forensics had gotten him nowhere. Nobody was that perfect. He took a risk using Kroc and Frankie. They'd gotten closer than ever before to the phantom they hunted but still had little.

He returned his focus to the words of those who had walked in the steps before him. He focused on the good in life. Case in point: Aurora's naked body.

"I feel guilty that you have to work all day while I get to play." She rooted through the shared dresser, giving him an R-rated profile view.

"Hazards of the job. I'll be happier knowing you are enjoying the holiday."

She stepped into blue panties that disappeared between the globes of her perfect ass. "Really?"

"Really. It's your family's barbecue, you should be there."

She selected a matching bra, put her arms through the straps, then hooked the back. "It is a tradition and grows every year. I think my parents expect over a hundred people to show. Can you imagine? It's more like a reunion than a family barbecue. Friends, neighbors, my parents' co-workers, everyone comes. Last year, my prom date showed up. I had to put on the dress I had made myself. Of course, my mother kept it."

Family picnic, to Cruz, did not include ex-boyfriends. He could picture her laughing as boys and friends alike encircled her, a single, beautiful woman. Vultures.

"What's wrong?" she asked.

He slid out of bed as she fastened the button on her silver pants. His hands were fast, pulling her back to his chest, her clothed buttocks against his morning cockstand. "Maybe I should go with you. Armed." He brushed aside her hair and nipped her neck.

She looked over her shoulder at him. "You're being silly."

He chortled at the thought of being something a benign as

silly with her being half-naked and talking about ex-boy-friends being at the picnic. "You aren't even in the right ball-park, baby."

She turned and took his face in her hands. "I love you."

"I love you. What time will you be back?"

"I don't know. I'll help clean up, then I want to stop at the store to get supplies for a project with the kids. Maybe the grocery store, too."

"Have fun, baby, but not too much fun." Cruz kissed her soundly on the lips.

She giggled. "Silly. Happy hunting, Detective."

There was no happy hunting, which was a good thing. He kept reminding himself it was a good thing. On Cruz's re-commendation, the commander had authorized overtime. Lots of overtime. Cruz knew exactly how many police offers were staked out around the city instead of picnic tables be-cause the chief made a point of telling him.

But nothing happened.

Nothing. Zilch. Nada.

A team had staked out the remaining limited access high-ways since two hours before sunset Saturday night. The rib cook-off was a rousing but uneventful success. So was the Greek Festival and everything else. Good weather put every-one in the mood for a party.

Except Cruz. He kicked the shit out of a garbage can, frustrated at the nothingness of the day.

Cruz walked in the door as his AA meeting was starting. He fixed a cup of coffee and settled into a chair, intending to lis-ten but he couldn't hear a thing. The stories and experience of the others were drowned out by the noise in his head. He sipped the coffee, found it cold. One by one, the others filed by him. Time was up.

Tuesday, May 29

Eight in the morning, Cruz was working his way through his second cup of coffee and headlines from around the region featuring the growing debate: sinner or saint.

Yablonski sat a few feet away, watching three televisions are once.

"How are you following any of it?" Cruz asked.

He stroked his beard. "I'm a talented guy, gifted with multi-tasking skills far superior to mortal man."

Cruz snorted a laugh. His phone rang. "Hey, baby, aren't you supposed to be teaching?"

"Zeus, I'm worried."

"What happened?" He sat up straighter, which had Yablonski doing the same thing.

"Jace Parker isn't in school today. His mother called in that he fell and broke his arm. I mean, maybe he did but... I'm worried maybe he didn't."

"Yablonski and I will do a drive-by."

"Thanks. I'll feel better. Love you," she said before hanging up.

"What do we got?"

"The kid, Jace Parker. Aurora said his mother called him off school because of a broken arm." He pulled on his bullet-proof vest, checked his weapon, then shoved two snack-sized candies in his pocket.

Yablonski did the same, except for the candy. "I'll drive."

Minutes later, they pulled in front of the Parker house. Jace sat on the driveway playing with cars. His left arm was in a cast from the palm of his hand to near his shoulder. His right cheek was swollen and bruised.

Jace jumped and then grinned when he recognized the man stalking up the drive. "Hi, Cruz. Do you have any candy?"

Taking a knee, he pasted a smile on his face while inside

he raged at the violence this boy lived with. "I might. What do you think? M&Ms or gummy worms?"

His blue eyes flickered with mischief. "Can I have both?"

"Yeah, but don't tell Detective Yablonski. He's a candy thief." He looked over his shoulder to where the bald man with a copper-wire beard walked around the car.

"I like him. He gave me crackers and pop."

"He's a good guy." He returned Jace's smile, then asked quietly. "What happened to your arm? Your face?"

Jace looked at the cracked concrete under his legs.

"Jace. I'm sorry, buddy."

His face lifted then, blue eyes true and honest. "You didn't do nothing, Cruz. I was bad."

"What are you doing here?" Hayley Parker stood on the front porch with a narrow glare that threw daggers at Cruz and Yablonski.

Yablonski laid a hand on Cruz's shoulder when he would have popped up.

"We have a few questions, ma'am. Is your husband home?"

"No, he's not, and I don't have to answer your questions."

"You do," Yablonski said, "but it's your choice to do it here or back downtown. You can have an attorney present if you want."

Hayley ran her fingers through her hair, taking thick fists of it and pulling. "Why can't you just leave us alone!"

Cruz stood now. "Who did this to Jace?"

She wrapped her arms over the stomach. "He fell." She said nothing else but looked around, desperate to get back in the house.

Yablonski stepped forward. "Let's talk about this downtown."

"No. No," she said. "What do you want to know?"

"What happened to Jace?" Cruz asked.

She spoke slowly, quietly. "He was naughty. He had to be taught a lesson, is all. Then he fell."

"Did you push him or your husband?"

She looked in his eyes. "I'd never hurt Jace."

"Where is he, Mrs. Parker? Where is your husband?"

"What are you going to do?"

Yablonski answered. "Child abuse is a serious crime."

"But, but, he didn't mean to do it. It was an accident. Tell them Jace. Tell them it was an accident."

With the full attention of three adults on him, Jace froze. All color fell from his little face, leaving the purple of the bruise that much more grotesque.

Cruz positioned his body to protect Jace from sight. "You don't have to answer, buddy. This wasn't your fault."

"It was yours," his mother threw with venom. "If you would just stay out of our lives, we would be fine."

Yablonski stepped closer, his whiskey voice soft. "Did he beat you, too? Are there bruises under that sweatshirt? This is your chance to break the cycle."

"By handing you my husband? What will I do without him?"

"Live. Provide a home for you and Jace. One without accidents."

Tears poured down her face. "I...I don't have a job. I can't feed us."

"There are people who can help," Yablonski said, holding out his hand. "You just have to ask. Tell us where your husband is. That's the first step." She hesitated but stepped closer. "Don't be a statistic. There's too many sad stories in this city. Be a survivor. Be an exception."

She looked between Yablonski and her house, Yablonski and her son, her son and his broken arm. She whispered the name of a bar.

"What's happening?" Jace asked.

"Daddy's going to go away for a little while, somewhere

he can't hurt us anymore."

Jace frowned. "Will they hurt him?"

"No," Cruz said, seeing a boy's concern for his father. "He'll stay in jail and appear in court. A judge will decide what happens but, no, the police won't hurt him. That's not what we do."

Cruz and Yablonski spent most of the day shuttling between meetings. The chief's office felt more like the principal's. The meeting in the commander's office was like being raked over the coals by an accountant. Numbers, numbers, and more fucking numbers. The temporary help he had for the weekend was gone. Yablonski stayed because of the inarguable tie to narcotics.

And just when Cruz thought his head was going to split open and spew out the few remaining brain cells he had, they went to a meeting with the community's religious leaders on the state of the Drug Head killings. Pastor Michael Ashford attended, his rhetoric toned down by his own experience with the vigilante. Father Alejandro Ruiz from Sagrada Familia was there. Cruz tried to dodge him before Catholic guilt caught him by the gonads. The meeting was four hours long. F.O.U.R. The only consensus was praise Jesus.

"I need a beer," Yablonski said, his beard twisted and bent to the side.

"Me too," Cruz said. Yablonski punched his arm. Hard. "Ouuuch."

"Not funny, you bastard. Let's go throw some darts. Call our ladies, eat some bar food, throw some darts."

Erin came straight from work wearing her scrubs.

Cruz leaned back when she'd have kissed his cheek. "You don't take care of anyone contagious, right? Maybe you should scrub first."

She grabbed his head and kissed him full on the mouth.

"Coward."

Moments later, a miniature tornado blew the door open. Bodies flew left and right as a Tasmanian Devil resembling his girlfriend tore through the restaurant. Cruz set his drink down just as a hundred and twenty pounds landed in his arms.

"Guess what? Guesswhat guesswhat guesswhat?" Aurora didn't wait for an answer. "I'm having an art show!" She radiated sheer joy. Pure happiness.

"That's wonderful, baby!"

"Oh. My. God!" Erin punctuated each word. "When? Where? We are so going, Matt."

"Okay, okay," Aurora said to calm herself. "I got a call from Urban Spaces. It's an upscale gallery in Tremont. They have a show starting June 15 and had an artist drop out. They invited me to take his spot."

Aurora grabbed Erin's hands. They jumped up and down together, howling like a couple of teenage girls.

"How did they get your name?" Cruz asked. The women looked at him, scowling. "I mean it's great. Rahhh." Jazz hands. "You're going to knock their socks off, baby. I just wondered how they found you."

"Frankie made the connection."

"Frankie? Pelletier?"

"Yes," Aurora said, jumping on heels not meant to leave the earth. "The mother of one of her high school friends owns Urban Spaces. She pictures she took the paintings I have in the house and shared them. Isn't that great!"

"Sure. Yeah. Did you know she was photographing your art?"

Aurora put her hands on his shoulders. "Stop. Just for five minutes, stop being a cop and be the boyfriend of an almost famous artist."

Those green eyes, as honest and true as the blue ones he had to look in this morning made him want to be a better man. He pulled her hard against his chest and spun her in a circle until they fell into a table with laughter.

"I've never done an art show," Cruz said. "What do we need to do?"

"I have two weeks to deliver twelve pieces. I've already decided on most of them. I have to call my mom and see if she'll loan me the painting I did for her birthday. Oh, and I have fabulous idea for a new painting. It's big. Like. *Big.* Hmm, I don't think it'll fit up the stairs."

"I'll clear out the garage. I'll build you a studio if that's what you need." When she locked her mouth to his, kissing him until he saw stars, he figured he'd finally said the right thing.

CHAPTER TWENTY-ONE

Monday, June 4

"Five more days!"

Cruz cracked open his lids to radiant green eyes. "I thought kids were the ones counting down to the last day of school."

Aurora snorted a laugh and ruffed his mess of hair. "Nobody looks forward to summer like a teacher. Why do you think we all took this job?"

She wore a crazy Azteca-patterned skirt and an off-white, sleeveless shirt that showed the figure he loved to touch. Her hair hung loose today. A yard of dark curls against the creamy backdrop. He fingered one hanging over her breast.

"You have a little time yet, don't you?"

She deftly slipped his grip. "What you have in mind takes more than a little time."

"I can be quick."

She snorted again. "That isn't something to brag about." She smiled when he frowned. "We'll have plenty of time tonight. I'll see you after your meeting?"

"Absolutely. Well..."

She held up her hand. "I know. Unless something comes up." Then she cocked an eyebrow, quickly undid two buttons and flashed him.

"What are you doing?"

"Giving you incentive to see that you're the only thing

that comes up tonight. Happy hunting, Detective." She ran out of the room, laughter trailing behind her. Since the invite to the art show, she'd been walking on air.

True to his word, Cruz cleaned out half the garage for her latest piece. She worked on it daily, which meant she was practically living with him. She didn't bring it up so neither did he.

The back door closed and then his truck door. Her car officially died the week before. He had considered bribing the mechanic to put the beast to an end, but he didn't have to. Aurora had loved the little car. Too bad it was held together by rust and memory. Last time he was in it, they hit a pot hole, and he got road rash on his feet. The last bolt finally gave, and his truck became unofficially hers, giving him one less thing to worry about.

While his professional life circled the toilet bowl, home life was damn good. He could think of nothing that would make it better. Love waited for him in the form of his coffee and microwaved Jimmy Dean breakfast sandwich. He sat at his dining room table, happy as he ate and read his daily reflection.

His phone rang. Dispatch. He took the call, then made one to Yablonski. "Meet me on the West Shoreway at the corporate limits."

"Shit," Yablonski said. "I hoped when we got through Memorial Day, it was a sign."

"I hear you. Get ready for a long day."

A tent was up to screen the audience. And there was an audience. The strip of land that was the center of attention buffered the West Shoreway from Edgewater Park, a beach front park on Lake Erie. The park was popular for walkers this time of day, most of whom were curious about ten police vehicles lined up like freight train cars.

Cruz stood on the edge of the scene, arms crossed, not liking a damn thing he saw. "Everything's wrong."

Yablonski mirrored his posture and attitude. "Not one thing is right. Isn't even a half-decent copycat."

"Did you recognize the victim?"

"No. I snapped a photo and sent it to my guys."

In the tall grass, the head sat, nose to the ground, near the bottom on a hill. The stake it had been impaled up still stood near the crest of the hill, which became the shoulder of the road.

Yablonski's phone chimed with a text. "D'Andre Latti-more. That name sounds familiar."

Cruz knew it. "My profile list. Tony Gentile and Ester Moorehouse."

"Yeah. That's right. Lattimore is the dealer accused of killing three teens including Gentile's younger brother and Moorehouse's son."

"Moorehouse said Lattimore was out and she was upset about it. Let's track her down. I'd like to know where she's been the last twenty-four hours. Gentile, too."

"Detectives?" Crime scene called. "Have something for you."

In the scrub brush that fought for space between the grass and the beach was a pool of vomit. Deep in the green foliage, it wasn't more than fifteen feet from where the head had come to rest.

The sand was thick and moved easily under foot, but at this transition point, from beach to grass, the sand was thinner, harder. "We have a boot print. Three of them." Cruz lifted his chin. "Eyes open, people. This suspect left footprints all over the scene."

"This is going to sound obscene, but it has to be said."

Cruz raised an eyebrow to his friend.

"A mess like this makes you respect the professionalism of the Drug Head Killer."

Cruz rolled his eyes, shook his head.

"Did you see the butcher job on the neck?"

"That's an insult to butchers everywhere."

"And vomiting on your own crime scene? Not even in the same league as Drug Head."

"Thank God for that."

"Goes without saying. Did you notice...this isn't the Cleveland corporate limit? That's another coupla miles at West One Seventeenth Street."

"This scares me, Yablonski. A copycat? Last thing this city needs is a pride of copycats deciding who deserves to live and who deserves to die."

A uniform met Cruz and Yablonski as they walked into the department. "Ester Moorehouse is waiting in interview."

"That's some fast work," Yablonski said, clapping him on the shoulder as he passed by. "How did you get her so quickly?"

"She was parading around the Justice Center. That woman can move. I pulled the file on Lattimore and reports from his cases. They are on your desk, Cruz. Made a fresh pot of coffee for you."

It was good when people knew you, Cruz thought, refilling his go cup with strong coffee. Then he picked up the pages Yablonski set down and read. Lattimore was a small-time dealer, selling to support his own habit. His sheet was filled with petty crimes dating back to his eighteenth birthday and, he expected, well before that. Lattimore's story was he was standing on the street corner, minding his own business, of course, when three teens approached him. They demanded drugs and, when he didn't have any, one pulled a knife and demanded money. Fearing for his life, Lattimore pulled the gun he has holding for a friend and had no idea it was stolen. Everything after that was a blur, then he was standing, and his attackers weren't.

Lattimore had run, concerned there could be others. The

woman whose garage he ran into called the police. The knife was recovered. The only prints on it were those of Jimmy Gentile. The gun was recovered. The only prints on it were Lattimore's. No drugs were found on Lattimore, Gentile, Moorehouse or their friend.

Lattimore was charged with three counts of manslaughter. He was assigned a public defender and refused to plea. He was held as his case proceeded. Dates were pushed back several times for various reasons. Bail had recently been posted by his grandmother.

File in hand, Cruz went to the interview room, pausing to observe the suspect through the glass. Ester Moorehouse sat patiently, her gaze on her hands. Her fingers drummed on the table top, the only sign of impatience.

"Good morning, Mrs. Moorehouse. This is Detective Yablonski." Cruz read her her rights, which got her full attention.

"Why are you saying that?"

"I have to, ma'am. Do you understand your rights?"

"I understand them. I don't understand why you're reading them to me."

"Ma'am, can you account for your whereabouts the last twenty-four hours?"

"Yes," she said. "Do I need an attorney?"

"It is your right to have one present."

She sat quietly, searching his face. "Why am I here?"

"D'Andre Lattimore was found dead this morning." He said it matter-of-factly, almost cruelly, watching for a reaction.

Ester Moorehouse jumped to her feet, her chair toppled to the floor. Yablonski leapt to his feet, hand on his weapon, ready to step in front of Cruz. Her gaze stayed riveted to Cruz's face, but her hands trembled. Her mouth opened, but no sound came out. The seconds stretched into a daunting silence.

Cruz broke the silence, but not the tension. "Mrs. Moorehouse, where were you from noon yesterday?"

Her hand went to her stomach, her fingers splayed over her figureless middle. "I...uh...I think. He is?" Her knees gave way. She knelt on the hard, cold floor. Her forehead rested against the edge of the table, her forearms encircled her head.

There was a sound then. The high-pitched laugh of hysteria. When she lifted her head, her eyes were wild, saliva dripped from her mouth. "Where was I? Where was I? I was here! Check your cameras. Eight hours a day I slept, four I ate and bathed, and the other twelve I was here. Marching and walking and walking and marching because what else does a childless mother do? I really want to know because, because it's over. There is nothing left to march for." Her voice faded, her chin fell to her chest and she cried. They were not tears of celebration, of a final justice, but the tears of a woman who had lost everything. "He's...he's dead?"

"Yes, ma'am," Cruz said.

"How?"

"It's under investigation."

"Did the Drug Head Killer get him?"

Cruz looked at Yablonski before answering. "It was made to look that way, but no."

"But he's dead. Just like that. It's over."

Neither Cruz nor Yablonski responded.

"I...I thought it would feel different." Her colorless face showed nothing but misery. "I was marching. Alone. That criminal just walked away while my son, while those boys never had a chance to grow up. It wasn't fair." Her voice cracked, rising in pitch as she struggled to talk. "I thought I would feel satisfied in the end. Something. But it doesn't fix anything, does it? My baby's still gone. My baby's still gone."

* * *

Gentile hadn't showed for work that day or the day before. His foreman reported he'd been acting strange for the last week and had gone as far as to have him drug tested. The results were negative. A black and white met Cruz at the home of Tony Gentile. Yablonski held the screen door while Cruz pounded on the front door.

"Anthony Gentile. Cleveland police. Open up." There was sound beyond the door. High pitched chiming, like the crashing of glasses. "Tony? It's Detective De La Cruz. I need to talk to you about D'Andre Lattimore." Heavier thuds. A muffled curse. Cruz was ready to okay the forced entry when the deadbolt turned. The white panel steel door opened, and Tony Gentile fell out, reeking of alcohol and vomit.

Cruz caught him before he hit the ground.

"It was awful. It was...it was..." Tony heaved, and Cruz tossed him to the side, letting him empty his gut over an overgrown azalea bush.

Tony's shoulders trembled, convulsed. He turned his head to Cruz, his olive complexion as pale as paste. His eyes were bloodshot, underscored by dark bags. "How does he do it? How does he stand it?"

Cruz didn't have to ask who he was talking about, none of them did. "You going to throw up again, Tony?"

"Maybe." He stood tall, fingers curled like claws into the banister, taking deep breaths. "I'm done."

"Let's go in the house and talk."

From booking, Cruz went to D'Andre Lattimore's grandmother. Faith Ernwell lived in a small apartment in a large building with hallways smelling of mold and a dried cocktail of life. The apartment was neat but sparse. There were no extras in her life, yet she had posted the bond. Sad eyes in a round face peeked under the chain on the door. He did his duty and walked away worried Gentile had killed her, too.

Now he sat in Montoya's office, feeling as though this one day had lasted three. There was no joy in arresting Tony Gentile. He had confessed, providing ample and graphic details. Crime scene collected the evidence from his home, his business, his truck. Sobering had driven Gentile into a dark place. Cruz put him on suicide watch for his own safety.

"Good work today," Montoya said. "You closed the case within hours and well before the six o'clock news. Ramsey was happy."

"I hope it discourages any other potential copy cats." Silver lining. "Anything new from Kroc or Pelletier?"

"You would have heard. The suspect has gone silent. Again." Montoya was annoyed. It came through in the flat, low tone of voice, the bite at the end of his words.

"Is there a problem, Commander?"

"Jesus, I want to say upfront I know it's bullshit. You have the chief and my backing on this."

He sat up tall, his mind racing through scenarios but settling on nothing. "What?"

"Internal affairs is looking into your relationship with a boy, Jace Parker."

Cruz stood. "What do you mean looking into? What relationship?"

"You arrested his father."

"Christopher Parker. He broke the kid's arm. Yeah, I arrested him."

"He has accused you of having an inappropriate relationship with his son."

Cruz stood there, waiting for Montoya to say it was a bad joke, but it didn't come. "That's disgusting." Outraged curled his upper lip. "I have done nothing inappropriate or improper with that or any other child."

"Prepare yourself, the internal affairs bureau will be thorough. My advice? Get an attorney."

An attorney. What the hell was going on. "Am I suspended?"

"No, pending the outcome of the investigation. Jesus..."

Cruz walked out of Montoya's office, out of the department, out of the building. He stood on the corner of Lakeside and Ontario and felt nothing. He was numb. How could anyone think that he...

He started to walk. Blocks later, the numbness faded as his mind began to work.

Betrayal. He worked his ass off trying to catch a serial killer only to be accused of the single lowest form of human behavior.

Anger. He wanted to take Christopher Parker by the neck and...and...

Frustration. Impotency. Helplessness. There was nothing to do but wait for it to happen.

The streets were nearly empty when his walk brought him back to the garage. The streets of downtown emptied fast on a weeknight. Folks headed home to families.

Cruz drove to the place that was home every Monday night. He was late. The parking lot had a dozen cars clustered near the entrance, but there was nobody outside. Cruz backed into a spot, put it in park. He didn't turn the engine off. He just stared at the plain brick building. Why did he come here week after week? The coffee was horrible, and the chair killed his back. What did he hope to find in there? Help? There was no help.

Cruz shifted the car back in gear.

Two hours later, he pulled into his driveway. He had run out of places to go. Aurora was home. He had hoped she would be out. With her sisters. With her friends. He wanted to be alone.

Aurora walked out of the garage wearing a pair of micro-short bib overalls and a neon pink sports bra. Cruz looked over his shoulder to where his leech of a neighbor would be watching. The curtains moved. He was sure of it.

"What the hell are you wearing?" He snapped at Aurora, hating the idea she was on display in his own backyard.

She looked down at herself. "Just an old pair of shorts."

"Where's your shirt? There's more of you uncovered than covered."

She flashed a saucy smile. "You usually like that."

"Not in my backyard!"

She ran her hand up and down his arm. "Bad day?"

"No. Shit, Aurora, is there paint on your hands? Damn it. This shirt is ruined." He tore off the shirt and stuffed it in the garbage can.

"I'm sorry. I wasn't thinking."

"No, you weren't but what's new. Did you think about making dinner?" He stalked to the back door.

"Why don't you jump in the shower, wash the day away." Her soft voice, full of concern, followed him. "I can make us something to eat, then we can sit and talk about what has you spitting nails."

Talk. That was the last thing he wanted to do. "I'm not hungry. A shower sounds good then I'm going to bed."

Tuesday, June 5

Cruz sat at his desk, the sun just cresting the horizon. He read reports from various departments and support personnel, wishing one of them, just one of them could write in English. What was happening to the education system that professional men and women couldn't put a noun-verb-noun together.

He pushed away from his desk hard enough to send his chair into the wall behind him, making a dent in the abused plaster. He swore under his breath as he stomped to the coffee pot. He'd made it himself. He'd drunk half of it himself.

He'd left the house without his starter cup. He'd showered and left the house inside of fifteen minutes. He hadn't read the daily meditation. He hadn't eaten breakfast. He hadn't kissed Aurora goodbye.

He'd just left.

With a fresh cup of coffee, Cruz crossed the room and stood in front of his murder board. He looked over the lives lost. Were they all winners? The pride of society? No. He could admit, privately, maybe some parts of society were better off without some of the characters. He adamantly believed justice came from a process with rules of engagement. Was the system messy? Yes, but it needed to be. Our fore-fathers fought and died, bled and wept for the right for have the complicated, fucked-up system that presumed innocence.

Cruz looked at the faces of the survivor. Officer Nick Kroc. Shouldn't he count Francesca Pelletier as a survivor? She had a connection to the suspect. He hated they hadn't found it. The damn woman had a ridiculous number of con-nections, even going back just a year. Her career as a re-porter. Her volunteering in hospitals. Her active connections to high school friends—one of whom she used to get Aurora into an art show—proving the power of those connections.

Crash!

Cruz looked to the sound, surprised to find a department at full speed. One of the detectives was bent over, picking up files and swearing under his breath. Campbell was a veteran homicide detective who looked like he swallowed a cocktail of ear wax and raw calamari.

"Need a hand," Cruz asked.

"Naw, I got it."

"You sure? You don't look like you got it."

"Fuck, Cruz. Some days. Some things..."

"It gets to you. What did you pull?"

Campbell collapsed against his desk. In his fifties, the cruelty people extracted on each other was etched in the lines of his face. "A double homicide. An elderly husband and wife killed, apparently for their prescription drugs. He was beaten to death. She was pushed down the stairs. Broke her neck."

The incidents of break-ins to residences and pharmacies for prescription drugs were on the uptick. The use of street drugs like marijuana, heroin and meth were down. Adderall, Vicodin, OxyContin were up. Notably up.

If the Drug Head Killer thought removing the retailers would eliminate the Cleveland's drug problem, he missed a basic of economics. Demand had not been eliminated and elements of it had been made desperate.

The hustle of the department was like bongos being played on his brain. He needed some space and found it in his car. Except in the quiet, he heard Montoya's voice, "inappropriate relationship with his son."

His stomach rolled. He wouldn't lose it, he hadn't eaten since...when? Oh, yeah, before he was accused of molesting a child. He'd left the house without his microwaved breakfast. He left the house hours before Aurora was awake. He thought of the way he behaved last night. He should explain, but he couldn't tell her, not until he'd cleared it up.

So, what was his plan? Sleep at work for the next God knows how many days?

That was a shitty plan.

He needed to act like nothing was wrong because there wasn't, not really. Internal affairs could investigate their ass off, there was nothing to find.

That was a damn good plan.

He dug out his cell phone and called Aurora, knowing it would go to voicemail. "Sorry about last night, baby. Needless to say, I had a bad day. Your painting looks great." He hadn't looked but was certain it did. "Meet me at Becky's for darts with Yablonski and Erin. I'll make up for being ass of the year. Love you."

Normal. Everything was nice and normal.

June 7

The people who use drugs are like that guy in the story. Faust. They trade bits of their souls for an hour of fake happiness, believing they can control the monster. It is sad that with the work Francesca, Nick, Jesus De La Cruz and I are doing, so many still fall. .

Some will never believe. Some will never retreat.

The two with me now are like that. I look into their eyes and the light is gone. Tonight I will grant their souls freedom and then post the signs at the gate of those who need it the most.

CHAPTER TWENTY-TWO

Monday, June 11

The call had come in near noon from a patrol officer. Two heads were found on the property of a tall public housing complex wedged between an elevated portion of the West Shoreway and Lake Erie. The prime lake front real estate would have been picturesque if not for the two-story-tall piles of salt and other materials that were the part of the lake front mines. Division Avenue at River Road. Not a part of town many Clevelanders could say they had been to. Two- and three-story buildings dotted the multi-acre campus resembling dorms at a university. Most windows were open as there was no central air conditioning; a few had small window units. The streets were nearly empty except for the predictable trash dumpster permanently parked in the public street at regular intervals.

The heads were mounted on Division Avenue in what had become the usual manner. Common stakes, one on each side of the road, impaled a head. One was a white male, early twenties. The other was the first female, also early twenties.

"Preliminary ID," Yablonski said, "Eric Hamby and Jessica Poole. We know these two. Boyfriend and girlfriend. Small time Bonnie and Clyde."

"Where are they from?" Cruz asked.

"Denison Avenue. West Eighteenth area."

"What's familiar about that?" Cruz pinched the bridge of

his nose. Then snapped his fingers. "Last week. The elderly couple killed in their home. Same neighborhood." Cruz directed Yablonski to the detective assigned to the case. "How long had he had these two?"

"Detective. You're going to want to hear this." An officer walked down the center of the street with three women in tow.

"Detective De La Cruz. I'm in charge."

The women introduced themselves. All were in their forties, dressed for a warm day on the Lake Erie shore. Two had faces scrubbed clean, the third wore make up with bright red lipstick. The shortest of the three took the lead.

"For your information, Detective, those heads were there yesterday morning."

Cruz blinked in disbelief. "Yesterday morning? But how?"

"Who do you think comes down here? Nobody but us. Who was to know and nobody was to tell."

Cruz looked around the crime scene. It was a city street with apartments lined up the road. "People must have come and gone. Somebody had to see. People had to be afraid."

The woman shook her head. "The only people who are afraid are the people who gots something to be afraid of."

"It was protection," the tallest woman said. "A warning. Nobody did nothin' yesterday."

Cruz paced away from the women. "Jesus Christ, Yablonski. Those heads were on the posts and nobody called it in. What the hell is going on?"

Crime scene arrived and got to work. Cruz directed his team into the housing complex to begin the arduous task of door to door calls. The managing authority was contacted and arrangements made to deliver copies of all surveillance tapes of the campus. The heads were taken with the posts intact. The scene was worked but, as was becoming too common, little was found.

Late afternoon had Cruz reading the files on Hamby and

Poole. Since turning eighteen, the pair had collectively been arrested a dozen times. The story was simple. They had a drug habit. When they needed money to support the habit they either one: sold drugs, or two: stole.

Back at the home of the elderly couple, the pair had left DNA under the wife's fingernails and on forks used for a midnight snack. But the police sent to arrest the couple hadn't been able to locate them just days after the vicious attack.

Cruz left Yablonski to the task of building the timeline while he did the next of kin notifications. Eric Hamby's father stood in the opened doorway, his feet planted wide, arms crossed over a T-shirt. "I knew this day would come. He's dead, isn't he?"

"Yes, sir. I'm sorry to inform you Eric Hamby was found dead this morning. The details of his death are under investigation, but you need to know only his head has been—"

"Drug Head got him? I told that boy. Over and over but there was never anything you could tell him. You better come in, tell me what's to be done."

"I need details, sir. When did you see Eric last?"

Jessica Poole's mother became hysterical, her stepfather stood though tears filled his eyes. "Did...did she suffer?" he asked.

"It's under investigation, sir." When the mother wailed with heartbreak, Cruz stretched the truth. "She didn't. Not to my knowledge. When did you see Jessica last?"

"Months," he said. "Jessie, well, Jessie didn't want..." He broke down.

Her mother looked up, tears streaming down. "She was so smart in school. She could have been anything, anything she wanted. When I heard about Drug Head, I had this bad feeling. She laughed at me, asked me for money. She swore and hung up the phone when I said no. That's the last thing I said to Jessie. No."

Hours later, Cruz drove by the building holding the Monday meeting. He didn't slow down. Another two hours passed, the sun was beginning to set as he pulled in his driveway. The garage door was closed, his truck parked directly in front of it. His house was quiet as a church when he walked in. No music blasting. No TV laughing.

Aurora sat at the dining room table, elbows set, hands clasped over her mouth. Her gaze was hollow, empty.

"Aurora? Baby?"

She jumped. She blinked, her gaze eventually settling on him. "I called you. A lot. You didn't call back."

Cruz took his phone out. Eight times beginning at 2:00 p.m. He'd dismissed the first, ignored the rest. "The case flared up. I couldn't answer. What happened?"

"A detective called from internal affairs. He wanted to interview me."

"Shit. You don't have to do that—"

"I already did. I went to his office this afternoon."

"Why?"

Her hands fell to the table with a thump. "Do you know what they asked me?"

Cruz stood at the opposite end of the table, his fists buried in his pockets. "Not specifically."

"It was disgusting, what he implied. I hated answering his questions. *Hated*."

"You should have call—" He stopped himself, realizing she had. It was he who should have. "It's going to be all right, baby." He went to her now, down on his knees.

"Why didn't you tell me?"

He blurted out the truth. "Because I didn't want it to be real. Because I could never hurt a child. Because it was easier to ignore than to face. I didn't think it would go anywhere. It's a ridiculous accusation made by a criminal who was pissed he's behind bars."

Aurora turned putting his body between her knees. "All the more reason to tell me. This is important to you—"

"It's just work. Work doesn't come here."

"Bullshit."

Cruz lifted his chin. "Excuse me."

"You heard me, Zeus. Bullshit. Your job is here every day. It's in our bed. Every night. Do you realize we have not had sex in weeks? It's like we're some old, married couple. I-I-I barely see you. You don't live here. You live at your desk or in your car or wherever else you hide."

"This is a big case. It takes a lot of my focus."

"It doesn't deserve all of you." She cupped his face. "Don't you see what it's doing to you?"

Cruz pushed away, came to his feet. "I can handle it."

"Well, I can't. I can't, damn it."

He took a step back though his features crowded together in anger. "Is that a threat? If there's something you want, just say it, Aurora. You want out?"

Aurora took a step closer, one hand over his heart. "I want you, and I want you to want me."

"I do want you. I'm just tired," he whispered.

"Call Oscar. If you can't talk to me, call him."

"I will," Cruz said, but it was a lie. He wouldn't call Bollier until he got his shit back together.

Friday, June 15

Cruz's alarm went off, but he was already wide awake. Aurora was in the shower and the tune of the morning was Journey's "Don't Stop Believing". She'd gotten up early everyday despite being out of school, showering and then walking comfortably naked through their bedroom. He rolled to his side, waiting for the show to start.

Aurora danced in, wrapped in a towel. She rolled him to his back, climbed on top, then kissed him. "It's going to be an amazing day."

"It is?"

Aurora propped herself up, her breasts straining against the towel. "My art show is tonight. You're going to be there, right?"

Cruz smiled into her worried eyes. "Wild horses couldn't keep me away."

She pursed her lips. "How about dead bodies?"

His hands ran up her ribs until his thumbs caressed the soft skin of her breasts. "I'll make an announcement there are to be no dead bodies after noon today. That gives me plenty of time before the seven o'clock opening."

"Do you want me to wait for you? We could go together?"

"No. You're going to want to be there early. I don't want you stressing over me. You're going to be great. I know it."

Cruz showered, feeling positive for the first time since Montoya broke the news about internal affairs. Yablonski and Montoya had been interviewed. Even Dr. Chen had made the list. Cruz was pleased the doctor was 'clearly' on his side. Let IA look. There was nothing to find.

He picked up his daily inspirations. He hadn't read the words of other AA members for five days. He'd never done that before. It didn't feel good. He read through the missed days, feeling like he was catching up on his life.

The meeting in the chief's office featured Cruz, Commander Montoya, and Chief Ramsey. No clinical experts to spout twelve-letter jargon. No public relations to spin the tale. No feds to get in the way.

"Where are we?"

Cruz spoke. "The evidence has placed the latest victims, Eric Hamby and Jessica Poole, at the scene of the Gertz murders. DNA collected from the female victim and from the kitchen matched Poole while DNA on the male victim matched Hamby. Accounts provided by associates indicate they likely went missing twenty-four hours after they killed the Gertzes. They were not reported missing. The suspect left little to work with, again. The various cameras around the housing campus were focused on doorways. Not the street. The residents closest to the sites have heavy shades pulled at night because of the bright street lights. No one claims to have heard or seen anything."

Ramsey curled his lip. "Have you seen the reports from the street? They are lauding him. Raising him up as the poster-child for drug control."

"Yes, sir. I heard about the heads." Morning television reported mannequin heads mounted at the entrances to neighborhoods and parks throughout the city and into the suburbs.

"This is getting out of hand."

"Yes, sir."

"I'm going to ask the FBI to take over."

"No." Cruz snapped the word, drawing fierce scowls from Ramsey and Montoya. "This is my case. Our case. There is nothing the feds can do that we can't."

"We're going on eight months, Detective. Eight months of dead ends and gang battles, protests and rallies, media and social bullshit." Ramsey rose slowly, his shoulders seeming to widen as he released the torrent held behind the hard-edged features. "A killer is trolling our streets with impunity! He goes where he wants, when he wants, toying with us. I am sick of playing his fucking games!"

"Then we'll change the rules." Cruz paced away, giving room for an idea to unfold. "We'll change the fucking game.

Listen, it's about control, right? Since we found Uncle Hall, we have been chasing after him. He sets a play in motion, we don't know the clock has started until we find a head. We tried playing a zone defense, but the city is too damn big to throw a net fine enough to catch one in a million."

Ramsey dropped his chin, looking like a wolf ready to defend his territory. "Do you have a point, Detective?"

"We engaged him with Kroc and Pelletier. We were able to confirm he is male and white. He is not untouchable. He just thinks he is."

Montoya nodded his head, interested. "What are you suggesting, Jesus?"

"We start playing offense. I'm going back undercover."

The room went silent. The only sound was the whirl from Ramsey's laptop.

Cruz held up his hands. "Before you say no, listen. This makes sense. He is approaching dealers. I'll go back in, my cover is still solid. I'll throw parties and make headlines and the bastard will walk into our arms."

Montoya looked at Ramsey. "I like the idea. Maybe someone from narcotics—"

"I'm the better choice. Come on, Kurt. Narcotics is already spread thin and they can't afford to burn a cover. Add to that, they don't know this suspect. I do."

"How about Yablonski? He's been with you for months. He's got the chops."

Cruz wasn't being put aside, not even for his best friend. "Absolutely, Yablonski has chops. He's also arrested half the people we need to draw in to make this look legit. Word will spread fast Cleveland police opened up a house. People don't forget Yablonski."

He interpreted the silence as agreement on this last part at least.

"I won't need much," Cruz said, the details falling into place. "We'll use Uncle's house. Mrs. Hall will let us. There's already a customer base to make it easy to establish the cover. The suspect knows the area, having already attacked Hall. It ups the odds he'd be watching."

Ramsey sat, steepled his fingers. "Maybe be irritated another demon-seed stepped into Hall's shoes. He could come at us hard."

"Which is what we want," Cruz said. "The harder, the better."

Ramsey pointed to Montoya. "You like it but you aren't buying it. What are you thinking, Kurt?"

"We can't ignore the situation." They discussed the investigation into Cruz's relationship with Jace Parker.

"It's ridiculous. It's the false accusations of a man who beat his own child until his arm broke." First Cruz fought for his case, now he fought for his pride, his reputation, his life. "There is no, I repeat, no validity to the accusation."

"And yet, process must be followed." Ramsey sighed heavily. "I'll make a call. If we can clear the record, I'll give you a month. If not, we'll go to Narcotics. The approach works for me. I like taking control of the game."

Cruz had some far and away hope that Ramsey's call would solve his problems. Instead, it brought it to his door. After lunch, Cruz sat in Montoya's office with a Detective Moss from internal affairs bureau. Moss was in his late thirties with a set jaw and a slight air that said everything around him stunk. The file in front of him was two inches thick.

What did they have in there that was two inches thick?

Moss opened the cover. "You first met Jace Parker on November first, is that correct?"

Cruz didn't like being on this side of the table. It was hard not to be sarcastic and rude. Having Montoya in there, standing on his side, helped. "Yes, it was the day after Halloween. I responded to a call from his mother that their home had been shot at Halloween night."

"Did you speak with Jace?"

"Yes. He was sitting on the porch when I came out of the house. I spoke with him about the incident the day before."

"Was anyone with you when you spoke to him?"

Cruz had to pause. Were any of the uniformed officers around at that point? "His mother and father remained in the house. I stayed close by because I was concerned about Mr. Parker's frame of mind. There were two uniformed officers at the scene. I can't say their whereabouts at the time of the conversation."

"Did you give the child candy in exchange for information?"

"No. Absolutely not. I did give the child a bag a candy from my nieces. He had missed trick-or-treating. While he ate the candy, he divulged the name of the man his mother suspected of shooting at her home. He gave me the name voluntarily. I was not interrogating a child."

The questioning went on for hours. Everything he had said or done with Jace had been made to feel dirty. Giving him the winter coat was made to sound like a sexual invitation. Aurora had told them he had a special relationship with Jace. The innocent comment was likened to sexual imposition.

For an hour, they talked about Jace calling and the chocolate rabbit that resulted. Moss asked details Cruz wouldn't have been able to answer ten minutes after the conversation ended. In the end, Cruz was clear on two points: his relationship to Jace was detective to child, proper and platonic, and Jace's father was an ambitious dealer with a hard-on for the cop who busted him.

At four-thirty, the interview wasn't finished but suspended until Monday.

Cruz walked out of the department. He was sickened by the allegations against him and felt betrayed by a department that took a criminal's side over his.

"Detective della Cruz."

Cruz looked up to find Sam Bell leaning in a corner, his head hung low, his eyes red. Any other day, Cruz might have cared. Not today. He walked past Bell without stopping.

"She's dead now. She dead, too."

And Cruz reversed direction. "Who's dead?"

"Melissa. Sleeping pills." The man looked lost, ripped of the only friend he had. "Some doctor gave 'em to her. She took 'em all. Thought maybe you should know."

"I'm sorry, Mr. Bell." He was, more than the words said. Cruz took out his wallet and handed Bell a card.

"A therapist?"

"She gets it. Tell her I sent you."

Tears streaked Bell's cheeks. "That boy was everything to her. He...he was her life."

Cruz got that, but his shoulders weren't big enough for another's grief. "She knew how good a friend you were. Call Edna."

He walked on then, needing to be out of this building and away from people needing things from him.

"Detective De La Cruz!" A different voice shouted his name. This one was excited.

He kept walking. He'd done his good deed for the day. Everyone else could piss off.

"Detective. Detective De La Cruz. Just a moment of your time." Soft-soled shoes closed in behind him. "Just a moment, Detective."

Cruz turned and faced a squat, bulldog of a man. He held a paper. "Whatever you're selling, I'm not buying." The man slapped the paper into his hand. "What's this?"

"You're being sued. See you in court."

Cruz looked at the paper, watched his fingers curl, felt the paper crumble.

"This guy bothering you, Detective?" A couple of officers ran to assist him.

"Yeah. Get him out of here." The server howled and railed as he was dragged out of the building. Cruz saw was his life flash before his eyes. Because that's what it meant when a cop was personally sued for five million dollars. Five with six zeros. The world he lived in thought it was a lot of money when there were three zeros. Six? That was an altered reality.

Who was suing him? Faith Ernwell, the grieving grandmother of D'Andre Lattimore, on behalf of her grandson's estate. Wrongful death.

Then he was in his car, but he didn't remember walking. His hands shook as he turned on the engine. The car left the parking garage. He didn't know where it was going. Up one street, down another, onto a narrower one. The car stopped in front of the home where the Gertzes died.

The two windows on the second floor had the shades drawn, two large eyes, closed. Summer didn't touch the house in mourning. No flowers bloomed. No grass grew. It laid in waiting, waiting for him to solve the damn case. He pounded on the steering wheel, each blow punishing bone. He needed...he needed...clarity. He needed to get all of the shit out of the way. He needed a place to think.

Ten blocks away was a joint called The Ugly Broad. It took a minute for his body to adjust. The light was too dark. The sound too loud. The scent too sharp. The bottles reflected the lights like a disco ball. An invitation to party. Just sit, let your hair down, relax. It was Friday night. The regulars gave him a look over but nodded as he sat. They recognized one of their own.

"What can I get you, buddy?"

June 16

The news reported that signs are being posted around the all city. I jumped in my car and found ten. It's hard to write in words. I felt like I won the lottery, found the pot of gold at the end of the rainbow, and was named king for a day.

I went down to Lake Erie, to the park where we would go on a hot day. It doesn't feel like this lifetime. I just sat there and enjoyed the amazing colors of the sunset.

CHAPTER TWENTY-THREE

Saturday, June 20

Palms pressed flat against the wall in front of him, the water pounded the back of his head. Cruz stood under the punishing stream, water so hot it scalded. Steam billowed from the shower. He couldn't see across the bathroom to the opposite wall.

He wanted to leave. Be somewhere else. Someone else. Leave the Drug Head Killer and internal affairs and the division painting him as a filthy monster. Just leave.

There was a quick rap on the door followed by Oscar Bollier's voice. "Aurora is here."

The door closed and for the first time since he'd become a man, he cried.

Aurora stood in the picture window, wearing painted-on faded blue jeans and a mossy green cotton shirt matching her eyes. She had high-heeled wedge sandals, the top of which matched her eyes also. Her hair was wild, natural. Curls rioted in all directions.

Cruz stood on the stairway, drinking in the sight of her, committing her to memory so he could keep her for always. He stepped down, and the stair creaked, giving him away.

She looked over her shoulder and then came to the bottom of the stairs. Her face was lined and her eyes red, a harsh setting for those emeralds. There were dark circles beneath them. Her lips were chapped, swollen.

"Are you hurt?" Aurora's voice was rough, as though it were the first time she tried using it. She met him on the landing, her hands pressing quickly to his chest, running down his sides, his arms.

Where he hurt couldn't be seen or touched so he simply said, "No."

"Good," she said. Then fast as a lightning strike, her hand slapped his face.

He took the hit. He deserved so much more. She retreated into the living room, and he followed her, a man marching to the gallows.

This was the end. This was their end.

She was the best thing he'd ever had in his life. He would miss her burnt toast, microwaved sandwiches, and off-pitch singing. His throat closed at the thought of never seeing her paint again, never hearing her call his name over a crowded room and having every turn to see who she loved, never making love...

"I...I'm sorry." His voice broke, matching the rest of him. It was a pitiful offering, he knew, but it was all he had to give her.

She spun on her stacked heels. "For what. Exactly."

He let out a deep breath. "Everything."

"Not nearly good enough, Jesus."

He winced at his name. He wasn't her Zeus anymore.

"For not being a better man." His voice was a whisper, weighted down by shame. "For letting you down."

"You did let me down. Last night was a big night for me. How am I supposed to feel when the man who means everything to me doesn't show?"

"Like you can do better." At some point, as he wallowed in self-pity, he remembered the art show he'd forgotten. He knew how much it meant to her. He owned it because he didn't deserve a pass. "I didn't mean to not show. I just—" he pinched the bridge of his nose, "—I needed some space to think, to work some stuff out."

"Without me? When I made the mistake over the ring, you made a point of invading my space, saying we had to work it through together. Now you have a problem and you close me out?"

Being accused of the most vile act wasn't in the same universe as being jealous over a ring. "You wouldn't understand."

Fire lit her eyes, tinted her cheeks. "Is this some kind of Latino he-man bullshit?" Her hands flailed as she ranted, nearly striking him again. "Because I'm telling you now, I'm not having it. 'I am the man, so I stoically endure the hardships of life, protecting the frail little woman from the ugly world.'"

"It is an ugly world. What's wrong with wanting to protect you from it?"

"Number one: I live and work in the real world. You not talking to me does nothing to shelter me. Number two: I'm a grown woman, competent, talented, and resourceful. I do not need a lover who doesn't think I'm capable of standing on my own two feet. Number three: It doesn't fucking work. You keep secrets from me, and all it does is build a wall between us. It doesn't protect me. It shuts me out!"

He tried again to make her understand. "You don't see what I see."

"And thank God for that. But you don't see what I see, and what I see is a good man being eaten alive in front of my eyes by the things he sees. It's going to kill you, and it pisses me off that you're going to let it."

"It's not like that—"

"It's exactly like that." She stomped her foot on the floor. "God...sometimes I just...want to take a two-by-four and hit you upside that thick skull of yours. I don't know what to do with you! Being patient hasn't worked. Being supportive hasn't worked." She growled deep in her throat as she looked to the ceiling. "Don't I mean anything to you?"

He stood there, taking the tongue lashing, knowing when it ended, he would be alone. He would let her walk, because it was the best thing for her, but he couldn't let her go thinking he didn't care. "You're everything to me. I need you just to breathe."

Her hands went to her hips. "It's not enough, Zeus. Needing me on a shelf where you take me down whenever it's convenient for you does not work for me. I need you to trust me, to share your life with me. Your whole life."

"It's...ugly," he said, having no better word.

"Do you think I don't know that?" Her voice hitched, climbing an octave. "I'm not afraid."

"I am."

"So, that's it? We're done? You're letting me go?"

He looked into her angry face and didn't see resignation. He saw determination, and dedication and more love than he knew existed in the world. Like a drowning man tossed a life buoy, he threw his arms around her to stay afloat. "I'm not letting go. Not ever."

"Are you going to give me all of you?"

He squeezed tighter, unbelieving this was real. "If it's what you want."

"It's what I need, Zeus." Her hands were in his wet hair, her mouth against his ear.

Tears came again as it sunk in there was more burnt toast and breakfast sandwiches and bad singing and art and sex in his future. He lifted his head, finding her lips with his, sharing the emotions he couldn't name. This was his promise, to give her all he was. In a kiss that was more about heart than body, he understood it was her promise to accept him.

She broke the kiss, then pressed her lips to his twice more "Let's go home. Everyone is waiting."

"Okay. Wait...what?" He stumbled stiffly along as Aurora pulled.

"You are coming, right, Oscar?"

"Definitely. I love a good intervention. Cruz may need a doctor with the mood Detective Yablonski was in when I talked to him."

Aurora chuckled. "I'd worry about Mari and his mother."

"My mother?" Cruz looked between the two.

"I better get my bag," Bollier said as he ran to his office.

Monday, June 18

"Why can't I go in?" Aurora stood in the hallway of the homicide department, hands on her hips, glaring at her mother. "I'm involved."

Catherine Williams, dressed in killer heels and a black suit designed to send her opponent to their grave, neatly side-stepped her daughter. "Of course, you're involved, Aurora, but this interview isn't a place for girlfriends."

Catherine was Caucasian with an attitude that matched her wardrobe. Her long, thick blonde hair was tied into a severe bun, adding to the lethal look. She was the polar opposite of her husband, Aurora's father, Ansel. The soft-spoken African-American accountant loved numbers nearly as much as his family. Ansel was the family's sturdy ship, navigating safely between ports. Catherine was the cannon looking for a target.

"Your mother knows what she'd doing, Aurora. I'll stay with you," her father said.

"Sit." Catherine used just her index finger to return Aurora to the chair. "Stay. Jesus, we need to talk before this interview. Is there a room we can use?"

An hour later, Detective Moss walked into Montoya's office brimming with confidence. He acknowledged Montoya, regarded Cruz as one might a cockroach, and then stopped at the power suit. "I don't believe I've had the pleasure," he said, extending his hand.

Catherine took a card from her pocket and put it in Moss's hand. "Catherine Williams, attorney for Detective De La Cruz."

"Catherine...Williams?" The smile fell from Moss's face as the name sunk in. He cleared his throat and returned to character. "I'm surprised a detective could afford a firm like yours, Ms. Williams. Pro bono?"

"Pro ass kicker, but if you're concerned about my finances, you can validate my parking." Catherine smiled, a snake preparing to strike.

Cruz looked to his commander, who smothered a grin.

Moss cleared his throat. "Shall we begin?"

In ten minutes, Cruz learned to not open his mouth until Catherine nodded. Damn, he was glad she was on his side. He swallowed a lot of pride when he agreed to let Aurora's mother lead his defense for the internal affairs investigation and the lawsuit. Funny, he never put it together that Aurora's mother was *the* Catherine Williams who was reputed to floss her teeth with unprepared prosecuting attorneys. She knew her law and had learned police procedure in a weekend. She backed Moss into corners, required him to re-word questions, and completely undermined the testimony of the drug-dealing, child-abusing father.

Two hours in, Moss looked like the one under the spotlight. His hair was pointing this way and that. He'd taken off his coat, and the pits of his dress white were stained.

Catherine leaned forward, speaking softly, almost motherly. "Detective Moss, your job is to investigate the allegations against my client. Child abuse is a serious crime and one that no one, least of all the Cleveland Division of Police, should take lightly. However, the testimony of Detective De La Cruz as well as that of Detective Yablonski and Ms. Williams has accounted for all of the time my client has spent with the minor. Crimes were committed by the boy's father, which is why he is in custody. It is beneath you to continue under the guise of an investigation to create a crime where one has not been committed."

Moss shook his head. "I assure you, Ms. Williams—"

The door opened.

"Excuse me? Is this the right place?" Hayley Parker saw Cruz and walked in the door, holding Jace by his unbroken hand. Aurora and her father followed.

Montoya came to his feet, annoyance pressed down his brows. "I'm sorry, Miss. This is a private meeting."

"I know. I'm Hayley Parker. This is Jace."

The boy's face lit up. "Cruz! Do you have any candy?"

Cruz stared at the boy, figuring out why he and his mother were there. "Not on me, buddy."

"How about your desk? Did Detective Yablonski take it all?"

He was a sucker for the kid. "Not yet. Don't tell him, but there are candies in my upper right drawer."

Jace looked up at his mother. "Can I? I know where his desk is."

Hayley Parker looked around the room. No one said no. "Sure, Jace. Come right back."

Hayley Parker looked good. Her face was fuller and healthier. Her eyes bright. Though still thin, she'd put on enough weight to fill out her clothes. Most notably, she smiled.

Montoya took the lead. "Mrs. Parker, what are you doing here?"

"Miss Williams called me. She said my asshat of a soon-to-be ex-husband accused Detective De La Cruz of abusing my Jace. It's not true. It simply isn't. The only person who ever put a hand on my son is his father." Hayley faced Cruz. "I hated you the day you arrested Christopher. I called you many names. I didn't think I could manage without my husband. But I have a job, helping women who have been abused. I just do the cooking, but they let me bring Jace, and they are all really supportive. I realized I belong there. With the help of the counselors, I've started the divorce proceedings. Thank you."

Cruz could not believe the sharp right his day just took. He looked to Aurora, overwhelmed that she thought to call Hayley and convince her to testify. Emotion clouded his voice. "This might sound odd, Mrs. Parker, but I'm proud of you."

"Call me Hayley." She stood a little taller. "Now. Who's in charge of asking the questions?"

"I am." Moss and Catherine said together.

Fifteen minutes into delicate questioning, Montoya's door flew open again, and Jace raced in, laughing hysterically. He ran to Cruz, climbing awkwardly onto his lap, one hand in a cast, the other filled with candy "Save me, Cruz. He's going to tickle torture me."

Yablonski appeared in the doorway, bearing his lower teeth like an old school werewolf. "Candy!"

Jace squealed and climbed to Cruz's shoulders, stuffing his mouth as he went. "Idon't havit. Nothing," he mumbled around a mouthful of candy.

"Yablonski," Montoya said, coming to his feet.

"Sorry, Commander." Yablonski stood tall and then backed out the door. "Excuse me, uh, us. Come on, Jace."

Cruz lifted Jace from his shoulders. Rainbow-colored drool smeared on the white sleeve of his shirt as the now first grader raced off.

"Well," Catherine said, standing. "I think we're done here."

"Agreed," Montoya said.

Moss sighed. "Agreed."

* * *

Friday, June 29

The coolness of the early morning did nothing to abate the heat. Cruz rolled, taking Aurora with him. He had made love to her the evening before and woke her in the middle of the night. Then she had woken him in a way that would steam the pages of *Penthouse*.

He found a rhythm that made her coo and was sure he could keep it up for a day or two. Easily. With her.

Fingernails dug into his back.

"Zeus," she cried in three syllables. "Now. Now. Now."

He put her legs over his shoulders and took them both over the edge. She locked her arms around his shoulders, holding him as he let her legs go. They tossed aside the sheets and laid locked together.

The alarm went off.

Aurora stilled Cruz's out stretched arm. "Just a few more minutes."

He kissed her temple. "Just a few," he said, hitting snooze.

The alarm eventually rang again. He turned the alarm off and slid out of bed into silence. He showered, dried his long hair without braiding it. He shaved his thickened beard into the artistic patches he'd seen on a rapper. He added morning toiletries to the small bag he had packed the night before and went down to his office. The daily inspirations sat on his desk. Opening it to the day's message, he read it. It talked to him about home and family and what he held precious.

He took a deep breath and put the book aside. Everything he was doing was for what he held precious. So, every man and woman could walk down a street without fearing a vigilante would judge them unworthy. He was doing it for his love, for his family. So, they could see what kind of man—

No. If the last week had showed him anything, it was that his family and friends accepted him as he was.

He was doing this for himself, to finish reclaiming his life.

He needed to return undercover, finish the job, and go out on his terms.

"I have something for you." Aurora stood in the doorway, wrapped in a short pink robe. "I know you said you can't take anything, you know, from this life. But..." She held out a leather string with a green cat's eye bound between two knots.

The polished stone matched Aurora's eyes. "Put it on me." He turned, lifting his black mane.

Aurora's fingers brushed the back of his neck as she connected the clasp of the leather. "There. Let me see."

Cruz turned around. The stone pressed against the base of his throat.

"You look...tough, Zeus. The hair and the goatee and my stone." Aurora choked up. "I love you."

"I love you, too." It wasn't enough. "Do you think, if I asked you to marry me again, you'd say yes?"

Her eyes became glassy. "I think I would." Hastily, she pressed her fingers to his lips. "Ask me when you come back." She smiled weakly and even that faded when a car pulled in the driveway. "Better get going. Matt's here." She gave him a quick kiss and left him alone.

He fingered the stone around his neck, picked up his bag, then walked out the door of his house. His Cleveland Division of Police car was in his garage. The truck Aurora drove pinned it in. He patted the back of it, entreating it to take care of her.

"I'm coming back." he shouted to the silhouette in the window. "I am coming back."

Cruz drove the tricked-out Escalade through the neighborhood Uncle Hall used to own. He parked it in front of a house no person in their right mind would pay more than twenty Gs for. The windows were darkened by shades except where they were torn. The screen door was off one hinge and cocked at a useless angle. The paint was in the process of pealing itself off the wood framed home.

He knocked on the front door.

A blurry-eyed man with a gun tucked into the front of his jeans opened the door. "We ain't fuckin' buyin'."

Cruz smiled. "That's not what I heard, my friend."

The blurry eyes widened, the pupils struggling to focus. "Tigre? Oh, holy fuck. *El Tigre*. I thought you got popped, like, two years ago."

"Nope. Still kickin'. Can I come in, Ray Ray? Don't like having my ass hangin' out in the wind."

Raymond Ramos, known as Ray Ray, had been Cruz's right hand man when he'd been undercover. He had given Cruz the nickname Tigre after an alley fight and the name stuck. Ray Ray was nearly the same age as Cruz and made what legitimate dollars he had delivering soft drinks for his uncle's distributing company.

"Come in, come in, come in." Ray Ray backed up, inviting Cruz in like an honored guest. The house hadn't changed much in the years. One of the chairs was new. A few more holes in the wall. "Oh, hey, meet my woman. Keisha," he yelled. "Come in here and meet El Tigre."

Keisha was young, barely legal, and she was high.

"Tigre," she giggled. "Meow. I like your necklace."

"Keisha, go get my friend a drink. I'd offer you blow, but we just finished it off. Gotta find a new bag man, you know what I'm saying?" He snickered, caught himself, and then smiled. He took the gun out of his pants and set it on the coffee table. "Sit down. How you still walkin' around? Thought Uncle capped you."

Fingering the scars at his eye, Cruz sat in the newer chair. "Nearly. Messed me up bad."

"How'd you get out of there? The cops showed up and everything went to hell. I couldn't find you."

"No idea how I got out of there." No memory was a blessing. "Woke up in a hospital with tubes going in and out. My face wrapped up like a fuckin' mummy. Almost lost my eye."

Ray Ray leaned forward, staring at the scars. "Shit, man. That's too close."

"When I got out, I had to put miles between me and Uncle. Serious miles. Didn't need him coming back at me while I was drinkin' my dinner through a straw."

"That was smart. You always was smart. Uncle was lookin' for you."

"Figured. I woulda if I was him. I had to ghost, you know? Went to Dayton. I gotta cousin that took me in. Started working down there."

"Whatcha doin' back here?"

"Heard Uncle met the reaper. Heard lots a people met the reaper. I came back to take back what's was mine."

Ray Ray clapped loudly. "Thank you, Jesus."

Cruz laughed at the unwitting joke. Keisha sauntered in and handed Cruz a beer. He took it a little too forcefully, over compensating for being hesitant to touch the damn thing. Keisha didn't notice.

He opened it but didn't drink. "I'm setting up in Uncle's old house. Thinking of throwing a little welcome home party for myself. You know anyone who wants to party?"

"Are you fuckin' kiddin' me? The entire mother fuckin' city wants to party. The fuckin' Drug Head guy's killin' my buzz."

Playing dumb and arrogant, Cruz snorted mockingly. "Who's this Drug Head guy? A snowman?"

"He's a killer. A no-good fuckin' killer and the police ain't doin' nothin' to stop him. He capped Uncle. Got Bear. People runnin', man. If they gotta place to go, they goin'."

"But not you?"

Ray Ray grinned as pat the gun on the table. "Drug Head don't worry me. I hope he takes a run."

July 3

Jesus De La Cruz has moved into one of the houses. His hair is long and he has a beard but I see him.

He calls the infected souls to him. He plays his music loud and stands on the street corner and they come to him.

He is like me, now. One soul at a time, we fight for the redemption of the city.

CHAPTER TWENTY-FOUR

Tuesday, July 3

It was déjà vu all over again. Cruz sat in Walter Stanislav's home, sipping the Cuban coffee. The house changed little since the day last November when he'd accepted the man's hospitality while waiting for Alvin 'Uncle' Hall's dogs to be contained.

Today they sat in the kitchen instead of the living room. The shades drawn, sheltering his meeting with the bald man with the wiry beard.

"We've been profiling every one you've come in contact with." Yablonski sipped the coffee, winced, then pushed it away. "You're a popular guy. It's keeping the boys and girls busy."

"Any hits?" He'd gone above and beyond to be a loud, visible beacon to anyone who wanted a piece of anything. Sometimes it seemed there was a line out his door.

"Nothing strong, not yet. You really think the suspect is going to show up at a party?"

"He was able to approach the victims without raising their suspicion. He had to be someone they were familiar with."

"I like the way you handled Dee Dee Reynolds."

"What were the odds she'd answer the call when Keisha miscarried?" The EMT he once thought could be his suspect had sliced through chaos like a hot knife through butter. "I never saw nothing like that, Yablonski. Dialing nine-one-one was the only thing I could to do."

"Do you think she made you?"

He gave a single shake of his head. "She had her hands full with Keisha and Ray Ray."

"I don't know. It's pretty hard to miss a guy like El Tigre."

Cruz rolled his eyes. "You aren't going to give me a hard time about that."

"Of course, I am. As your friend, I'm duty bound to use it against you for the rest of your life."

"Shit. Well, don't tell Aurora."

Yablonski grinned. "Too late."

"I saw the mayor's speech on TV," Cruz said, turning back to topics that didn't choke him up. Working undercover never bothered him before, but then he'd been alone. There was no one to miss or be missed by. He had thirty days to make an arrest. Today was day 8 "He's committed a lot of resources to July Fourth events."

"Ester Moorehouse has amped things up and joined forces with Pastor Michael Ashford for a community forum. It managed to get a lot of people in a room that hadn't been together before. The county prosecutor talked about treatment and rehabilitation being tools to improve people's lives and reduce prison populations. The mayor announced an initiative rewarding addicts for staying sober with tuition-free classes at any of the higher institutions in the city."

"Any? Case Western Reserve included?" Cruz raised a skeptic's eyebrow.

"That's what the man said."

"Now that's going to be a culture shock."

"Are you still planning a party for tonight?"

"I gotta get his attention. Working street corners isn't doing it."

"You don't know that. Just because he hasn't killed you yet doesn't mean he isn't planning it. You watch your ass."

Sixty people filled the house, turning it into a slice of hedonism. The beer he carried was warm and full. He'd done what he had to do to sell that he was back and legit. It was easier to pull off the lie in a big group like this where no one cared about anyone except themselves. Cruz could stagger and slur his words, laugh and ramble, and no one was the wiser.

One on one was harder, especially with a social guy like Ray Ray. Cruz was surprised the guy took a piss alone. So, he did what he had to do. He'd come to hate the feeling of his head being disassociated from his body. He needed to be in control, as much control as the Drug Head Killer was in.

Too many people to watch. The big ones and little ones he mentally moved aside. He wanted to the average ones, the white ones, the ones who blended. That outted a black woman with her hair cut boy short and a Hispanic man whose hands were too smooth to be described as rough or hairy. He had two potentials. The first was a white man turned down by two women, so far. His smile never faded, he just adjusted and tried again.

The second white man had ropy muscles, greasy wavy hair, and a beard trimmed to a perfect triangle. He leaned against a wall, watching the room.

Cruz looked everywhere but at him. The man had the right stature, the right build but didn't blend in. It was the danger in the set of the dark eyes that set off Cruz's internal warning system. Cruz was armed. A handgun in an ankle holster. A knife in his pocket. He had intended them for show but would use them if it came down to it. The guy stayed where he was, talking to those who drifted his way. Cruz let him stay there, waiting for him to approach.

After midnight, the front of the house lit up with red and blue lights. Cruz shifted the little white girl off his lap and went out his front door. He met the cops down at the sidewalk, wanting to keep it private. A few of his guests staggered onto the porch but weren't willing to go the last twenty feet. "'Sup?"

The two uniforms approached without recognition. "We've received complaints about the noise, sir. You have to turn it down." One of the officers looked past Cruz to the porch. A few of the wasted partiers were making lewd gestures.

"It's the fourth of July. A day made for partyin'." He held his hands up in surrender when the officer took an aggressive step forward. "We'll keep it inside." He walked back to the house, ushering everyone in. He turned the music down from eleven to four, which sounded like a whisper after hours of blaring sic beats.

The corner with the watcher was empty except for three bottles.

Two more hours and people started dropping. Some left, more slept where they sat.

Ray Ray stepped over a pair of legs on his way to the door. "Nobody throws a party like El Tigre."

"You don't have to go, man. Crash here."

"Next time, man. I gotta special delivery to make. Early. Won't pay to be late, you know?"

"That dude was right, this was the place to be. Yo, Ray Ray. You leavin'? Can I catch a ride?" A light skinned Latino in a Cleveland Indians T-shirt came down his stairs.

At first Ray Ray didn't look like he knew him, then he flung his arm around the slim man. "What the hell. I'm feeling generous tonight. See you later, Tigre. Great fuckin' party."

Wednesday, July 4

The cell phone in the case with skull and crossbones rang. Light fought through Loretta Hall's curtains to mess with Cruz's eyes. He squinted, forcing his pupils to focus on the screen. He didn't recognize the number.

"Yeah," he said, draping his arm over his eyes.

"Tigre?" A woman sniffled. "This is Keisha. Ray Ray's girl?"

"Keisha. Right. Right." He looked at the clock. Half past eleven. "What's going on?"

"Is Ray Ray there?"

"I don't think so. He left after two this morning. You want me to check?"

"Yeah. I'm worried on accounta he hasn't called. He always calls."

Wearing the thin cotton pants he slept in, Cruz opened his bedroom door. A dozen people slept in his house. Two were in the little bed that had been Alvin's. Boy, girl with the sheet around their waists.

"Time to get up and out." Cruz pounded on the bedroom door, earning him groans and curses from the sleeping couple. There was a guy on the stairs. Two on the couch. One on each chair. The floor here, there, and everywhere. None of them were Ray Ray.

"Sorry, Keisha. Not here."

"Tell me the truth, Tigre. Did he go home with another woman?" Her voice trembled as she asked the question she feared most.

"No, Keisha. He said he had to work. What the fuck? It's a holiday."

"It was just a half-day for some of their best customers, but he didn't show, Tigre. His uncle's pissed."

"Maybe he's sleepin' it off somewhere."

"Maybe," she said, but she didn't sound like she believed it. "He doesn't just disappear like this. Not without a call or text."

"Meet me at Ray Ray's house." He ended the call as he got busy cleaning house. "Party's fucking over. Out."

One guy rolled over and put a pillow over his face. Cruz

took a handful of shirt and another of jeans and dragged the bastard off the couch.

"I. Said. Out."

The rats scrambled off the ship. Five minutes and he was alone. Walking amid the detritus, he retrieved his cell phone from the top of the kitchen cabinet.

"Yablonski. Ray Ray left here two this morning, girlfriend just reported him MIA. He works for his uncle's distributorship. I'm on my way to the girlfriend. Going to convince her to bring you in."

"I'm pulling the video from last night. One hell of a party, my friend. Got him. Who is the little guy with him?"

"No idea but find him. ID the man in the corner, too. Got a couple of beer bottles with his tag on 'em."

"On it."

It took some work to get Keisha to come up with the idea of calling the police. Cruz played the Drug Head card. The nineteen-year-old had been a bundle of nerves but was going to play the wait-see-cry-pray game.

Yablonski responded to the call with a uniformed officer. Cruz stood behind Keisha, projecting he-didn't-give-a-fuck-what-was-going-down.

"Can I call you Keisha?" Yablonski asked, sounding more like a guidance counselor than a cop. "What is the name of the company Raymond works for?"

"Cuyahoga Distributing. His uncle owns it. Angelo Ramos."

"All right. The officer is going to give Uncle Angelo a call while you and I talk about Raymond. What time does he usually go to work?"

"He leaves around four. He has to load the truck before he starts his deliveries. A lot of the restaurants want their deliveries early."

"Does he have a regular route?"

"Mostly. Sometimes there might be a special order or if

someone's sick, you know."

"Do you live here with Raymond?"

She shook her head. "But I stay over a lot."

"Can you tell if anything is missing? Did he come home?"

"I, uh, don't know. I didn't look around like that."

"Could you do that now for me?"

Cruz stayed where he was, looking like he'd as soon stick a knife in his friend's kidney as talk to him.

"You got a problem with me?" Yablonski asked, sounding like he wanted an excuse to stand on Cruz's throat.

"You ugly. You white. You cop." He ticked off his fingers. "Guess you out, *pendejo*."

Yablonski ground the fist of one hand into the mitt of the other. "Watch your language, boy."

Keisha ran down the stairs. "His work uniform is gone. The pants and shirt he wears."

The officer came back in the front door. "Detective."

Yablonski held up his hand. "Keisha. It would be helpful if you could find a recent picture of Raymond and something personal of his. Toothbrush. Comb. Anything like that."

When she ran off, the officer came up to Yablonski and stood close enough Cruz could overhear.

"Raymond Ramos came in, loaded his truck, and was gone before anyone else arrived. One of the dispatchers came in at six. Ramos didn't answer any calls—cell or radio. Didn't make any deliveries. The truck is GPS equipped. Angelo Ramos found the truck parked on Train Avenue. No sign of his nephew."

There was a moment for the unspoken to sink in.

"I'll get his cell number from her," Yablonski said. "Maybe we'll get lucky and get a ping. Did we get an ID on our partiers?"

"The hitchhiker is Miguel Mendez, nineteen. Was picked up on a DUI the day after he turned eighteen. I have the address. The other guy is Anaconda Chavez-Brown—"

Yablonski whistled low and long.

"You know him?" the officer asked.

"We haven't been formally introduced, but he has a reputation."

Keisha ran back in. "Do these work?" She held out a snapshot taken at a Christmas party, his toothbrush, comb, and ball cap.

"Perfect. I'll need his cell phone number. There is a chance we can trace him."

She gave it up instantly. "What else?"

"I have your number. We'll get to work and call you when we know something."

She blinked up at Yablonski. "That's it?"

Yablonski rested a supportive hand on her shoulder. "You've given us a lot. A lot more than most people. Let us do our job."

Then they left. Cruz stayed where he was, hating that others were doing the work. Keisha rubbed her eyes, looking around for something to do besides cry.

"Fuck this, Keisha. Let's go look places where the cops can't."

It took hours, but they looked everywhere. Flops even cockroaches considered too nasty to live in and dark nooks of fancy buildings. The shadows. The streets. The holes people crawled in to escape. Everywhere. They didn't find Ray Ray.

A small porch projected off second floor on the rear of the Hall house. Cruz stood on it, watching the sun melt into the horizon. Blue gave way to purple, streaked with brilliant red and orange. It looked like a painting and he thought of Aurora. Impatient firebugs set off illegal fireworks, bright splashes of light against a cotton-candy sky.

The vivid orange of the sun grew in intensity, and then it was gone.

The phone in his hand vibrated. Cruz answered with a single word. "Where?"

* * *

Thursday, July 5

"Do you have any idea, any at all what a thing like this can do to an event? The Burning River Festival. How in the hell did he get a head in there? The mayor is irate!" Ramsey paced his office, his longs legs making short work of the room. Not many people had the balls to chew out Win Ramsey, and few who did lived to tell the tale. Since Ramsey couldn't kick the mayor's ass, he kicked Cruz's and Yablonski's. "And now you stand here, after everything we invested in this little operation, and you tell me we have nothing?"

Cruz stood tall under the tongue lashing. Ramsey wasn't saying anything he hadn't thought of himself. "We have a lead. Raymond Ramos left the Hall house with a Miguel Mendez. We have him in interview. Mendez indicated Ramos was meeting a buyer. He didn't have a name, but we are looking into a man named Anaconda Chavez-Brown. Video showed the two men, Chavez-Brown and Ramos, huddled in conversation."

"We are working with the Districts to locate Chavez-Brown," Yablonski added.

Special Agent Bishop slid a file to Yablonski. "I had our analysts run the list of names you sent me. Everything we have is there. I'll tell you the money led nowhere. My DEA contacts have been tracking Chavez-Brown since he left Arizona a year ago. They suspect he's moving into Cleveland, taking over orphaned territories and running out any challengers."

"I've seen the DEA's reports," Yablonski said. "Chavez-Brown is sadistic and brutal in his tactics. I don't like him showing up like this."

"I want this son of a bitch in my jail. Do you hear me?" A fist the size of sledgehammer slammed onto the desk. "Now get out of my office and catch the bastard."

Yablonski paced with Cruz down the empty corridor. "Do you think Chavez-Brown is the Drug Head Killer?"

"The timing is right." It was hard to turn away from a suspect when there were so few.

"I've read everything there is to read, Cruzie. My gut says the guy would have no problem with the killing but the time and the patience for the staging? No. And he wouldn't have let Kroc live. And he wouldn't have reached out to the reporter. Physically, he fits the mold but everything else? I don't see it."

Cruz came to a halt, thinking. Wishing his read had been different. Anaconda "The Snake" Chavez-Brown had been busted for breaking and entering, theft, and assault. Nowhere on his resume was the word slick. "Probably," he said. "Still have to follow up on him."

"Absolutely," Yablonski said as they started walking again. "Now what? Another party?"

"I was thinking something more direct."

Shock and then outrage colored Frankie Pelletier's voice. "Say that again. You want what?"

"We want you to run a story to bring the suspect to me." He paced the area around his desk, figuring out the words to get her to do what he needed.

"Hold on. I have to get somewhere private." A minute of silence. "Did you break up with Aurora?"

"No. Of course not."

"Well I'm not driving a killer to her door. How could you even suggest it? Don't you have any feelings for her?"

"Hold on a minute, Frankie. I've gone undercover. I'm living in a wired house in Cleveland."

"Okay. I was worried you turned into an asshole. Let me think this through. You want me to run an article about how not all the drug dealers are running out of the city?"

"Yes. I want to get in his face, show him I'm defying him. Get him to come after me."

Silence again. "I don't know about this, Cruz."

"Come on, Frankie. We know he reads your work. At least talk to your editor, but I need it soon. Tomorrow."

"Let me think about it. If I'm going to make up a story, I need to think about it."

Cruz let her disconnect the line without arguing further. She had printed the fax inside a thoughtfully-worded article. She would do the same with this. Nothing would be made up about the story.

He went to the murder board where Ray Ray's picture now was. It made him sick to see it there. The man had been in his house hours before he was killed. Ray Ray was the closest thing El Tigre had to a friend. He might have been an unambitious user, but he was loyal to his friends, a dependable deliveryman to his uncle, and a loving partner to Keisha. His life wasn't perfect, but it was *his* life.

Guilt blossomed. Cruz should have made him stay. Ray Ray would be alive if he had made him stay. This was one death he had had the power to prevent.

He shook his head, tired of feeling the weight of guilt for everything. If he had made Ray Ray stay, who's he to say what Drug Head would have done? Maybe grabbed Ray Ray later. Maybe grabbed somebody else. Cruz was sure there was a logic going on in the suspect's head, but he hadn't unraveled it. Yet.

Yablonski came into the room. "I have to go over to Narcotics. Fifteen minutes and we'll head out." He tossed a newspaper on Cruz's desk. "Check out the arts section."

"The arts section? You going soft on me?" But he opened it and Aurora smiled at him. The article about the art exhibition took half the page. The picture of the artist and "Moon Struck", the super-size painting from his garage, took the other half. On the following pages, three more of her paintings were featured, more than any of the other artists.

His chest swelled with pride, and he made a decision. This was the last time he was leaving her.

Friday, July 6

Cruz read the article online. "The Economics of the Drug Trade." Frankie had written a superior piece, utilizing statistics compiled by Narcotics on the shift in local economics associated with the exodus of the snowman. He barely recognized the picture of himself on his porch, looking like an angel kicked out of hell. He was quoted as saying his moving back into the city was good business. The demand was high and the supply low, which made it a great place for a guy who could take on the risk.

He frowned as he read it. It didn't sound street enough. Supply. Demand. Risk. Not street words. Why didn't he catch it when he was talking?

The doorbell rang using the code for a buyer. The house was still a mess from the party. No worry about cleaning, it added to the image.

A woman was on the front porch. Cruz guessed her to be his sister's age, though she looked a hundred years old. "I'm looking for an abe."

Cruz didn't say a word but went into the house and came back with a few dollars' worth of happy. Beyond the woman, two houses down, sat a black van.

"Walk with me." He turned the woman around and, hand on her elbow, made her walk down the stairs.

"I got a man. He gonna mess you up you mess with me," she said, her blurry eyes wide.

Cruz let her go, straining to see the license plate. The cars parked on the street were too close together. Then the van swerved into the driving lane and laid rubber on the road. He ran at the van, hit his fist off the side as it sped past him. It was a stupid, impetuous thing to do because it put him on his ass while the van raced away.

The woman hurried to the street. "You okay, Tigre?"

"Get the hell out of here." Cruz snapped, then sprinted into the house, answering Yablonski's call.

"What the hell was that?" Calm was a thin veneer.

"Tell me you caught that."

"Caught what? You leapt off the porch like a fucking puma."

"He was here, Yablonski. He was right here. I hit the van."

"What? You were hit by the van?"

"No. I hit it, with my forearm. I want cameras set up on the street. Today. If we don't have them, call Special fucking Agent Bishop. Let him be useful."

July 7

Francesca and Jesus De La Cruz are doing it. They are spreading the warning and bringing the infected to that house and they come like mosquitos drawn to a bright light.

I want to know more about him. After feeling like the only soldier in the fight, I can't help wanting to just...hang out or something.

I know that can't happen. It's against the rules.

But maybe...

I found a young soul and sent him to Jesus De La Cruz. If he can't, then I'll do my job.

I would like to rest.

No. I will not let evil trick me into blindness. I will stand until this sword is taken from me. This is my choice.

CHAPTER TWENTY-SIX

Saturday, July 7

Cruz made an art form of being obvious and flashy. The corner where he worked had become the most popular in the neighborhood. At the house, he blasted the stereo until he couldn't hear his own thoughts. Twice a day, he walked to the store three streets away, strutting like a thoroughbred out to stud. He greeted those bold enough to approach him with a broad smile and full supply of goods for sale. Every customer left happy and photographed…and sometimes fingerprinted.

Yablonski did not like those walks to the store and clucked at him like a mother hen. Some ol', same ol' got them nothing. He pushed the envelope with Kroc's interview and they got a result. Two contacts led to confirmation of gender and race. He was pushing again. Hard. He wanted the suspect in handcuffs in hours. Not days, not weeks. Hours. He'd have a personal conversation about Ray Ray before the guy saw the interior of the interview rooms or booking or any other public building.

He was so close, he could taste it. Yesterday he'd come within feet of the suspect. The guy was watching him. He'd be coming. Soon. And Cruz would be waiting.

He stretched out his stride as he walked to the store. The sun blazed high in a cloudless sky that day, pressing temperatures into the nineties. He itched for the action. He bought an energy drink and hit the street, taking the long way back. At a playground, stopped to watch kids shoot hoops on asphalt hot enough to melt rubber.

The skull and crossbones phone vibrated. A text message. *Intruder at house.*

Is it our friend? If it was the suspect, every car the Cleveland police owned would be on the little street in minutes. But, if it was just a junkie looking for a free buzz, it wasn't worth blowing his cover.

Not confirmed.

"Damn it." He texted back. *Stand by. Will investigate.* Thunder rolled overhead as he ran back to the house. He'd gone farther than he realized. Cruz wasn't a runner. He hoofed back to the neighborhood, then slowed to a strutting walk, catching his breath as he rounded the corner. A dealer of El Tigre's stature didn't run unless he had a damn good reason. If eyes were on him, sprinting to the door would worry those eyes. Maybe give them reason to think something was up. His head was held high as he walked through the gates he'd been leaving open to let people know he was open for business. The minute he was in the house, his phone rang.

"We didn't get a clear visual on the face," the officer on duty said. "Baggy pants, black hoodie. He went through fast. Five minutes tops. He hit the kitchen cabinets, freezer and refrigerator, under furniture, both bedrooms, bathroom."

"Did he get anything?"

"He was stealing everything he could."

Cruz studied the refrigerator and the greasy print on the handle. His breath escaped like a released balloon. "He hit the leftover pizza and gave us a nice print. I'll collect it and drop it at Stan's, but it's not him. He's not sloppy."

He walked through the house taking inventory. His visitor took everything he found that could be physically ingested. Pizza. Beer. Bottle of Jager. Small bag of weed. Toothpaste.

Cruz collected the prints, delivered them to the neighbor who was getting a thrill being part of the investigation, then returned to the fugly red room to sulk. Two Latinos showed up, looking for a party. He indulged them because it was his job, but even they figured out he wasn't fit for human consumption. He passed out—figuratively, not literally—in front of the television, then staggered to bed sometime between night and morning.

Sunday, July 8

The sun woke his wore-out ass by going LED on the bedroom. He stared at the ceiling, dejected. He wanted it yesterday. Instead he was still here, up for another day of playing king of the losers.

Was this ever going to end?

He reached for the paper...

He reached for the newspaper that had Aurora's picture...

The newspaper that had Aurora's picture folded so she smiled up at him was missing. Cold washed over him like an Arctic shower. He called his babysitter, who answered on the first ring.

"Was someone else in the house yesterday?"

"What? In the house?"

"Was there someone here beside the idiot who stole everything he could eat?"

"The alarm tripped just that one time."

"The alarms are only on the doors, right? What if he came in some other way?" He was out of bed. All the windows in the house were open. It was July in a house without air conditioning. The screens in the front room, dining room, and the odd room off the dining room, were all intact. The kitchen window, the one over the table, was neatly cut along the frame. "Shit. Roll back the video. He was here. The fucker was here."

"Already on it. Yeah, we got him. Shit. He went in not five minutes after you left."

"Tell me you got his face."

"Dark hoodie. Gloves. He's going through the house. Cocky bastard is acting like he has all the time in the world. He's not touching anything. Looks like he's checking the place out to buy it. He's going upstairs. He came out of your bedroom holding something. He tucked it into his sweatshirt."

"Fuck!" Cruz raced back upstairs, taking them two at a time. He dropped to his knees next to his bed and removed the cell phone he'd taped to the underside of the frame.

One. Two. Three rings. Voicemail.

"If you're looking for Aurora, well, it's not your lucky day. But leave me a message and I'll call you back real soon."

"Aurora, it's Zeus. Call me. *Now*." He killed the line and barked back into his police issue. "Get someone to my house. He may be after my girlfriend."

"How would he know your address?"

"How does he know anything!" He recited the plate number for his truck and then the waiting started.

After a minute, a literal minute, he was going to explode. He couldn't sit here waiting to find out if Aurora's head—"I'm going after her."

Running down the stairs, he called her again. This time, she answered on the second ring. "Well, I guess this is my lucky day, I—"

"Aurora. Where are you?" He cut her off.

"Slavic Village. I got the most a-mazing call. I'm meeting a buyer. I just pulled into the parking lot." She named a restaurant he'd heard of but never been to. "The buyer said he saw the article in the paper and wants to talk about 'Moon Struck.' He didn't exactly make an offer but hinted at five thousand. That's five with a thousand after it."

He struggled to keep the rational part of his brain in the lead. "Did he give you a name?"

"Oh, my God, so his name is Michael D'Angeles. Is that epic or what?"

"Get out of there, Aurora." Panic shoved rational thought to the ground and stepped on its throat. "Don't ask any questions. Just turn the truck around and drive away." The sound shifted to the speaker phone, and he heard the engine start.

"Where am I going?" The unbridled joy in her voice had been replaced with unmitigated fear.

Where was she going? He couldn't send her to her family or his. Too risky. "Ritz-Carlton. Valet the truck. I'll meet you in the lobby. If you're there before me, stay in a busy, well-lit area."

"Okay," she said, then only the sounds of a city at midday filled the space between them.

"Aurora? Have you seen a black van?"

Her voice trembled. "I, uh, just passed one. Do you want—"

"Just come to me." Cruz was in the Escalade, pushing the envelope on traffic laws. "You're doing great, baby. Just come to me." He dug out his undercover phone and called Yablonski. "Get a car to the Slavic Village." He named the restaurant. "We're looking for a single white male. He is waiting for Aurora."

"Shit. Are you sure? Is she there?"

"She's headed to me." Cruz's private phone beeped; the call had disconnected. "Fuck. Hurry, Matt."

"Who is it? Anaconda Chavez-Brown?"

"I don't know. Maybe. Detain every single white male. Lock them all down."

By the digital clock on the dashboard, it had only been sixteen minutes since he left the house. He parked the

Escalade in front of the hotel, tossed the keys at the valet, and ran into the hotel.

"Sir, your ticket. You'll need it to get your car back."

Cruz slowed enough for the valet to catch up and hand him the ticket, then he was through the revolving door and in the lobby. He didn't see her. He searched the restaurant and the bar. He called her but didn't hear a phone answering. If she was here, he would have heard her phone ringing. He was closer, he told himself, he should have beaten her to the hotel.

The call rolled to voicemail.

Why didn't she answer?

Fear was as real and tangible as the picture window Cruz paced in, as the thick carpet under his feet. It was the little devil on your shoulder, telling you you were shit, and your whole life was shit, and you were going to live a lonely, shitty life alone.

A truck turned a corner, driving right at him, too fast. The valet leapt back as the tires squealed to a stop, and then he spun around as the woman driving ran past him.

Cruz said every prayer he'd ever learned as he sprinted out the door and captured Aurora in his arm. She held on, her feet dangling inches from the ground.

"Tell me what is going on." Her voice trembled as much as her body.

He needed a moment to hold her, to convince himself that she was here and whole. "I'll tell you everything once we're inside." Reluctantly, he set her on her feet but kept her tucked under his shoulder. He found a secluded place for them in the nearly empty bar. "The suspect...he found your picture. I'm fairly certain it was he you were going to meet."

"My picture? But how?"

He named himself the fool he was, taking responsibility not lessening the impact of his mistake and the near result. "I'm guessing the gallery has you on the website. He had your name, your story. It wouldn't take much for him to get a phone number."

"Are you sure it's him? Maybe it was just an art lover who wanted my painting?"

Feeling how much she wanted it—both the sale and appreciation—he put his arm around her, tucking her close. "Maybe but the timing is too coincidental."

She stilled and eventually shook her head, snapping herself back from wherever she had gone. "I don't know how you deal with this."

Yablonski joined them. Three single, white men were detained and then released. Two weighed more than two hundred fifty pounds, the third was missing an arm. The street detail had pulled over nearly a dozen black vans and SUVs. No Anaconda Chavez-Brown. Nobody wore a sign saying "I am the Drug Head Killer." No van filled with headless torsos.

It was unanimous that Aurora would not be staying at her apartment. Yablonski considered putting her in a police-secured location. Aurora wanted to stay with a friend.

Yablonski crossed his arms over his barrel-chest, daring Cruz to disagree.

Aurora pushed out her bottom lip and gave him puppy eyes.

"I love you, Aurora. When it comes to the house, our social life, and ninety-nine percent of everything else, I'll give you your way. But not in this. You'll go with Matt and do what he says for as long as it takes to shut this bastard down."

"Zeus." Aurora breathed his name with compassion, love. "Nothing is going to happen to me."

"Damn right. And I want your cell phone. He has this number. We'll get you a new one."

***

Cruz had been back in the Hall house thirty minutes when a courier came to the door. A courier. In this little throwback neighborhood. He couldn't have been more surprised if a leprechaun knocked on his door.

The envelope he was handed had his name clearly printed across the front. Detective Jesus De La Cruz. Cleveland Division of Police.

"Fuck."

If this was from who he thought it was, then the glue on the envelope could give him the DNA sample he'd been looking for. He went to the kitchen for the knife. Inside was a single piece of paper, cut to fit inside the envelope. Printed neatly in the center was an address.

He called Yablonski. "I've been made."

"By who?"

"Pick me up. We have an appointment. Bring plenty of friends."

The address was a familiar one in the Slavic Village neighborhood, the same one where Aurora's elementary school was, the same where she was called to meet the "art buyer." The closer they got, the more the hair stood up on Cruz's neck.

"This isn't going to be good," Yablonski said.

"I hope the boy isn't here."

Yablonski parked in front of the home Hayley Parker shared with Jace. Everything was normal and was all the more eerie for it. Backed by six officers, all in body armor and heavy weapons, they approached the house. They covered the front and the back doors.

Cruz knocked and raised his voice. "Mrs. Parker? It's Detective De La Cruz. Cleveland police. Open the door."

Silence answered wickedly.

"Hayley? Open the door."

Now it dared them. Cruz signaled, and the house was entered.

"We got a body," an officer covering the rear called. "Female."

"Search the house," he called out as he made his way to the body. "She has a son. His name is Jace." He squatted by her head, grief and regret swamping him. "You were so close, so close to getting out of this bullshit. What the fuck happened, Hayley?"

Calls of "clear" sounded throughout the house. He stood, relieved he didn't have to look upon the small body. Now, hope beat within his chest. "Jace? It's Cruz. Come on out, buddy. It's safe."

The house was searched. "No one, Detective."

"He's small and clever," Cruz said. "We have to check everywhere. Literally. Under the front porch. Attic. Everywhere."

The house was searched again. Inside and out.

"Send out an Amber alert. Jace Parker. Age five. Blond hair. Blue eyes. Weight fifty pounds. Blue cast on his left arm."

"On it," an officer called out.

Cruz went upstairs. The bedroom Hayley used had a queen-sized bed shoved into a room made for a full size. The bed was made. Clothes were folded in the drawers or hanging in the closet.

The smaller bedroom belonged to Jace. A twin mattress laid on the floor, but the bed was neatly made. A small number of trucks and action figures were scattered on the floor. Not messy so much as used.

Cruz opened a drawer in the small dresser.

It was empty.

He pulled a second drawer. Empty also. Cruz furiously pulled open drawers finding nothing by lint and dust. The closest held extra blankets and more toys, but no clothing hung from the dozen hangers.

On the bathroom sink was a cup with one pink toothbrush. One toothbrush, not two.

Cruz walked down the steps slowly. This didn't make

sense. This wasn't the Drug Head Killer's M.O. at all.

"What the hell, Cruzie? Hayley Parker was stabbed with a knife. She had defensive wounds on both hands. There were wounds on her back and the killing wound over her heart."

"This isn't our suspect. Who knew where I was? Hayley didn't, and she didn't send that letter. Who has Jace?"

Maybe he hadn't been made, at least not by the suspect. But who knew who he was? The Stanislauses. Aurora. Maybe someone recognized him but didn't give it away.

Who would kill Hayley Parker and take off with Jace?

The obvious answer, Christopher Parker.

Cruz waved over one of the uniforms. "Check that Christopher Parker is still locked up. The rest of you, start with the neighbors. The missing child is the priority." He squatted down next to Hayley, squinting as the light reflected oddly off her forehead. "Yablonski. Look at this."

Yablonski came next to him. "What is that? Wax? There's some on her mouth, too."

Cruz leaned over her, changing the angle. Small crosses of oil, on her forehead and lips reflected the light differently. He looked around the kitchen and spotted a bottle of cooking oil next to the sink. "Someone gave her last rites."

It was the judicial system's worst nightmare. A small-time criminal released on bond goes after the wife he abused, kills her, and vanishes with his son.

Every cop in the city was looking for Christopher Parker.

Every programmable billboard, every television station, every radio station broadcast the description of Jace Parker.

Cruz sat at his desk looking at the picture he'd gotten from the school yearbook Aurora provided. He ached somewhere deep inside. Jace had never gotten a break in his young life. His nieces came to mind and the home his sister and brother-in-law provided. Not perfect but just what every kid should have. Happily imperfect.

Needing to move, needing to do something, he pushed to standing. "I'm going back to Uncle's," he said to Yablonski. "I'll take my shit and work from there."

"Are you sure?"

"No. But at least there, I'm doing something."

"Has it occurred to you he sent you to Parker's house as a warning? You could be next."

He was smart enough not to tell his friend that was the point. "Then we better be ready."

Cruz drove back to the Hall house barely seeing the road in front of him. His head flipped through image after image of people he'd come in contact with since that first November day. There were so many. Who would have recognized him and sent him to Hayley? How did they see him without being seen in return?

He ran through names.

Loretta Hall. No.

Gerard Wallace. White, cocky, slim build. Not a no.

Walter Stanislav. Maybe. He was wily. Cruz could see him directing the way to Hayley. But how would he have found her? She was across town.

L'Tonya Simmons. Nope. In jail on arson charges.

Lydia Hernandez. He just didn't see it.

Melissa Mayes. Dead. A victim by extension.

Sam Bell. Capable of causing trouble, but his dark skin got him off the hook as their killer.

Tony Gentile. In jail on murder charges

Dee Dee Reynolds, Roger McCormick, Ester Moorehouse, Felix Sidowski. The women got the gender pass. The men had an undeniable motive. The auto mechanic was a straw away from the camel's back breaking. It wouldn't be pretty when it did. McCormick deserved a second look. Maybe that straw snapped eight months ago. The butcher, on the other hand, had his shit more together than Cruz did. It didn't ring for him. There needed to be some deep-seated, unresolved issues behind these killings. Sidowski conquered his demons. The officers camping at the Stanislav home had expanded the list another six months, adding ten more names to be interviewed.

Anaconda Chavez-Brown. Unaccounted for.

He felt a failure again, making him angry and mean. He parked the gas-hogging truck and used the remote to shut the gate. He was fucking closed. He didn't care how bad anyone was jonesing for a fix. He left his laptop where it was. If he touched it, he'd throw it through a window.

He needed a drink—a shower. He needed a shower and to call Aurora. Fuck the rules. Something had to give or he'd freakin' blow and take half the city with him.

Something caught his eye. A shadow. A blur.

He spun, going low, catching the man about to attack him around the waist. He pinned the arm that held the knife, but the attacker had enough room to poke a few holes in Cruz. The shallow bites kicked in Cruz's survival instinct. When it came to flight or fight, for Cruz, it had always been fight.

Hard. Dirty. Often.

With momentum on his side, he took the attacker to the ground. His face landed near the attacker's, and he bit him Mike Tyson-style. The attacker roared, fighting to dislodge him. He locked his legs around Cruz. They rolled over the coarse ground. Cruz's head bounced off the concrete drive-way. The knife dropped. They rolled, Cruz ending on top. Fists flew in the limited space. A right cross stunned Cruz, giving the attacker the opening he'd been looking for. He wrapped his hands around Cruz's throat and squeezed.

Cruz clamped onto the thick wrists, unable to dislodge them. He gouged at the eyes, scratched at the face, punched at the nose. The grip didn't slip. He looked around for something to use. Determine to squeeze the life out of Cruz, his assailant didn't notice the hand that reached the dropped knife. The eyes with murder in them went wide when that knife was sheathed in his throat.

The hands around Cruz's throat released immediately. He rolled away, gasping for air, rubbing his throat, barely hearing the life and death struggle the man next to him waged...and lost.

A shadow fell over him. Cruz reached for the piece on his ankle, then he recognized the officer. "Find out who this asshole is."

The cop squatted down as sirens grew louder. "It's Chavez-Brown. Ambulance is on its way. Just lie still."

He fought to his feet. Like hell he was staying still. "Cancel it. I'm fine."

July 8

I can't stop crying. I'm soaking the paper and my hand is shaking and it won't stop. I can't see through the tears.

I have a son again. I don't deserve a second chance, I know that, but I will not let him down. Jace needs someone to protect him, to stand against the evil that he lived with in his own house. He cries for his mother.

If you are looking down, Jason, I want you to know he'll never replace you. He may use your name but he'll never be you. I hope you will think of him as a brother, one I could never give you. Look out for us. Be our guardian angel. I'm taking him away from here, to a place where no one can hurt him. Some place good. Some place safe.

My calling has changed. The sword has been passed to my successor. Jesus De La Cruz.

CHAPTER TWENTY-SEVEN

Monday, July 9

Ray Ray's girl Keisha picked Cruz up from the hospital and delivered him to the Hall's house. Cruz refused to stay the night, and Yablonski refused to take him back. The cuts and contusions weren't anything he couldn't take care of himself. He didn't need as many stitches as the overzealous resident put in. The chatty little bastard should join a quilting bee. He'd have skipped the whole experience if the officer watching hadn't called in support at the first sign of blood.

His official phone rang around half past six in the morning. A restless night and aching body made him sloshy, slow answering the phone.

"Detective. We have another head," an officer on the scene said.

"Where."

"In front of City Hall. In one of the big planters. There is a letter addressed to you."

In ten minutes, Cruz stood with Yablonski looking for the last time at the face of Christopher Parker. Cruz opened the letter with gloved hand. He read it twice and then handed it to Yablonski.

Yablonski read it, brows pressed together. "Is this…is this how it ends?

Jesus De La Cruz,

I wanted to do this in person. After all the time we've worked together, I would have liked to have sat down and talked about the battles the way other soldiers do. I have been proud to be the sword defending the city but my time is over while yours is just beginning. I saw you in battle. You were magnificent. You have picked up the sword that I had laid down. I'm proud of you.

Thrust into hell Satan and all evil spirits who wander our city for the ruin of souls. Stand in front of them. Defend them. Protect them. It must be done for our people to have a chance at a good life.

I will pray to St. Michael every day with you in my mind. I will pray for the health and happiness of your family. They are your strength.

Vaya con Dios.

Michael D'Angeles

CHAPTER TWENTY-EIGHT

Tuesday, July 10

Cruz commanded the audience in the chief's office. "Christopher Parker was released from custody on Friday, July the sixth. On Sunday, July the eighth, he killed his wife, Hayley Parker. The knife he used to kill her was turned in by a restaurant owner in their Slavic Village neighborhood after customers reported it in the parking lot. The prints on the knife were Parker's. The blood was Hayley's."

"Is that where he killed her," Dr. Chen asked.

"No," Cruz said, "he killed her in their home. How the knife came to be in the restaurant parking lot is not known. The restaurant in question is the one which Aurora Williams was invited to by a so-called art buyer. This shortly after someone broke into the house we used and stole a photo of her."

Ramsey looked at him sternly. "That we will discuss later."

Cruz could only nod. "The buyer gave her the name Michael D'Angeles, the same name used to sign the note left with the head of Christopher Parker. While the name is phony, the man is very real."

Chen raised two fingers. "You are certain this man was not Chavez-Brown?"

"Chavez-Brown, the man who jumped me outside the Hall home, was dead before Parker's head appeared in the City Hall planter. We will complete the investigation, but it is likely Chavez-Brown was only interested in territory."

"Clearly," Chen said, accepting the logic. "Do you maintain that Michael D'Angeles is the suspect? The Drug Head Killer? Perhaps he is the accomplice we theorized about."

"I am certain the person Aurora Williams spoke to was our suspect. She indicated he was soft spoken, having a voice that was mild but male. There is no physical evidence to support an accomplice, male or female."

Ramsey sat behind his desk, his powerful hands folded as he listened. "How did Parker meet D'Angeles?"

"What is known is that Parker did meet D'Angeles and their meeting ended violently. In the end, he was decapitated. The head was left facing the road. Cameras in the area captured an apparent homeless person shuffling through at five yesterday morning. The person was bundled up, despite the warm temperatures, and carried a backpack. He sat on the planter and arranged Parker's head. The video is not that clear, but no one else approached until a woman arriving early at City Hall made the discovery. Parker is with the Medical Examiner. We are awaiting results."

"What about the boy?" Chen asked.

Cruz ran his hand over his braided hair. Hadn't he asked himself that question every minute of the last day? "Someone anointed Hayley Parker's body in the Catholic sacrament of Last Rites. I don't think I'm going out on a limb when I say that someone was not her husband, which puts at least one other person in the house." He took a deep breath. "Jace is gone, his clothes are gone, his toothbrush is gone. And, if the letter is to be believed, our killer has hung up his saw."

"You think the suspect took the child?" PIO Hyatt asked distastefully. "What would be the point?"

Yablonski tossed out answers like snowballs. "A hostage. Leverage. A cover."

"How much danger is the boy in?" Ramsey asked.

All eyes went to Chen. "The boy doesn't fit the pattern

the suspect demonstrated. It puzzles me that he took the boy at all. We cannot dismiss a scenario in which a new player has the boy. A neighbor. An aunt."

"We are exploring those options," Cruz said flatly, no hint of censure or impatience. Just a cop, going by the book. "So far, nothing has panned out."

"I don't like where this heading," Ramsey said.

"We are continuing to investigate. Roger McCormick, who we first interviewed during the spring, is currently under doctor's care for depression. Felix Sidowski sold his business a few months ago, and, according to the man who bought the business, has been traveling. Research further back into past crimes identified six new names. Four of those are promising."

Chen sighed, resignedly accepting a concept. "Clearly, it is important for the boy's sake that we get him back. But we have to consider a new problem. Based on his letter, the suspect has shifted the reality of the archangel to you, Detective. He may have expectations of you. He may have a new role, one in which we do not know the rules, once again."

Ramsey stood, walked from behind his desk to look out his window. "Detective De La Cruz, is this chapter in our history over?"

Cruz walked to the window, standing next to the man he followed as life continued on in the city below. "History is a story told through the lens of time. We have no option but to wait and see."

EPILOGUE

Friday, July 27

It was another sad, unnecessary death. Mrs. Teresa Aguilar, eighty-five, lived alone in a home with no air conditioning. There was no one to notice the symptoms of dehydration and heat stroke. She died in her favorite chair five days prior.

In his car, air conditioning blasting, Cruz typed in the information he had as he drank from his go cup. The coffee was hotter now than when he left it.

He'd gotten three calls while he'd been in the house.

His commander. Call when able.

Yablonski. Information on another case.

A number with no caller ID. He played the voicemail.

"...a real horse. I'm not allowed to give him candy but he loves apples. I named him Cruz because he has long black hair twisted together, just like you. I'm getting good at riding. I'm not allowed to make him run yet but really soon we are going to go super-fast. And then we can run with barrels and go on camping trips and I get to learn how to rope calves. I really like it here. Maybe you can come and see him and ride him." A soft voice whispered in the background, then Jace's voice shouted in his ear. "I do! I want ice cream! I want ice cream!"

The phone hit the floor with a crash. The recording captured the sound of a resilient boy's laughter and the close of a final door.

ACKNOWLEDGMENTS

The expertise of many people went into creating this manuscript. Any mistakes in this story are wholly my own. I am indebted to Vinnie for your help understanding mental illness and drawing it into this storyline and to Kara for advice given on DNA and witnesses. A big thank you to Trey R. Barker for help with terminology. Thanks to Denise for coaching me through policing and to Kristen B for acting as our interpreter. Deepest respect and appreciation to Mike for sharing his experiences with alcoholism. You inspire me. Finally, many thanks (and apologies for the typos) to my reading team Matt, Traci, Denny, Elaine and Karen.

TG Wolff writes thrillers and mysteries that play within the gray area between good and bad, right and wrong. Cause and effect drive the stories, drawing from twenty-plus years' experience in civil engineering, where "cause" is more often a symptom of a bigger, more challenging problem. Diverse characters mirror the complexities of real life and real people, balanced with a healthy dose of entertainment. TG Wolff holds a Master's Degree in Civil Engineering and is a member of Mystery Writers of America and Sisters in Crime.

tgwolff.com

On the following pages are a few
more great titles from the
Down & Out Books publishing family.

For a complete list of books and to
sign up for our newsletter,
go to DownAndOutBooks.com.

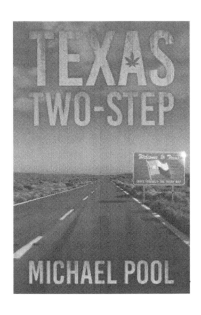

Texas Two-Step
A Teller County Novel
Michael Pool

Down & Out Books
April 2018
978-1-946502-56-8

Cooper and Davis are a couple of Widespread Panic-obsessed Texas ex-pats growing some of Denver's finest organic cannabis. At least they were, until legal weed put the squeeze on their market. When their last out-of-state dealer gets busted, they're left with no choice but to turn to their reckless former associate Sancho Watts to unload one last crop in Teller County, Texas.

What ensues is an East Texas criminal jamboree with everyone involved keeping their cards so close to their vest that all the high-stakes dancing around each other is sure to result in bloodshed.

White Heat
A Duke Rogers P.I. Thriller
Paul D. Marks

Down & Out Books
May 2018
978-1-946502-73-5

Winner of the 2013 Shamus Award for Best Indie P.I. Novel!

He had to make things right... He had to find the killer...

P.I. Duke Rogers finds himself in a combustible situation in this racially charged thriller. His case might have to wait...

The immediate problem: getting out of South Central Los Angeles in one piece during the 1992 "Rodney King" riots...and that's just the beginning of his problems.

Dead Guy in the Bathtub
Stories by Paul Greenberg

All Due Respect, an imprint of
Down & Out Books
978-1-946502-87-2

Crime stories with a dark sense of humor and irony. These characters are on the edge and spiraling out of control. Bad situations become serious circumstances that double down on worst-case scenarios. A Lou Reed fan gets himself caught on the wild side. A couple goes on a short and deadly crime spree. A collector of debts collecting a little too much for himself. A vintage Elvis collection to lose your head over. A local high school legend with a well-endowed reputation comes home.

This debut collection is nothing but quick shots of crime fiction.

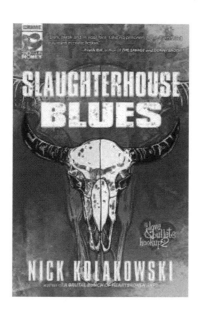

Slaughterhouse Blues
A Love & Bullets Hookup
Nick Kolakowski

Shotgun Honey, an imprint of
Down & Out Books
978-1-946502-40-7

Holed up in Havana, Bill and Fiona know the Mob is coming for them. But they're not prepared for who the Mob sends: a pair of assassins so utterly amoral and demented, their behavior pushes the boundaries of sanity. Seriously, what kind of killers pause in mid-hunt to discuss the finer points of thread count and luxury automobiles? If they want to survive, our fine young criminals can't retreat anymore: they'll need to pull off a massive (and massively weird) heist—and the loot has some very dark history...

Made in the USA
Middletown, DE
05 March 2019